Glitter
& MAYHEM

www.apexbookcompany.com

Glitter & MAYHEM

Edited by

John Klima,

Lynne M. Thomas, &

Michael Damian Thomas

An Apex Publications Book
Lexington, Kentucky

GLITTER & MAYHEM

ISBN: 978-1-937009-19-9

Cover Art © 2013 by Galen Dara

Title Design © 2013 by Galen Dara

This anthology is dedicated to

Arachne Jericho and

all of our glittery Kickstarter backers.

This party is for you.

Table of Contents

Introduction
Amber Benson

"There will be Glitter / There will be Mayhem / We will drink your solid gold milkshake / Drink it down to the very last drop."

The Venue: Club Apex
The Theme: Glitter and Mayhem
In Attendance: Anyone Who Is Anyone
RSVP: Be There or Be Square

To the uninitiated, it may look as though you're holding a book in your hands, but don't be fooled by the pretty cover: there is a party in these here pages. What you've got, my friends, is an invitation to the bash of the epoch—an event that will go down in the annals of time as an occasion you don't want to say you had the opportunity to go to and then somehow missed.

If you decide to redeem your place at the bar, be prepared to have your body and soul sucked into the roller derby-disco ball-sex, drugs and glam rock 'n' roll-alien-debauched-glitter-party monster-EXTRAVAGANZA of the ages. It'll be a sensuous assemblage of lipstick-smeared kisses, cleavage, glittering costumes and sexy boys and girls all looking to hook it up as they twirl their glow sticks and roller skate past you.

I know you might have some misgivings as you step inside: there is no "plus one" on this non-transferable ticket. So if you're here, you're going it alone—but then so is everyone else you'll meet. Just ignore the red velvet rope and the bouncer from Hell. You're one of the golden. *You're on the list.*

Come on in and have a drink. Lose yourself in the crowd. Let the music steal any thought as you rock your body to the stylin' beat of an androgynous DJ in a shiny, silver lamé jumpsuit. Go mirror ball blind. Have another drink—once you've downed the first one, the rest come at a more modest price—and whatever you do, *don't* keep your hands to yourself.

Yes, it's all so much easier if you go ahead and give in to the glitter and mayhem. One hell of a trip past the lips, the teeth, the tip of the tongue, but more than worth it.

With that said, you just have to remember one thing: you've entered this party at your own risk. Having your mind blown can lead to other, more permanent kinds of brain damage. Oh, and a rather robust and insatiable appetite for hardcore speculative fantasy.

Not that that's such a bad thing.

We hope you have a bloody good time tonight…because even when you leave this party, well, the party never leaves you.

Sister Twelve: Confessions of a Party Monster

Christopher Barzak

It didn't take with me, the world and its rules, the things it expected of me. In the end, that's the only reason why I find myself still here after all these countless years, and still I refuse to leave the scene. If you drop a beat, I'm on it. If I hear the slightest scratch, I'm ready to spin. If my shoes give out, if I split a sole or break a heel, it doesn't matter. I kick them off and keep on dancing like the music and my body can't be put on pause.

We have a date—the music, the dance floor, and I. We're going to move all night long if we have anything to say about it.

If I gave a damn about the world, though, and what it wanted from me, I'd be sitting in a high-backed chair right now with my needlepoint in my lap, collecting a fine layer of dust as I concentrated on a difficult stitch. My father liked seeing us girls do things like that. "Nothing more beautiful than to see a young lady with her head bent over a hoop," he used to say as he passed through our room, where my sisters would be sitting in that exact position. Then he'd notice me heaped in the corner chair, where I'd pulled my legs under me and sat hunched over the yellowed pages of a novel, and he would *tsk*. Seriously, he would *tsk*. Once, he told me, "You are quite fortunate to have been born last of all my daughters."

"Why is that?" I asked, placing my finger upon the sentence I was just then reading before looking up into his disappointed face, eyes blinking beneath their furry salt and pepper mantle. The gold crown on his head was tilted a little to the side, as if a beggar or a drunkard had just accosted him.

"Because the youngest child always gets away with more than his or her older siblings," was his answer. Then he turned to walk away.

"Is that luck, Father," I asked, "or is it just the intelligent observation of others going through life experiences before you have, and then analyzing the results of their conclusions, that leads to smarter decision-making?"

"Tsk-tsk," said my father. Looking over his shoulder, he shook his head as if I were a bitter pill his advisor forced him to swallow each night for the sake of his health.

The youngest child is also supposedly the one everyone likes (except the older siblings, of course, because they tend to feel jealous of all the attention diverted to the baby). But whether any of that is true or just psychoanalytical bullshit doesn't really matter. What matters is that, somehow, that psychoanalytical bullshit sometimes maps on to your life in a real way; and at those times, if you're a person who's able to be honest with yourself, you have to sit around and think, *Well, okay, maybe I should pay attention to what this is telling me?*

In my case, yes, almost everyone liked me, except for my sisters, who I always felt either hated or thought little of me, because of both my prolonged innocence and also because of the way I often stupidly pointed out the flaws in their thinking without realizing how embarrassing that might be for them. Really, my pointing out their flaws was a symptom of my innocence—back then I thought it was a *good* thing to be honest with people, no matter what—but that explanation doesn't excuse the hurt I must have caused them. In the end, what matters is that I too often told the truth as if it were as ordinary as the air we breathe, and because of that I could sometimes make my sisters feel like the lowest creatures in existence.

"I told you so." Those were the words I often found myself using with my sisters in the year after my brother-in-law, the soldier who I'm sure has gone on by now to be king in place of my father, discovered our secret. "I told you so, I told you so," I would tell my sisters in the eleven months that passed during the year after that man brought a halt to our dancing.

2

I said this so often because I so often realized things that my sisters never noticed, and they always made me feel like a stupid little girl when I said things like, "Shouldn't we wait to leave until we hear the guard snoring?" or "Shouldn't we maybe tie him to his chair anyway, just in case he's fooling? That way, he can't follow us down into the clubs."

They laughed at me, my sisters. They said, "Oh child, you are always so afraid." But I wasn't afraid. I was never afraid. I was just observant and cautious. I knew that soldier had something on us, I just didn't know what.

Turns out, he had a cloak that could make him invisible, and he had some wisdom from an old crone he'd met in the woods on his way to our castle to solve the secret of our nightly disappearances for our father. The wisdom the old crone gave him was this: *Don't drink the cup of wine they'll give you at the end of the night, but make them think that you did.*

It was good advice, really. Old crones know a lot. They've seen shit go down that most young people only hear about in songs and movies. The wine that we gave to our nightly guards, to our would-be-saviors and suitors, was always drugged. It put them dead asleep within minutes of sipping it twice, and while they were nodding off in the corner, their minds growing black as a bog, my sisters and I—well, the twelve of us would go out dancing.

It started when I was sixteen, us all going out in the middle of the night like that, coming home in the wee hours of the morning with our shoes completely in tatters. It started after my oldest sister found the secret passage beneath her bed, while she was looking for an earring she'd dropped as she undressed from a particularly dreadful ball that evening. My father was trying to marry her off that year; at twenty-eight Sister One was far beyond the age by which most princesses would have already got hitched. Sister One didn't really want to get married, though. She had nightmares about diamond rings and multi-tiered white cakes, and some mornings she'd wake up screaming. But she endured my father's matchmaking because she had to. She was a dutiful princess, Sister One, even if she hated her duties.

So we were all back in our room, exhausted after a night of "Pleased to make your acquaintance, I'm sure," and glad-handing every major royal who-de-who and every minor foreign ambassador my father introduced us to, when my oldest sister dropped her left earring and knelt down to look beneath her bed for it, only to alarm the rest of us when she said, "What's *this*?" as if she'd found something either terrible or else terribly exciting. All of us stopped fiddling with our laces to look over our shoulders at her where she was crouched on the floor, her head stuffed under the bed. "What's this then?" Sister One said again, and she scurried under the bed like a common rodent.

She came out a few seconds later, gasping for air like she'd just come up from swimming underwater, and begged us to help her push the bed aside. None of us knew what was going on, but we were sisters—we did things for each other when one of us asked a favor—so we lined up on one side of the bed, all twelve of us, and gave it a good shove.

All of us gasped, too, when we stepped back and saw the glowing silver outline of a door etched into the flagstones before us. "Look here," Sister One said, and she put her hand upon the center of the outlined door. The floor began to shift, stone grinding on stone, and seemed to lower a little. Sister One looked up with a wicked grin cutting across her face; then she looked down and put her hand on the center of the stone door again, making it grind ever so dully as it moved lower and lower, until we could see nothing but a few of the top steps of a staircase leading down into thick darkness.

"What is it?" one of my other sisters asked.

And Sister One said, "A secret passage, clearly!"

Just then, a soft sound flowed out of the passageway, like dandelion seeds blown upon a current.

"What's that?" one of my other sisters asked.

And Sister One said, "That? That, my sisters, is music."

I could tell you about what happened next: the stairwell that led us down to a forest of silver, and a forest of diamonds, and a forest of gold. I could tell you about the strange things we saw there, and how we stumbled in a wondrous unison, somehow balletic, all the way through those well-groomed woods until we reached a shore where twelve boats knocked against a dock that stretched out into the water. But all of that is just precursor to what drew us further into that underground world where, in the distance, a castle stood upon an island, illuminated as if by a self-producing glow. Music poured from its high-arched windows like it was the very water that flowed up to the shore to crash upon the sand before us.

4

It was only then, when the water-music crashed to foam in front of us, that we noticed the young men—our underground princes—waiting in the boats to ferry us across. They were all decked out in tight pants of dark crimson leather and white shirts that opened all the way down to their navels, with gray cloaks thrown over their shoulders like smoke. Their hair, ashen-colored from this distance, curled around their ears. I couldn't help myself. The first thing I did when I saw them was to trace the bare skin at their necks down to their waistlines with my eyes and to swallow hard. The music swarmed around their bodies like sparks, bursting, snapping, and my feet began to twitch involuntarily, my hips to sway like the boats on the water.

Each of us climbed aboard one of the twelve boats and sat at the opposite end from our underground princes, our hands folded in our laps like we were going to still make an attempt at a sense of decorum; and though it probably only took a few minutes to cross that narrow strip of water to the island, I thought I might rend my dress from my body in anticipation of our arrival. I was like a vampire, those creatures of myth I'd read about in the novels I'd read in my father's library. I smelled blood on the air. It was really only the musical notes coming from inside the castle that made me so unnaturally thirsty, but I wanted to lap those notes up like a vampire laps up blood all the same.

Our spooky princes took our hands and walked us away from our boats up the wide stone steps to the front gate of the castle, where the music grew louder and our steps grew lighter, it seemed, the further in we went, as if we had begun to walk on air. We passed through sconce-lit passageways, their fires flickering gold-leaf upon our faces, until suddenly one of the princes stopped at a door that thrummed so hard, it seemed ready to fly off its hinges, and when he opened it, out burst an ear-shattering sound like I had never heard before.

Light—pieces of light—broke into my eyes. On my skin, too, a moment later, light scurried over my flesh as I held my hands out in front of me. When I looked up again, I saw a room full of people, moving to the beat of the music. People of so many different colors wearing so many different strange styles of clothing: silver skirts that hugged their bottoms, earrings that brushed against their collar bones, black lace bras (!), sequined shirts (on men!). They were all dancing, and their movement was as strange as their fashion. They were all either too far apart, throwing their arms into the air or kicking their heels back, or else they were far too close, where no space could be seen between their bodies. Some even pushed their backsides against the waists of their dance partners and, seeing this in particular, I couldn't help but raise my light-speckled hand to my mouth, which hung open like an untended gate.

I laugh at this memory now. I laugh at how innocent I truly was. How little I knew of what the world had to offer beyond the confines of my father's kingdom within its place in time and space. What a gas! What a lark! What a blast! What an epic evening! Even that—all of those bits of language—would have been limited to, "Quite enjoyable indeed!" prior to my underground dancehall experiences.

Our spooky princes took our hands and drew us out onto the crowded dance floor, where all of us began to move in unfamiliar ways. Our hips out, our hands in the air, our hands gripping those warm bare waistlines of our princes even. The song the DJ was playing kept repeating the phrase, *Get down like you're underground,* and I backed up against my prince, like I'd seen a woman with pink frizzy hair and a face made up like a geisha do with another woman, who was dressed in a dark pinstriped suit and a bowler hat. My prince put his hands on my waist as I ground against him, slid his fingers down my thighs, and for the rest of the night we did not speak a word. We just danced. As one song slid into another, we just sighed.

At the end of that night, my sisters and I knew we'd return. Despite being covered in a slick of our own sweat, despite our dresses and shoes being hopelessly ruined, we knew we'd go back as soon as we could. So after our underground princes led us back to our boats and poled us across the river to the forests of diamonds and of gold and of silver, Sister One stopped at the bottom of the stone steps that led up to our room and said, "Sisters, if we are to ever visit this place again, we must not speak a word of what we saw and what we did this evening. Understand?"

We all nodded, and one by one we made solemn vows. "I will never ever," Sister One said, and then Sister Two, and then Sister Three, and then Sister Four, and so on, down the line we pledged, until it came to me, and I completed the previously unspoken end to our sentence: "I will never ever speak a word of this place or what we do within it."

What happens underground, stays underground.

My sisters all looked at me and grinned. It was one of those moments that, looking back, I can see how I didn't always frustrate them with my innocence, but could sometimes charm them with it.

Which brings a tear to a girl's eye, of course, wading around in the warm pool of good memories. They make one nostalgic though, those comforting waters, and there are plenty of memories that are not so pleasant in all of our histories—so let's move on.

As I recall, our maids and our father were all upset by the state of our dresses and by the ruined remains of our shoes, which we left in a pile in one corner of our room like a heap of garbage. We were questioned over and over, but all of us held fast to our secret. "No, Father, I haven't the faintest clue," we all said, feigning ignorance. "We were all asleep and dreaming. Surely someone must be attempting to make a joke of us."

Our father, of course, accepted this excuse. At least he accepted it at first. But as we continued to disappear each night and to return each morning with our new shoes in the same tattered condition as the day before, he grew both wary and weary, and eventually he offered one of our hands in marriage to the first man who could uncover the mystery of our shoe-problem.

"Really," said Sister Three on the afternoon of that public announcement, "why does it have to be a man? Why does the reward have to be marriage to one of us? What a jerk. I'm totally getting my drink on tonight. He can't stop me."

"For real," said Sister Nine, and the two of them high-fived each other.

This is when we began drugging those who came to sit in the ante-chamber of our room, so that we could continue going down into the castle beneath our father's castle, where the choice of clubs to visit, we learned soon after returning several times, were infinite.

It was on a night when our spooky princes led us down a different passageway from the one we'd taken on our first few trips that we learned that the underground castle held more rooms to dance in than we'd initially realized, and that each room belonged to a different time and a different space in the world above. Instead of the disco of our first few visits, it was a hip-hop club, and then a country line-dancing bar, and then a death metal hall. Door number one, door number two, door number three, etc. They went on and

on down the castle hall, and behind those doors, we could be anyone, we could be anywhere, we could be anywhen.

There was Studio 54, for instance, where our matching sisterly princess dresses made us into immediate stars on the glitter-covered dance
floor, and where I discovered the most wonderful substance called angel dust, which I smoked with a beautiful Asian woman whose dyed
blond hair surrounded her head like an angel's halo. That evening, I
danced with her instead of with my spooky prince, who had slumped
down on a couch with his head in the lap of an artist who had become
famous in his own time and place for painting soup cans, my prince
told me later, as he poled me back across the river. And when we finally reached the stone stairs that would take us up to our room again, my
sisters raised their eyebrows at me and tittered playfully about my
naughty choice in dance partner. They had already begun to abandon
their princes over the course of our nights out, too, much more quickly
than I'd dared to do, but they were surprised, I think, to see that I'd
done something outside of my usually cautious procedures.

Then there was the Viper Room on Sunset Boulevard (I <3 you
Johnny Depp!!), and of course the Copacabana. There was XS in Las
Vegas, with that glorious pool in the middle of the floor where we all
dove in headfirst and did a tribute to the Busby Berkeley films we'd
watched on a dancehall friend's mobile phone one evening over Bloody
Marys at an all-night diner. We touched the bottom of that pool and
watched the bubbles of air escape our mouths to rise to the top of the
water, which we burst through a moment later, crossing our hands
above us, over and over, to the roaring applause of our fellow clubbers.

And there was the Roxy. And—oh my God—the Ministry of Sound
in London. Whiskey A Go-Go, where I drank far too much whiskey and
go-goed myself into a silly stupor, was sick all the next day and stayed
in bed, nursed by Sister Eight, who had decided not to drink that night
and made sure to bring us apple juice for breakfast and chicken broth
for lunch and told our father we'd all caught the same illness after
drinking water from a brook in a nearby forest.

Womb, in Tokyo. Wow, that night's a broken mirror. CBGB's, when
we were feeling punk and wanted to tease our hair up into Frankenstein's wife's crazy beehives and wear jeans with holes in our knees.
Berghain in Berlin—oh Lord, you don't even want to know the shit I
saw go down in some of the rooms of that former power plant gone

fetish leather. They only played techno in there, and the place was nothing but dark room after dark room with strobe lights blinding you momentarily. Luckily Sister Six scored us some ecstasy and all was good after we swallowed those smiley-faced pills.

There was the Paradise Garage, too, of course, which my sisters were fond of because it was located on King Street. They thought it was clever to go dancing at a club that reminded us of our father, who was totally tearing his hair out about our ruined shoes and constant daytime sleeping at that point, not to mention all of the would-be suitors he kept having to behead when they couldn't discover the mystery of our ruined shoes each morning. We felt bad about our suitors' deaths, my sisters and I, but honestly, they should have minded their own business and left my father to do his own dirty work. And really, what kind of idiot tries to follow in the footsteps of the multiple men who had tried before him and ended up beheaded? Clearly, they weren't the brightest of the bulbs in the kingdom.

It was the Limelight, though—this old church turned club in the heart of Manhattan—that stole my heart more than any other club we went to. There, my sisters and I came with our faces painted to look like butterfly wings, or like strange monsters. We wore purple or blue long, stringy wigs, and ripped up our princess dresses so that we looked like down-and-out rich girls who got lost on their way home from the prom and were led astray by big bad wolves instead of knights in shining armor. The music was techno and industrial, the drugs were always upbeat. The mirror ball in the center of the dance floor spun and broke light against our painted faces, like that first night we'd gone dancing in the underground castle, and oh, everyone there was so ready to laugh and twirl and pretend to be somebody that they weren't in real life.

I understood that, the pretending. Back home in my father's kingdom, we were quiet and reserved. We bowed and we handed over our hands to men who kissed them, and we batted away compliments as if we were not worthy of praise. We ate only a third of what was put on our plates for dinner, and we drank only one glass of wine in front of anyone. At social occasions, we danced with old men who would slip their hands around our waists like we belonged to them, and when we pulled away, they would raise their brows and question us about whether or not we wanted to upset our father.

Politics. Fuck politics. My sisters and I had found our own kingdom to belong to. And at the Limelight, that Gothic-styled church in the
middle of Manhattan, we could feel like we were still in our father's
kingdom but also in our new home, among the party monsters with
whom we shared our revels.

The sad thing is, our story is a fairy tale. That can't be dismissed. And
no matter what anyone tells you about fairy tales, most of them don't
really have happy endings. Not the real fairy tales, that is. Not the ones
that really happened.

What happened to us was, the old soldier I've already mentioned
came to my father's castle and took up the challenge to find out how
our shoes would come to be ruined every night like a ritual, and he had
a couple of things going for him that the beheaded suitors before him
hadn't. He had that cloak of invisibility the old crone in the woods gave
him, for instance, and the advice she'd also given when he told her he
was going to take up the king's challenge: *Don't drink the cup of wine
they'll give you at the end of the night, but make them think that you did.*

Old crone, wherever you are, I will totally slap you across the face
for this treachery if ever I come across you. What did we ever do to
you? Did you hate us because we were happy?

So the soldier found us out. Didn't drink the drugged wine we gave
him. Pretended to fall asleep. Put the cloak of invisibility over his
shoulders and followed us down into the forests of silver and gold and
diamonds. Slipped onto the boat with my spooky prince and me. Saw
us dancing with an array of unseemly characters at the Limelight. Saw
me with too much vodka and a little bit of pot in my system, lifting up
my dress in the middle of the dance floor. Jesus, that was a great night,
regardless of what followed.

The thing was, I knew someone was shadowing us that night, I
just couldn't see him. I knew it and twice I said to my sisters,
"Something is wrong here. I feel as though someone unseen is
among us."

And of course my sisters either pursed their lips skeptically or
threw their heads back in laughter. "Stop worrying!" they said. "You're
such a downer!"

But he found us out, that soldier, and he explained our secret to
our father the very next morning, after we returned, before we

could even put ourselves to bed and pretend like we didn't know what he was talking about.

"My daughters," our father said when he learned of what we'd been doing. "How dare you sneak about like thieves in the night? How dare you dance with anyone who offers a hand like a common harlot?"

"But Father—" Sister Ten said, clasping her hands together as if she were praying.

"Enough!" our father thundered, and we all cringed, wishing our mother had not died in my childbirth, for it would have been nice to have a mother there right then to soften our father in this moment. "Your underground nights have ended," he told us. "And you will no longer live in this room. It will be sealed off, in fact, and starting tomorrow, one of you will marry each month until a year has passed and all of you are living a proper life. I've been too easy on you all. Let you now answer to husbands!"

He let the old soldier pick which of us he wanted to marry, like we were the carcasses of dead chickens hanging up in a shopkeeper's window. Which one is the plumpest, the juiciest? My oldest sister, of course, Sister One, who he'd been eyeing up the entire time my father scolded us.

Father married her off to the old soldier the next day. The eleven of us were her bridesmaids. Most of us looked down at our feet as Sister One made her vows to the old soldier. We put the tips of our fingers to our eyes to wipe away any tears before they might show.

After that, I watched each of my other sisters married off to dukes and lords and even one given to a blacksmith whose work my father admired. We were his property, traded and bartered for political gain and finely crafted weapons. It was as if he were preparing to go to war with an enemy that had not yet revealed its existence. I suppose we were his enemies. Our betrayal of his trust made us disgusting to him.

Each wedding was a brief and sad affair, except for Sister Eleven's. By then nearly a year had passed and she had had time to get used to the idea of this inevitability, and had persuaded my father to at least allow her some consideration in the selection of her husband. My father appreciated Sister Eleven's embrace of her fate, and allowed her to choose between three suitors of his picking. I suppose that was an option of sorts. Sister Eleven knew to accept this and not to dare complain.

They married in the spring, under a blossoming cherry tree.

I was next, of course, but unlike Sister Eleven, I had not become accustomed to the idea of marriage as punishment, even if I could choose between a handful of my father's selections. All those months barred from the underground castle, I tossed and turned on my bed, thinking of the many people with whom I had danced and the many experiences I had enjoyed (even the bad ones), and burned as if I had a fever. And on the night of Sister Eleven's wedding, when I cried out in my sleep while I dreamed someone was suffocating me with a pillow, I knew I could not do as my father commanded. I knew I would once again have to betray him.

My father had had the door to our old bedroom barred shut from the outside, and a guard patrolled that hall now more often than they used to. So it would be no use trying to pry the door open. I only had one real option. I would have to climb up the vines that covered the wall on that side of the castle, and flit through our old room's window like a moth.

I waited until the eve of my wedding, which was to be a marriage with a middle-aged archduke who smelled of horse dung and had brown spots on his teeth; when the clouds passed over the moon of that early summer night, casting everything in darkness for several minutes, I began my ascent.

Hand over hand, foot braced in the nooks and crannies of the thick vines on the wall, I made my way up to the windowsill within fifteen minutes, just before my arms grew so sore I thought I might fall, and had only enough energy to pull myself over the ledge and drop down into our old bedroom, where the thud of my landing echoed through the lifeless room.

Before me were our empty beds, the covers pulled up and made as if they were waiting for someone to return to them, as if the girls that usually inhabited them were just out for the night, dancing, and any minute now they would come running up the stairs from the under-ground forest of silver, holding their laughter tighter as they ascended, and would finally put themselves to bed. I nearly cried, remembering how it had been not so long ago, recalling the feeling of freedom.

But I didn't let myself waste too much time, and quickly went to the stone door and placed my palm upon it, sighed with relief as it be-gan to grind and lower itself to reveal the stone staircase that would lead me back to the underground castle. Back to my spooky prince, who minutes later caught me in his arms as I ran toward him, out of breath, then poled me across the river, where we ran up the stairs of the underground castle, our hands linked between us, and disappeared into the dark of the cavernous entrance.

In a castle underground, in a place where time and space don't exist in the ways that we're used to, a person doesn't age. You just are. You exist, but outside of the laws of nature. I spent the timeless passage of what would have been years for someone locked into a particular world doing nothing but dancing. I went to all of my sisters' and my favorite clubs, night after endless night, and slept my days away in a room not unlike our old bedroom. A hostel sort of room, it was, where the homeless types like me who had taken up residence in the underground castle would go to sleep when they didn't go home with a dance partner from another world for the evening. We were fugitives from our own circumstances, fleeing the cage of fate in which our origins would entrap us.

My sisters all got married. That's the end of their stories, like all the bad punch lines to all the bad knock-knock jokes that somehow still manage to breathe in the world. A typical fairy tale ending, only not so happily after all.

But me? My ending is different. I picked the lock on time and space, and escaped my fate to live outside of the rules of a particular world. I live alone, but at least I'm free.

I've seen so many worlds now. I've seen so many things since I became a wanderer. And though I often feel the weight of guilt lower upon my shoulders when I think of my poor sisters back in my father's realm, married off to husbands who are little more than jailors, I can't say I'd do anything different. I feel the guilt, and then I accept it. I confess this great sin—the fact that there's no way I could have lived out the ending of their fairy tales, that I abandoned them to the fate I would have been assigned as well—and roll it all up as a message in a bottle.

The river that flows by the underground castle flows through all the worlds in all the times that exist in the universe. I cast the bottle into it and watch my story bob as it floats its way into eternity. And then I turn, called by the music in the castle to return to it.

One day, if you find these words and read them, know that I have quite a different ending than my sisters. Know that I'm happy, despite having to call myself a person who has run away.

And if you ever find your own secret passage into the underground, you can be sure that I'll be the girl you see in every club you ever visit. The one on the floor with the mirror ball spinning above her, showering light down on her hair and shoulders as she twirls and whirls. I'll be the one who never stops dancing.

Apex Jump

David J. Schwartz

Roller derby is like life. Some days you're jamming along, barely feeling your skates touch the floor, handling the curves without a thought, and then some blocker comes out of your blind spot and you're careening into the infield struggling to tuck in and fall small. It's like life because after that happens you've got to check for breaks, ignore the rink rash, and get the fuck up.

Derby is also like life in that it *becomes* your life. We practice three times a week, we have meetings every Tuesday, and we do appearances for publicity and charity. Well, that's how it was on the team I was on before, which was in a major metropolitan city that I moved out of under such circumstances that I no longer refer to it by name. I usually just call it Hastur. If you get that joke, consider yourself high-fived.

Here in Alexandria—which the locals charmingly refer to as "Alec," as though the town was their sarcastic younger brother—there aren't quite as many opportunities for public appearances. There isn't even a proper rink for us to skate in, so we hold our bouts in an old Quonset hut out beyond the power plant. On the Monday after every bout at least one person comes up to me at work and tells me they were going to come but they couldn't find the place. Under other circumstances that would sound like the Minnesota version of a polite excuse, but I believe it. The top of our wish list is a neon sign, but we need to make some money first.

Which is why we agreed to this away bout with the Stellar Swarm Rollergirls. Really, it's why Lewd-a-Fisk agreed to it. Lewd-a-Fisk is our Events chair, and she said the money was too good to pass up. Transportation provided, a 60/40 revenue share—the 60 going to the winner—and 5k guaranteed? That's more than the Douglas County Rollergirls made all last year. We're a volunteer-run non-profit; we could use the bump. It's one of those things that might be a little too good to be true, which is what Joan Deere starts saying to Lewd-a-Fisk at around 3:30, when the bus that was supposed to take us to Lyra is an hour and a half late.

"This guy didn't say he was a prince or anything, did he? That he was coming into an inheritance in a few weeks? You didn't front him five hundred bucks so that he could pay you back with interest?"

"Come on, Joan." Lewd-a-Fisk is my derby wife, which doesn't mean what you probably think it does, at least not in this case. It's just sort of a buddy system, really, and I feel obligated to stick up for Lewdy even if I'd rather be on my couch having a margarita and watching some awful science fiction thing on cable. Instead we're waiting—fifteen skaters, minus the usual volunteers and camp followers—in front of our Quonset hut headquarters in the blaring heat of a Minnesota August. You'd never think it—at least, I never did—but the summers here are as brutal as the winters. We'd wait inside, but it's even hotter in there.

"Look, I met Mr. Kevinson, all right?" Lewdy says. "He's a bit eccentric but he checks out. I called the Babe City Rollergirls and they sort of laughed, but they said he was legit."

"Something's not right, because I've never heard of Lyra, Minnesota," says Spermicidal Tendencies. She's been saying it for two weeks now, ever since we put this on the schedule, but before anyone can tell her to shut up, a rumble and a gasp echo across the asphalt, and a bus pulls into sight. It looks like it was painted by the Electric Mayhem under the competing directions of Ziggy-era Bowie and Graffiti Bridge-era Prince. It's the kind of thing you can't possibly take in all at once.

It hisses to a stop, and the door swings open to reveal a person wearing silver coveralls, a furred cape, and a battered white top hat over shades and a veil of curly black hair.

"Sorry I'm running a skad late," the person says. I don't like to make assumptions about anyone's gender, and there's more than a little bit of mixed signals at work here. "Let's get your baggage into the hold and take off." I don't see their hands move, but they must have pressed a button somewhere, because the luggage compartments underneath pop open.

Lewdy steps up to say hello, so I guess this is the notorious and objectively eccentric Mr. Kevinson. A few of the girls are staring. You've got to be a little bit open to freakiness to be a derby girl, but Mr. Kevinson is not the sort of person you see in Alexandria, ever, and some of the team comes from towns even smaller than that. As the resident big-city veteran of queer proms and fetish nightclubs, I figure maybe this is a good time for me to take the lead.

"Mr. Kevinson." I offer my hand and he covers it with both of his. His skin is brown and warm. "I'm Huggernaut. I hope we can still make the bout on time."

"Lickety-split." Mr. Kevinson's voice is like Barry White and Dusty Springfield licking honey off of each other. He smiles, or at least he forms his mouth into a crescent; his eyes are hidden behind dark sunglasses and there's something synthetic about the way his skin wrinkles. Too much makeup, I decide, and stow my gear underneath.

Normally we prefer to convoy to the away bouts in our own cars, but Mr. Kevinson had told Lewdy that parking was limited at the facility, so we agreed to be driven. It's a luxury we're not accustomed to, or at least it seems that way until we're all settled in and the restraints drop down over us. Not bondage-type restraints, but roller-coaster-type restraints, padded steel that pushes down against my shoulders, lets up slightly, and then locks into place. Lewdy and I are seated right behind the driver. I try to kick at the back of his seat, but it's too far.

The girls start swearing, but they're quickly drowned out by a sound like when your dog barks at the vacuum cleaner, only amplified about five hundred times, and that's when it occurs to me that maybe the name Stellar Swarm is more descriptive than we realized and perhaps Lyra is not a town in Minnesota after all.

"It'll just be a skad," says Mr. Kevinson, as the ground falls away and Gs press me against my seat and push the breath out of me. Barry and Dusty continue to make sweet love as the light outside fades from bright and humid to blue and vaporous to cool and glitter-dark, but I'm not really hearing what Mr. Kevinson is saying because I'm distracted by thoughts of A) death, B) interstellar slave trafficking, and C) bloody retribution against the Babe City Rollers if I'm ever within a light year of Bemidji again.

Lewdy and I find each other's hands and squeeze. Since we're right behind the driver's seat, we get a full view of Mr. Kevinson as he stands up with his back to us and shudders. There's a click, and then the cape bulges out and falls away as something like an oversized Weeble floats out from behind it.

You know what I mean when I talk about Weebles, right? Those egg-shaped, bottom-heavy toys from before cable? I spend a lot of time with these girls, and the time I feel oldest is when I drop some joke or some cultural reference and I get silence and blank stares. I say girls—it's in the team name, after all—but our ages range from nineteen to forty-seven. Anyway, I'm old enough to remember those Weeble commercials, the ones where they wobbled but they didn't fall down, but this is a little different, because there's something *inside* the Weeble. It's maybe two feet high, and I'd say it resembles a weasel except that it's blue, has one leg, appears to be hairless, and is steering a floating egg.

It hovers in the aisle just out of my reach while the body with the cape and the hat sits back down in the driver's seat. "I apologize for the deception," it says in a voice like Dusty reaching orgasm while sitting on Barry's face. "Sadly, we find it to be necessary for your planet. Lyra, as you may have realized by now, is not a town in your fine state."

Spermicidal Tendencies shouts from the back of the bus: "I fucking *told* you!"

"It is, rather, what you on your planet refer to as a Dyson swarm, surrounding a largely overlooked star in the vicinity of Vega. I own a roller derby club in the swarm, which is where you'll be skating tonight. I assure you that the terms of your contract will be honored, you will be well treated, and you will be returned to your planet by no later than 0800 local time tomorrow morning.

"We'll be traveling about twenty-nine light years, which will take approximately thirty minutes. I suggest that you relax and enjoy the journey."

We start making some alternative suggestions, but before Mr. Kevinson—if that is his real name—can be properly insulted, things get weird. I don't mean implausible or unlikely, I mean *trippy*. Everything gets bendy and indistinct, like we've all been colored outside the lines. I feel Lewdy's fingers squirming in my own, and I try to let go of her hand, but it's like our knuckles are fused and the bones in my arm have disappeared. I spend a few minutes trying to untangle us, and I should be panicking, because this is wrong in so many ways, but it's not freaking me out like it should. I'm so liquid that a part of me is worried that I may have pissed myself. I'm thinking about the way Mr. Kevinson has a body that he can just float out of whenever he likes. Maybe he's got other bodies around, or maybe he can make alterations to the one he has whenever he feels like it.

This is something I think about a lot, because I wasn't born in a girl's body. Notice that I don't say I wasn't born a girl, because I fucking *was*. I spent twenty-eight years thinking I was trapped in my body before I got up the courage to start changing it. Sometimes I wish I hadn't waited so long. Sometimes I wish I could mold myself like Silly Putty, to be more of the person I know I was supposed to be. So that's what I spend the rest of the trip to Lyra doing, thinking malleable thoughts.

It doesn't work, but when we come out of whatever-that-was I feel calm. I turn and look at my hand, which is still clasped with Lewdy's and in no danger of becoming bonded. I squeeze her hand and smile at her in a way that I know I'm going to be embarrassed about once I come down from this hyperspace drug.

Mr. Kevinson's voice comes over the speakers—I don't see the blue weasel anywhere, so maybe he's floated back into the driver. "Ladies," Mr. Kevinson says, "welcome to the Lyra Swarm."

It's like a disco ball, if you made each of the mirrors the size of a small planet, put a gap of about ninety-three million miles between each of them, and put the light on the inside. That, and either put them in fixed orbit or create some insanely complex and dangerous orbital matrix, and make about a third of the mirrors solar collectors that transfer energy to the rest of the swarm wirelessly or through some other ingenious and unlikely technology. Hey, I may teach drafting at a technical college, but I read.

"Technically I think that's a bubble," I say.

"True, Madame Huggernaut. It started as a swarm, but over the centuries it's become a bubble. Over a trillion beings live here, of more than ten thousand species. Which reminds me: in a compartment in the seat arm you'll find some translator putty. Stick it between your cheek and gum and the nanites will do the rest. Now I hope you'll forgive me if I'm quiet for a moment while I dock with the Apex Jump."

The putty he mentioned looks pretty much like chewing gum. I slip it into my mouth and feel it start to dissolve. It tastes like pickles.

Lewdy elbows me in the side. "Don't put that in your mouth! It might be a Roofie!"

"Oh." I reach into my mouth, but the putty is already gone. I guess the hyperspace high has worn off, because all of a sudden I feel like dirt. It's almost fifteen years since I transitioned, but I was socialized as a man for almost twice that long, and I still have blind spots about being a woman. Fortunately, Lewdy seems to be wrong; as far as I can tell the putty hasn't done anything at all.

Mr. Kevinson steers us toward a platform in the shape of a massive banana yellow skate wheel. The outer rim of the wheel is lined with what I assume are docking bays, and we maneuver toward one of these with more grace than I would expect of a bus. The bus slows, straightens, and sets down with an efficiency that's almost insulting to the blissful experience of getting here. The docking bay door clunks shut and air fills the space so quickly that the windows fog up.

The restraints release and lift away, and the door hisses open. I struggle to my feet—it's a little bit of a surprise to find they're still there—and stomp to the front of the bus. Mr. Kevinson's vehicle/body is strapped in, but clearly there's no one there. The head tilts to one side, and when I pull aside the fur cape there's a cavity in the back the size of a three-foot egg.

"Where is he?"

"Mr. Kevinson had some urgent business to attend to." This new voice is like playing cello with a piece of French toast. I turn around and see an...alien, I guess I have to say. It looks kind of like if you took a short, somewhat rotund man with a heavy beard, glued long white hair everywhere that the beard didn't cover, and then shaved the beard.

"Who are you?" I say.

"I'm Mrs. Danielson," the thing says. "I'm your liaison."

I stand there for a second wondering why it is that this five-foot-tall space yeti speaks with a Southern twang until Lewdy elbows me and whispers, "Since when do you speak space yeti?"

"Go take your putty," I tell her. To Mrs. Danielson I say, "Give us just a moment, please."

"Certainly."

The team is staring at me like I'm going to start vomiting fire hydrants. "We're not in Kansas anymore, all right?" I say. "I don't know how the fuck to get back. We need to be able to communicate. I'm fine. Take the putty."

"I was supposed to text my folks directions to the place," says Spermy.

"If you can get a signal here, go ahead," I say. "Just tell them to hang a left at Hercules."

So they take the putty, or at least some of them do, and the rest of them at least pocket it. Then we file out and start unloading our luggage while Mrs. Danielson shakes everybody's hands.

"You're being stupid calm about all this," Lewdy tells me.

The truth is I'm freaking out, not with fear, but with excitement. I probably should be scared, but I'm in outer space! I'm a *space traveler*; we all are. Neil Armstrong hasn't got shit on us. Well, except for the part where he and Buzz and Michael Collins did at least some of the driving. Any one of us could take him on skates, though.

"If you'll just follow me, I'll show you to Locker Room 12B," says Mrs. Danielson. "It will go more quickly on skates."

We look at each other for a moment. Then: "Lace up," says Joan Deere, my co-captain. "We've got a bout to win."

Ten minutes later Mrs. Danielson leads us out of the docking bay and into the most spectacular spectacle you've ever laid spectacles on. The interior of Apex Jump, as it turns out, is ringed by a mile-high wall of docking bays, habitats, and terraces, and centered upon an open, multi-level concourse leading to and from a glass-dark hub that extends all the way through the platform like a black tower. Sun shines on vegetation growing in parks the size of parking spaces and hanging from trellis-like awnings. Vendor carts stand under these, veiled by leaves and flowers, selling things that resemble food in every way but their colors. Other vendors hawk programs, glowsticks, smart tattoos, branded clothing, mood-altering substances, and a thousand other things.

The vendors themselves are even more interesting than their wares. Two balls of light hover over a display of crystal cylinders, extolling their virtues in waves of color that I somehow understand as words. A bowl of water the size and shape of a basketball holds a murky, bubbling liquid from which five slithery appendages rearrange a display of holographic video projectors. Something I take to be a marble pillar spins with a stony rumble as we approach and offers me an ice cream cone. But none of that captures the strangeness, because we are weaving through a crowd of beings of every size and color and shape and substance, walking or slithering or crawling or hopping or flying or skating, or floating along in vehicles like Mr. Kevinson's egg except filled with liquids or gases of unearthly hues. Some resemble animals or objects that I can name, some I'm not even sure I *see* in any real way, they are so far outside of any context that I know.

Something with wings and eyestalks and a tail about twelve feet long lurches into my path, and I have to brake to avoid running into it.

"Oh my God," it says, or at least the translator nanites tell me it's saying, "are you Huggernaut? I saw the streaming footage of you skating against the Windy City Rollers when you were still on the Hastur team." It doesn't say Hastur, of course, but like I said I don't speak the name of my former dwelling place, not even when I'm repeating fan squee from creatures who live twenty-nine light years distant.

Somehow, this is the most normal thing that has happened to me since I stepped onto Mr. Kevinson's bus.

"Hi," I say. "Yes, we're here to skate against the Stellar Swarm."

"I'm sooo excited that you are here!" it says. "Good luck tonight! I'll be cheering for you."

Lewdy elbows me as we resume following Mrs. Danielson through the crowd. "You've got fans on Deep Space Nine?"

"Like I knew? Besides, this shit is more *Farscape*, if you ask me."

Let me be clear: I love Lewdy, but I am not *in* love with her. She has a husband and a little girl, and I love them too. When I moved to Alec I was angry but I was also really damn sad. I don't want to get too much into it, because it still hurts. Let's just say: I *had* a derby wife, a real one. And then she decided that not only did she not want to be my wife anymore, she didn't want me in derby. For a long, excruciating season I fought her off the track as she turned our friends against me. Not all of them, just enough that I could see that it was tearing the league apart. What hurt the most was that when I left, no one tried to talk me into staying.

I moved to Alec because it was far away and they didn't have a team. Except that it turned out they were starting one, and they nearly wore out my doorbell asking me to join. It took some convincing, but I'm so glad I said yes. Like I said, life knocks you down and you get the fuck up. Lewdy and the other girls gave me a home, and this one I plan to hold on to.

"This way," says Mrs. Danielson, pointing. "Take it all the way down and turn left. I'll be by to check on you before the bout."

A minute later we're zooming down a lazy spiral ramp in a line. The gravity here must be a little less than Earth-normal, because we don't pick up enough speed for this to feel dangerous. Joan turns the descent into a back-to-front, the girls at the rear passing all the way to the front, each in turn. It's a good idea; focusing on the drill helps keep the sensory overload of the station around us at bay.

When we roll out on Level 12 we find ourselves on the outer edge of the dark tower at the center. We veer left and race down the hall, backpacks, duffels and all. We roll into Locker Room 12B and the door shuts behind us and whispers, "Going up."

My apartment in Hastur would fit into Locker Room 12B about a dozen times, along with a day spa, a juice bar, and a deli, all of which are also in here. There's a buffet as long as a semi trailer and a makeup artist, and vidscreens showing non-stop derby.

"I am never leaving this place," says Spermy.

"All right, let's shit, shower, and shave," says Joan, who sometimes has delusions of being a drill sergeant. We let her get away with it. She gives the orders and I run the practices, mostly.

I don't know exactly how a sonic shower works, but if you have any problems with limp hair it's the way to go. If we had sonic showers on Earth all the shampoo brands that talk about giving your hair extra body would be discontinued. It's like a piano concerto for your hair, only lighter and fuller; it's a harpsichord organ concerto for your hair.

I confess that this is mostly what I am thinking about when Mrs. Danielson shows up to give us her orientation speech: I am thinking about the fact that my hair looks dynamite, and will up until the point where I stuff it under my helmet. I'm tuned out until I hear her say something about Apex Jump being a WFTDA-certified facility.

"I thought the WFTDA was pretty much Earth-based," I say. WFTDA stands for Women's Flat Track Derby Association, the governing body for the DIY roller derby revival.

"In that I'm afraid you are mistaken," she says. "I believe the acronym takes on a different emphasis in your language, but out here it is known as the Wider Federation for the Targeted Dissemination of Anarchism. We are advocates of anarcho-syndicalism, or the cooperative self-determination of autonomous communities.

The horizontal structure of a roller derby league is in many ways a prototype of anarchistic community-building."

"I have no idea what that means," I say. "I studied civil engineering, not poli sci."

"Is this still a women's league?" Spermy asks.

"There are as many as thirty-one genders among the galaxy's known species, depending upon how you count them," Mrs. Danielson says. "But yes, the Stellar Swarm Rollergirls are all just that—girls. Would you like to see them in action?"

She cues up tape of the Stellar Swarm Rollergirls skating against the Oly Rollers. The aliens aren't any one species—there are lizard creatures, bearish creatures, and something that looks like a cactus that I hope isn't quite as pointy. They don't look that big next to the Oly skaters, but they're fast as hell.

"Oh my God, did you see that, that broom-thing?" Spermy asks. "It cut past Rettig to Rumble like she was standing still."

"She," I correct her. "She cut past Rettig to Rumble, not it."

Lewdy raises her hand. "Mrs. Danielson, how many Earth teams have skated against the Stellar Swarm?"

"Almost three hundred."

"How many have won?"

Mrs. Danielson shrugs. "Oh, don't worry about that. Just do your best and have fun."

"What's the spread?" asks Joan.

"I believe that currently it's 170 points."

My heart plummets into my gut like a sinkhole has just opened up in my liver. I think back to the first roller derby world cup, just a couple of years back. Since the derby revival started in the US, we were able to field the strongest team, but the teams who came were there as much for the camaraderie as the competition. I wasn't there—I was in Hastur, watching it streaming with some of my teammates—but I remember something that happened after the US/Scotland bout, which the US won 435-1. I remember it because they interviewed the Scotland jammer who had scored that one point, and she was fucking ecstatic to have lost by 434 points. At its best, derby is like that—you skate hard, you hit hard, but you win or lose with grace and love.

I'm not sure I have that kind of grace and love in me. I did, before everything in Hastur went to shit. Nowadays, I'm less sure.

"We've never lost by 170 points ever," Joan huffs. "Turn it off."

"We've lost by 150," Spermy says, which is true. The Minnesota Rollergirls All-Stars were kind enough to visit us last year, and they knocked us all over the Quonset.

"We've never lost by 170 points, though, and we're not going to start now. We're not going to think about covering the spread. We're going out there with the same goal we always have—to *win*."

There's more to the speech, and it's inspiring and all, but it's a little disjointed and it works better in person. As Joan delivers it the girls are performing their pre-game rituals—painting their faces, stretching, cranking loud music through their earphones. Lewdy and Frida K.O. are playing cribbage. Minnesota Vice is sprawled out on a bench, napping. My own pre-bout ritual is a visualization thing. I picture the opposing team as a skyscraper, myself planting charges inside it and detonating them with a hip check in passing. It's a simile, you dig? You may have noticed I like similes.

A three-headed gasbag that looks a lot like a walking bagpipe reports that we have thirty minutes. I must be getting used to this place, because I just nod and say thanks.

Five minutes out we blast the Dixie Chicks' "Sin Wagon" on Spermy's portable sound system, drowning it out as we sing along. Then we do our huddle and skate into battle.

The skate dome of Apex Jump is enormous. The track looks regulation, with the benches in the infield, but the auditorium floor alone is five times bigger than our Quonset hut. We roll out between the bleachers to a sound like nothing I've ever heard. An airplane engine is loud, but unless you've heard one running in an enclosed space I don't think you can understand the effect. This is sound that puts pressure not just on your ears but also on your entire body. If you'd ever been in a sonic shower, maybe it would make sense.

Above the rafters there's an upper deck, and above that more upper decks. One of them looks like it's full of water, and all of them are full of the same *Monster Manual* of creatures that we saw out in the body of the station. Up above, the sun—whatever sun this is—shines down through a ceiling that filters its light in wild disco patterns. Through the crowd noise I recognize the strains of our unofficial theme song, David Bowie's "Queen Bitch," and I'm ready for a fight.

We do a circuit around the track, and Mr. Kevinson's voice announces each of us by our number and name. There are people here (if I can call them people, and why not) with signs with our names on them, in English. Something that looks like an enormous fat ladybug is wearing one of my Hastur jerseys.

"They fucking love us!" Lewdy screams in my ear, and I smile because what the fuck is there to say.

Then the Stellar Swarm Rollergirls appear.

Have you ever been set up on a date by a friend, and you get to the place early, and when the person walks in you just know it even though you're thinking, "Oh no, it can't be them, they're way out of my league and this is just going to be embarrassing and what was my friend thinking?" That's what this feels like.

"At least they're all bipeds," I shout at Lewdy.

"Didn't you hear Mrs. Danielson? She said we were in the Class Three Biped Division. There are like two dozen divisions—Quadruped, Heavy Tail, Mixed..." She keeps listing them, but the crowd is too loud, and I'm trying to study the competition, here. I'm one of the two main jammers on the team—Spermy is the other. If the two of us can't score on these things, we don't have a chance.

Joan hands me the jammer star first. Derby works like this: each team has a jammer, who starts behind the pack and tries to lap the other team before their jammer can lap your team. If you're the first jammer through cleanly, you can call off the jam any time. For every player you lap you get a point. It sounds simple, except that the other team has four players trying to block you, slow you down, or force you out of bounds. It helps if you're fast, which I am. It can also help if you're small, which I am, although that can also mean getting knocked around a lot.

The other team's jammer is the cactus woman. She holds out a gloved hand, and I shake it. I brush across a needle as I do so, but the needle is soft and hair-like, so I should probably revise the cactus idea but then the whistle blows and we're off.

Oh Hell No of the Northern Brisbane Rollers has said that derby is like playing speed chess while bricks are thrown at you. There are a lot of tactics in derby, but not a lot of time to think about them, so you either have to know what to do instinctively or you have to trust your teammates to scream out what to do. Right now my goal is to get through the scrum of opponents and my own teammates and get ahead. But before I can even get around the first turn the cactus is through, and when I juke over toward the inside line to follow, one of the bears sends me sliding into the infield.

I check for breaks, I ignore the burn in my legs, and I get back up. I manage to slip between a pair of defenders right around the second turn, but my opponent laps the pack and scores four points before calling off the jam.

And that's how it goes. Spermy gives up nine points to the broom woman. I take the third jam and manage to stay close, but they still take three. Frida takes the next jam and gets called for a track cut penalty; while she's in the box the Swarm bring the score up to 41-0.

Lewdy sits down next to me, panting. She's a big girl but she's in condition; these creatures are knocking us flat. "I didn't even know their jammer was there until she was past me," she says.

The penalty runs out, and Spermy puts us on the board, taking two points to their four. I start to notice that the Swarm isn't moving quite as fast either, and I manage to take a lead jam, four points to none. Our blockers are learning our opponents, making them work harder to get through. But they're still getting through.

At the half it's 102-17. The crowd is still enjoying it, apparently, but when we retreat to the locker room my legs feel like rubber. A very nice lady with six arms and twelve eyes hands us some kind of sports drink. I take a sip and immediately feel human again.

"What is this stuff? I feel great!" says Minnesota Vice.

"It doesn't matter," says Spermy. "If they gave it to us, they gave it to them too. They're going to come out just like they did at the start."

"Did you see that block I put on the one with the shell?" Lewdy asks. "I hit her as hard as I could, and I was the one that got knocked out of bounds."

"They're good," Joan says. "Let's end that train of thought right there. What do we have in our favor?"

"Gravity," I say. "The gravity isn't as strong here, is it? Has anyone else noticed that?"

"We're not exactly floating up toward the ceilings," says Spermy.

"No, but you know those jumping drills I've been making you do? I think we should be all over that."

As game strategies go it's a bit one-note, but it's worth a shot. It's not going to do any more than even the odds a bit, but for the sake of pride we need to have a better second half than we did a first.

I put myself on the line for the first jam, again. For a moment I remember that the crowd is there and that this is the biggest venue I've ever skated in and probably ever will. Then I settle into myself and focus on what I'm doing.

Apex Jump isn't just the name of this roller derby space utopia, it's also a derby move. You can't cross out of bounds with your skates on the floor, but at either end of the oval, where the track bends, you can legally leap from inbounds to inbounds, passing *over* a section of the infield, without being penalized. That's an apex jump, and that's what I do when I catch the back of the pack.

There's a Prince song playing on the speakers as I take off — "Let's Go Crazy," I think it is. A good omen for a Minnesota team. The crowd noise is pressing down on me, but I feel it under my feet too, buzzing through the ball bearings and the soles of my skates, surging as I catch air, at least a foot higher than I've ever managed at home. I've got the light of a distant red sun shining off the sparkles in my eye shadow and all day today not a single person has asked me whether I was a boy or a girl. I still get lonely sometimes, and there's still a Hastur-shaped hole in my heart, because when you love a place it lives in you just the same as you live in it. But I'm with my friends and an alien with an enormous tail went all fangirl on me a couple of hours ago, and I'm going to nail this jump and I'm going to skate my tits off.

We lose, of course.

The final score is 170-54, and I'm proud as hell. The Stellar Swarm take most of the second half to adjust to our new strategy, and by the end we're almost gaining on them, but I wouldn't give us better than an 80-point spread for a rematch.

So the Swarm do their victory lap and then they skate over and slap hands and hug us, and the crowd gives us a standing ovation. If you were the sort of person who wanted to believe in things like universal love and sportswomanship and compassion, you might get a little teary standing there in this moment. Maybe.

I'm weeping like a faucet, myself.

The afterparty...if the station was like a bacchanal when we first skated onto it, the afterparty is like a saturnalia. The girls that drink get drunk, and the girls that get high have plenty of options. I mean, we're all athletes, but we party. The Swarm are fearless and hilarious and they are full of stories of all the other Earth teams that have visited Apex Jump. I start taking notes but then I lose my pen and then I'm making out with this furry little mama from some planet I've already forgotten the name of. Her lips taste like apricots. Then at some point we end up at Mr. Kevinson's place, and I'm trying to get him to sing "Can't Get Enough of Your Love" while I sing "Breakfast in Bed" and Lewdy is laughing so hard she can't breathe, and that's about all I remember.

When I wake up Mr. Kevinson is ready to drive us back home, all of us except Spermy, who is dead serious about never leaving and is planning to try out for the Stellar Swarm.

"You should stay too," she tells me. "You hate it there even more than I do."

I don't know what to say. Do I hate it? My home planet? I hate Hastur, and I hate transphobic assholes, and I hate evangelical Christianity, but there are just as many things that I love. I love Tilda Swinton and pasta with pesto and Istanbul and the New Pornographers and *The Vampire Diaries*. I love dogs and thrift stores and swimming in lakes and bonfires and Lewdy's laugh. Goddammit, maybe I *am* in love with Lewdy. That complicates things.

"I'll come and visit," I tell Spermy, "but I'm going home."

"Okay," she says. "Tell my mom I'll call her tonight and explain. I met this plasma cloud last night who works as a long distance carrier." She's playing it cool, but when I hug her she loses it.

"I'm not dying, I'm just twenty-nine light years away!" she yells, and we laugh, and we get on the bus, and we're gone.

Not only does Mr. Kevinson pay us seven grand for the bout, a couple of days later a new sign shows up outside the Quonset. We don't know what powers it or what it's made out of, but I'm pretty sure that the words "HOME OF THE DOUGLAS COUNTY ROLLERGIRLS" are visible from space.

With Her Hundred Miles to Hell

Kat Howard

I had been dreaming of honey. Golden, like the sun. Thick and sweet, late summer distilled.

Then. The numbness and burning of the sting. Skin that swelled around the poison beneath, too-hot and ill-fitting. Breath that wheezed through a closing throat, and death, just on the other side.

I woke up. Honey, sweet on my lips, and an echo of buzzing in my ears. A crackle, a rustling, and dead bees spilled from my sheets to the floor.

That wasn't even the strangest thing.

When I touched the bodies, I dreamed of flight. A waking dream, but sun and wind and the hum of the hive just the same.

The last dreams of the dead bees.

Change, like death, tends to happen in only one direction, and is not lightly undone. The death of the bees was only the first dreaming death. It was not the last.

You could go to Hades six times. That was the rule. There were reasons for it, as anyone who knew anything about mythology would tell you. The Erinyes guarded the door, and they would remember your face, and your sixth night there, dancing in Hell, that would be your last.

I'm not kidding about the Erinyes. Or the Eumenides, the Kindly Ones, as the people who thought they could bribe or talk their way through the doors one more time called them. And sure, Cerberus would have been the more usual thing, but a slobbering three-headed dog draws a different sort of clientele than fiercely sexy women in miniskirts and boots.

If you ever saw the snakes they wore, just beneath their skin, you had bigger concerns than getting turned away at the door.

Aside from the Furies who kept the riffraff out, Hades was invitation only, the invitations small red pips of a pomegranate, made from glass, the name of the club etched onto them. Invitations were coveted: everyone, it seemed, wanted to go to Hell.

Hades was full of the beautiful and the damned, and there was exhilaration, there was glory, in thinking that was who you were, too, even if only for six nights. Most people who walked through the door would have gulped down an entire pomegranate, condemned the left-behind world to an eternity of winter, if it meant only that they could stay.

"Hello, Morain," Tisiphone said. She kissed me on the cheek, then waved me past the line of people waiting to get in. Hades was where I worked, so I needed no artful invitation, nor was I bound by a six night limit.

I still died, just a little, as I walked through the doors.

What do you dream, when you are alone in the dark? Be honest, now. Take out those secrets, those velvet wants, those blood-drenched desires. You need not show them to anyone else, but look at them. Know them. Roll yourself about in them until your hair is mussed and your skin is sticky.

Now, imagine you could have that dream always. Whenever.

Imagine.

And think about what you might give to have it.

Clear your mind of whatever you think of when you think of Hell, because if walking into Hades were like walking into some medieval Inferno, Virgil or no Virgil, no one would go.

Or maybe some would. There will always be some who will revel in feeling that they are the apotheosis of evil and ought to be either punished or celebrated accordingly, in screams and agonies, even if those screams and agonies are their own. But there wouldn't be lines down the block, even with the Greek name slapped on the sign and myths as bouncers.

No, walking into Hades was like walking into a live performance of all of the sin you were told would send you to Hell. It was the opulent decadence of a Renaissance palace, the wildness of a bacchanal. It might be Hell, but it's also a nightclub.

I paused at the edge of the dance floor, let the music sink into me, slide under my skin, and course through my blood. The hanged man spun from the ceiling, crooning about being undead, undead, undead to the dancers below.

The pieces of the dream had held together well, though I thought he would be sore when it wore off.

That was the other reason to come to Hades. To live, temporarily, in a dream. Here, you could dream whatever you wanted. They were made for you, little faceted jewels that you swallowed like Alice drinking and eating in Wonderland. And for that space of time, here in these walls, the dream was real. Tangible. Yours.

That was a thing worth dying a little bit to have.

That's why I don't have to stand in line, or trade a pomegranate seed to get in. I dream those dreams, collect all the fractal pieces of them from myself, so they can be shaped into whatever the current desire or fashion is. So long as I come here to dream, I can blacken entire calendars' worth of nights in Hell.

I walk past the bar, the edifice of glass, all edged and polished to glitter in the lights of the club, to better reflect the dreams and desires of those who spend small deaths to be here. As I pass, I nod at the bartender, Tantalus, who can neither eat nor drink from what he serves. Please. Don't look shocked. You read the name on the door when you walked in, and if you think there aren't those who came here to watch others suffer, you haven't been paying attention.

Behind the shine and the lights, there is a door. The man with coins for eyes opens it for me, and I step into the shadows. I walk down until I can no longer hear the bright discord of the club, walk further until the bass no longer thrums through the soles of my shoes, walk until there is only silence and darkness.

A dream can be given to someone else. Of course it can. Here. An assortment, each designed to exacting specifications. Reach in and take one. Oh, and you don't have to give it away if you don't want to. Keep the dream for yourself. Just swallow it down. Perhaps you'd prefer it mixed into a drink.

No?

Something specific, then. Well, there are certainly the usual flavors. Flying is popular. A visit from someone long-missed, either living or dead. Sex. Nightmare. Both together.

More specific even than that? Well. Possible. Anything is possible. But it will cost. Be certain of what you want, and be more certain still of what you are willing to pay.

I don't sleep when I dream, not here. I have to be awake as the dreams unspool so that I can collect them. It's not painful, not really. Imagine the drawing-off of poison. Any pain there might be is overwhelmed by the feeling of purgation, the knowledge that when this is over, things will be better. That I will be clean again.

When I had walked far enough, I sat before Mother Night. This place, like all undercrofts and hidden spaces, was hers, and the dreams born here became hers as well. She was the one who told me what to dream, who gave me the list of what the dreams required.

I say list. It was never written down.

Today it was a key, and a scrap of fabric, lush red satin. I drank, as I always did, from her offered cup, and it tasted like wine, like cinnamon, like rue.

I curled into a hollow, and I dreamt. The dream fell in pieces from my eyes, like tears, and I collected it in the cup from which I drank.

"Is there another dream?" I asked.

Mother Night leaned forward, close enough that her hair brushed my skin. It smelled of winter, of midnight, and of the cold light of the stars. It felt like secrets. She angled my face toward her, and looked into my eyes.

"How many deaths have you spent at the door?" she asked.

I knew. I knew to the exact number, and I suspected she did as well. Too many, and I could die permanently. Or the dreams could change again. The connection between both was too close to see the boundary separating them.

So I did not lie. But I thought of my bed, covered in bees, in butterflies, in the velvet and leather of bats. There were things I needed to atone for.

"Not enough," I said.

"For now, it is. No more dreams tonight."

The walk back up from the underground at Hades always seemed to take longer than the trip down, as if the mythology had been invoked so many times that it overrode the physics of the space. There were times when it felt I walked ten minutes down, and a hundred miles to return.

Still, there was only one way out, so I walked back to the light, the music, the crowd of people who had died, just a little, to be there.

No. There are things that cannot be done, even in dreams.

You think you are the first person to ask? To come here, to this place of all places, and ask that question? Console yourself at least with the knowledge that you will not be the last.

I can give you a dream with her in it. But it will be a dream. There will be nothing of her beyond that dreaming, neither here, nor elsewhere, whether you look back when you wake up, or not.

The door to the underground of Hades slides shut behind me, and I kiss Charon on the cheek as I walk past him back into the life of the club. He doesn't react. He never does. Just once I'd like to see if he could blush, if it were possible to knock the coins from his eyes.

There was a glass waiting on the end of the bar. There was always a glass waiting on the end of the bar. Ambrosia and pomegranate seeds. Six of them. He was waiting as well. Hades, who collected deaths, even the small ones that came out of dreams. "Your dreams would be yours again."

I met his gaze, and touched the rim of the glass to my lips, as I always did. The air in the club paused. Then I set the glass back down.

"They already are." Most days I called them a curse, but they were mine.

"As you say, and so it must be true." The glass disappeared, replaced by an Archangel, tasting of ice and hazelnuts, and this time when I toasted Hades, I did drink. Then I leaned against the bar, and watched bits and pieces of my dreams come to life.

That night, I dreamt while sleeping. When I awoke, there was a pile of feathers at the foot of my bed, and I knew what my dreams had killed.

If I dreamed sleeping, there was always a small death when I awoke. I gathered the corpse of the sky-colored bird. For a moment, there was the sensation of air through feathers that weren't mine. "I'm sorry," I said.

I was. I was sorry every time it happened. Working at Hades helped, bled off the worst of the poison in my dreams, the thing that made them fatal, but I couldn't control them. The deaths still happened, as if death and sleep had somehow become confused in their roles, and were sending me the wrong gifts.

When I climbed out of bed, I discovered I was wrong. It was not just one bird.

Small, feathered bodies, flightless now, littered my floors. An entire flock.

It was a thing done in the dark. Such things always are.

"What sort of dream is it you want, hmm? Something to make someone love you for the night? Or a night of terror for the lover who traded the scent of your skin and the sound of your breath for someone else?"

"Death. A dream of death."

A hiss of breath being drawn in through teeth, and a rustle of fabric. "Such a thing will cost."

"I will pay."

"Very well."

No noise in the darkness then, but scents. The sweet rot of over-blown roses, the thick dark clots of earth, the warm iron of blood, so fresh the very air smelled red.

Red was the color of the small, faceted stone that dropped into the outstretched hand. "There is your dream."

"And the cost?"

"You will know it when it is asked."

Hades looks different in the light of day. It looks less real, without the artificially lit darkness to give it dimension, like a film set after the production is over.

Coin-eyed Charon guarded the door. As he always did, as he had everywhere this threshold existed for the crossing. I passed through it into darkness, and I did not look back.

I walked down and down and down, and waited for the shadows to embrace me, to cast their cool fingers over my skin, to veil my eyes from the deaths in front of them. All I saw was thousands of feathers, wings that would no longer fly.

"Give me something to dream," I begged Mother Night.

She held silent, immobile.

My eyes burned with salt. "Please."

"Very well," she said, and the serpents came.

They wound around my hands and feet, slithered through my hair. I drank from her glass, and it burned like acid and tasted like bitter almonds. I drank it like it was champagne.

I had just drained the dregs from the cup when the dream exploded from me, flinging me backwards. My head cracked against the wall, and I dreamed someone's death.

The snakes moved beneath my skin, and fell from my retching mouth. I crawled to my hands and knees, and vomited the dream in the shape of serpents.

When I finished, sticky with bile and vomit, I handed her the dream, safely in the cup. She tucked it on a shelf behind her, then said, "Again."

I took the offered cup.

By the time I stumbled my way back out of the underground at Hades, night had fallen and the club was full of beautiful people. At that moment, I was not beautiful, and I did not care.

The glass, as expected, was on the end of the bar. Ambrosia and pomegranate seeds. My mouth was rancid with my own bile, my throat raw from vomiting snakes and worse. I picked up the glass, watched the light turn the contents neon colors, and thought about drinking.

"The dreams would stop, if you drank." The air around me darkened at Hades' words, and there was comfort in the darkness.

"Because I would be dead." That was the choice, and the peril. Back before stories began, Mother Night had two children. Death, who named himself Hades, and an incarnation of Sleep, whose name is no longer spoken. The incarnation can be filled, of course. You know the stories.

Six seeds from a pomegranate. Don't look back.

People always do. They think they know what they want, until the moment of change stands before them.

Still, right now, my own blood under the nails I hadn't torn from my fingers, vomit drying in my hair, and an apartment full of small deaths to return to, my own death sounded momentarily tempting.

"Life ends in death. For everyone."

"Yes, but not tonight."

I didn't stay to drink, or dance, or watch other people have my dreams. I just went home.

I don't think about what I would dream if my dreams were my own. If sleeping and dreaming didn't mean waking up surrounded by death. The very idea struck me cold—what if dreaming about something, someone, on purpose made the dream reach out to them? Dream of a lover, and it would not be dead birds I would find in my bed.

I have never wished anyone sweet dreams.

I woke with the sheets sticky with sweat, wrapped around my legs like ropes. A small green snake slithered from my hair. I sat up slowly, unwinding myself from the tangled sheets, expecting to see a massacre of serpents scattered about the room.

Nothing.

My throat was still ravaged, and the inside of my mouth tasted like scalded honey. I gagged, retched, and brought up another snake, the color of poison. It braceleted itself around my wrist.

A knock on my door. I ignored it—I was in no shape to see anyone. I wasn't even sure if I could speak without snakes dropping from my mouth.

The knocking came again, louder this time. Robe clutched around me, I opened the door.

Tisiphone, clothed in vengeance.

"Morain, I am charged to bring you to Hades." No glamour to soften her voice now. This was one of the Erinyes speaking. Her voice rang like bronze, and I had to will my feet to remain unmoving.

"What is it?"

"Better that you come," she said.

"Can I change?"

"Better that you come now."

The other Erinyes, Alecto and Megaeara stood just outside the door of the club, faces as dire as Tisiphone's.

"What happened?" I asked.

They said nothing, but opened the heavy door. "Go inside," Tisiphone said.

The death of the door sucked the breath from my body, but it was what I saw inside that dropped me to my knees.

Hades was full of the dead. The corpses of all of last night's mortal revelers littered the floor, their finery tatted and dull in the pale light of morning.

"Is it you, Morain, who has done this?" Tisiphone asked, her voice like a sword, like a scale. It fell on me, and I could not have spoken false, even had I wanted to.

"I don't know," I said. "But I can tell you."

They nodded permission, the three avatars of vengeance, and I began laying my hands on the bodies. As I touched them, their final dreams filled my head.

Some I recognized because I had birthed the pieces of them — love, sticky like cinnamon hearts; fame, all lights and leather and a rock song for a soundtrack; dancing, naked and glorious, in a green wood. Some dreams were things I recognized not at all, just bits and pieces of lives filtered through night and sleep.

Fragmented as the dreams were, they were what I tried to concentrate on. To see only those images, to not think of skin too cool beneath my fingers, of eyes that fixed on nothing, of the stench of a room peopled with death.

There was a noise, as I worked. A clinking that I couldn't place. Too irregular to be a machine. I looked around and saw Charon, weeping. The noise was the coins that fell from his eyes.

Then. A man. Like any other who came to Hades, and like none of them. I didn't recognize him. But oh, I recognized the snakes and the poison that poured out of his dream.

A dream of death.

I could not move my hands. My skin went numb, too-hot, as if I had been bee stung, and my vision as red as the heart of a pomegranate.

As red as the seeds in the glass that was pressed to my mouth.

I drank.

Death was a lot more like a nightclub than I expected it to be. Somewhere in the back of my memory, Bowie was singing about the heart's filthy lesson, and I wanted to tell him I had already learned that. I was ready for the exam.

"You're not dead, dear. Not yet. Open your eyes and have a drink with me."

It was a voice I was used to obeying, so I opened my eyes, and reached for the glass. Mother Night, who looked nothing like I had expected.

"I was dead."

"Perhaps. You can be, if that's what you choose. Or you can be something else."

"I ate the pomegranate seeds." A dream or a death. That was the choice of the drink, and if I was here, it wasn't a dream.

"Which means only that you ate them. Ravaged maidens and endless winters make for good stories, true, but for bad lives."

We finished our drinks. My mouth tasted of honey. "Thank you," I said.

"For what?" she asked.

"The dreams."

She smiled. "The dead don't dream, Morain."

"I know."

When I left that place, to walk back to my dreams, I took the longer path. I did not look back.

Star Dancer

Jennifer Pelland

It was the summer of 1984. I'd just gotten out of college and had moved back in with my parents in Chicopee. If I wanted to hang around with fellow lesbians, the only ones around were the Smithies up in Northampton. How bad were they? They used "Sapphic" unironically.

Don't judge me. A girl gets lonely.

I was desperate to leave. Go to London. Maybe San Francisco. Or I suppose New York City. Somewhere where my taste in music was more interesting than my taste in sex partners. In other words, anywhere but Chicopee.

But for now, I was stuck with the Smithies, heading to a party that was going to have a belly dancer, of all things. She called herself "Shahrazad the Star Dancer." I was pretty sure that was a stage name, although in Northampton, one couldn't assume. The Smithies were all twittering about how she represented female empowerment and the reclamation of our bodies or some such shit. I was just hoping to watch a hot babe writhe around some stranger's living room and then go home with a raging case of metaphorical blue balls and enough masturbation fantasies to get me through the rest of the month. With any luck, she wouldn't dance to Duran Duran. I fucking hate Duran Duran. The music coming out of London had been so much better before they'd gone all *Tiger Beat* and dragged everyone else along with them.

Yeah, scratch London from the list.

So here I was, in that aforementioned stranger's living room, surrounded by hairy-legged hippies who were passing a joint around. As usual, I stood out from the crowd in my Alien Sex Fiend T-shirt and thick black eyeliner.

"You're objectifying yourself, Cass," one of the Smithies said, pointing to my spiked dog collar.

"Gotta pee," I mumbled, and made a beeline for the bathroom. Time to pop some MDMA to make this party more palatable. My gay friends in college called it "Adam," and I'd heard some people starting to refer to it as "ecstasy," but all I knew was that this shit had totally made my Chemistry degree profitable by my senior year at UT Austin.

Austin. I'd liked it there. Too bad it was surrounded by Texas.

The MDMA had kicked in by the time the belly dancer arrived. I could tell it was working because I didn't care that I was surrounded by Smithies anymore. In fact, I was starting to think about asking one of them out. I had the sneaking suspicion that the one who was wearing pants instead of an Indian broomstick skirt was hiding a pair of shaved legs. Yeah, my standards were getting pretty low now that I was back home.

The glittery dancer set up her boombox, and promptly dropped to the floor and started doing inhuman things with her abs.

No, I seriously mean inhuman. I may have been a Chem major, but I'd taken enough Bio to realize that the human body didn't have that many abdominal muscles. Never mind the fact that her arms didn't appear to have bones and her hair was undulating under its own power.

I looked around the room, but no one else seemed to be bothered by any of this.

Had to be the MDMA, right?

Shahrazad got up from the floor and started doing a killer shimmy as she danced in a circle around the room. She stopped directly in front of me, planted her navel inches from my nose and started undulating on top of that shimmy. That's when I realized that she wasn't actually wearing glitter. That was her skin.

I looked up, mouth agape, into eyes greener than any I'd ever seen before.

She winked.

Too soon, the show was over, and Shahrazad pulled a caftan on over her spangly costume, much to the dismay of the Smithies.

Then, to their further dismay, she walked over to me and handed me a business card.

"What are you?" I whispered.

"See you tomorrow. Midnight."

I looked down at the card. It was for the Agawam Rollaway.

"Belly-dance party at the roller rink?" one the Smithies asked. "We're totally there!"

When I looked up again, Shahrazad was gone.

"Uh, can someone give me a ride to the bus?"

As I sat on the Peter Pan bus, staring out at the median strip of I-91 as it hypnotically floated by the window, I clutched the card in my hand and wondered what the fuck I was getting myself into. Like, what if they were doing an all-night "Thriller" skate tomorrow? Wasn't that the kind of thing the Geneva Convention protected me from?

As always, I'd timed my drug trip perfectly. My brain was straight by the time I got off of the bus. I headed to my beat-up, second-hand Pinto, and stuffed my fingers in my ears as the boys from Westover did a low, fast fly-over. They'd been doing a lot of night runs lately. I blamed Reagan. Mind you, I also blamed him for stubbed toes and hangovers and shoulder pads coming back into style.

I drove back to suburbia, to the room I rented over my parents' garage.

To Boring-ville.

I had to get to London. Or New York. Or Tokyo.

But for now, I guess I'd have to settle for the roller rink.

I was awoken by my windows rattling to the tune of another Air Force fly-over. Shit, I'd overslept. I had to open the store in half an hour. I put a new coat of eyeliner over the smeared remnants of the previous night's, ran my fingers through my hair to re-spike it a little, then tossed on last night's clothes, stuffed a baggie of MDMA in my pocket in case one of my special side customers came to the store, and climbed into the Pinto to head to Eclipse Records.

Working at a record store sounds a lot more interesting than it actually is. Well, it might be a cool job in Boston or Cambridge or New York City. Here, I mostly peddled Duran Duran, A Flock of Seagulls, and this new chick named Madonna. She wouldn't last. Some days, I thought about dipping into my stash to get through the workday. Then I remembered that I had no way of restocking it, and chugged coffee instead. Someday, I'd be able to set up a new lab. When I had the money. Which at this rate would be never.

When I got home, my parents were out for the night. There was a note on the fridge saying they'd gone to the movies, and that I should have the leftover pizza. Score one for me. Eating leftovers alone was easier than going through the dinnertime question gauntlet. "Are you still sending out résumés for real jobs?" "Any luck finding a roommate so you can move into your own apartment?" "Will you stop dyeing your hair black long enough to look like a normal human being for your brother's wedding?"

Honestly, though, they weren't bad people. For starters, they were public school teachers, which is one step away from sainthood if you ask me. And they'd mostly accepted my lesbianism. But it's damned hard to feel like an adult when you're living in your parents' house. At least Mom had taken over my old bedroom to make it her crafts room. If I'd had to live there instead of over the garage, I probably would have slit my wrists in despair. Of course, why she'd taken over my old room instead of my brother's might have had something to do with the lesbianism thing. I guess she preferred a shrine to football trophies over a shrine to cunnilingus.

I killed time watching TV, then it was back to the Pinto, back to I-91. And then it was midnight, and I was stepping out of the car, staring at the darkened and thoroughly closed Agawam Rollaway.

Another Air Force flyover thundered past, this one so low to the ground that I reflexively ducked.

Well, this was a wasted night. And I'd even worn the studded leather jacket and belt that matched my collar. I pulled the card from my jeans pocket and was about to throw it to the ground when suddenly, a door opened, and spinning disco-ball light spilled out into the parking lot, stopping at the toes of my scuffed, second-hand combat boots.

A glittering Amazon of a woman stood in the open doorway, so tall and gorgeous that she would have made Wonder Woman herself weep with jealousy. "She's waiting for you."

I strained to make out the music. Oh, thank God. *Not* "Thriller." In fact, I was pretty sure it was Depeche Mode. Eh, that would do.

As I stepped through the door, the Amazon grabbed my arm, twisted it behind my back, and slammed me against the wall. "You've seen things you weren't supposed to," she hissed in my ear.

Okay, so I was beginning to suspect that I'd been pretty stupid to come here without letting anyone else know about it. Wait, the Smithies had seen the card. They'd come to my rescue, right? Oh God, they were probably all stuck up in Northampton with pot munchies right now.

"Let her go."

Shahrazad wafted into view, sparkles spinning around her like a cloud of demented fireflies, and I'm pretty sure I started gaping again.

"This isn't possible," I mumbled. "I'm not even high this time."

"No, once you see me as I truly am, I can't fool you ever again. Celeste, I told you to let her go."

I could literally feel the Amazon's reluctance as she dropped my arm and stepped backwards.

I shook out my arm and watched Shahrazad's hair flutter in the complete and utter lack of breeze. The light from the disco ball was interacting in the most mind-bending ways with her glitter cloud. I blinked hard, but it didn't help. "What are you?"

"My dear, it's all in my name."

She'd called herself "Shahrazad the Star Dancer."

Shit.

"It seemed like a harmless enough descriptive. I had no idea you had such pharmaceutical sophistication on this part of your planet."

"So...um...you came here from another planet to belly dance?"

When she laughed, it sounded like wind chimes. "Oh, how I wish it were that simple. I came here to hide. Will you help me stay hidden?"

Behind me, the Amazon growled.

"Celeste, I'm sure we can trust her." She turned her hypnotic green gaze back to me and asked, "Can we?"

I swallowed hard. "Lady, if I told anyone, they'd lock me up in the loony bin."

Shahrazad smiled. "Wonderful. Now let me show you what else I've discovered I'm good at."

She led me into a room that I know wasn't part of the Rollaway, if only because of the wave of nausea that crashed over me as I walked through the door. "A phase junction," she said. "Pay it no mind." She laid me back on a pile of subtly undulating pillows, and I stared up through a faceted glass ceiling at more stars than should have been visible under this much light pollution.

"How—"

"No talking," she said. She nimbly undid my jeans with her teeth, then proceeded to reduce me to a gibbering wreck with her tongue, all to the continued strains of Depeche Mode.

Yeah, I'd protect her secret. Especially if there was more of that waiting for me.

Celeste the Amazon growled at me again as I staggered out into the parking lot toward my Pinto. I probably wouldn't be able to walk straight for a week. And there, at last, were the Smithies. "Sorry we're late," one of them said, rolling out of a VW bus that reeked of patchouli. "Did we miss anything good?"

I just laughed and climbed into my car.

I went back to the Rollaway every night that week, and every night, I walked back to the car with rubbery legs and a stupid grin on my face. Somehow, Shaz (as I now called her) managed to get her phase thingie to cover the entire building, so on nights when the Rollaway was open late, I sat back and watched two entirely different realities sharing the rink. In the regular old reality, the Smithies, pimply teenagers, and the occasional creepy old guy skated around in circles to the most insipid pop crap out there. In Shaz's reality, she rocked out to rhythms so complicated that they hurt my well-medicated brain. I'd thought Shaz was unreal on bare feet, but on roller skates, she was something else altogether. I swear, sometimes she was skating a good foot above the actual floor.

"What are you on?" one of the Smithies asked me.

"Nothing I'm going to share with you." Which is exactly what I would have told her even if I *weren't* helping hide a belly-dancing alien.

Shaz skated over, her lip in a fetching pout. "You never skate with me."

"Lady, I can barely walk when I'm around you, never mind skate."

That night, she finally let me show her my own talents. Did I mention that she tasted like smoke and honey? Holy shit, she was something else.

As she was the one lying bonelessly on the pillows for a change, I chucked a pair of pillows aside, rested my elbow on the comfortingly solid floor, and asked, "Seriously, though, why are you here? On this planet?"

"I told you, I'm in hiding."

"By taking belly-dance gigs? That's not really hiding."

She rolled onto her stomach, showing me her magnificent sparkling ass. "Oh, I know," she said. "I can't help it. I suppose I'm too much of a diva to stay hidden away entirely."

I forced myself to look at her undulating hair. If I kept staring at her ass, I'd lose all ability to think. "Another thing—your English is perfect. The fact that you just busted out the word 'diva' and used it correctly—"

"I studied your language before coming here," she said. "Really, I can't believe you care about—"

"*Why* are you hiding?"

She sighed. "I just want to dance and have fun."

"Seriously, just answer the question."

"I did. I just want to dance and have fun. Those things are...discouraged where I come from. Especially for someone in my position."

I looked down at her position. It was tasty.

She noticed my scrutiny and smiled.

I couldn't help myself. I had to show off all over again. I was picking sparkles off my tongue the entire drive home.

The next morning, I stood groggily behind the counter of Eclipse Records, hoping that the large cup of Dunkin' Donuts coffee I'd just chugged would kick in before I had to deal with any customers.

No such luck. The bell over the door rang, and I looked up to see two young punks walk in.

Well, that was a refreshing change for Chicopee.

And then I noticed that both of their mohawks were vibrating.

Ah. I knew what that meant.

They shuffled up to the counter, hands stuffed in the pockets of their artfully ripped jeans, their skin glittering madly as a beam of sunlight hit them. The one with the green hair said, "Hey, we heard you could hook us up with a belly dancer."

"Like Siouxsie Sioux style? I don't think we have anyone like that around here."

"No, like traditional style."

I raised an eyebrow. "I didn't take you for the traditional anything type."

Their mohawks vibrated even more rapidly, and I pretended not to notice.

The blue-haired one said, "Well, it's our mom."

"It's for our mom," the green-haired one said.

"Yeah, that's what I meant."

Hmm. Whatever species she was, they didn't get stretchmarks.

"Yeah, sorry. I can't help you. But if you want the latest from The Cure—"

"Actually, do you have any Madonna?"

I gave him a pointed once-over. "Aren't you a little over-dressed for Madonna?"

He had the decency to blush at that. At least, I think that was what it meant when someone like him turned gray.

They hadn't been gone more than ten minutes when the bell rang again. This time, it was three military guys. I think Air Force. And me with a pocket full of MDMA.

Shit.

The oldest one removed his hat as they walked through the door and tucked it under his arm. "Excuse me, are you Miss Labonté?"

"Ms. Labonte. I'm a feminist, and this isn't France."

"I'm Colonel Gagnon. May we have a word with you?"

"I'm working."

"We're your only customers."

"So buy something."

He nodded at the youngest of the soldiers, and the kid started duti-fully browsing through the cassettes.

"Now, Ms. Labonte, have you seen anything unusual lately?"

"This is Chicopee. I'm the most unusual thing here."

He placed his hat on the counter and gave me an appraising look. He lingered briefly at my chest, but I chalked the attention up to the fact that I was wearing a homemade "Smash the Patriarchy" T-shirt. "Perhaps in a neighboring town?"

"I really doubt we have the same idea of what constitutes unusual."

"And I suspect you doubt that I even have the same ability as you to *see* the unusual."

The small lump of pills in my right pants pocket suddenly felt as large as a grapefruit.

"You'd be right, of course. But Captain Ireland here has a differ-ent perspective."

The third man stepped forward, stared intently at my temple. "Are you wearing glitter?" he asked.

"Uh...I'm dating a stripper." The military hated lesbians, right? Maybe that would scare them off.

"Captain Ireland had a rather checkered past before joining the Air Force. He sees things a little differently than the rest of us do. And clearly, he sees something in you."

I laughed nervously and tried my best to avoid catching Ireland's eye. "Well, so long as he's clean now. I'd hate to think the Air Force was sticking junkies into cockpits."

"Interesting," Ireland said. "So you know drugs are the key to seeing them."

Oh, fuck me.

I opened my mouth to sputter out some half-assed rebuttal, but the Colonel held up his hand and said, "Just tell us where she is."

Wait, maybe I could still make this work.

"She? I thought you were talking about those two guys that were just in here. You know, the glittery guys with the colored mohawks? The *vibrating* mohawks?"

Ireland's eyes lit up. "So there are more—"

Gagnon held up his hand. "Not in front of the civilian." He turned to the third soldier and said, "Lieutenant, we're leaving."

The young lieutenant came up to the counter with a Joy Division cassette. "I'd like to buy this."

Maybe there was hope for the military yet.

Ireland took another long, appraising look at me, then asked, "So, what have you taken?"

"Lots of pills," I said with a shrug. "You know how college is. I never bothered asking what they were. Figured I was better off not knowing."

"Pills," he mused. "Not peyote?"

"God, no. Give me medical-grade pharmaceuticals any day. Nature's got no quality control."

"Hallucinogens? Amphetamines? Soporifics?"

"Sometimes all at once. I lost track. You know. College."

I rang up the lieutenant's purchase, and Gagnon handed me a business card. "If you see these young punks again, or anyone else like them, call me. It's crucial that we locate them."

"National security, eh?"

"Planetary," Ireland said.

Gagnon shot him an irate look. "Not in front of the civilian."

The three men left, and I tossed the business card into the trash. Then my knees gave out and I found myself on the floor, legs tucked against my chest, perilously close to being in the fetal position.

Suddenly, this alien girlfriend of mine was starting to seem like more work than she was worth.

I spent the rest of my shift trying to figure out what the fuck to do. Call the Rollaway? First off, the Air Force was probably tapping the store's line. Secondly, what the hell was I supposed to say? "Hi, can you please hand the phone to the woman who's living in a slightly different dimension in the middle of your rink?" Yeah, that wouldn't work so well. And with my luck, they'd have a digital phone and know to dial *69 to figure out who'd called, resulting in a one-way trip to the loony bin for me.

Driving out there was just as bad an idea.

And what about her kids? Shit, what could *they* do to me? My brain kept running through every gory sci-fi movie I'd ever seen, which at least meant that I was occasionally consoled by thoughts of Sigourney Weaver in her skivvies.

Besides, what did I really owe Shaz? Sure, she was awesome at cunnilingus, but it wasn't like we were going steady or anything. We were just fuckbuddies. You could hardly blame someone for going back on a promise to a fuckbuddy when military and interstellar hunters were involved.

And speaking of which, how the fuck had they both even connected me to her?

I still hadn't figured anything out by the time the store closed, so I drove home, hoping for another note pointing to leftovers, and instead found my parents waiting for me at the kitchen table.

"The Air Force was here," Mom said. "They wanted to get into your room."

"Did they have a warrant?"

"We didn't ask for one."

"So," my father asked, "when were you going to tell us about the drugs?"

Oh, great. They'd found them. "What I put in my body is none of your business."

"When it brings the military to our house, it certainly is."

"Did they call the cops?"

"No, but I would have myself if they hadn't confiscated the lot."

"Confiscated? Goddamn it!" I raced out of the kitchen, across the backyard, and up the stairs to my little garage apartment. The door was hanging open, and I expected to see the place ransacked, but apparently, the Air Force was good at doing very tidy searches, because the place looked untouched.

But when I looked under the bathroom sink, my stash was gone.

The only MDMA I had left in this world were the pills in my pants pocket.

I heard footsteps behind me, and turned to see my parents both staring at me with clear disapproval. My father shook his head and said, "You're selling, aren't you?"

"Well, I sure as shit can't anymore," I said. "They took everything!"

"Under our roof?"

"Of course not," I said. I shouldered my way past them and ran down to the car. "At the store."

"Don't you come back, young lady!" my mother yelled.

"Stop treating me like an after school special! I'm an adult!"

I slammed the car door closed, shutting out whatever ridiculous retort my mother threw back at me.

Fuck being followed. I didn't care anymore. I was going to the goddamned Rollaway. Let the Air Force and Mommy's Little Punkies come along for the ride. I'd wanted excitement, hadn't I? Who needed Tokyo when I had this?

When I got to the Rollaway, Celeste the Amazon was in the parking lot, pulling a fresh cigarette from her jeans jacket pocket and lighting it off of the butt of her previous one.

"Where the fuck is she?" I asked.

"You don't wanna know."

"I've had the Air Force *and* her kids asking about her today. They're probably both on my tail right now."

Celeste flicked the butt to the pavement, ground it out with her toe, and took a long drag from her fresh cigarette. "I told her this would happen," she said, smoke wafting from her nose and ears.

"You're not mad at me? I thought you were her bodyguard or something."

She snorted, and I swore I saw tiny tendrils of smoke coming out of her scalp. "Nah, I'm her big sister, and I'm officially done looking

out for her. She can take care of her own sorry ass from now on."
She bobbed her head toward the door and said, "Have at her."

I stormed into the Rollaway, hanging a right at the phase junction,
and found Shaz dancing naked in the middle of her pillow room, surrounded by kneeling Smithies. Shaz was ecstatic, glimmering with
sweat and sparkles, her hair practically throwing sparks as she flung
her head back and forth. Shit, she was right. She *was* a diva. How had I
fallen for someone so damned high-maintenance?

One of the Smithies turned to me—the one I'd actually thought
about asking out—and cried, "We are in the presence of the goddess!"

"She's just a naked lady. For fuck's sake, I could be a goddess by
those standards."

"You're not seeing her with true sight. Have one of these." She gestured toward a plate of suspicious-looking brownies.

Oh great, the Smithies had discovered hash.

The song ended, and the Smithies broke into wild applause. Shaz
smiled down at their fawning faces, looking for all the world like she
was getting high off of them, then finally noticed me. "Cass!" She flung
her arms wide and said, "Ladies, make a path for her."

They parted like she was Lady Moses.

"I met your boys today," I said. "And the Air Force."

Her skin went gray, and she raced down the Smithie corridor and grabbed
me by the forearms. "You didn't tell them where to find me, did you?"

"I'm pretty sure they were all smart enough to follow me."

As if on cue, we heard Colonel Gagnon ordering the evacuation
of the Rollaway through a megaphone. "We have the building surrounded. Come out with your hands up."

Oh God, I was officially living in a bad movie, and that line was the
proof of it.

Her two sons snuck into the room and gaped at Shaz. "Mom!" the
green-haired one squeaked. "Stop it! You're embarrassing us."

"I'll do no such thing! This shape is beautiful!"

"How did you get past the military?" I asked.

"We didn't. You can come in now."

Colonel Gagnon marched in, flanked by half a dozen heavily-
armed soldiers. Celeste walked in behind him, arm-in-arm with Captain Ireland, who was clearly tripping balls on my stolen MDMA. "I
love everybody," he mumbled.

"Yeah, it wears off," I said.

Shaz glared at her sister, hands on her hips. "What the hell do you think you're doing?"

"Even I have my limits. Her, I could take," she said, nodding her head toward me. "But them?" She looked at the Smithies and shuddered.

"I love them alllllllll!"

Gagnon shook his head sadly. "Lost another one," he muttered. "'Best minds of my generation destroyed by madness' indeed."

I kinda felt my sanity snap at that. Next thing I knew, I was standing on a pile of undulating pillows holding the plate of hash brownies over my head and screaming, "Who the fuck are you people, how did you find me, and why is that soldier quoting Ginsberg?!?"

"At ease, Ms. Labonte," Gagnon said. He held out his hand and said, "Now give me the brownies and nobody has to get hurt."

"Not until I get answers!"

"And if you don't get them, what exactly are you planning to do with those brownies?"

"I...Fuck." I handed him the plate and let out a long sigh. "I have no fucking clue."

Celeste lit a fresh cigarette off the one she was currently smoking and handed it to me. I took a long drag, remembered I didn't smoke, and decided I didn't care.

Gagnon led his stoned Captain to a cushion, and asked me, "So, who are the aliens?"

I pointed to Shaz and the boys. Celeste pointed to herself. "We're the royal family of don't even bother trying to pronounce it," she said. "Little sis here is the queen. But she wanted to be a dancing queen instead and convinced me to help her escape. Stupidest mistake I've ever made."

"As for how we found you," Gagnon said, "apparently you're shedding glitter that only the chemically initiated can see. Captain Ireland followed the trail to the store, and I suspect the princes did too."

I glared down at Captain Ireland. He hugged a pillow and professed his love for it.

"We've lost too many good men in this line of service," Gagnon said. "Captain Ginsberg was only one of many. You should try reading 'Howl' now that you know that. It takes on a whole new level of meaning."

"I...I think I will."

"As for why this unit exists, ever since we started sending radio broadcasts out to the stars, we've been overrun with aliens coming here to party. Most come to the U.S., or the U.K., because we're the ones putting out the most broadcasts—"

"Which makes it easier to learn the language," Shaz said.

"—but we're seeing more and more head for Latin America."

"We almost went there," Celeste said. "But someone decided she liked roller skating more than the samba."

"Shut up!" Shaz snapped.

"Oh, make me."

"And how did you two know she was belly dancing?" I asked the boys.

"Educated guess," the blue-haired one said. "She watched a lot of *I Dream of Jeannie*."

The green-haired son said, "Look, mister, please just let us take our mom and leave your nice planet alone."

"Never!" Shaz cried. "I'll never give up dancing! This shape is liberating!"

The soldiers trained their weapons on her.

"The jig's up, sis," Celeste said.

"Ooh, now that's a dance I never tried."

Celeste rolled her eyes, then walked over to her sister and yanked a hunk of metal out of her ass.

Shaz's form immediately collapsed into a gelatinous ball. I'd been going down on that? Ew.

"Their species is boneless," Gagnon said. "That device gives them human form. But it relies on neurological flim-flammery that an appropriately medicated brain can see right through."

"Now do you understand?" Shaz burbled. "How can I dance in this shape?"

"The United States government formally requests that you figure that out back on your home planet. Now, would the rest of you please?"

"Gladly," Celeste said. She pulled a half-empty pack of smokes from her pocket, handed it to the Colonel, then pulled down her pants and yanked a chunk of metal out of her own ass. The boys quickly did the same, and then Gagnon pulled Ireland to his feet and ushered us all off of the ship.

I watched, incredulously, as it uncoupled from the Rollaway and peeled off into the sky.

"Your country thanks you," Gagnon said.

"Can my country get me a new place to live? My parents kind of kicked me out."

"We can do better than that. How would you like a job with benefits? You seem to handle it better than most." He cast a pointed glance at Captain Ireland.

"I'm a lesbian. I don't think that's legal."

"In your case, I think we can make an exception."

So I finally got that exciting life I'd been looking for. Nice pay, good benefits, and I only have to wear the uniform a couple of times a month when higher-ups come for a visit. The rest of the time, I get to travel the globe, get wasted on new and exciting pharmaceuticals, hit underground parties with truly excellent music, and look for aliens. I've finally gotten to go to New York, San Francisco, London, and even Tokyo once, and all on the government's dime. You'd think that other countries would have their own alien-hunting programs, but apparently they're content to use ours. We're the ones with the missiles to back up our deportation threats, after all.

Although we don't deport them all. For instance, Nick Rhodes from Duran Duran is here on a legitimate interstellar work visa. Who knew? And I managed to convince the U.N. to grant Iggy Pop political asylum. Apparently, his allergy to shirts is a death penalty offense on his home planet. And Madonna—ugh, don't even get me started. Her species lives *forever*. And now that she's gotten her tentacles into the music business—

Shit, I probably shouldn't have mentioned the tentacles.

Anyhow, if you'll excuse me, I'm off to listen to this new sound we intercepted that we're calling "dubstep." Don't worry, it'll be declassified as soon as we figure out how to keep people from guessing right off of the bat that it's not from this planet. Shouldn't take more than a year or two.

Of Selkies, Disco Balls, and Anna Plane

Cat Rambo

Here's Anna Plane and I all through high school: a bushy-haired, white geek girl with a tattered fantasy paperback in the rear pocket of her jeans and me, Arturo, an equally geeky Hispanic theater boy.

Here's us a few years later, dividing time between jobs we hated and the college classes those jobs paid for. Still best friends (of a sort), still sharing trials and tribulations, still with an unspoken question between us, mostly on Anna's part, because I knew the answer.

And here's when I finally answered it, and broke Anna's heart.

South Bend, Indiana, didn't house many dance clubs, even in the height of the disco scene. *Saturday Night Fever* had made it more mainstream, but most of the citizenry still regarded disco with a touch of suspicion as a breeding den of sex-borne illness and drugs, even though it was already dying at that point in 1982.

Not so for Anna. Disco was everything she'd ever dreamed of, the glitter and glitz of an ersatz fairyland. She watched *Dance Fever* every weekend. She could tell you the latest steps, the Top-40 hits, the name of every member of ABBA.

She hadn't been that way in high school. She'd scorned the school dances, saying they were just a way for the popular kids to reinforce their social presence and make everyone feel like shit. But something about disco drew her.

Even though we'd drifted away from our former closeness, divided by differences in class schedules and then, increasingly, in our interests, I did keep in touch. That's how I found out what she'd been hiding.

It was one of our TV nights. She had a fancy laser disc machine, and a stack of every sci-fi or fantasy movie available in that format.

We settled in with popcorn on the couch. She shared a shitty little apartment over on Colfax Avenue with a woman, Dionne, who worked at Waldenbooks but who I had yet to see read anything more than the back of a cereal box, and was usually over at her boyfriend's.

We sat around and shared our troubles in between throwing popcorn kernels at the screen during the cheesy moments. The restaurant she'd been working at had just closed down, so she was looking for a new job.

Dionne had already informed her Waldenbooks wasn't hiring, she said wryly.

I shook out the ink-pungent folds of the *South Bend Tribune* and we went through the ads, circling them, imagining new jobs, new existences for her.

There really weren't that many opportunities out there. Finally we gave up and lapsed into conversation, trailing off into "Remember when?" and asking "What happened to..." as though we'd been out of high school three decades rather than three years.

One of the apartment's oddities was that each of the two bathrooms was reached by going through its accompanying bedroom. I'd gotten used to it, and so when need called, I wandered into Anna's bedroom.

So much of it was familiar to me: the old type drawer hanging on the wall to hold several scores of lead figurines, the bookcase devoted to gaming manuals, the Han Solo poster facing off with the black-light poster of a woman turning into a tiger I'd gotten her. Stacks of paperbacks.

When I noticed the closet door partly ajar, I wasn't tempted to go look. What clothes could Anna have that I didn't know? Hell, I'd been with her when she bought half of them.

But something unexpected peeked out, sparkling like the Witch's Slippers in *The Wizard of Oz*: a length of ruby sequins hanging where it had snagged on the doorknob, as though she'd put it away hurriedly, perhaps when I'd arrived.

What was it?

I drifted toward the door, stood for just a breath looking at that red material. I reached for the doorknob as gingerly as though petting a dog I was unsure of.

When the door swung open, the disco dress blared forth, a slinky thing of red spangles and lycra. Black hose were draped over the shoulder, lacy things with a line of crimson crystals along the back. On the closet floor sat two high-heeled, strappy black Armani shoes.

It stunned me. Was it a gift for someone? A costume?

An entire outfit meant it could only be for her.

I hadn't realized she loved it that much. I'd thought she was content to watch dancers on television, not that she pictured herself there, the dancing queen, in the midst of it all.

You don't hide things from your best friend. I pulled it out, and went back into the other room, holding it in front of me like a flag.

Anna turned almost as red as the dress. She said, "Why were you going through my things?"

"It was hanging out! How could I not notice something that color?"

She stood up, scattering popcorn kernels, and snatched it from my hand. "You had no right!" She marched into the bedroom, disregarding the popcorn crunching beneath her heavy steps, and replaced the dress.

Returning, she stood in the doorway, folded her arms, and said, "It's just in case."

"In case Donna Summer happens to lose her luggage?"

Her chin came up, pointed at me. "In case I want to go out. I do go out sometimes, you know."

"Where?"

"I went to Cinnabar's, till it closed," she said. "They had good dance music."

I knew how I could make things up to her for all my absences of late.

"Go put it on," I said. "We're going dancing."

Along the way, I explained the guidelines to her. "Look, Anna. You have to know, this place, it's got great music and fabulous people and everything, but there's something else. It's a gay bar."

She blinked. "South Bend doesn't have any gay bars."

I laughed at her. "You'd be surprised. Jeff showed me this one. Best place for dancing I know."

She didn't ask the obvious question. I could see her burying it. If she didn't ask, I didn't have to tell her, did I?

I loved Anna, but not in that way. There wasn't any need to rub her nose in it.

"What's it called?"

"Diana's Hunt."

"Why?"

"You'll see." I eyed her dress. "You'll fit right in."

Her face was unhappy. "You think I look ridiculous."

"It's just not what I expected."

She turned to stare into the night sliding past the car window. "Sometimes," she said softly, maybe to me, maybe to herself, "you want to be someone else."

From the outside, the place didn't look like much. A gravel parking lot clustered with cars, a loopy-lettered, red neon sign that simply said "Diana's," and a sign on the door, "21 and older only." Anna trailed me, our footsteps crunching over the gravel.

I wondered if I was making a mistake. I hadn't shared this part of my life with her before. It didn't feel right.

But when I glanced over my shoulder, she was a flash of red in the parking lot lights, tall and beautiful.

She held herself differently in that dress, no longer the too-tall, slump-shouldered girl everyone assumed played basketball in high school. Now her shoulders were back, and despite her hesitation, anticipation gleamed in her eyes.

I liked this new Anna. She seemed happier.

So I swung open the door, and the music reached out and pulled us in.

The bar was named for its owner, Diana. I could tell Anna had never seen anyone like her before.

Diana was short and swarthy, and of indeterminate age. She kept her hair butch short, wore jeans and T-shirts with a men's tuxedo jacket over that, sleeves rolled up to mid-forearm to expose three silver bangles on her left wrist. She was muscular, broad-shouldered. She was an ex-roller derby queen; she'd skated under the name Morgan le Fleet.

Her lover, Clementine, kept the music playing from a booth toward the back. Most of the light system was homemade or scavenged theater lighting, but one piece shouted the bar's intent the minute you walked in. Suspended from the metal rafters high above hung a great mirror ball, at least four feet in diameter. It was positioned over the booth, casting a cloud of falling, glittering light around Clementine.

She was dark-haired like Diana, but milk pale. Her hair fell to her shoulders, sleek as a seal's pelt, framing a narrow face. She was beautiful but intense. She had a way of looking at you as though she expected, maybe even demanded, something. You had the feeling she was on the verge of scorning you for failing to live up to that demand.

When we came in, she was playing Alicia Bridges, demanding that we celebrate the nightlife. The sapphire lights shining on the disco ball drew purple sparkles from Anna's dress as she stepped up beside me.

I heard her take a breath as it hit her. From the name, I'd expected something very different, say, classical Greek to the core, the first time I'd come, with Jeff in a pack of other theater people. Instead, an amazing assemblage of souvenirs of other times, other places covered the walls, things Diana had found or been given. A three-foot-tall statue of the Virgin Mary hung over an enormous silver guitar, while next to it were a pair of gilded roller skates. A spear-gun was mounted with two bright blue flippers behind it.

There were spotlights, a stuffed giraffe head, pink flamingos, luchador masks, clown faces, and a Civil War-era sword with dusty tassels hanging from its stock. Christmas lights *everywhere* glittering off the faces of the rhinestone-covered ukulele and the matador's suit and a huge plastic mosquito that Diana joked was from her hometown in Upper Peninsula Michigan, which someone had glued a fake moustache on.

The air was full of cigarette smoke, and underfoot the floor sucked at our steps, sticky with the spills from sugary mixed drinks.

I'd worried unnecessarily. Anna, at least the new Anna, wearing unfamiliar clothing, fit right in. We'd never done anything harder than the occasional joint or whiffet—or so I'd thought—but when we got separated, I saw her near the bathroom door, doing a line of coke someone had offered.

There were plenty of people making out on the dance floor or in darker corners, but the Hunt wasn't about sex. It was about being there, about feeling the thump of the four-on-the-floor beat going through you, shaking you down to your bones, rearranging your atoms.

It was about being part of the glittering crowd, feeling tribe members all around you, caught up by the music, moving any way they could. Mostly men on the dance floor, but the women danced too. Here, everyone was just another body jostling close to yours.

And when Sister Sledge came on, and "We Are Family" began, Anna was there, singing and waving her arms with the rest of us.

I relaxed. She belonged.

It mattered to me because the Hunt was one of the happiest places I knew. A place where you could forget all your troubles, and live in the moment. Where all you had to worry about was keeping time with the music. We knew disco was dying but none of us were going to give it up anytime soon.

My happiness that Anna fit in didn't mean I was thrilled when Diana offered Anna a job there, though. They'd been talking at the bar, which was busy and shorthanded. By the end of the night Anna was there behind it, shoulder to shoulder with Diana, serving drinks.

Diana wasn't flirting with her, of course. I never saw her have eyes for anyone but Clementine.

I can't say the same for Clementine. Diana and Clementine were inseparable, but you never got the impression Clementine was particularly happy about it. It was an odd match. She stayed in her booth spinning records. Diana waited on her personally, bringing her drinks throughout the evening.

I never saw Clementine thank her.

When the evening started to die down, I stayed and helped clean up afterward, since Anna had driven. Diana slipped me twenty bucks for my help, which was nice.

But it was even nicer to see Anna happier. Sure, I felt a little jealous. The Hunt had been mine, and here she was taking it over. But that thought made me feel mean and dog in the manger-ish.

I could let her have the Hunt, after all. Maybe she needed it more than I did.

When we left the club, it was close to two in the morning, one of those hot Indiana summer nights, where the air feels like the cicada buzz is stitching the heat to your skin. The parking lot was almost empty.

That is, except for the three women on motorcycles.

They were in the parking lot, watching the bar. They didn't even really look at us as we went past, which was odd, because everyone at the Hunt was always friendly.

I didn't think much about it at the time, only noticed them because of the big rumbling Harleys they rode. Their black gas tanks were painted with an odd Celtic knotwork design.

As I got into Anna's car, the leader looked at me. She looked enough like Clementine to be her sister.

After that I didn't go to the Hunt so much. It wasn't that I didn't want to see Anna. In the process of uncovering her red dress secret, I'd edged a little too close to one of my own.

In 1982, in Indiana, you didn't talk about certain things. I'd seen the word "homophobia" for the first time in a *New York Times* article, but I knew what it was already. It wasn't that I didn't trust Anna. But I'd kept the secret to myself for so long that I didn't know how to say it anymore.

I kept telling myself that she must know. I'd taken her to a gay bar, for God's sake.

She said, on one of our TV nights, "You never come down to see me at work."

"I've been busy," I said.

She gave me a look that said, plain as day, I know you're bull-shitting me but I won't push.

I decided to distract her. I edged closer to her on the couch. I said, "Do you know what I'm really in the mood for?"

I regretted it as soon as I said it, but I could already see what she was hoping for in her eyes.

I pulled back, just a touch, and said, "I'm really in the mood to read a really good science fiction book. Will you lend me a couple to take home?"

I felt like such a shit.

So guilt drove me down to the bar, a couple of evenings later. I sat there and chatted with her, listening to "Kung Fu Fighting" and "Do You Think I'm Sexy," abandoning my stool every once in a while to go dance. She was happy I was there. I could see that in her eyes.

And she seemed to be getting along fine with Diana and Clementine. When I mentioned a new song I'd heard, she got Clementine to play it for me.

Every once in a while I'd see some woman flirt with her. Anna was surprisingly adept at handling that, friendly but professional, without making them feel rejected.

She'd never had good luck with men. I wondered if she was tempted to try something different. She never said anything about it to me.

Of course she wouldn't.

Summer wound down, and we entered heat-mad August, days of sweat and sunshine so hot you didn't really want to move. When evening started falling and the air cooled off a little, your energy would return.

One way to burn some of that off was to drive up to the Michigan dunes, build a fire, and get drunk on the beach. I went up one evening with Anna, and a bunch of other high school friends. I didn't particularly like them or want to hang around with them, but Anna made me promise to come.

It was what I had expected: a lot of beer and a couple of bottles of Jaeger getting passed around. We knew a spot that was technically private property, but the owners of the house far above were rarely there to disturb us.

We sat on the soft sand around a fire made from the wood we'd brought and I watched the stars far out over the lake, wondering when I could gracefully excuse myself and slip away.

That was why I was the first person to see something out in the water, coming toward our fire. Several somethings, leaving long dark vees as they swam.

At first I thought they were fish, or seals, or something stranger. Not people. But as the heads came up out of the water, I realized they were human. Women, three of them.

As they came closer yet, I recognized the women who had been on the motorcycles. I would have leaned over to say something to Anna about it, but she was on the other side of the fire.

Late-night beach campfires have their own rules. So we just nodded to the women when they came up, moved over to make room for them, passed out beers.

They didn't introduce themselves to the group, but I saw one talking to Anna.

After it all broke up, I walked with her to the cars. I said, "Who was that woman and what was she talking to you about?"

She laughed. "All sorts of crazy things. We got to talking about fantasy books, and she asked what if all of that was real?"

"What if it was?"

"I wish. That'd be something wonderful. To learn there was actual magic in the world."

She paused before getting in the car.

"It was nice to spend some time with you," she said.

"It was," I agreed, a little too cheerfully.

There was a long moment where she looked at me. I took a step back, waving.

"Catch you around," I said.

"Sure," she said. "Sure."

Classes started again. I was in two plays that semester, plus a staged reading, so things got busy and I didn't see much of Anna in between the demands of work and school. A few times I went down to the bar to talk to her, and she always seemed glad to see me.

Clementine approached me there on a Saturday night.

We'd never really talked before. She was always too busy spinning records and keeping the light show going. That homemade, cobbled-together system had its idiosyncrasies. The light never seemed to reach certain corners. But Clementine knew how to use it, knew how to turn the whole place into a fairyland full of sparkle and madness.

She was taking a break, giving someone else a chance to handle the music. I came up beside her and she looked at me, silently, as always. I never had seen her smile.

She said, "I like your friend Anna."

I was surprised. These were perhaps the first words she'd ever spoken directly to me. I glanced over at her. She was watching Anna behind the bar.

I did see her smile then, for the first time, a small, secretive smile.

A few days later, Anna called because her car had broken down and she wanted me to drive her to work at the bar. We always did favors for each other. I said, "So when should I come pick you up?"

"Oh, you don't need to. I have a friend picking me up."

There was something odd about the way she said it. I didn't know quite what to make of it. Usually we analyzed her dates and relationships at length.

So, it was a little bit snoopy of me, to come in later that night and stay till closing time. Something wasn't right.

When she left, I trailed out the door after her, unobtrusively. I stood out in the smokers' corner, pretending to have a last cigarette before going home.

I watched her get on the motorcycle behind the woman who looked so much like Clementine.

Was *that* who Anna was sleeping with?

I couldn't help but ask the next day when I ran into her at lunch.

I said, "Hey, so you've gotten to know that woman from the beach?" as I set down my tray beside hers on the table.

She said, popping her yogurt open, "She has a lot of interesting things to say."

I quirked an eyebrow. "About?"

"Magic," she said, and blushed.

"Is she teaching you magic?" I teased.

But her face was serious as she shook her head. "No. Her kind of magic can't be taught."

"You're serious?" I knew Anna was crazy for this sort of thing: dragons and unicorns and wizards. Not enough to believe in any of it.

"There is more," she said. "Have you ever seen Diana doing anything odd?"

"Odd how?" There was still incredulity in my voice.

Her lips firmed and she shook her head. "Never mind."

"Look," I said. "I don't know what's going on, but don't let that woman scam you."

Familiar Anna looked at me with something new in her eyes.

She said, "Do you think Diana is a good person?"

That made me blink. "Why would you ask that?"

"I heard some things."

"Like what?"

"Do you think she would do something really bad?"

I leaned forward, exasperated. "What are you trying to get at?"

But instead of explaining, she said, "Do you know that there have been seals sighted in Lake Michigan?"

I scoffed. "Right. And some whales too."

"I looked it up," she said. "No photos, but three or four sightings, all in the Upper Peninsula. Do you know what a selkie is?"

At my head shake, she explained. "They're people who can turn into seals. According to lore, when they change into a human, it's a matter of stepping out of their sealskin, which they have to hide somewhere. What if I told you that Clementine is one, and that the only reason that she stays with Diana is because she has to, because Diana has her skin hidden somewhere in the Hunt?"

"I'd think you were working on a book."

"But I'm not."

"All right. So let's posit that Diana has somehow gotten Clementine's skin..."

"Melissandra says Diana's a sorceress, she stole it away by magic. Someone has to make her give it back. But she can't be killed, Melissandra says, unless it's with an object that Diana owns. It's a geas or something."

I couldn't help rolling my eyes, I swear I couldn't.

Anna's face closed. Her eyes went down to the table. "I need to get to class."

The next day I went down to the Hunt, on one of Anna's days off. I wanted to watch Diana, to see if there was something behind all of this, or if it was all just Anna's fevered imagination.

I ordered a drink from Diana. She said, "Haven't seen you much lately."

I shrugged. "How's Anna working out?"

"I know she's your friend, but she's..." Diana hesitated. "There's something off about her."

I wanted to say, More off than believing you're a sorceress who's stolen a selkie's skin? But I didn't need to tell her that. Anna was harmless, even with weird ideas stuffed into her head.

"I think she stole some things," Diana said. "Tell her to bring them back and all's forgiven."

Had Anna been rummaging around in an insane search for a mythical seal skin? But I just nodded, and settled back to observe the bar.

I'd never really watched Diana before. The only time she had any expression was when she was watching Clementine.

Doting and fond and desperate, all at once.

Who was the woman pursuing Anna and what was her connection to Clementine?

I finally realized what that expression was on Diana's face. I'd seen it before, when Anna was looking at me, too tired or unaware to hide it.

That was when Anna came in with the spear gun.

I don't know that people would have noticed so quickly without Clementine. She must have been watching, knowing Anna was coming. The moment the door swung open, the Pointer Sisters stopped telling us how excited they were, and the lights swiveled in two directions, picking out Anna at the door and, across the room, Diana at the bar.

They stared at each other long enough for me to take a breath.

Anna stepped forward, wearing the red dress. Its light leaped up to meet that of the mirror ball. Bits of bloody light skated over the faces of the crowd and glinted on the spear, with its wicked, sharp vanes.

She said to Diana, "You had no right to enslave Clementine."

Diana's face worked. She cast a look at her lover, who stood in the booth, her face impassive and blank as the mirror's absence, reflecting nothing.

Anna took three more steps. "You need to let her go."

"I can't," Diana said.

"Can't? Or won't?"

Dian's expression hardened. "Won't."

I was standing halfway between them. I started toward Anna.

She waved me back with the spear gun. "Don't interfere, Arturo."

"You don't want to do this," I said. "Think of all the trouble it'll cause. You're throwing your life away on a crazy story someone's spun you."

Her face was untroubled. "The selkies will protect me. They can't come in the bar, but I can act for them."

"They lie," Diana said. "They twist and mislead, the fae." She was staring at Clementine.

Clementine said, "I will be freed."

"Without your skin?" Diana said softly. "Life with me is less preferable than wandering the Earth looking for it?"

"Yes."

I edged closer and closer to Anna. I was shaking, my heart pounding. There's something about a gun, even one without bullets, that raises the tension level in a room.

She noticed me even as I reached for her.

We grappled desperately for a moment while everyone screamed. I don't know which of us pulled the trigger, but the spear didn't hit Diana when it launched. It went wild, the sound bright and brittle in the room, and then the enormous mirror ball exploded as the spear shattered it.

Everyone screamed. Shards bounced with a ting off the silver guitar and chipped a dimple in the Virgin Mary's cheek. A luchador mask was torn from the wall, landing in a heap atop a pile of shards.

Something previously contained in the mirror ball's heart fell, a dark armload of folds that made Clementine's face light as she ran to it.

Diana said, hoarsely, "Clemmie, no."

Clementine didn't even look back as she slung it around her shoulders and went to the door.

Anna walked toward me, shards of mirror crunching beneath her feet. She didn't seem to notice that she still had the gun in her hand, she was looking at me so intently. Watching my face for some sign that was lacking, apparently.

She said, "They promised me something if I did this thing for them."

I asked, "What did they promise you?"

"They promised me you. But that's not going to happen, is it?"

I shook my head.

"And it's not because you like some other girl, some other woman better."

It wasn't a question, but I shook my head anyway.

She took a deep breath, squared her shoulders. She said, "Because you don't like women."

"I like women," I said. "But not like that."

We'd been coming to this moment for so long.

Somehow I had always thought we could avoid it. I'd skirted around its edges, hiding in half-lies and omissions.

She looked back over her shoulder, at Diana, who was standing in front of Clementine's booth, looking at it. The bar owner looked old. And tired. Anna turned and walked away from me, went to Diana. She said something to her I didn't hear, and Diana said something in reply.

Sometimes you love someone and they don't love you back. Or they don't love you the way you want them to, even though every cell in your body knows they're the right one for you. Maybe you do what Anna did for so long, waiting even though you know, deep down, it'll never come. Or maybe you do what Diana did, taking love by what might be trickery, might be force.

You'd think it would have drawn Diana and Anna together, that frustration. That sorrow.

And those of us who are loved? We know. Sometimes we care. Sometimes we don't.

Sometimes we ride away on a motorcycle, rumbling down a moonlit road, headed back up to Lake Michigan. Hair whipping back in the wind. Never looking back at all.

Sooner Than Gold

Cory Skerry

I tug on clean underwear in case I get arrested, paint my makeup perfectly because there's nothing sadder than a grown man in badly applied eyeliner, and climb out my apartment window, onto the fire escape.

I can't be late to this assignment, and if I go through the lobby, there's a strong chance the night doorman will have a thing or two to say about the video footage of our card game last night. I forgot there was a camera pointed at the lobby desk.

The asphalt below reeks of garbage and piss; about half of the latter is probably mine. Don't judge. If I'm drunk enough, there's not even any point in aiming for the toilet.

My boots land softly as I hit the ground, but the ladder clangs as my weight slides off. I look back up at the enchantment, where it strings out between my leg and the trunk in my apartment.

It's a violet chain so thin it looks like I could break it with my fingers, glossy and iridescent like niobium. It burns where it enters my skin, a pain so bright and cruel it took me a week to learn to sleep again.

Sometimes I think about finding some woo-woo psychic to tell me what it is or try to remove it, but I'm afraid the person at the other end of the chain will find out I tried.

Desert heat radiates from the ground, warming the soles of my boots, and I worry about pit-stains and failing hair gel. I shouldn't have worn my jacket, but I cut a better figure with something to embellish my shoulders. And I need to look sharp. I can't use my charm at a drag queen convention if I look like a microwaved cat turd.

I give in and hail a cab, where I endure five minutes of crackly radio commercials and a Celine Dion song. My reward is AC while I sip from my flask and neurotically check the book for new directives.

The book is old, like grandpa-times-three old. The worn leather cover is flexible and shiny from years of use, but the gilt edges of the pages haven't rubbed away. Sometimes I flip through all the paragraphs of nonsense, written in languages I don't recognize, but I usually just open to the page with the ribbon bookmark, the one page that's in English.

The book says the same thing it said when I woke up this afternoon:

> *GlitzCon Ball. Saturday night, 8:00 p.m. Pluck the thorns of the black lily.* **Do not touch her with your bare flesh.**

This cryptic bullshit is sometimes worse, sometimes better, but it nearly always works out in the end. I tuck the book back in my pocket as the cab rolls up to the convention. The side mirror shows my still-flawless makeup before the cab pulls away.

Inside the hotel, I follow signs to the ballroom entrance, where the bass from the party is rattling the doors. An employee holds up a warning hand. She has enough cakey makeup and sparkly rings to be a GlitzCon attendee, and she's old enough to be my mother.

This isn't the only entrance for me, but I want to see if I look as good as I think I do, so I'll try it.

"Where's your con badge?" the Sparkly Cougar asks.

"I don't have one," I say.

"Then—"

I step back, cock a hip, and hold out my hands in the universal gesture for "I'm unarmed." It works even when you're not talking to cops. "But that room is full of horny, middle-aged queens, and you know what they like even more than bitching about how painful their shoes are?"

I use both thumbs to peel back the fitted black cloth of my coat, exposing my all-black rockstar outfit: lace shirt, pierced nipples, edges of a mystery tattoo creeping up above the low-slung waistline of my skinny jeans. I'm going for "slutty Japanese pop star" tonight.

"This."

Sparkly Cougar reluctantly chuckles.

I grin. "I know, right? Come on, honey, you *know* no one is going to complain."

She rolls her eyes, but she laughs and opens the door for the best thief she'll ever meet.

I stroll into pandemonium. The stench of perfume, sweat, fuzzy teeth, and wine is almost too heavy to breathe; the requisite flock of disco balls spin stars across the crowd and the electronic music booms and whirs beside the cacophony of hundreds of gaudy floral costumes. One queen is wearing a ball gown that looks like a giant upside-down rose; another has a bouffant wig with real miniature pansies planted in it. Daffodils, lupines, orchids...None of the elaborate, garish costumes are a black lily.

I don't see any black *anything*—I stand out like a goth skidmark.

I had this coat tailored just for me, a slim-waisted frock style with buttons made of real antique coins: pieces-of-eight from a treasure chest I never should have stolen and definitely never should have opened. Still, without the chest I wouldn't have had the cash to pay the seamstress, and now I have over thirty hidden pockets to stuff with jewelry. Even though I'm here for the thorns of the black lily, nothing says I can't nab some extra rock candy to pay bills, like rent and booze.

I wend my way through the garden of glitter, searching for others in male clothing. Dudes or not, their jewelry is more likely to be real.

I pretend that I've tripped on a drag queen's train, stumble into a fat fellow whose tie tack looks like it might be real diamonds, and walk off wishing I dared snatch the matching cuff links. But even though I did put on clean underwear, I don't want to risk getting caught.

The author of the book is *not* pleased when I'm delayed by jail.

I try not to think about that, instead searching for a black flower costume. There must be a thousand attendees in this cavernous geode of a ballroom, plus at least fifteen hotel staff, ten live parrots hanging in gilded cages by the garden-themed photo set in the back, and two service dogs for one old lady. After forty-five minutes of charming my way through the crowd, winking when someone slaps my ass and leaning over to kiss fingers while I tease off rings—that shit works, I'm telling you—I'm still the single smudge of goth couture in this florist-shop LARP.

It's been almost two years since I failed to steal what the book directed.

I am *not* going to fail again.

Even the AC can't stop me from sweating now, and I pat at my hairline with my handkerchief. My mascara is waterproof, but that only goes so far.

The fucking book can't be specific, can it? No, it just gives me riddles. Maybe I'm looking for a small enamel lily pin on someone's lapel. Maybe the book means black as in African American, wearing a lily costume of any possible goddamned color.

Around the room again, and again. Checking lapels, checking skin colors against costumes, panicking every time I see people trickle out the doors.

I head for the nearest door—it's actually the one I came in—and place my hand on the knob. Options blur through my mind: the elevator, the emergency stairs, a utility closet. I choose the last, and when I open the door, that's where it leads.

I shut the door quickly behind me, because I don't want anyone following. Now if they try to open the same door, it will lead into the hall, where it actually goes. Relieved, I take a deep breath of the closet's comparatively fresh air. Just a faint odor of pine, bleach, and the musty suggestion of a mop put away while wet.

Two doors' distance is all I get. Don't ask me how it works, or why I can do it, but if I lay my hand on a knob or a handle, I can choose if the door opens into the following room, or any of the rooms that annex that same room. Sometimes it's a dead end, like this closet, because there's no other door to open. I've chosen the wrong door and gotten arrested before—it's a bit like trying to solve a maze with a pen instead of a pencil. You just screw up sometimes.

Like sometime, you might go into a room no other human could have found. Maybe you take a chest that wasn't meant for a human to have. You smugly carry it back to your apartment, but the moment you open the lid, a chain snakes into your leg. The pain is phenomenal. You dig through the chest, looking for something to cut yourself free, but there's nothing but gold coins and one crappy old book in a language you can't read.

The intangible chain stretches all the way to the hardware store, where they think you're a psycho case when you start hacking at the linoleum floor by your feet with garden shears, and then an axe, and then a sledgehammer. The cops mace your crazy ass, but you barely even feel it because your leg is getting worse. You say you were angry and drunk, and you agree to pay the damages, and you go home in defeat.

You can't even tell the truth to friends or your now-ex-boyfriend, because they can't see the enchantment.

There is no sleep. Not for days. You consider amputation, start looking up methods on the Internet. Turns out there are fetishists for everything, and their utter batshitness might be your gain. But before you pack your leg in ice to induce a frostbite so severe the doctors will be forced to surgically remove your curse, you wonder about the book.

You open it again, hoping there's something in there, something to explain, even if it's just a picture. It's gibberish until one page, the page that says:

Nautical exhibit at museum at midnight. Brass spyglass from a 1728 wreck. **Place it in chest.**

You know which museum has the nautical exhibit. What do you have to lose? It doesn't hurt any more to walk than it does to stay in place. And you miss stealing, since you've been hiding in your apartment biting a pillow and swallowing a plethora of Vicodin tablets that do absolutely nothing.

The moment you place the spyglass in the chest, it slides through the wooden bottom, like it's sinking through water.

The pain in your leg becomes bearable. It doesn't disappear—It never fucking disappears, *never*—but you can pass out now. You sleep, and you don't wake up from a dream about being savaged by a shark or stepping in a bear trap or being allergic to only one of your socks.

So you steal what the book tells you, and you put it in the chest. Gold coins ooze up from the other side, breaching like whales, until there's a stack to replace your offering.

The burning subsides for a time, but the book always makes more demands.

Now that I have the privacy of the closet, I pull the book out and look again. It says what it said before, plus one more word.

NOW.

I jam it back into my pocket, take a deep breath, and step back into the bouquet of B.O. and carcinogenic perfumes. I arrange a smile on my face with all the care that a florist takes with a wreath for a state funeral.

Maybe I'm not looking for a person. Maybe the "her" was a statue, or a painting. I close my eyes almost all the way, so I just see a blur of light and color through my lashes, and scan the room. When a dark patch appears, it's just one of the service dogs I spotted earlier, a saggy-bellied lab standing guard by her owner's feet. Before I can dismiss her entirely, however, I spot a glint of silver on her service coat.

Hundred bucks says I know that dog's name.

They're leaving right now. The door shuts behind them.

I duck around huge hats and ponyfalls, poufy skirts and trailing scarves. When I exit the ballroom, they're nearly to the elevator.

No, no, no. I break my practiced saunter and jog down the hall toward the woman and her dogs. I hate drawing attention, but I don't have a choice.

I slow as I approach, creeping up behind Lily's wagging tail. The pin comes off of her embroidered "Service Animal" coat easily, though the sharp edges puncture the pads of my fingers.

Lily's tail brushes across my cheek as I get to my feet.

She spins and snarls. Her elderly owner hauls at the leash, her face calm as her four-legged companion tries to get close enough to chew my nuts. I don't have to pretend to be terrified.

I clench the pin in my hand, trying to pretend it's not cold as a polar bear's butthole. It's not the first object I've been told to steal that has strange properties, but it's the first that numbs my fingers until I can't even tell if they're still gripping it.

"Holy shit, your dog is psycho!" I yell, backing away.

"You probably deserve it," the woman snaps. Her other dog growls low in its throat, but it doesn't struggle to reach me the way Lily does.

I flee, my heart beating faster than the electronic music in the next room.

Good. Now I'll go home and throw this pin in the chest and waste Glenlivet by drinking it fast until I pass out. I open the book — still the same message—and tuck the bloody pin under the cover. When I get frisked, they never seem to be able to find the book, so it'll be safest there.

I no sooner finish tucking it into my breast pocket than someone with a beautiful Spanish accent says, "You're not supposed to pet service dogs."

I glance over my shoulder, just to be sure it isn't security.

It's a queen, maybe. I can't tell; she's lanky, with a Roman nose and overpainted lips. She could be female with strong features, or male with delicate ones. She has blood-red extensions, high-quality toyokalon bound into a messy ponytail to show off her impossibly thin hoop earrings and her black leather choker.

She's the only other person wearing black, a simple velvet dress powdered with glitter. I didn't see her in the ball room, when I was looking for black costumes.

I realize I'm staring, and shrug. "Service dogs don't bite. Pretty sure that lady bought the coat on eBay so she could smuggle her fleabag into tea parties," I say. "It's like a fad with old bitches. Give it a few centuries; we'll be doing it, too."

She narrows her eyes but doesn't speak, as if she can't decide if she's offended or not.

"Nice being lectured by you," I say, and head for the stairwell.

I hate elevators, because I can't open the doors with my hands, so if I'm trapped in an elevator, there's nothing I can do. Luckily, I'm my own elevator. I haul back the stairwell's heavy fire door and it opens straight to the parking garage.

My footsteps echo alone for long seconds before I hear the elevator door open behind me. Heels click on the pavement, and I glance back to find the goody-two-shoes with red plastic hair.

"You're leaving already? Not enjoying the convention, then?" she asks. She trots closer, inviting herself to walk along with me.

"Drag isn't my scene. I'm way too pretty to pretend to be a woman," I reply. The chain is hurting more. I'm taking too long, and the book's author is angry. I look for doors to get outside faster, but most of them are on cars, which won't do the trick.

For a moment, I imagine going back into the convention with her and having a drink. She has style, and it's been a long time since I hung out with anyone I wasn't stealing from. But the book doesn't leave room for socializing in the schedule.

"What's your name?" she asks, toying with the silver disk hanging from her choker.

"Could you piss off? I'm not interested in anything with tits, even if they're fake."

"My name's Lily," she says.

I'm too slow. I turn to look at her, my mouth opening to ask a stupid question, when she reaches down on the ground and grabs the violet chain.

She pulls, hard, and I thump onto my back.

Even though I think I'm still awake, everything is black and sparkly. It's like her dress, like the sky, and then I keep blinking until my vision focuses again on the ceiling, with its emergency sprinkler system nozzles and sleeping moths. My head hurts and my leg hurts and I think I forgot how to breathe.

I don't understand how she can touch the chain when I can't, but I also don't understand how she was a dog. The collar is the same, though. I remember now.

The pavement scrapes by beneath me as she hauls me by the chain toward the elevator. Some people getting into their cars glance over, then studiously pretend not to notice so they don't have to get involved. To people who can't see the chain, this looks like a psychotic tantrum, like I'm scooting myself toward Lily.

"Stop," I plead. It's barely audible, just a croak.

"I'll stop when you give me back my pin, you insufferable bag of dicks. If you were scared of me biting you, just wait until you see what I can do with this tether."

"I can't—" I start, but I lose my breath again when she whips the chain around a few times, like a jump rope. I curl forward, retching. She lets go, and I lie gasping like a landed fish as her fingers poke through my pockets. She flings jewelry on the ground as she finds it, and finally, gives up.

"What did you do with it?" she asks.

"I gave it to someone," I say. The pin is cold against my heart, reaching through the book and the coat.

I know my mascara is smeared now, waterproof or not. I have to remind myself that as bad as this is, it will be worse if I don't put the desired item in the chest. I just need to get to a door.

"I need the silver thorns to do my job. That 'old bitch' is down one body guard until I can change back into a dog. I've killed for her before, and I'll do it again."

"Please, it's too late."

"You're a wretched liar." She swings the chain around, lifting me off the ground, and slams me into the back of a lime green Escalade. The crunch is either a rear window or all of my bones.

This time the flashing lights are colors. Blue, red. There's glass in my hair and everything tastes like blood.

There are cameras, I remember, in the parking garage.

I force my eyes open, past the prodding cops, and see them escorting Lily away. She glares over her shoulder, yells about theft.

I'm not sure if I'm coughing or laughing.

They frisk me, looking for her pin, but it's in the book where they can't find it. They do find the other jewelry I stole—well, what Lily didn't already throw on the ground—and they handcuff me.

Fine. If I have to pick from: getting murdered, not putting the pin in the chest, or getting arrested, this is my best option.

They don't care enough about me to call an ambulance, and after a few minutes, I have to admit I probably don't need one. The injuries they can measure are just a mild concussion, a split lip, and some bruising.

The book is still in my jacket, and they make me wear ghastly jail jammies, so I spend all night wondering what the page says now.

The first time I failed the author, the book gave me a countdown for fixing my mistake, and when I gave up, because I didn't understand how bad it would get, the book told me to go into my kitchen, pull out everything with a skull-and-crossbones sticker on it, and pour myself a cocktail.

I had no intentions of doing it, but that's when I found out the chain reached deeper inside than just my leg, than even my flesh and bone.

My hands mixed every cleaning product I had into the glass I usually use for scotch. My mouth opened, and I poured it down my own throat. The slop burned as it passed through me, for days, from my lips to my asshole. It crept through my veins and flavored my breath, blurred and stung my vision.

When I couldn't take any more and tried to slit my wrists, I did bleed, but it smelled like Pine Sol and trickled out like rust-colored syrup. It didn't change my condition. When I tried to leave my apartment, or use the phone, my hands refused.

I was so alone that Death refused to visit, and even my own body was on someone else's side.

I keep my lawyer's business card laminated in my wallet, and I call him with my usual lies. He gets me out late on Monday morning, and I'm in too much of a hurry to sit through his warnings and advice. In the cab on the way home, I open the book.

Place thorns in chest. **Fifty-four minutes until punishment.**

I pull out the pen I stole from the front desk at the police station. I don't know if this will work, but I'm desperate. Bracing the book against my knee, I write:

black lily touched my skin, tried to kill me for the thorns. got away but can't steal for you if dead. what now?

My words disappear, but I don't know if that means they've been read. I stare at the page until the cab pulls up outside my apartment building. I am too sore to go up the fire escape.

The doorman I cheated holds up a hand, like I'm traffic he's directing, and says, "Hey, you owe me forty bucks, or—"

"I'll get it for you tonight, when your mom pays me," I say, eyes still on the blank page. I open the stairwell door and step straight into the fifth-floor hallway, where he can't follow fast enough to kick my ass.

As I walk toward my apartment, text appears on the page, showing up in strokes as someone writes each letter.

Place thorns in chest. **Thirty-three minutes until punishment**. *Stab her with iron knife.*

I stole an iron knife with a silk-wrapped handle months ago and put it in the chest. My teeth creak against each other. I don't know where to get another. Who would even want a knife that rusts?

I shut the book and fumble with my keys. I don't know if I could even use the knife—I can't imagine stabbing Lily, stabbing *anyone*. I'm a thief, not a murderer.

I can't wait to put the pin in the chest so I don't have to worry about it anymore. My leg feels like one solid cramp. I'm so distracted that I don't smell the perfume until I close the door behind me.

I look up in time to see Lily grab the violet chain and flip me onto my back again. *At least it's carpet*, I think.

"You left your filthy face grease on my tail, so I had your scent," she says. She's dressed much as she was Saturday night, in a short black dress and pumps.

I'm not playing this game again. "I'll give it to you," I say. I thrust out my palms, my favorite no-weapons signal.

She crosses her arms.

"Let me get it." My sore muscles tear like wet paper as I struggle to my feet.

"You sure made a shitty deal," she sneers.

I pause on my way to the chest. It looks like a normal steamer trunk, against the wall under an expensive-ass painting that I also stole, next to an even expensiver-ass plasma screen, which I actually bought because for once it was easier than stealing.

"Deal?"

"This isn't a deal?" she asks, quirking an eyebrow. She dangles the chain meaningfully.

"No. I just...I stole that chest," I say, pointing. I explain about the chain and the book.

I open the chest, because I want to show her the gold—prove I'm not lying—and see the same iron knife I stole months ago, with the chartreuse silk tied around the handle. The author must be loaning it to me.

Lily flops down on my couch, setting her shoes up on my glass coffee table.

"You foolish mortal. Do you know what you could have gotten, if you'd asked instead of stolen?"

"What?"

"A contract with a clause stipulating when your service ends. We make fair deals, you know. We always have."

"What are you?" I whisper. I've watched TV; I've seen movies; sometimes if no one is looking I even read comics. I don't want to say any of the silly words out loud, like demon or faery.

She snorts and shakes her head.

"Me? I'm someone who can actually kill you. I'll just wait for you to start chugging Drano-on-the-rocks again, and then offer a quick death in exchange for my pin...unless you want to take me back to the hotel and show me where you hid it. I smelled you in that utility closet—is that it?"

Lily pours herself a couple fingers of scotch and sips it, watching me. I reach into the chest and slide the knife into my sleeve. It's cold under my fingers; I imagine sinking it into the soft hollow at the base of her long throat.

I'm suddenly so nauseated I almost fill the chest with half-digested jail food.

"How do I get this chain off?" I whisper. "That's all I want."

"Good luck, bitch. Pretty sure you have to kill the bastard writing in the book."

I pull out the book, flip it open again, stare at the words.

Four minutes until punishment. *Place thorns in chest. Stab her with an iron knife.*

My only idea is desperate, and *stupid*, but what do I have to lose?

I hold the book over the trunk and shake it. The pin falls out. The bottom of the trunk swallows every silver thorn before Lily has even gotten to her feet.

Her face crumples with rage, and even if she can't turn into a dog now, her bared teeth could have fooled me.

"Help me kill him and I'll get your pin back," I say quickly, half of a second before she yanks the chain toward her. If I can't make my plan clear she might kill me, so I force myself to explain even though every word is a scream.

"I can...control doors," I gasp. "I can get there."

She scowls. "That could take forever."

"It won't."

I'm more scared of this plan than I am of Lily. The last place I want to go is the place where the pain comes from.

After an interminable moment, Lily drops the chain.

I'm too shaky to stand again. I kneel at the coffee table and reach for my only glass, which has her lipstick prints on the rim and a finger of scotch left in the bottom.

She slides it out of reach. "Start talking."

"Okay." I gather my thoughts, trying to ignore the glass. "I can get there and steal the pin back. I just need you to protect me the way you protect the old lady."

She shakes her head. "The book's author has a dog, I'm sure, and she'll still have her pin, because some *slutty mortal crybaby didn't snatch it.*"

"I am not slutty!"

"Could've fooled me, Captain Nippleparty," Lily says, pointing at my torn shirt. She stretches, rolls her head to pop her neck, and gets to her feet. "Okay. If you can get the pin back fast enough for me to use it, I'll keep the dog from eating your face. But you're on your own with the book's author."

She grabs my hand, and I feel a thrill at the touch of her strong fingers, until she casually kicks the violet chain on her way toward the front door.

I pull her back.

With my other hand, I close the chest's lid and grip the cold brass handle. I feel through the possibilities: the tiny wooden room it usually opens to, or the bigger room beyond.

"Maybe you're not as stupid as you smell," she says.

I open the lid/door, step in, and we both fall through, linked by our hands.

We land on a desk carved of glittering white stone.

I don't have time to look around: in a chair in front of the desk, so close I can smell his graveyard breath, there's an old man with butter-yellow eyes and Count Dracula hair. His waxy, colorless skin reminds me of a maggot.

For just a moment, he looks like he got fisted with an ice cube — and then his eyes drop to see the violet chain coiled on the desk's smooth surface. He smiles and lays one palm over it.

Pain. I'm on my belly instantly, swimming across the desk. My hands claw at the stone, at Lily, at the still-wet pages of the book he'd been writing in, as if somewhere I might find the switch to turn it off. My boots encounter momentary resistance, followed by the music of hundreds of coins clinking, rolling, and spinning on a marble floor.

I crane my neck at Lily, just in time to see him strike her face with the side of his fist. The quill with which he'd been writing stabs into her cheek, dribbling black ink down her jaw.

In one smooth motion, she slides off the desk and lands in a defensive crouch.

As she backs away, the clicking of her heels multiplies. It's a dog trotting up behind her. Woolly and beige, like an old couch, it seems harmless until it bares its teeth. The rumble in its throat sounds like a power tool.

This was stupid, so stupid. I should go back through the chest. My left elbow bumps against it, so I know it's still here on the desktop. Just shut the lid, then open it once, tumble through into my apartment. No doubt I'd be punished, but at least I'd be far away, where I belonged.

The plume hanging out of Lily's cheek quivers as she stands between the book's author and his canine mercenary. Then the dog jumps on her, its paws on her chest, tearing into her arm when she swings at its face.

It's hard to focus, but I force my right arm flat on the desk so I can reach into my sleeve.

The book's author watches Lily go down to her knees, his face expressionless. I draw the iron knife, and before I can change my mind, before I can get sick again, I slam the blade into the side of his neck.

The blood that dribbles out is iridescent, like a parking lot puddle. He paws at the knife with both hands, but a moment later he goes limp and molds to the contours of his chair like wet laundry.

The pain fades, but it doesn't go away. I don't have time to worry about that, or the fact that I just went from thief to murderer.

It's my fault Lily's here.

I dig through everything I knocked off of the desk, coins and the inkwell and a bunch of jewelry, but I don't see Lily's pin. I have to get it to her—a dog against a dog has a better chance than she has now.

I can't find it. The dog snarls louder behind me and Lily curses. I glance back to see her holding it at arm's length by its collar, its teeth gnashing the flesh of her arm as if it means to chew it off.

No time to keep digging. I scan the room. It seems carved from a single block of opalescent white stone, even the desk. Sourceless frost-tinted light shows me shelves and shelves of familiar items. I spot a broken pocket watch that worked back when I stole it, a hat pin I remember sneaking off of a mannequin in a porn store window, and finally, the brass spyglass I stole from the nautical exhibit.

That's the one I grab.

Lily's blood is slick under my shoes as I dash over. I swing the spyglass at the dog. I don't want to hit it, but its mouth is foaming with Lily's blood, blood she never should have had to spill. When the brass strikes the top of the dog's skull, it yelps, falls to the side, and is too dizzy to get up. I know how it feels. If I tried to pull the knife out of a dead man I would have passed right the eff out—I'm barely hanging on as it is. I swallow the gush of about-to-puke saliva and breathe through my nose.

Lily stands, her lacerated arm dripping more blood. "Where is my pin?" she asks.

"I don't know. Why am I still chained?"

"I don't know."

We stare at each other, she without her pin, me still attached to the chest by the violet chain.

"Let's load the chest with all the coins and jewelry," I say. "When we get back, we'll sort through it all."

I take off my coat and rip out the lining to bandage Lily's arm. When it's wrapped tight, she helps me pile handfuls of treasure onto my coat, all of it stained with ink and blood. We lift it together and dump the contents into the chest, over and over until there's not a coin left.

"I can take you back through," I say, "so you can go to a hospital."

"You'd trust me in your apartment with all that cash?" she asks. She starts to grin, winces, and yanks the quill from her cheek. "How come you're not going back that way?"

"I have to own both chests until I get the chain off," I say. "I can't bring it through itself—I don't know what'll happen—so I have to go back the long way."

Maybe I don't hide my dread well enough. Her eyes are sharp and dark as she looks at the chest, already empty, and then back at me.

"No, thanks," she says. "I think I want to see what's through door number two." I fight the urge to hug her—I'm covered in enough blood as it is.

I grab one end of the chest, and she grabs the other, and we walk toward the door. I caress the cool handle, considering the possibilities. None of them will take us home, but you don't get through a maze without hitting a few dead-ends.

I choose a hallway, and then another door, and another.

Subterraneans

William Shunn & Laura Chavoen

In that summer of '84, Tuesday nights were usually Tuts, and Wednesday nights were Exit. Most Thursdays would have been Neo, but Shirley was tired of being predictable. That's why they ponied up their five bucks apiece to the scary guy on the door at Medusa's.

"But I'm not going to know anyone here," said Caroline, hanging back in the doorway.

The rumbling bass from upstairs pounded in time with the angry pulse in Shirley's ears. She grabbed Caroline by the arm and pulled her inside, out of the sticky August night. "That's kind of the point," she hissed. She didn't want them to look like posers in front of the bouncer.

"But everyone's gonna be at Neo..."

Shirley folded her arms in the dim entry hall and gave her room-mate a stern look. Her eyebrow was sore, but she tried not to touch it. "Be a little adventurous for once." She started up the rickety staircase, not waiting to see if Caroline would follow.

Above, flashing red lights and a screeching cacophony beckoned. Medusa's was a four-story former tenement block on Sheffield, in the Lake View neighborhood of Chicago. Shirley figured it must have been abandoned before the current owner picked it up for cheap and started knocking down interior walls. She thought she could still smell plaster dust beneath the cigarette and pot reek.

She stopped in front of a mirror at the top of the long staircase, excited. Her private superstition was that whatever song was playing when she first arrived at a club was an omen for how the night would go, and she *loved* the song blasting from the room on the right, "Scary Monsters." Through the door, a crowd of people in cracked leather and ripped jeans danced like marionettes to the strident, aggressive music. Their shadows cut spooky canyons through a shifting haze of hot, angry colors. More dissonant sounds churned from a warren of rooms to the left, and grainy gray light leaked down from the top of the next staircase.

Her roommate crowded suddenly against her. "I don't like this," Caroline whined, almost shrieking to be heard.

Shirley took a moment to inspect herself in the crazy light, with her leather jacket, plaid skirt, black Doc Martens, and all those piercings. She touched the new ring in her left eyebrow, which yielded a pleasurable spike of pain. She fiddled a moment with it, making sure it lay even with its two neighbors. Beside her, Caroline was looking tiny and timid in her ripped T-shirt and black spandex miniskirt. Not quite right for the surroundings, but not quite wrong, either. Being Asian and beautiful made up for a lot.

"Look at us. Perfect," Shirley said, swallowing a mouthful of envy. "Now come on." She dragged Caroline through the doorway and into the churning crowd.

They made a little pocket for themselves on the dance floor. Shirley groped for the rhythm with her feet and hips and elbows. The people around them, with floppy or spiky hair dyed black, didn't pay them much mind. Eyes closed, Shirley let herself shake like the guitars were buzzsaws in her brain.

"This could be the theme song for this place," Caroline said, leaning in close.

Shirley bared her teeth with what she hoped was ferocious menace. "Which are we—scary monsters, or super creeps?"

Caroline shuddered, swaying back and forth. "New Bowie's so much better than this."

"'Let's Dance'? Ugh, that sucks. He totally sold out."

"Did not."

"You just want to be his little China girl."

"I'm Taiwanese," Caroline said, punching Shirley in the shoulder.

Shirley grinned and turned in a tight circle as she pumped her arms. Caroline with her blood up was always more fun than killjoy Caroline.

It didn't take long for Shirley to work up a sweat. After several more songs, Caroline pantomimed thirst. A lot of people on the dance floor had plastic cups in their hands.

"I'll find something," Shirley said. "You'll be okay?"

Caroline gave her a thumbs-up.

There was a counter with a throng around it in the far corner of the room, near the DJ, but Shirley decided to see what she could find elsewhere. Not just liquid, she hoped, but maybe a new friend who wouldn't mind standing her a line of coke.

She shimmied her way back to the door and made a cursory tour of the rest of the floor. The other rooms were smaller, darker, louder. Strobes filled one, whirling starfields another, creepy ultraviolet light and jumbled couches filled with shadowy loungers a third. It all seemed pretty cool, but that pearlescent light from the upper floors beckoned.

As she climbed the stairs, "8:15 to Nowhere" by Vicious Pink was subsumed by New Order's "Blue Monday." She felt like she was breaking into the layer of calm air above a thunderstorm.

It was more open upstairs, cooler. To the right was a room like the one below it, with people moving sinuously in the gray-white light to sounds that could have been recorded on a factory floor. To the left was a large area filled with ranks of dark couches, nicer ones than downstairs. Maybe a dozen people were lounging here, some passed out on the couches or the carpets. Shirley wondered if she'd just stumbled onto the heroin floor. She'd always wanted to try horse...

She started picking her way through the open area. At its far end was a portable chrome bar, and in the corner on a raised platform sat a small grouping of armchairs and loveseats.

She didn't get a chance to check out the people sitting there, though. Before she was a third of the way across the room, the guy behind the bar caught her eye. He was the first blond she'd seen in here, and he wore a black dress shirt with a skinny, gray-striped tie. He could have been as old as, say, twenty-eight. And he was *watching* her.

Not just watching, though. He was trying to be *seen* watching her. Seen by *her*.

As she caught his gaze—his blue, blue, electric blue gaze—he tilted his head to one side and swallowed. Shirley felt suffused with warmth, with longing, with being wanted...

And Shirley feels herself shoved suddenly aside—straitjacketed and stuffed in a corner. She can't move, but she *is* moving—turning, heading back down the stairs to the dance floor. It's like someone else is driving. Caroline rushes up to her, asks about the drinks, but Shirley sweeps them both out onto the floor where they dance with abandon to the mechanical beat for what might be hours. Several times young men try to insert themselves between them, but every time it happens she shoulders past the guy and blocks him out. At last, she takes Caroline by the hand and the music ratchets them up the stairs to the gray lounge and Shirley watches in puzzlement and then horror as she backs her roommate up against a structural pillar and kisses her.

Caroline shoves her, *hard*, with both hands.

Shirley stumbles backward. Something wrenched unpleasantly at her brain.

"What the *hell*?" Caroline snarled, wiping her mouth with the back of her hand. She glared at Shirley with disgust, then whirled and fled down the stairs.

Shirley, confused, was too dizzy and exhausted to follow. Shakily she turned, in search of a place to sit. Across the room she saw the guy at the bar look down suddenly, a smirk on his lips. He brushed his eyebrow with his left hand, fingertip lingering for a moment, and busied himself mixing something.

Fritz, she thought, wrinkling her brow. *Your name is Fritz*. But how did she know that?

"I know there's good work in you," said Joseph Lyon, adjusting his round glasses. Through the floor-to-ceiling glass behind him, peaceful water reflections rippled up the faces of the buildings on the north side of the Chicago River. "Now go back out there and bring it to me."

Shirley nodded once and stood up. She was biting the inside of her lip to keep from showing any emotion. She closed her art director's door carefully behind her as she exited his office. She stopped at her cubicle only long enough to snatch her purse from the back of her chair, then walked straight out to the eleventh-floor elevator lobby and stabbed the down button. She couldn't breathe. She had to get out in the open air, escape that constricting skin of metal and glass packed tight with water coolers and coffee machines and bullshit.

It was barely ten on a Tuesday morning, and already it was shaping up to be the worst day since the fiasco at Medusa's. It wasn't bad enough that her newest layout for Chevy had gotten munched in the rollers of the wax machine, ruining all her careful work from the day before. On top of that, Joseph Lyon had called her in to inform her, in his smug, patronizing way, that Heinz had rejected all her paste-ups for the new mustard campaign.

When the elevator doors had closed behind her, Shirley let out an inarticulate howl. *God*, what an asshole he was! That was *excellent* work she'd turned in, but Joseph Lyon wouldn't know good art if it beat his balding head in, shoved his glasses down his throat, and strangled him with his own stupid tie. He probably hadn't even *presented* her designs to Heinz.

Only eight months in this job, barely a year out of art school, and already she wanted to slit her wrists.

Shirley felt like she was suffocating. As soon as the elevator doors opened again, she fled through the high-ceilinged lobby into the gathering heat of Upper Wacker Drive. She couldn't even complain to her one real friend, because Caroline still wasn't speaking to her after what had happened at the club Thursday night. That made life at their cramped Bucktown apartment uncomfortable, to say the least.

The pedestrians on Wacker all seemed listless, heat-baked. Two blocks west, Shirley rested her face against the cool plate-glass window of a stereo shop, behind which a fat television was replaying yet again the clip where that idiot Ronnie Raygun joked about bombing Russia.

"Fuck, I wish I were somebody else," she said.

She straightened up but stopped, fascinated to see the way her ghostly reflection in the window overlay the president's face almost perfectly. There he was, with his slicked-back hair and wrinkles, wearing her silk scarf and bone satin blouse, his face studded with all her bright steel jewelry.

And that was when the weirdest realization clicked.

As she hauled Caroline up the stairs, the first song Shirley heard was "Love Puppets" by the Legendary Pink Dots. She grinned. It was *definitely* going to be a good night.

Caroline folded her arms when they reached the top, her face a mask of defiance in the gray light. Being a Tuesday, this would normally have been a Tuts night, but Shirley had convinced her they needed to try Medusa's again, to get things straightened out. "You better not try anything," Caroline said, practically shouting to be heard.

By way of answer, Shirley led Caroline into the lounge on the left. Several people were lolling in the chairs on the riser in the far corner, one of whom jumped up and descended to his spot at the bar. Shirley tried to arrange her features into a hardened mask as they approached him.

The blond man flipped his hair back. "This is a private party area, ladies," he said, mustering an uneasy smile. He had a slight accent, but it was hard to tell what kind over the music.

Shirley put both hands flat on the chrome surface of the bar. "That's okay," she said. "We're *here* to party in private."

"Um," said the man, who tonight wore a faded gray T-shirt. "Okay, then. The club's dry, but in here you can just grab a beer from the tub and slip your cash through the slot. Honor system."

If she were at Exit or Neo, she'd know exactly how to ask for what she was looking for. Plus, at Neo she knew John, who'd always said he could get anything she needed, for the right price.

But in this place, she was at sea. "I don't want a drink," she said, trying not to stammer. "Whatever you did to me the other night. That's what I want."

The man glanced sideways at the group on the riser. "I don't know what you're talking about."

Caroline beside her was tapping her foot, and now she grabbed Shirley by the arm. "Thanks for ruining my night *again*. Let's go."

Shirley shrugged her off. "Oh, you know," she said, staring into the man's perspiring face. "You most definitely know—*Fritz*."

"This is totally bogus," Caroline said. "I'm getting out of here."

But the man was shaking his head with a rueful snort. "No, wait," he said, raising a hand. He finally met Shirley's stare. His eyes *were* incredibly blue. "You really want that again?"

Now it was Shirley's turn to snort. "Are you kidding? I don't want it *done* to me, dickface. I want to *do* it. I want to be someone else."

She held the man's gaze for a full fifteen seconds, never wavering. Caroline looked back and forth between the two of them until the man at last looked down and let out a sigh.

"Okay," he said, waving a hand. "Let's go present you to Seph."

"Shirley, what's going on here?" whispered Caroline as they followed the blond man over to the riser in the dim corner. "Are you *crazy*?"

"Maybe," Shirley said. "We'll see."

But she didn't think so.

The man indicated they should wait a pace back from the riser while he trotted up the two steps. He spoke in the ear of a woman with flowing black hair who was facing away from them in a leather armchair. After a moment the woman turned and peered at them around the side of the chair.

Her skin was very pale and her eyes very black, though either or both could have been a result of the grayish lighting. Her gaze narrowed at Shirley, who had the peculiar sense of being looked *through*. The woman next studied Caroline, who flinched.

Then she looked up at the blond man, spoke a word or two, and dismissed him with a wave. Caroline hugged herself, rubbing her arms as if she were slowly scrubbing them. Shirley could understand why.

The man rejoined them. "Okay, you're in," he said, leading them to a vinyl couch in the middle of the room. "Commando Mix" by Front 242 was playing now, and a triumphant Shirley found it hard not to strut in time with the beat. The man took an armchair at a right angle to the couch and sat forward with his skinny ass barely on the cushion.

"What are your names?" he asked.

"This is Caroline," Shirley said. "I'm Shirley."

She waited for the inevitable *Laverne & Shirley* comment, but it didn't come. "My name *is* Fritz," he said. "Kudos."

"Seriously?" Caroline asked. "Like Walter Mondale?"

Shirley elbowed her, but Fritz simply opened his right hand. In his palm lay two mottled brown pills. Shirley touched the pocket of her jacket, where she'd stuffed the two hundred bucks she'd gotten from a cash station on their way over.

"How much?" she asked.

Fritz shook his head. "We're not making money here, just having fun with a few clever friends." He held out his hand. "Here."

Shirley reached for one of pills, but Fritz closed his fist and pulled it away.

"But there are rules," he said. "First, these pills never leave the club. Second, your *mounts* never leave the club either."

"Our mounts?" Caroline asked, nostrils flared.

"You'll see."

But Shirley thought she knew what he meant. "And what's third?"

Fritz held the pills out again. "There *is* no third rule. Just have as good a time as you want."

She picked one up. It felt rough and a little heavy, like a pebble.

"So, we call these subs," Fritz said. "They're from Greece."

"Why subs?" Shirley asked.

"Short for substitutes, I think." A guy in pinstriped jeans set two cold bottles of Schaefer down on a low table in front of them, then vanished again. "Anyway, the best way to do them's to have one ready in your mouth when you spot the person you want to ride. Catch their eye, and swallow at the same time you make eye contact. Might be easier to wash it down with the beer your first time."

Caroline snorted, eyeing her pill like it might suddenly hatch in her hand. "And then what happens? The two of you, like, switch places? Like *Freaky Friday*?"

Shirley regretted having tried to explain the feeling in those terms, but Fritz only shrugged. "It's not a swap," he said. "I've *seen* that done, but it's not a move for virgins. Now, ready to try?"

The rational part of Shirley's brain was with Caroline, telling her they were being fucked with, but she was shivering nevertheless, and her palms were sweating. She nodded.

"Good. You first. Hold it on your tongue and pick up the beer. Now look around."

The sub tasted a little like mown grass and a little like dirt. Shirley looked out toward the opposite dance floor. Two guys with mohawks and ripped leather jackets had just reached the top of the stairs, and one of them was squinting into the gray light of the lounge. With her free hand Shirley waved at him. As he peered back and they locked eyes, she took a quick swig of the Schaefer. The pill scraped its way down her throat, and...

And suddenly she's standing at the top of the stairs, looking at the fat, beer-swilling girl on that sofa over there, trying to figure out if she knows her. When the realization hits that that's *her*, she turns away in disgust—and exhilaration.

The music is much louder here. Her companion has a stubbly face pitted with acne, and smells like a locker room. She punches him on the arm. "Holy shit, man," she says around a tongue that feels thick and foreign. "Check out that foxy China girl in there." She points at Caroline.

A moment later the guy's eyes widen. He turns to her, mouth open in shock. "Shirley?" he says, astonished.

"Caroline?" she says back.

Then they both squeal like little girls, grabbing each other's hands and jumping up and down on legs weirdly muscular and powerful.

Medusa's soon became a twice-a-week thing, and then a three-times-a-week thing. Though they never became a part of the group in the corner, Fritz seemed to take a real liking to Shirley and Caroline. At least, he seemed to take a liking to Caroline, and to tolerate Shirley, but as long as it got them their fix of subs she figured she had nothing to complain about.

In the meantime, she gave herself a guided tour of the vice inhabiting every nook and cranny of the club. She danced like mad with the group doing speedballs on the main floor, dropped acid with the lamers in the booths near the DJ on the third floor, and smoked this new thing called crack with some really nice kids up in the back rooms of the fourth, all without leaving the relative safety of the gray lounge. She even got to sample heroin at last in the midst of a blissed-out huddle in one corner of the building's dank, half-finished basement.

But more than the access to no-consequence highs, Shirley loved the sex. She liked to wait for groups of two or even three people to appear at the top of the stairs, looking furtive or giggly on their way to one of the restrooms or random dark spaces at the back of the building. She might ride the girl into the back room, or maybe the guy, depending on her mood. She'd never been with another girl herself, but she came to love the borrowed feel of hard nipples against her palms, the rush of slickness against her fingers as she hastened a girl toward orgasm, even the taste of those juices through someone else's tongue. And oh, did she learn what the big deal was about male orgasm.

She learned even more the time or two she rode her way into a guy-on-guy encounter. And if she went farther with any of these folks than they might have gone on their own? Well, what of it? It wasn't like everyone involved didn't have a good time, and when she dismounted after any- where from two to twenty minutes, like removing her hand from a glove, there was no harm done. Maybe an awkward question or two in the mind of the mount, and a new resolve to kick the drugs for a while.

What was most fascinating to her, though—most reassuring, and occa- sionally most depressing—was simply getting to sample the vast but amazingly familiar range of emotions through which her fellow clubgoers swam and sometimes flailed. It helped her feel like less of a freak.

The nights when Cabaret Voltaire's "Sensoria" played first always turned out to be her favorites.

As summer gave way to Chicago's too-brief fall, Shirley found it harder and harder to keep her mind on her job and off her clubland adventures. It was late September when Joseph Lyon summoned her to his office for another chat.

"You started here with a lot of promise, Shirley," he said, as sun warmed his office and cast his eyes into shadow. "But your work's been mediocre in general, and lately I've sensed a kind of...*distraction* settling over you."

Shirley blinked hard at the man across the desk, this paunchy clown who, if he'd ever had any artistic talent to start with, had let it be systematically ground out of him over twenty years in the business. She found herself wondering if he still even had any of those recognizable human emotions she'd discovered inside so many other people.

"I'm sorry, Mr. Lyon," she said, slipping into the persona of someone who gave a shit. "It's—it's been a rough time for me. I'll try to do better."

"Don't worry, we'll work out a progress plan to keep you off pro- bation," he said, taking off his glasses. "In the meantime, won't you please call me Joe?"

"Guess what?" said Caroline, eyes shining. "We finally did it."

Shirley pulled off her cherry-red, twelve-hole boot and picked up one of her rental skates. "Do I want to hear this?" she asked dryly.

Caroline clomped and rolled around in front of her, swaying to whatever moldy disco song was playing out on the roller rink. "No, I don't mean *that*. I mean, that too, but no. Fritz and I did it, Shirley. We *swapped*."

"Interesting," Shirley said, nodding, as she laced up her skates. In truth she felt a stab of envy. Caroline had been arriving early at

Medusa's for a while now, and even going on nights when Shirley didn't. Shirley would have liked to try a swap, but no one ever asked her. "How was it?"

"It was *awesome*," Caroline said. "So amazingly intimate." She rolled back and forth in front of Shirley's bench. "So what are we doing here tonight?"

"Something else awesome." Shirley had lured Caroline here to The Rainbo late on a Monday night with the promise of something fun and different. She gestured out at the rink, where a spinning disco ball spread glittery shards of color over the handful of skaters. "Don't you get tired of riding young, boring people every night? Look at *this* place! Everyone here's so much more...you know..."

"Old?" Caroline suggested.

"Well, I was going to say mature. But 'old' works."

Caroline folded her arms, tapping one skate on the concrete floor. "But aren't you forgetting something? The subs are at Medusa's."

Shirley had dressed a little differently than usual for tonight's adventure. She had on satin men's pajama pants, silver with black and white stripes, that she'd hemmed into shorts for herself, plus a white T-shirt, a wide black belt, and white lipstick. She reached into the little white purse slung over her shoulder and took out two brown pills, displaying them proudly on her palm.

"How did you get those?" Caroline exclaimed.

"I have four," she said with a sly smile. "Once a week I've been palming one and pretending, so we could go out on our own sometime and, well, do something like this. So let's roll out there and get a feel for the scene."

"The feel is *old*. And lame."

Shirley laughed. "Okay, let's get an old, lame feel for the scene, and then we'll pick our mounts."

They tottered onto the rink to the strains of "Heroes," which at least wasn't too cloying a song. There were fewer than a dozen people out on the boards, and it didn't take Shirley long to single out the one she wanted to shoot for. He was at least forty, with longish hair, widow's peak, bushy, gray-shot sideburns, and cream-colored three-piece suit. He was apparently there alone, but damn, could he skate! Especially during the disco numbers, he would leap and pirouette and glide backward and do a squatting, spinning thing that reminded her of John Travolta and Dorothy Hamill simultaneously.

She wanted to skate like that.

But Caroline had picked out an aging diva wearing a tennis dress, sparkly tights, and a rainbow headband, and they both agreed she would go first. Shirley sat on a bench in the locker area with her arm around Caroline's shoulders, her roommate slumped against her like a sack of potatoes as she rode. At Medusa's it might be possible for *two* women to sit slumped glassy-eyed and catatonic without drawing attention, but not here. As it was, Shirley offered a shrug and an embarrassed smile to the one couple who dropped through to change into their skates.

After ten minutes Caroline blinked, sat up, and grinned. "That was so cool," she said. "Try it, try it!"

Craning her neck, Shirley spotted her target out on the rink, then waited for the man to come sweeping around the curve of the low wall on his way past them. When he did, she cheered loudly and clapped. They locked eyes as the man sketched a little bow, and Shirley swallowed the pill, and...

And now she's flying around the rink, *flying*—not thinking about the moves but just letting them happen, jumps, spins, sweeps, one after the other in a sequence that seems like it might never end. And as she rides this improbably graceful body, she becomes aware of the memories overlaying this space, already ancient in its incarnation as the Kinetic Playground, the legendary rock club where she fucked herself up to bands like Zeppelin, MC5, Deep Purple, Vanilla Fudge, and the Mothers.

And with that comes the sadness and the loathing for herself and all the things she's done and all the things she's lost, and her legs pump even harder because it's all she can do to outrun those feelings and they're not supposed to follow her here, not to this place, not those firefights and the guts and the mud and the Viet Cong and the pit and the bamboo and the battery cables and the not those not those get out get out get out *get out GET OUT!*

Shirley spasmed and tumbled over backward, and it was all Caroline could do to keep her from cracking the back of her head on the concrete floor. Shirley pushed herself shakily to her knees. Unlike her usual graceful dismounts, this time she'd been forcibly *expelled*.

"Are you okay?" Caroline asked.

Donna Summer was feeling love now on the sound system, while across the rink the shaking man in the three-piece suit was leaning over the wall with both hands braced to keep himself from falling over.

Shirley wiped spit from the corner of her mouth. "God, am I glad we're young," she said. "Let's get the hell out of here."

The next night Shirley had to work a little late thanks to some stupid remedial assignment Mr. Lyon had saddled her with—paste-ups for a Kotex Light Days campaign. Shirley brooded as she walked from the El, knowing Caroline would have been at the club for a while already. A monkey could have done those designs, and wouldn't have had to put up with any gross insinuations from its boss, either.

It was fully dark, and the air was chilly. When she turned the corner from Belmont onto Sheffield, she saw a big crowd ahead gathered outside Medusa's, all looking up and pointing. She hurried up the block.

"What's happening?" she asked the first person she came to, but then she could see for herself with awful clarity.

A woman out on the wide ledge beside an open fourth-story window. A small woman, dancing and singing, as if oblivious to the danger yawning at her feet.

Oh, God.

"Caroline!" Shirley screamed.

People in the crowd were yelling up at Caroline, telling her to get back inside, and hands were straining out the window to reach her and pull her back to safety, but she spun away, nearly losing her footing.

"Caroline, no!"

But she recovered, spread her arms with a grin, and made a dainty bow to the people below.

Shirley was shoving her way through the crowd, trying to get to the front door, when the voices around her started screaming in earnest.

She looked up in time to see Caroline topple backward off the ledge, arms spread gracefully as she fell. People were scrambling to get out of the way, when it looked for all the world as if Caroline had expected them to catch her.

The hours stuttered past in a strobing kaleidoscope of images, each seemingly unconnected to the last. The shrieking crowds, the shrieking ambulance, the shrieking family at the hospital who blamed her and didn't want her anywhere near their daughter. She wasn't sure how long she'd been at Vaughan's Pub when Fritz slipped into the booth across from her.

"How is she?" he asked.

Shirley peered up from her whiskey through gritty, blurred eyes. "Fuck if I know," she slurred. "Where fuck've you been, anyway? Wha'fuck *happened*? Who rode her out that window?"

Fritz's nostrils twitched. He breathed in sharply, then took a slug of Shirley's whiskey and slammed the glass down again. "The rules, Shirley," he said, looking at the scarred surface of the table. "You took subs out of the club."

The corners of Shirley's frown trembled. "So this is Caroline's punishment? Jesus, what's mine?" She looked around, suddenly nervous. "How'd you find me, anyway?"

"It wasn't *her* punishment," Fritz said, drilling her with his blue gaze. "It was *mine*! I'm the one Seph blames, Shirley! You think this is some game? You don't know what she *is*. She feeds off the energy we generate, stores it up. That club is her prison, and when she's strong enough to break free..."

"What?" Shirley said.

He stood up abruptly. "They made *me* do it," he said, glaring down through the dim, yellow light. He finished her whiskey, then stood with his fist dancing in the air, white-knuckled around the empty glass. "Don't come back to Medusa's."

And he turned and stalked out.

She found herself at work sometime in the late morning, unchanged, unshowered, unable to make sense of the work on her drawing table. She felt numb inside.

Until, that is, she sensed herself being watched and looked up from her sketch to catch Joseph Lyon staring at her across the bullpen through the glass wall of his office.

She still had two subs left in her purse. Without thinking, she pulled one out and popped it into her mouth as she met her boss's impassive gaze. She wanted a glimpse inside his...

Head. That's what she wants from the heavy girl who's no longer quite as heavy as she was a couple of months ago. Her performance has been going from bad to worse, so now the only question is if there's any way she can get head from the girl before inevitably firing her. Or maybe she can even fuck her first. That would be better.

The thoughts are so focused and all-consuming that it takes her a moment to realize it's *herself* she's staring at from her office across the bullpen. When she does, her formless rage finds *its* focus.

She touches the heavy stirring in her gabardine trousers, the bulge that's beginning to stiffen and rise. It strains painfully against her zipper, so she slaps the glass with one hand while she undoes her pants with the other. Faces swivel toward her from all around the bullpen, and now her cock is free as she pumps it to the rhythm of the gasps and shrieks and hoots from beyond the glass. Some people are frozen openmouthed outside her office, others are turning their faces away or reaching for their phones, but she doesn't care. Oh, a part of her cares, but that part is crowded to the back of her skull, blithering in horror. Meanwhile, a geyser is gathering like a clenched fist deep in her loins, the pain of it white-hot and delicious, and in only a few more strokes its eruption will become inevitable whether she wants it to or...

And that point of no return was when Shirley slipped clean out of Joe Lyon's head, slipped her sweater on, and slipped out of the office for the day.

That evening she stalked into Neo like a broken old fighter. She hadn't been there since summer, but "Work for Love" by Ministry told her to expect only a so-so night. The new-wavers bouncing and strutting all around her in the reddish-orange light seemed criminally cute and dorky. She wished she could somehow turn herself into one of them again.

The song finished up as she skirted the dance floor. "Now a deep track off the brand-new Bowie record," said a DJ who sounded approximately thirteen. "Check out *this* 'Neighborhood Threat.'"

She found John in his usual place, ensconced in a small, dark booth near the payphones. Someone had just sat down with him, a kid with spiky orange hair, but when John looked up he seemed startled by whatever he saw in her expression.

"Sorry, you're going to have to give me a couple more minutes," he said to the kid, shooing him out of the booth. When Shirley sat down, he took her hands across the table, saying, "I heard what happened to your friend Caroline." He looked no older than anyone else in the place, a moon-faced kid hiding behind his wooden Ray-Ban Wayfarers. "I'm really sorry. How is she?"

"Not awake," she said, squinting against the sting in her eyes. "Back's broken, among other things, but they won't really know the extent of the damage until she wakes up. *If.*" All this she'd learned from calling the hospital, since Caroline's family still hadn't allowed her to visit.

"I heard it happened at Medusa's," John said, shaking his head. "That place is bad juju. We miss you guys here."

Shirley rubbed her face. "Look, John, I need something."

"Sure. Anything I've got."

She pressed her lips together in a thin line. Her hand shook as she took a slip of notepaper from the left pocket of her jacket and slid it facedown across the table.

John lifted the top edge of the paper and read what was written there. He went white. "Jesus," he said, sliding the paper back. "Shirley, I don't have this."

She stopped his hand with hers. "You told me once you could get anything."

He looked at the facedown note like he was going to throw up. "Yeah, well...I mean, I can *get* this, sure. But I don't think you can afford it."

Shirley reached into her right pocket and let John see her wad of bills. She'd cashed out the last of her savings and taken as much of an advance on her credit card as she could. She had more than a grand in her hand. She put it away again.

John sighed, but this time the slip of paper vanished into his hand. "This could take a couple of days," he said. He didn't look her in the eye.

"Tomorrow," she said. "No later."

He nodded, then reached out and touched her wrist as she slid out of the booth. "What are you doing, Shirley?" he asked.

She stood up. "John," she said with a grim smile, "I'm only dancing."

The bouncer at Medusa's the next night looked shocked to see her, but he didn't stop her at the door. Climbing past the main dance floor, Shirley tried to disregard the omen in Gene Loves Jezebel's "Upstairs," a track she had no use for.

Upstairs in the gray lounge, Fritz saw her coming and rushed out from behind the bar waving his hands at waist level.

"I told you, Shirley," he said, blocking her path through the middle of the room, "you can't *be* here. Get out."

"They took her off life-support," she said. "Out of my way."

Fritz's face came near to crumpling. "Please, you can't."

An imperious snap made them both look toward the riser in the corner. Seph, the black-haired woman, was standing, looking at them both. "Let the girl pass," she said, and her voice cut smoothly through the music and murmurs of the room.

"Shirley, whatever this is, don't do it," Fritz hissed.

But she slipped past him and continued to the riser, where she climbed the steps like mounting a scaffold. An ominous series of backmasked synth tones washed the room, trembling and delicate.

Shirley didn't glance at the four or five other people seated in the group. She had eyes only for Seph, whose loose black gown trailed all the way to the floor. Pale, pale skin rendered her beautiful and terrible at once, and her tresses moved in an unseen breeze as if each ringlet had a mind of its own. Shirley faced her from six feet away.

"Seeking revenge, are we, dear?" The woman's voice was like the bell that tolls to open a tomb. "You'll find it a simple dish to prepare but not so easy to serve."

Every instinct told Shirley to run, but maybe she'd never been good at doing the smart thing. "I never had a chance to try a swap," she said. "I guess I knew if I didn't ask I'd always wonder what I missed out on."

Seph laughed. "You must know," she said, tilting her head to one side, "that whatever you may have planned, I'll know about it once I take residence in your head. You can't surprise me."

"I only want to know what it's like, just for one minute. Then I'll leave and never come back." Shirley narrowed her eyes. "Or are you that afraid of me?"

The woman's brow clouded. "Fine." She snapped her fingers. "Subterraneans, please," she said to one of her attendants, who hopped up flourishing a wooden pill case. "Let's delve beneath the surface, shall we?"

The music swelled with gentle motion, and a counterpoint of low, multi-tracked voices entered. The woman chose a pill, and the attendant held the case out to Shirley.

"No, thanks. I brought my own." Shirley raised her left hand, her last sub pinched between thumb and forefinger.

"On three," said the woman, staring deep into Shirley's eyes. "One, two, three."

The woman popped her pill, and Shirley did the same, together with the capsule she'd held hidden behind her next three curled fingers. She dry-swallowed, never breaking their locked gazes...

And she watches as a mocking smile spreads over her own metal-studded face. Then the eyes widen, the gasping begins, and the face she's lived with every day of her life convulses in terror. Her former hands clutch at her former throat, and that's when Shirley turns away.

"She tried, she lost," Shirley says with a careless wave of her hand, sashaying on sandaled feet past the choking girl. "Finish her."

She hears the thrashing body collapse behind her as she descends from the riser. There's no need to explain that she swallowed two full grams of potassium cyanide along with the sub. The woman in her former body will know this by now, one way or another. Shirley's still afraid Seph might make the jump out, but with every stride toward the staircase this becomes less of a possibility. Cyanide poisoning is not nearly as quick a thing as the movies make out, but within another minute or so Seph will have lost consciousness and it will be over—if the attendants haven't killed her by then.

The music crests again. A breathy saxophone stumbles blindly through the surreal soundscape, pursued by a handful of lyrics that seem at first to make sense but ultimately don't. By the time Shirley reaches the bottom of the stairs, Bowie's voice is lost in the babel of other sounds from other floors.

By the time she reaches the cool street and the million possibilities for her new life, it's all just a distant, thumping growl in the night.

The Minotaur Girls

Tansy Rayner Roberts

Only the hottest girls in town got picked for the Minotaur.

Like everyone else when I was fourteen, I wanted it desperately. I wanted to be like willowy Amber Sanders who was taken by the Minotaur the year before. Maybe I could dye my hair from mousy brown to fire-engine red, and attain the mythical, miraculous status of *glitter*.

My mates and I weren't even glitter enough to get past the velvet rope. Thin Lizzie and Fat Lizzie and Chrissy and me, we tried a few Saturday nights, but it was humiliating to stand there in our best silver bubble-skirts and white tights, frizzed-high fringes and skates hanging around our necks, hoping that the door bitch would let us past.

We never even saw the door bitch. The lads on the door wouldn't let us past the first rope to get to her. We were too young, too wide-eyed, too daft.

So unglitter.

We skated in the park instead, wobbling around the bike ramps and hoping not to ladder our tights. If we couldn't have the silver lights and pounding music of the Minotaur, at least we had this.

If we practiced and practiced, if we were hell on wheels, it wouldn't matter how we looked, right? The Minotaur would beg us to join them.

Sometimes Thin Lizzie's brother Sean and his bogan mates would join us, and sometimes they had beer. They didn't care that we were young—I think they liked trying to impress us. Eventually we paired off, for pashing and groping. This was practice too, I told myself, as I tried to keep Richie Mason's wandering hands from going too far past my bra.

A Minotaur girl had to be good at everything.

One Monday, Fat Lizzie wasn't in class. The rumours were flying around the school by lunch. She had been seen, walking into the Minotaur in broad daylight. Wearing their uniform, the crisp white mini-dress, and brand-new silver skates.

Our mate had been taken, and she hadn't even said goodbye.

"Why her, though?" said Chrissy as we ate dim sims at the corner shop after school. "She's...well, you know."

"Fat," said Thin Lizzie, who wasn't especially thin.

We sat in quiet reflection of how horrible it must be to be slightly fatter than your friends.

"Must have been the boobs," Chrissy decided, and we all agreed. Fat Lizzie filled a bra like no one else.

"Listen to us," I said. "Talking like she's dead. She's on the inside, isn't she? She's still our mate. Do you think she'd let us in one night?"

There was a long silence, as we thought about that.

"She won't want to know us now," said Chrissy. "No one ever comes back."

I practiced skating even harder. The Fat Lizzie thing gave me hope. It might be my turn next. So I went to the park even when the others couldn't be bothered, and I rolled and spun and did every trick that I could.

Notice me, notice me, notice me.

One evening, I spotted a boy watching me on the bike ramps. He had a nice shirt, all silvery, and when I stopped and matched his stare with my own, I recognised him.

He used to hang out with Thin Lizzie's brother Sean last year, before the boys started noticing us. I didn't remember his name, maybe Ade or Ollie. He'd gone missing a while back and everyone thought he shot through to the big city, looking for work.

It had never occurred to us that maybe the Minotaur took boys too.

They had made him beautiful. His hair was like frosted snow, and his eyes a bright jewel-blue that didn't exist in real life. He had the perfect jeans, fitted to his hips like they were sewn on to him. Glitter all the way.

He lounged on the edge of the ramp. And oh, he was watching me.

I did a flip and skidded up the slope to land near him, breathing harder than I wanted to. "Hey."

"You're good," he said. His voice was beautiful too. It reminded me of expensive soap and Milli Vanilli.

"I practice a lot," I said, and could have kicked myself. You're not supposed to show how much effort it takes to be good. You're supposed to be floaty and gorgeous and not even try. "I mean, it's the best park for skating. I'm Tess."

Did I sound desperate or what? I flopped down next to him, not looking at those beautiful bright eyes, pretending not to care that I sounded like a dropkick.

He didn't tell me his name.

"You're one of them," I said. "A Minotaur boy."

He smiled softly. Sunlight gleamed on his hair. Glitter on a stick. "Is that what you call us?"

"What do you call the rest of us?"

A gentle shrug. "We don't think about you much at all."

Anger burned through me. "Say hello to Fat Lizzie for me. I used to be her friend." I pushed myself up, rolling down the ramp, wanting to get away from him as fast as I could.

Something flashed in the air in front of me and bounced, ringing on the ramp. I skidded and leaned down to pick it up.

A silver coin with a Minotaur printed on it, and the words Admit One stamped on the back. I'd never seen one before, but older girls giggled about them sometimes, the tokens that get you past the velvet rope. Two prefects had once had a slap fight in the quadrangle over one they had found in the street.

The coin was warm in my hand. I looked up, shielding my eyes against the sun reflecting off the boy's frosted hair. For the first time in my life, I felt brave.

"I have two friends," I said loudly. "I go with them, or not at all."

The Minotaur boy stared at me for a moment, and then he began to laugh.

Glitter is an attitude, not just a look. I had never felt as glitter as I did that day I showed Chrissy and Thin Lizzie what I had for us. Three perfect silver coins. Minotaur tokens.

"Unbelievable," breathed Chrissy.

Thin Lizzie was frowning, turning hers over in her hand. "What did you do for this, Tess?" she asked finally.

My cheeks went hot. "I skated really well in the park, and he gave them to me."

Thin Lizzie's eyebrows went up. I hated her in that moment. If she was going to be a mole, I didn't want her to have the coin at all.

Was this why Fat Lizzie never got in touch, when the Minotaur took her? Did she think we would be bitchy about it?

"You don't have to come," I muttered.

Thin Lizzie smiled. "Of course I'm coming."

"This is so awesome," Chrissy squealed. "What are we going to wear?"

We touched our skates up with silver paint, and shared a brand-new frosted lipstick. My hand was hot from holding on to the coin all the way to the club. The lads on the rope let us through, and we found ourselves stumbling through a dark corridor toward the door bitch.

Her fringe was sprayed so high it almost brushed the top of the doorway. I'd never seen anyone with a nose stud before, and tried not to stare at it.

"You're the ones Ari invited," she said, taking in our carefully assembled outfits. I waited for her to kick us out for being so unglitter.

Ari. His name was Ari.

The door bitch pulled back a dark curtain and the air was thick with music, a pounding beat that made my teeth hurt. Silver lights blazed out at us.

"Skates on, chickadees," said the door bitch, and gave Thin Lizzie a push so she ended up in front of us, sliding on the polished floor. "Ante up."

We had made it to the Minotaur, and it hadn't cost us anything.

Skates on. Ante up.

It was bigger inside than I had ever imaged. Ramps ran up the walls from room to room, and the lights dipped and spun from an impossibly high ceiling, making the shapes and the curves change every time. It was the best skating rink ever, times a million.

I lost Thin Lizzie. She was ahead of us, and plunged down a chute with some other girls, screaming and laughing. By the time Chrissy and I got there, Lizzie was nowhere in sight.

"We'll stick together, yeah, Tess?" Chrissy said, and I nodded reluctantly. The music was loud and amazing, with a beat that got inside my arms and legs. I didn't want her holding me back. I wanted to dance and skate and kiss boys and drink pink drinks and...

Chrissy seemed small.

We skated together, down a long channel into a high-ceilinged room where skaters flipped and tumbled their way up the walls, and a bright silver disco ball threw rainbow refractions against them. The ball spun, and the world shifted.

Sometimes when the light fell on them, they didn't look gorgeous at all. They looked like monsters. Their eyes glowed and their limbs undulated. Their sprayed hair became flowing lion manes, their lipsticked mouths became beaks, and there were snakes coiling everywhere, from their scalps to their pubes.

When the light shifted, they were beautiful again.

I still wanted to kiss them.

A tall monster with dreadlocked hair and kicky pink skates screeched up in front of me, grinning like a demon. I let her pull me into the maze of ramps. I did my best tricks and she laughed, clapping in delight. I spun and whirled, and if there were feathers flying from my arms now, I hardly noticed them.

I wasn't a monster or anything. Not yet.

Pink Skates tugged me into another room, and I lost Chrissy altogether. I didn't care. This one had a bright purple disco ball that cast grape-coloured shadows. The walls were soft and padded like the room was one big lounge suite. Someone gave me a drink and I gulped it gratefully before the sting hit the back of my throat and I realised that it wasn't water. It was like acid going down but then it warmed me up all over and I drank more of it.

No one was skating here, or if they were it was a long and lazy dance. Mostly they were pashing, limbs tangled together, heads tipped back against the soft parts of the walls, hands vanishing under layers of designer clothing.

I felt my face flame red with embarrassment. I don't know why. I hadn't cared at all that time Thin Lizzie and her first boyfriend started heavy petting in the park while the rest of us were right there, talking about which of the Coreys was cuter.

Some of these people were going further than heavy petting, but it was dark and the music was loud, and I didn't want to stare.

Kids were gaming in here too, with silver tokens like the ones Ari had given me. Several beautiful Minotaur Girls leaned over a green baize table, flipping coins back and forth for the customers. I didn't understand the game.

I still wanted to play.

Pink Skates turned and kissed me. My head fell back against the cushiony padded walls. I was so light, my skates were the only thing holding me down. She tasted of raspberry lipgloss.

"Bet you can't guess my name," she whispered.

Whoops and hollers awoke me from my daze. I pulled away from her, but no one was looking at us. The skaters and the gamers and the make out artists all looked up, pointing and hooting at a boy in a cage that hung from the high ceiling, gleaming like a mirrorball.

"Go on," Pink Skates said, more urgently. "Bet."

The boy was not laughing. He flinched as they threw bags of cellophane confetti which burst against the cage.

He was Ari, the silver boy who had given me the coins.

"What did he do?" I breathed. Why were they punishing him?

Pink Skates gave me an odd look. "He won at the tables, and this is his prize," she said. "I'd love to be in the cage. Everyone looks at you. Guess my name, or you lose the bet."

"Rose," I said at random, the pinkest name I could think of.

"Wrong," she laughed, and kept on laughing until she could barely breathe. "I win!"

"What are you—" I started to say, and then something slammed into my chest. I gasped through the pain, falling to my knees. It hurt. My breasts were on fire from the inside out, and my stomach cramped like I was having five periods all at once.

Pink Skates did a pirouette in front of me, glowing with light and happiness. "Standard ante," she said. "A year of your life. You should be more careful who you bet with, chickadee."

"Why me?" I demanded of her. The pain began to ease, and I struggled to my feet.

"Why not? Baby dolls like you taste good. Fresh meat." She skated away, still laughing.

This was the Minotaur. Music so loud it hurt, bored kids causing pain for kicks and, oh yes, being taunted in a glowing mirrorball cage was some kind of reward.

All I'd ever wanted to do was skate.

Somewhere in the dazzle and the brightness, I heard a scream. Was that Chrissy? I should never have left her alone.

I forced my way through several rooms of skaters and dancers and gaming tables and ramps, dazzling lights and dark shadows. Hands plucked at me, but I shook them off and kept going. "Chrissy!"

I found her in a ball pit below a beautiful glass ramp that looked like something Cinderella would have skated down.

"These people are skanks," Chrissy said breathlessly as I helped her climb out from under the writhing bodies. "Some of the girls were kissing other girls!"

"Yeah," I said uneasily. "Let's get out of here."

I had seen a big purple EXIT sign before, but I wasn't sure where.

"Going somewhere?" jeered a voice.

Thin Lizzie. She had come in here with us less than an hour ago, but I guess she'd made some new friends. She stood with them now, chewing gum and staring at me.

"I'm over this," I said defiantly.

Thin Lizzie glided forward, daring me to push her or prove my uncool in some other way. "They say I can stay if I stop you both leaving," she said. "I can come every night. Maybe earn my ticket into being a real Minotaur girl. Don't spoil this for me, Tess."

"I want to go home," Chrissy whined.

"You'd like it if you gave it a chance," said Lizzie. "Don't be such a chickenshit."

I faced her down. "If this place is so glitter, why are they trying to stop us leaving?"

But I knew that already. They didn't want me shouting my mouth off about how gross the Minotaur really was.

An older boy, with dark eyes and a smile I might have thought was charming about fifteen minutes ago, put his hand on Thin Lizzie's shoulder. "You can leave, babe," he said to me. "Anytime you want. But first you have to skate."

They took me to an arena deep in the Minotaur, with a plain round skating rink. A spotlight fell on me and I wondered for one laughable moment if this was some kind of reward, like it had been for Ari.

Teenagers leaned over balconies and sprawled across banks of velour seats.

The Minotaur girls stood at the edge of the rink, beautiful and silver and nearly identical. Never mind the spotlight, I was blinded by their pearly white eyeshadow. There were a few boys with them too, just as pretty.

My eyelashes prickled with sweat, and the audience took on other shapes before my eyes. Monsters all, teeth and claws. Laughing, sneering, glittering monsters.

I searched the crowd for one friendly face, but Chrissie stood with Thin Lizzie, their fingers entwined. She wasn't going to save me.

So I skated for the monsters. The lights grew brighter, and the music pounded in my ears only slightly louder than my heartbeat. I spun and whirled.

I could see the monsters more clearly now. Thin silver threads flowed from their wrists and ankles, spiralling upwards into the ceiling. Every time one of them moved or jerked a head, I saw a thread tug at them.

I kept skating, pulling out every trick and flourish that I knew. A chime rang out above the music, and the Minotaur girls joined me on the rink, wheels flashing.

While I was skating, I was one of them.

I slowed, and immediately saw the difference. The Minotaur girls turned toward me with sneers and suspicion. I sped up, did a twirl or two, and they relaxed.

No way I could do this forever. My skates felt like concrete blocks on my feet.

Thin Lizzie and Chrissy skated together. They did not look at me. Thin Lizzie's threads were almost as bright as those of the real Minotaur girls, and Chrissy's glowed as she gained confidence.

If I stayed longer, I might not want to leave either.

A silver shadow poured from the ceiling to the floor. Everyone skated around it, pretending it wasn't there. It was a rope ladder, made of those threads they all wore. A silver ladder of knotted threads. It couldn't take my weight, surely?

But it was a chance.

I spun and danced and sped around the rink, not aiming for the ladder at all. I even let a Minotaur boy or two catch my hand and twirl me around. Non-threatening. Part of the show.

Then I skated backwards until I felt the soft brush of the thread ladder against my back.

I grabbed hold and climbed, pulling it up behind me. Up and up, and I hardly needed the ladder after a while because the silver threads were a thick tangle up here, twitching in the air. I climbed and climbed, and finally grasped something solid instead of that diaphanous ladder. It was a hanging cage. The knotted ladder ended here. I could see where the web of threads had been torn around us, to make the ladder.

"You," said a whispered voice, and I saw the boy Ari staring out at me, his thin fingers grasping the bars. "Is it you?"

He was so pathetic, my stomach swelled up with anger against him. "Why did you give me that coin?" I hissed. "Why did you bring me here? This place is horrible."

Ari was still beautiful, but not nearly as glitter as he had seemed that day in the park. "I didn't have a choice," he said. "The Minotaur made me do it. But I hoped...it might be different this time. Maybe you could break this place wide open. Someone has to."

I hadn't thought of that. Could I close down the Minotaur once and for all? "Everyone would hate me," I said in awe at the very idea of it.

Ari smiled with bright teeth and yeah, I'd still let him kiss me. "They'd never forget you," he said.

I broke two fingernails getting his cage open. I had to use a skate to bash at the lock until it broke and Ari could get out. We climbed together, up the chain that held the cage, and it wasn't long before we spotted a railing at the top of the Minotaur. There was a balcony running around the inside of this upper part of the building, and we clambered across the web of threads to reach it.

If we fell, we would be caught in those threads like the net under a trapeze. So many threads, each plugged into a beautiful monster.

Ari was right. We had to blow this place wide open.

"Where are we going?" I whispered.

"Control room," Ari said back. "There's always someone pulling the threads."

"Like—a big boss?"

"I can't answer that," he said, as I climbed over the railing. Finally, solid floor under my feet. He didn't once try to help me and I wasn't sure if that was wonderful or really annoying. "A different girl pulls the threads each night."

"How does all this happen without someone in charge?"

"It's the Minotaur," said Ari. "The building is alive. It wants us to have a good time and put on a show. It loves roller skates, who knows why. If we make it happy, it rewards us. So we do."

We were outside the control room now. It had a wide glass window but I couldn't see much in the darkness.

Ari hung back.

"Aren't you coming in?" I asked.

"I don't think I can." He lifted his feet and hands. Pale threads veined away from him and down over the edge of the balcony. "They always grow back," he said sadly.

I ran inside the control room and slammed the door behind me. "So," I said aloud. "Who's pulling the threads tonight?"

"Tess?" said a small voice. "Is that you?"

As my eyes got used to the darkness, I saw her at the far end of the room. She sat on an ordinary office chair, the kind that spins around. Every inch of her body had a silver thread growing out of it. They lashed into the walls and floor and ceiling.

Fat Lizzie. I hadn't seen her in weeks, but she looked different. Gaunt and angry and so, so scared.

"What have they done to you?" I breathed.

"It's not they," she said. "There isn't a 'they.' It's the Minotaur. She hates us all."

The floor shuddered under my feet. The Minotaur didn't like us having this conversation. And since when was the Minotaur a she?

"What happens if I cut you out of those threads?" I asked Fat Lizzie.

"They grow back. Faster. And they hurt."

I turned to the control banks, all those switches and dials. I pressed a button, and a screen flicked into life slowly, in grayscale. Another screen, then another. You could see the whole Minotaur from here, every room and ramp. The girls and boys were skating, gaming, kissing and groping.

"Not much of a show," I said aloud. "What if I make it more entertaining?"

The floor stopped rumbling under my feet. The Minotaur was curious.

"You can't beat the Minotaur, Tess," said Fat Lizzie. She sounded stretched thin. "She won't let you."

That stung. Ari thought I was special. Why was she so certain I wasn't? "Why not?"

Lizzie didn't answer. Her hands moved back and forth, plucking at the silvery threads that spun out through the walls and floors.

I left the control room and went back out to the balcony, where Ari lay trapped in his own tangle of silver threads. "Why me?" I demanded. "Why did you choose *me* if I'm so useless?"

He shook his head, staring up at me.

"Why am I the only one without silver threads sticking out of me?" I tried. This time, when he didn't answer, I flew at him, tearing at the threads. He yelled with pain as I pulled them out. When the last of them snaked away off the edge of the balcony, Ari sat there, breathless and rumpled but able to talk to me again.

"What are we going to do?" I demanded. I was no use on my own. I should be part of a group, with Lizzie and Lizzie and Chrissie bouncing our every word and thought off each other until everything made sense.

I missed them so badly.

"Don't ask me," Ari snapped. "This is your game, not mine. Don't you get it? You're the hero and I'm the fucking damsel in distress."

Something rang a chord in my mind, so very familiar. "What do you mean, game?"

"Ante up, lay your bets, roll the dice," he said in a sing-song voice. "I laid my bets on you, Tess, and you're not exactly paying off."

"Who am I playing against?" I hissed at him.

He glanced past me, and shuddered. "The Minotaur."

I turned, not sure what to expect. My worst fear was that it would be one of my girls, Thin Lizzie or Chrissie, that I'd have to fight them. But it wasn't anyone I knew.

She wasn't tall. She was old like Mum, and I felt a familiar shock as I gazed at her, like meeting a long-lost aunt for the first time. She was fitter than my mum, with better hair. She had a really great suit, all purple velvet and pale pink lace, like something Prince would wear.

"You were right the first time, Tess," said the Minotaur. "There is a boss."

"I knew it," I said sourly. "No way a building is this mean all on its own."

"That's not exactly true. I am the building, and the building is me — the Minotaur and her maze. Bet you can't guess my name."

"I'm not falling for that again."

"Fair enough." She grinned at me, like she was my age. I wish I could remember where I'd seen her before. "My name is Teresa Maree Holland. Or it was, before I became the Minotaur. So long ago."

I felt small and stupid, and that made me angrier. "That's my name."

"Obviously."

"You expect me to believe that...you're me?"

"No, sweetheart," the Minotaur said, all patronising like the teachers at school. "You're *me*."

"That's not *true*," I flung at her.

She smirked at me, and I knew that expression so well that it chilled my insides. I'd practiced it in the mirror before coming here to-night, so I'd look like the confident one instead of tagging after Thin Lizzie like I always do. "The reason you don't have threads sticking out of you is because you are all thread, my darling. That's what I made you from. Time to come home, chickadee."

The Minotaur reached out to me, and I felt something tug inside my stomach. It was true. I could feel how my whole body was made of threads, coiled tightly to make my limbs and blood and skin. If she pulled hard enough, I would dissolve into whorls of thread, spinning and dancing in the air. I wasn't real, I didn't mean anything, I was temporary...

"No." I wrenched myself away. "I'm not you. I don't care what game you're playing..."

"Aces high," she said with a wink. "But you're more of a two of hearts, really. A three at most. Naïve enough to let one of my girls win a year of your life, which I'm rather put out about. I had plans for that year."

"I'm *me*," I said, enraged. "I'm Tess, I'm a real person."

"I was like you once. More than once. So fresh-faced. I mean, look at your adorable baby-doll body. Life was so glitter back then. All I wanted to do was skate, and go with cute boys, and cruise with my friends. Look at me now—I'm living the dream."

"Apart from being old," I shot at her.

She looked triumphant. "You don't think I went to all this trouble just to see a younger version of myself scampering about, do you? Look at you, my dear, all fire and outrage. Big fringe, short skirt. The power of youth. I made you, and now I'm taking you back, like I do every time. Every Minotaur does, when she grows old."

Every time. This had happened before. The knowledge fell into my head like a brick. It wasn't just her, not just this Minotaur. Kids like me, all over the world, eaten and absorbed by desperate middle-aged wannabes like her. She smiled at me, like a real mother might, and I knew it was true. I knew a lot of things I couldn't know unless it was all true, and I was the next version of her.

The Minotaur didn't want to pull my body apart into threads of nothing. She wanted to climb inside it, steal it for her own. Where would I be? Would I be her? I couldn't imagine anything worse.

"You are...so...*unglitter!*" I howled at her.

She actually laughed, as if the word meant nothing.

I don't know what they were about, those other girls. I don't know how many of them—of me—trudged obediently to the slaughter, letting the Minotaur take them and reshape them and put herself inside their young bodies so she could do it all over again, and again, and again.

What did she do to them, to make them not want to fight for their lives? I thought about my friends, and the last time I was truly happy, that day in the park when we were all together. I was ready to fight.

I was aware of every thread in this body of mine, every mote of skin and drop of blood. She had built me for one purpose, to be the next Minotaur. She wanted to rule this world of skates and dance music all over again, to control the silver threads, and so she must have built that power into me in order that it would be there when she stole my fourteen-year-old body. Fifteen-year-old. That was a hard one to get used to.

I could see it all, just as I felt her reaching out to me, into me, awakening that power so that it would bring her home.

And I snapped the threads. Every time she reached for me, I severed the connection. She frowned and tried again, but I beat her back. *My body, my threads. Mine for the keeping.*

Mine to destroy.

This time, when she came at me, I yanked every thread in the place. I felt Fat Lizzie in the control room, hanging on to the threads for dear life, and I begged her to trust me, to let her burden go. They slipped from her, every thread, and snaked toward me.

The woman who thought herself the Minotaur howled, trying physically to prevent the threads from reaching me, but her power was weak, and every thread made me so, so strong.

I called to them, the Minotaur girls and boys, the teens who just wanted to skate and play games, the audience, my friends, even Ari. *Come to me, give me your power, share it all with me, and I will set you free. Ante up. Bet on me.*

Offered a choice between my older self and a teenage girl who looked much like them, they chose me.

The look on the Old Minotaur's face when she realized she had lost was awful. I felt kind of bad for her. But that didn't stop me setting those kids loose on her.

You thought you were free of them, grown-ups with their rules and stupid lectures. But she was here all the time, telling you what to do.

They didn't like that, the Minotaur kids. They climbed to us, up the webs of silver threads, hungry and desperate and furious. The happy fun place was lost, the music had stopped, and they remembered now that they had homes and families and lives that had been stolen from them. That they had been stolen from.

They ate her alive, the horde of beautiful silver children with shiny hair and totally glitter outfits. They tore her to pieces, and I let them do it.

Afterwards they looked at me, all docile and obedient, with the blood of my older self still staining their mouths, like they wanted me to be in charge. They thought I would be better than her, because I was young like them, and they did not know how to go on from here.

Would I be the one to give them back their eternal skate party, their games and glamour and mirror balls? Would I make it all better?

"We're going to burn it down," I told them. "It's going to be so glitter. The most glitter ever. And after that, you can go home."

The Minotaur burned, and the fire engines came, and there was nothing much left after that except charcoal and crying teenagers. I found my skates in the sparkling rubble.

"You did it," Ari said to me. "You broke the spell."

"Yay for me," I said flatly.

The parents came, one by one, to drive their kids home. Thin Lizzie's mum cried when she saw her. Chrissy's dad looked really fierce. Fat Lizzie's parents just looked relieved.

Ari and I waited, until they had all gone home, and it was just us.

I hadn't expected anyone to come for me. That Mum and Dad I thought I had, when we talked about our parents at school, or in the park...if they had ever existed, they belonged to the original Tess, generations ago. Gone now.

I didn't ask why no one had come for Ari. He didn't seem surprised.

"What now?" he asked.

My charred skates still had silver paint on them. "Let's go to the park," I said.

"And do what?" he said in disbelief. "Skate? After all this?"

"It's the best park for skating."

I knotted my laces together, hung my skates around my neck, and took his hand. We would skate a bit, and talk, and maybe kiss for a while. We would fall asleep on the cold grass of the park. And I would leave him there, before it got light. Where I was going next, I couldn't take him.

There were other Minotaurs in the world, in other towns. I knew that now, and I knew how to stop them. I had to locate the girls that were just like me, help them unravel the truth and the power within their own skin.

Skates on.

Ante up.

One thread at a time.

Unable to Reach You

Alan DeNiro

Julian tries to do good, he really tries to help people who Google in desperation. He runs a website that allows people to post phone numbers that anonymous callers call from—pre-recorded messages, sometimes hissing, machine noises, or nothing at all. Sometimes these are demands for credit card numbers, car insurance advertisements, foreclosure notices, promises of beautiful timeshares, lottery-winning announcements, threats of unpaid speeding tickets requiring one's presence in Hawaii. The people who post these numbers—as anonymous to Julian as the ghost callers themselves, but friendlier—find solidarity on his site. The site also has a PayPal tip jar, which has received a total of $35.50 in the one-year lifespan of his site. He keeps waiting for a thousand-dollar donation, but so far he hasn't come across any angels on the Internet.

But it's not for the money that he does this. Sometimes, he's been able to track the phone numbers to shady operators and scam artists and report them to the Better Business Bureau. If not, though, he still thinks that listing the numbers help countless people that he's never met. In that sense, Julian sees his site as a full extension of his life, in which he tries to be helpful. *Mindfulness*, like his book on meditation tells him. He is mindful of the perils of the Internet. During the day he is an independent shipping contractor, delivering short-run packages throughout the city in his Mercury Tracer. His shift supervisor Chester once called him "the stupidest smart person he's ever known." He lives in a furnished basement apartment and is about twenty years away from a theoretical retirement age, though he has no money to retire on.

He usually drives from eight to three—he would drive more, if they had more hours and packages for him—and on one hot, long summer afternoon, he arrives home and checks the most recent numbers posted on the site, which is the highlight of most of his days. In a new thread, a few people have posted a number that scares him. It's his own. And the reports are all different.

"All I hear is heavy breathing and then a man mumbling something about a credit card APR."

"A crackling w/ dog barking in the background. When I asked who it was they hung up."

"STATIC," yet another call report says. "Then THREE successive high-pitched beeps, five seconds apart. I could hear a noise in the background, like someone using an electric can opener."

Julian checks the number posted three times, and verifies that it's his. His cell phone, a pay-as-you-go phone because he doesn't want to spend too much on a plan, is right next to his computer keyboard. He checks his outgoing calls. Nothing unusual. To his sister, to his auto mechanic, to his credit card (to plead for an extra month).

"No," Julian says. He sets the phone down and picks it up again quickly. He looks through every conceivable folder inside the phone's data system. Nothing to suggest that he had made those calls at those timestamped times. He had his phone with him at all times. There was no chance of accidental dialing. Could there have been a duplicate number? Unheard of.

He checks his email. A few people have sent his new phone numbers. He allows the computer illiterate to email questions to him, if they can't figure out how to post them. He replies with his boilerplate:

"Hi there. Here's the link you can use to fill out the form. Be sure to search and see if your harassing number is already included on a list. Thank you!

"P.S. This site is an all-volunteer effort. If you would like to donate to keep this site operational—no matter how small the amount—it would be greatly appreciated!"

Then he logs into his site's admin panel and double-checks the IP addresses of the people who have logged complaints about his number.

He does a geographic search. The calls were logged all over the map: Fresno, Grand Rapids, Orlando. Not one single person, pretending to register multiple complaints. Julian feels a chill on the back of his neck. He hears a pounding on the basement door, which startles him. But it's just the people upstairs having sex.

Julian decides maybe it's a fluke. He emails his best friend, Harry, who works third shift in a call center in South Dakota, and forwards the call reports to him. He is the most frequent commenter on the site, and the only person he has really gotten to know from his efforts. "???" is Julian's subject line. Then he plays a few rounds of Minesweeper and goes to bed.

The next morning, it's worse. Much worse. He is late for his shift because he spent an extra hour in panic in front of his computer, looking at the call reports that his patrons have posted.

"WTF, srsly? It's someone making monkey sounds & then saying they are from the Texas Department of Corrections and that I have a bill for my prison stay."

"Someone in a robot voice starts shouting at me to stop prank calling him."

"Can someone help me? I am scared. Looks like this creep has struck lots of times. Just heavy breathing and a sawing noise. Wish I could find out where this CREEP LIVES."

There are about ten more reports. Already, his own number is #12 on the "Most Frequently Calling Numbers."

By the middle of his day and his third package run, he's wondering if his shift supervisor Chester is somehow the one who is prank calling with his phone number. He wouldn't put it past him. During his lunch break—Wendy's, which he eats inside his parked car—he checks his email and Harry has replied to his.

"Julian!" he has written. "This is bad. But you know that ppl can spoof your number or any number they want?? There're sites where they can sign up for it and enter, say, your number so it looks like you're the evil prank caller?? You don't know this? Well, what would you do without Harry, lol. Anyway, I think someone's out to get you. Got to run but let me know if you need anything else.—Harry."

Julian looks out the window, at the people going in and out of Wendy's, people driving into the strip mall. Who would hurt him?

There's a knock on his car window. He screams and his value fries go flying into the passenger seat. He's embarrassed by the high pitch of his voice. It's a man wearing a Goodwill suit that's one size too small. His hair is newly shorn. He's holding a sheaf of newspapers. Slowly, Julian rolls down the window.

"Free paper," the man says. "Free paper. Written by the homeless. All money goes to the homeless."

"I don't have any money," he says. His phone rings. It's a number he doesn't recognize. He ignores it.

"Fair enough," he says. "Fair enough, sir." Then he keeps walking. Julian quickly rolls up the window. Julian lived out of his car for a few weeks, a few years ago, before he moved in with his sister for a year, letting him get back on his feet before he could find a job. The homeless man makes the rounds in the parking lot, until an assistant manager comes out of the store and has a few words with him. He shakes the papers at the manager but he moves on.

It could be someone using a used phone and a public internet connection, Julian wonders as he watches this scene.

Back at home, he looks at his site. His number is now #9.

"Will the owner of this site PLEASE report this SOB to the BBB?"

He checks the voicemail he received while in the parking lot. "Whoever you are, just stop calling," a woman says. "Just shut the fuck up, you sick fuck." Julian sets down the phone. He doesn't list his name on his voicemail. "Hi, this is [THE NUMBER]. I'm not here right now please leave a message." He is his number. He erases the message and then cleans his apartment from top to bottom in order to try to calm down.

It doesn't work.

He gives a report to Harry of recent developments. "What should I do?" he writes. As he writes, his throat constricts.

Harry writes back ten minutes later. "Uh, difficult to say. I would either switch your number, call the police, or can you figure this out on your own? I don't know, have you Googled your own number?"

Julian hasn't. He says goodbye to Harry and Googles his own number. He never felt the need for that before. The effort unsettles him. There are about seven pages of entries. Most are junk, pages of number strings from Vietnam or China, or requisition numbers for industrial parts for sterilizers or optical scanners. Nothing suspicious at all. Only one site catches his eye, five or six pages down: griefgraveyard.com.

He takes a deep breath and goes there, going to the main site first, taking out the string of numbers and letters following the website name in the address bar. The site isn't like anything he's been on before, a site for other people with different types of lives than his. The background is black and the font is white and gothic. There are lots of blurry photos of men and women much younger than him, with all sorts of different hair colors than his brown-gray—purple, blue, bleached yellow—and with lots of piercings on the lip, nose, and next to the eye. It's not clear what the purpose of the site is, except for these various people to gain "ascension points."

"PROJECT: SYBERIAN CANDOR, sponsored by Fun-Co" is the title of the exact page where his number resides; there's a long list of other numbers there. There is a large and blurry profile picture pic, although it couldn't have been an actual unadulterated photo, of a woman with blue spiky hair and sunglasses and wide wings tucked behind her. The wings are leathery and brown, with tiny feathers along the edges. The expression on her face is one of knowing a secret that's horrible and also kind of funny. The screen flickers, like it's getting an electrical surge. Julian stares at the woman with wings for a couple of seconds, and starts to feel woozy.

The furnished basement spins and grows dark in stop-motion.

When his head clears, and the light comes again, he finds himself without a body. He is floating in the middle of a dim, windowless room, with light coming from faint halogens set in the ceiling. There are dozens of people dancing. There is sludgy music with a cavernous beat; even though he hears it distantly, like a train approaching from miles away, he senses that the music must be thunderous for the dancers. They are the same people Julian saw on the griefgraveyard website, and they are in a frenzy to the music—arms and legs intertwining, tearing at each other's clothes, revealing tattoos of insectoid larvae hatching and werewolves feasting on throats and slinking dragons burrowing into gaping mouths. The women and men kiss, the men and men kiss, the women and women kiss. A DJ, high on a stone dais in the far corner, has his turntables on an alabaster altar with dark green fluid staining the surface. Julian takes a second look at the DJ and, though the man is wearing only a pair of shorts and thigh-high boots and has a reptilian tail, Julian recognizes the man who was selling newspapers in front of the Wendy's. He worries that he might be recognized, but no one pays any attention to him.

The woman with wings in the center of the room unfurls them, and everyone else takes a step back. Julian floats toward her; he is both horrified and thrilled by her presence. Someone hands her a silver chalice and a black-bladed knife. Tipping her head back, she cuts a vein in her wrist and catches blood that looks like motor oil in the chalice. Julian expects them to pass around the chalice and drink the blood, but instead everyone circling around her pulls out their cell phone and dips their cell phone in the blood when it's their turn. When everyone had done so, they all start dancing again with their cell phones held aloft, screens lit. He had seen people do that on television before, on *Ryan Seacrest's Rocking New Year's Eve*, where a band wearing jumpsuits he didn't know was performing. Drifting closer to the throne, he sees that the number on each of their screens is his own. And while each phone was dialing, the plastic of the phone had absorbed the blood.

Without thinking, he tries to shout at them to stop. No voice comes out, but the winged woman cocks her head and looks in his direction. In the mirroring of her sunglasses, he sees that, here, he is a gray cloud, vaguely human-shaped and glimmering with pinkish traces.

She points at him and shouts in a language he can't decipher.

But her face surprises him. Because she looks frightened. She looks frightened of Julian. The room begins to pulsate and the light whisks away again and he wakes up on the floor of his basement apartment, blood streaming out of his nose. His computer had rebooted. It's hard for him to breathe. When he's able to calm down again, and stuff his nostril full of tissue, he wants nothing more than to stumble to bed, and he does.

He doesn't want to think about what had happened to him. But rather than feeling confused and scared, a peace falls over him as he sleeps. The peace doesn't dissipate in the morning when his boss wakes him with a call, wondering where the hell he was, did he know he's two hours late—

Julian mutters something and hangs up. When he goes into the warehouse to pick up his packages, his boss's voice is shrill yet distant, like the griefgraveyard people (if they were people) had been for him. He doesn't spend much time in the warehouse, and lets his boss's voice drift away as he walks back to his car. He delivers his packages in a daze, trying in the abyss of his mind to consider what really did happen to him, like attempting to solve a complicated chess puzzle without a board in front of him.

During his lunch in the Wendy's parking lot—no sign of the DJ—he emails Harry. He doesn't give all the details but tells him to check out griefgraveyard.com and see what he thinks.

An hour later Harry gets back to him with an email flagged "urgent."

"Um Jules," it begins, "that site wouldn't load for me. I mean, there's a website THERE, it just kicked me out. Does this have to do with the prank calls?? I checked the domain registry for you. They use GoDaddy. No help. But, uh, I hate to say this but your number is Number ONE on the call chart. If it gets this bad the police might investigate? Be careful okay?"

Julian guesses that they are escalating. When he gets home that night, he eats his Hungry Man dinner and sits down in front of his computer. Taking a deep breath, he goes to griefgraveyard.com.

The site is there—he has no trouble accessing it—but he keeps expecting something to happen, and nothing does. He blinks several times, focusing on the picture of the winged woman, but nothing happens. After an hour of this he grows frustrated and stalks away from the computer, and decides to take a drive in the moonlight to clear his head. There's a chill in the air but he rolls down his windows anyway. His skin tingles. Soon he's on the outskirts of town: empty office parks, scrub woods, and drainage ditches. He stops his car in a rideshare parking lot on the edge of a small forest in the middle of nowhere, and gets out. The moon is full above him. He looks at his hands. Is there anything inside of him that could cause him to transport to the place of "SYBERIAN CANDOR"? He doesn't know. He walks to the edge of the woods, which actually look like a tree farm, the plantings of the pines angular and even. But there are mushrooms on the edge of the woods, with colors like angelfish. He is taken back to his time as a kid with his mother, when they lived in the trailer, before even that was taken from them. They used to take walks in the woods by the railroad tracks, and she would point out all the mushrooms, good and bad. He was embarrassed by her most times. She smelled. She could barely dress and feed herself, much less Julian. But in the woods she was lucid, strong.

Then when he was fourteen, she disappeared. When Child Protective Services came to pick him up, he heard the case workers mumble between themselves phrases like "psychotic break" and "hallucinogenic divorce from reality," which he wasn't supposed to hear.

He picks the angelfish mushrooms at the stem and cradles them on the walk back to his car, where he wraps them in newspaper. There is a white car that has entered the park-and-ride when he was in the woods, still running. Driving it is a woman with blonde hair, whom he has never seen before. He can't get a good look at her face, but he sees that she is smiling at him. He feels like he should be unsettled, but he isn't. He's about to go over and see what she wants, but she backs up her car and guns it back on the state highway.

Back home, it's two in the morning. He makes a tea with the mushrooms, his memories of his mother's actions in their tiny kitchenette taking over. Sitting back down at his computer, he waits for the tea to cool a bit and then drinks the entire cup in a few gulps. It's bitter and sour.

"Something's going to happen," he says to himself.

And it does. He blinks. The darkness of the computer monitor widens and elongates in all directions and swallows him up. He begins laughing. When he can see again, he's back in the cavernous dance space, though there's no music or movement. All of the people are naked and sleeping, huddled together in the center of the room, bodies slick and intertwined. Everything is dim. Julian doesn't waste any time. Hovering close to the ground, he moves close to one of the men on the edge of the throng, and then sinks down. He enters the body. He feels warmth and light and color. The man gasps and trembles but Julian quickly puts a stop to that. Quietly, Julian stands up and stretches the body, lean and taut and unlike his own in all ways. No one else stirs, and Julian begins walking to the dais and the altar. The room is *warm*. It smells like the mushroom tea he just drank. The turntables are empty, and there aren't any power cords. He touches the smooth marble of the altar, and the green stains. The stone pulsates and he flinches.

He looks down and sees something stuck on his thigh. No, stuck inside his thigh. A slit in his skin; he reaches down to touch it and then pushes his hand inside. It doesn't hurt. He pulls out the man's phone. The screen shows icons for a browser, an air hockey game, a weather app, and a "Manual" doc. Opening the manual, he sees it's in a swirling, hieroglyphic script, but he is able to read it:

Zukaratharakghnakhawgrynath d/b/a Fun-Co
ORIENTATION MANUAL
Position of Employ: Ectophage Transmission Technician/
    Dancer
Version 62.41.7 (Brass Scarab Clearance)

Welcome, invaluable team member! This manual will guide you through everything you need to know to perform your tasks ably and efficiently in service of the Unspeakable Leviathan. Yours is an especially important link in the chain that leads to the completion of the following Fun-Co team goals:

- Worship of our Dark and Merciless Overlord through impeccable work ethic in our efforts to satiate Its eternal hunger.

- Be the extra-planar leader in trans-life recapture hacking.

- Fun! (It's in our name!). You will be dancing. *A lot.*

A list of procedures and protocols that he doesn't understand follows.

Then he calls Harry. Harry had told him to never call him at that number, except if it was the direst emergency. Julian figures that if this doesn't qualify, nothing would.

"Hello?" Harry says. There's the rush and thrum of call center activity behind him.

"Harry. This is Julian." His voice is coming out all wrong though. Like he is a hyena trying to speak.

"Oh God, it's happening to me. Fuck. Fuck. Look, whoever you are—*leave Julian alone.*"

"No, Harry..."

But Harry hangs up.

The pile of bodies begins to stir. The winged woman crouches and stands. She growls. Julian looks for an exit, even though he has no idea where he can possibly escape to. The winged woman is handed her black knife and she begins a running leap toward Julian, stepping on the other confused sleepers that haven't quite woken up yet. Julian dives off the altar before the winged woman can reach him. But he realizes: why is he afraid? He waits for the winged woman to center herself again, his arms outstretched, and when she's standing only a few feet away from him, he takes the knife from her hand. She is too surprised to resist. He slits his own throat.

As he collapses and his vision darkens, he is happy. He has never been happier.

He wakes up on his knees, straddling his hogtied and gagged boss. He looks wildly around; he's not home. He's in someone else's living room. His boss's living room—smaller than he thought it would be, a condo with cheap wood paneling and high ceilings. The blood comes out of his nostrils in rivulets and he swears.

His boss is shrieking.

Standing up, wobbling, Julian goes to the kitchen and washes his face in the sink. He has no idea why he is in his boss's house. He doesn't even know whether anyone else is in the house, whether there's a family upstairs cowering in terror. The sky is just beginning to brighten with dawn.

There is a honking on the street in front of the house, and he startles. Julian wants to ignore it, but he goes to the front window and peeks out. It's the woman in the white Corolla, whose face he could barely see in the gray morning light. She rolls down the window. She looks to be his age—maybe a bit older—with streaks of gray in her blonde hair, and wide violet eyes. She's wearing rings on each finger, each with a different gemstone.

"Julian," she calls out, as quietly as she can. "You need to come with me. You're not safe here."

Julian puts a hand on his forehead. "Who are you?"

"I'm here to help you." She pauses, like she doesn't want to say more, but is forced to by circumstances. "I'm here to help you take down Fun-Co. But you can't do it without me."

He nods. He is floating inside, as he takes this role of provocateur upon himself. He starts to go down the front stairs but she says, "And bring Chester. We need him with us. I'll help you."

Julian doesn't hesitate. He doesn't hesitate anymore. They haul him into the trunk of her Corolla and slam the lid shut.

"What about my car?" Julian says.

The woman puts a hand on her shoulder. "Leave it. Taking him and taking my car will buy us a little bit of time."

Julian pauses. "Where are we going, exactly?"

She smiles. "South Dakota. To your dear friend Harry."

Her name is Emory. They drive all day, only stopping a few times for bathroom breaks and food and gas. They don't give Chester anything; they don't really talk about it. Through hills and flatlands, prairies and strip malls unconnected to any towns, past collapsing barns and burnt farmhouses. He expects her to speak more, to explain herself, but she says little. When he asks her what Fun-Co actually *is*, she doesn't say much. "Clearly we are in the realm of the supernatural. And you have seen more of it than I have. What's important is that they were using you, and others like you, as conduits between their world and…this one."

"Why, though?" Julian asks.

She shrugs. "If we knew that, there might be an easier way than what we have to do."

Julian also notes what he had read in the "Training Manual" about the "Unspeakable Leviathan."

She laughs. "That could be code for their leader. Their CEO, if you will. I'm sure you have Its direct attention now."

With twilight arriving, they come upon the call center—a white warehouse with wheat fields on three sides and a gas station on the fourth. There is little else around. Julian thinks the call center looks like a mausoleum.

They stop the car in the gas station parking lot, and Emory pulls a pill box out of her purse. She stares hard at Julian. "Now the power is in your hands," she says, opening the pill box. Inside are a dozen of what look like black aspirin. "They are going to be ready for you. They don't want you in. But with my help they won't be able to stop you."

"Okay, but what do you need Harry for?"

"The call center. It's the only place where the ritual can take place. They are using your phone number to try to break you and the work you are doing; only by using a phone hub like this will you be able to break through the defenses."

He pauses. "How do you know this?" he asks. "I mean, about the work I do?"

She sighs, but not unhappily. "I'm one of your biggest fans. I admire your site so so much."

For a few moments, doubts absorb into him like the winged woman's blood into the dancers' cell phones. But he chases them away. He doesn't want to doubt himself, or the fact that his life and work—forever ignored—is truly worth admiration. And since everyone on the Internet is more or less a stranger, it makes sense for a stranger like Emory to admire him.

"Open your palm," she says. He does, slowly, and she places all the black pills in his hand. Taking a deep breath, he swallows all of them and she gives him a sip of water.

There is no taste at all to them.

"Hold on," she says. "Hold on."

Things begin happening quickly after that. His awareness of what happens comes and goes. He feels like he is nine feet tall, somehow scrunched into his Corolla, as Emory backs the car across the state highway, through the parking lot of the call center, crashing the trunk of the car into the front doors.

They exit amongst the smashed glass. Emory pops open her trunk. Julian sees that Chester is unconscious. She sighs and gives him a shot from a needle she had in her pocket. He wakes up after that, and Julian cuts his legs free. They hoist him out. The receptionists flee deeper into the building.

Julian and Emory pick their way through the broken door, trailing Chester behind on a rope. Green, glittering hoops appear in the air and disappear again. Julian grabs Emory's hand and she squeezes it. They are in concert. Julian feels himself beginning to know what Emory is thinking, and he imagines that the same is happening to Emory. Two security guards come rushing toward them from a side hallway. Their faces are molten, like steel in a blast furnace. Their bodies glow orange. They don't look quite human to Julian. Emory shoots them with a revolver. Blue bullets fly out. They fall. Julian doesn't stop. Everything is easy. They walk over the bodies, but as he's walking to the main open room of the call center, his senses are darkening. He is not going to the griefgraveyard, though—he is only darkening in the here and now.

Time passes and, when he remembers again, and can see things again, he is in the middle of the call center, computers circled around him, Chester at his feet. Julian isn't wearing clothes, and Emory is on top of him. He has just come inside of her, and she is still rocking on top of him, her breath seething. Her veins are blue and raised, and her skin is flushed and her head is tipped forward. Julian still feels the pills working inside of him. Green hoops rise above the two of them all the way to the ceiling. Emory disengages and Julian looks around. All of the computers have the griefgraveyard site on their screens. No one else is in the room besides Chester and the other man, although he can hear sirens, distantly, and a bullhorn.

"What's happening?" he asks, rubbing his head.

"You are almost ready for your passage," she says.

The other man starts rolling around. It's Harry, Julian realizes. It has to be Harry. Harry is younger than Julian thought he would be. For some reason he had considered Harry to be kind of his twin in loneliness, but Harry appears to be the kind of fun-loving, assertive guy who always had little to do with Julian as he was growing up and navigating life.

"Remove his gag," Julian says. Emory hesitates for a second, but then does so.

"Julian?" Harry says. "Julian, please."

Emory kneels down next to Harry, putting the revolver next to his forehead. "This is a Fun-Co nexus," she says. "This is why I brought you here. I didn't want to alarm you about your friend, but he's one of the intermediaries tasked to keep tabs on you."

"Like the DJ," Julian says.

"Not exactly like the DJ," she says. "He exists in both places. But close enough."

"This is crazy," Harry says. "I don't know what she's talking about. At all." Julian kneels down as well and looks into Harry's eyes, trying to discern something there.

Harry's irises glitter. Julian shakes his head sadly and reaches out for Emory's hand. "I'm ready," he says.

She smiles. She leans in to give him a hungry kiss. He can feel her tongue licking his face. "Don't worry about them," she says, motioning toward the walls, the outer world where the police await. "I'll take care of them. Go."

He nods and starts to take in deep breaths, and then spin around, looking at each monitor. From the vestibule of the building there are shouts and smoke grenades. A momentary fear passes over him but it dissipates as soon as the darkness from the monitors truly settles over him, and after a few moments, his head feels like it's in his stomach, and it snaps back again, he is back in the realm of Syberian Candor.

He is the same glittering cloud, but everything else is different. The halogens in the ceiling are harsher and brighter, like a bar after last call trying to get the drunks to go home. The turntables are gone, all the dancers are gone. The altar is still there, but in the light he can't see the green stains. In the center of the room—which is more cavernous than he had realized, now that all of its walls are in full light—is Emory. She is cross-legged on the ground and trembling. At first he thinks that she is upset. Perhaps she arrived here by accident. He drifts toward her to comfort her, but then sees her stand. Her legs grow taller. Her skin becomes gray and oily. She turns toward Julian. Her chin splits open twice, revealing two small mouths there, each with a row of tiny fangs. Her hair lengthens into thick red knots, down to her waist, and her pupils widen until her irises are extinguished.

Julian stops in front of her. She manages to smile. He recognizes that smile of hers, even in her current form. She looks like she is ready to devour his form, but then he hears a phone ringing—an old fashioned ring—and Emory pulls a phone out of her elongated thigh.

"Yeah," she says. She holds out a finger to Julian as if to say, "I'll be with you in a minute."

"Yes, it's all done. Worked like a charm. No, he's not going anywhere. It was a little too easy. I know. Yeah. Listen, we're going to keep this locus unascended. Cut our losses. Yep, exactly. We've already repurposed the dancers into..."

Emory says a name that Julian finds to be unpronounceable.

"Anyway—no. No, you listen to *me*. I am your Eternal Overlord. The blood of all things should fill my stomach and fill my veins, et cetera, et cetera. Remember that? Okay. Good." Emory sighs. She's already walking away. "Well, we've had worse."

Julian races after her. Emory turns around. She stares at the cloud without pity.

"I'm not exactly sure how you found me to be so trustworthy," she says. "But it was a pretty bad decision."

She shimmers through the wall closest to her. He tries to do the same but is repulsed. Then he tries to retreat back to his own body, to return to the world, but he can't. He doesn't know how.

He tries to shout but can't.

He is left with his thoughts and little else. Over and over—he has no conception of time—he tries to make something happen but nothing does.

Not wanting to perceive anything, he enters the stone altar and remains asleep. He is not at peace but he is, at least, dormant.

Ages pass. Or perhaps they do not pass at all. He is awakened by vibrations like slow earthquakes. He jettisons out of the altar and sees the DJ again, the old DJ, playing several records at once. The lights are dim again. None of the dancers are the same; they all wear white robes. And the music is a drone, sounding like a distant bombing raid through the perceptions available to him.

They are all dancing in a circle, arm in arm. In the center of the circle is his mother: tall, braided hair, with the robe swirling around her.

More than anything, she looks innocent. Julian moves toward the circle, trying to see whether any of these dancers have phones.

There are so many things wide open to him, and so few.

Such & Such Said to So & So

Maria Dahvana Headley

It was late July, a dark green mood-ring of a night, and the drinks from Bee's Jesus had finally killed a man.

The cocktails there had always been dangerous, but now they were poison. We got the call in at the precinct, and none of us were surprised. We all knew the place was no good, never mind that we'd also all spent some time there. These days we stayed away, or not, depending on how our marriages were going, and how much cash we had in the glovebox. There were no trains nearby, and if you ended up out too long, you were staying out. The suburbs were a dream, and you weren't sleeping.

There was nothing harder to get out of your clothes than Bee's Jesus. We all knew that too. Dry cleaner around the corner. You'd go there, shame-faced and stubbled at dawn, late for your beat.

"Ah, it's the Emperor of Regret," the guy behind the counter would say to you. No matter which Emperor you were. All us boys from the precinct had the same title.

"Yeah," you'd say, "Emperor of Regret."

The guy could launder anything. Hand him your dirty shirt, and he'd hand you back a better life, no traces, no strings, no self-righteous speech.

I was trying to get clean, though, real clean, and the martinizer couldn't do it. I knew better than to go anywhere near the Jesus, but

I could hear the music from a mile away. Nobody wanted to let me in anymore. People doubted my integrity after what'd happened the last time. The last several times.

The cat at the door was notorious, and had strict guidelines, though lately he'd begun to slip. Things weren't right at Bee's. Hadn't been for a while. They had to let me in tonight. This was legit police business.

"C'mon, Jimmy, you can afford to look sideways tonight," yelled one of the girls on the block, the real girls, not the other kind.

"I'm here on the up and up," I said, because if I came in on the down and down, the place wouldn't show. But I'd seen it as I rolled past, lights spinning. Gutter full of glitter, and that was how you knew. Door was just beyond the edge of the streetlight, back of the shut-down bodega, and most people would've walked right on by.

But I knew what was going down. Somebody in that bar had called the police, and reported a body, male, mid-thirties, goner. I was here to find out the whohowwhy.

"You the police?" the caller had said. "It was an emergency three hours ago, sugarlump, but now it's just a dead guy. They dumped him in the alley outside where Bee's was, but Bee's took a walk, every piece of fancy in there up working their getaway sticks like the sidewalk was a treadmill. So you gotta come get him, sweets. He's a health hazard. Dead of drink if you know what I mean."

We did know what she meant, most of us, and we crossed our hearts and needle-eyed, cause we weren't the dead guy, but we could have been, easy. We were fleas and Bee's Jesus was a dog's ear.

Me and the boys duked it out for who was taking statements and who was caution-taping, and now it was me and my partner Gene, but Gene didn't care about Bee's like I did. The place was a problem I couldn't stay away from. I kept trying to get out of town, but I ran out of gas every time.

"What're you doing, Jimmy?" Gene said. "You're trying to sail a cardboard catamaran to Cuba. Not in a million years, you're not gonna get that broad back. Cease and desist. Boys are getting embarrassed for you."

I was embarrassed for me, too. I wasn't kidding myself, she was what I was looking to see. I was trying to put a nail in it.

Gloria was in that place somewhere, Gloria and the drink she'd taken to like a fish gill-wetting. Bee's Jesus was Gloria's bar now.

Ten years had passed since the night she sat on the sink, laughing as she straight-razored my stubble, and lipsticked my mouth.

"Poor boy," she said, watching the way I twitched. "Good thing you're pretty."

Gloria was a skinny girl with bobbed black hair, acid-green eyes, and a tiny apartment full of ripped-up party dresses. In her cold-water bathroom, she melted a cake of kohl with a match and drew me eyes better than my own. She'd told me she wouldn't take me to her favorite bar until she'd dressed me in her clothes, top to tail, and I wanted to go to that bar, wanted to go there bad.

I woulda done anything back then to get her, even though my Londoner buddy Philip (he called himself K. Dick, straight-faced) kept looking at her glories and shaking his head.

"I don't know what you see in her, bruv. She's just a discount Venus with a nose ring."

She was the kind of girl you can't not attempt, already my ex-wife before I kissed her, but I knew I had to go forward or die in a ditch of longing. It was our first date.

I saw her rumpled bed and hoped I'd end up in it, but Gloria dragged me out the door without even a kiss, me stumbling because I was wearing her stockings with my own shoes.

Downtown, backroom of a bodega, through the boxes and rattraps, past the cat that glanced at me, laughed at the guy in the too-tight everything, and asked if I could look more wrong.

Actual cat. I tried not to notice that it was. It seemed impolite. Black with a tuxedo. Cat was smoking a cigarette and stubbed it out on my shoe. It groomed itself as it checked me out and found me wanting.

"Come on, man, go easy," Gloria said. "Jimmy's with me."

She was wearing a skin-tight yellow rubber dress and I was wearing a T-shirt made of eyelashes, rolling plastic eyeballs, and fishnet. It didn't work on me. It wanted her body beneath. She was a mermaid. I was trawled.

"You expect me to blind eye that kind of sadsack?" the cat said, and lifted its lip to show me some tooth. Its tail twisted and informed me of a couple of letters. N-O, written in fur.

"Better than the last boy," Gloria said, and laughed. The cat laughed too, an agreeing laugh that said he'd seen some things. I felt jealous. "I'll give you a big tip," she said to him.

I was a nineteen year-old-virgin. I'd never gotten this close to getting this close before.

Gloria picked the cat up, holding him to her latex and he sighed a long-suffering sigh as she tipped him backward into the air and stretched his spine.

"Don't tell anyone I let the furball in. They'll think I'm getting soft."

"I owe you for this," she said to the cat.

To me, she said "Time to get you three-sheeted."

I was pretty deep at this point in clueless. Underworld, nightlife, and Gloria knew things I had no hope of knowing. She was the kind of girl who'd go into the subway tunnels for a party, and come out a week later, covered in mud and still wearing her lipstick. I'd been in love with her for a year or so. As far as I was concerned, the fact that she knew my name was a victory. She kept calling me Mister Nice Guy. Years later, after we'd been married and divorced, after Gloria had too much gin, and I had too many questions, I learned this was because she'd forgotten my name.

She tugged me around the corner, through a metal chute in the wall. For a second I smelled rotting vegetables and restaurant trash, cockroach spray, toilet brush, hairshirt—and then we were through, and that was over, and we were at the door that led to Bee's.

Gloria looked at me. "You want a drink," she said.

"Do they have beer?" I asked. I was nervous. "Could I have a Corona?"

The shirt was itchy, and she'd smeared something tarry into my hair. I felt like a newly paved road had melted into my skull and gum-stuck my brain.

Gloria laughed. Her eyelids glittered like planetariums.

"Not really," she said. "It's a cocktail bar. You ever had a cocktail, Mister Nice Guy?"

"I've had Guinness," I said.

She looked at me, pityingly. "Guinness is beer, and it's Irish, and if we scared any of that up, it'd be interested in you, but I'm not sure you'd want it. It's heavy and gloomy. You don't want the Corona either. You don't want what Corona brings you. It makes you really fucking noticeable at night."

I liked Guinness. I liked Corona. I liked wine coolers. I wasn't picky, and I knew nothing about drinking. Whatever anyone poured me, I was willing. I had never had a cocktail. I didn't know what Gloria meant.

She opened a door, and we were in Bee's. Bright lights, big city, speakeasy, oh my God. My face banged into a trombone, and the player looked out from behind the instrument and barked.

"Get your mug outta my bone," he said. He was a dog. A bull-hound. But I was cool with that. Dogs, cats, and us, and it was all completely normal and fine, because I was with Gloria, and I trusted her.

I didn't trust her. I didn't know her. She was a broad. She was a broad broader than the universe, and I wished, momentarily, for K. Dick and his encyclopedic wingman knowledge of bitters, bourbons, and cheap things with umbrellas. I wished for his accent which lady-slayed, and which made the awful forgivable. Or so he swore. K. Dick was more talk than walk.

I did need a drink.

Full brass band. Wall-to-wall tight dresses and topless, girls and boys in high heels, everyone cooler than anything I'd seen before. There was one gay bar where I came from. I knew of its existence and looked longingly at it from across the street, but I couldn't go in. I wasn't gay, and I wasn't legal, and anyone having fun inside it had kept the fun there.

Now, though, I'd lucked into Bee's, and Gloria shoved me up to the bartender, through the dancers and the looks. First curious, then envious as they saw the girl I was with. I tried to get taller. My shoes were a flat-footed liability. Gloria was wearing steel-toed platforms that made her six inches my senior. I looked like I lived in a lesser latitude.

"What you drinking tonight, Glo?" the bartender asked.

"Something with gin," Gloria said.

"You sure?" he asked. "Last time wasn't what you'd call a pretty situation."

The bartender had an elaborate mustache, and was wearing a pith helmet covered in gold glitter. I could see a whip protruding from over his shoulder. Around his wrist, a leather cuff with a lot of strings attached. I looked at them, and saw that they connected to the bottles behind the bar.

Gimmicky motherfucker, I thought, imagining myself as K. Dick, cool, collected, suave. I'd be a Man of Mystery. No more Mister Nice Guy.

"The lady will have a gin martini," I said, and the bartender looked at me. I wasn't sure if gin went into martinis, but I looked back, gave him a glare, and he snorted.

"Dirty?" he asked, sneering at me. I didn't know what dirty was. It sounded bad.

"Clean," I said, and Gloria grinned.

"And what about you, Jimmy?" asked Gloria. "What are you drinking?"

The bartender held out his hand to her and she spit her gum out into it. My tongue crawled backward like an impounded vehicle.

"I'll order for the boy," she said.

"You always do," said the bartender, and flicked his wrist. A bottle of gin somersaulted off the shelf and onto the bar.

"You sound like you got a beef with me, Such & Such," said Gloria, uncurling one half of his mustache with her fingertip.

"Not a beef," he said, his mustache snapping back into place, and nodded at me. "But you bruise the merchandise. And that shit is not my name."

"George," Gloria said, and rolled her eyes. "Make him an Old Fashioned for starters."

He moved his wrist and the bourbon slid over like a girl on a bench, the way I wished Gloria would slide over to me.

The music was louder than it had been, and the cat from the door was onstage now, walking the perimeter, eyeballing everyone and occasionally laying down the claw on an out-of-hand.

The bartender turned around and made my drink, and I heard a noise, a kind of coo. Then another noise like nails on a chalkboard.

Such & Such handed me a heavy glass full of dark amber liquid, cherry in the bottom. Gloria had a martini glass full of a silver-white slipperiness that looked like it might at any moment become a tsunami.

The bartender pushed them across the bar.

"Cheers," he said. "Or not, depending on your tolerance, Nice Guy. Should I call you Mister?"

"Yes," I said. Then I didn't know what to say, so I said. "Call me Lucky."

"You're not a Lucky," the bartender said. "You think you know a damn about a dame, but you don't know dick about this one."

I hardly heard him.

Gloria ran her finger around the edge of her glass like she was play-ing a symphony, and her drink unfolded out of it, elbow by elbow until a skinny guy in a white and silver pinstriped suit was sitting on the bar, looking straight into Gloria's eyes and grinning. Pinkie diamond. Ear-rings. Hair in a pompadour, face like James Dean.

I heard the bartender snort, and followed the chain on his wrist to the vest pocket of Gloria's gin martini.

My drink was already out by the time I stopped staring at hers. For a moment, I didn't know if she was a drink or not, but then I saw her wringing the wet hem of her amber-colored cocktail dress. She looked at me, and pulled a cherry stem from between her teeth. Her bracelet, a thin gold ribbon with a heart-shaped padlock con-nected her to the bartender's chains.

"You lovely So & So," said my Old Fashioned, her accent Southern belle. "Ask a girl to dance."

Gloria was already gone, in the arms of her white-suited martini, and I caught a glimpse of her on the dance floor, her black-bobbed head thrown back as she laughed. I could see his arms around her.

I'd misunderstood the nature of our evening.

Resigned, I took the Old Fashioned's hand. She hopped off the bar and into my arms, her red curls bouncing.

"You can call me Sweetheart," she said, and lit a cigarette off the candle on a table we passed. "But I don't think I'll call you Lucky. You came with Gloria, didn't you?"

"Yeah," I said. "She's great."

"She's trouble," the Old Fashioned said. "She likes her drink too much."

I looked onto the dance floor to see Gloria but all I saw was a flash of yellow, a stockinged thigh, and Gloria's acid-green eyes, wide open, staring into the silver eyes of the martini.

I spun my drink out into the room. The music was loud. The brass band was all hound dogs. I found that I could dance with my Old Fash-ioned, dance like I couldn't dance, swing like I couldn't swing. Her dress stayed wet at the hem, beads of bourbon dropping on the floor as the cat from the front door scatted with the band. I leaned over to kiss her shoulder, and tasted sugar.

"Oh, So & So, you're such a gentleman," she said, and spun me hard to the left, suddenly taking the lead. I kissed her mouth then, and her lips were bitter, a sharp taste of zest, the lipstick bright as orange peel.

She bent me backward and I could see her laughing, looking over me and at another girl on the floor, tight, sequined gold-brown dress, same kind of red curls. "Want another drink?"

"No," I said, overwhelmed. The room was spinning away from me, and there was Gloria out of the corner of my eye, now dancing with three guys and one girl, all in matching silver-white suits.

By morning, I was being led around the dance floor by five redheads, and my mouth tasted bitter. I had sugar all over my clothes, and I was wet with bourbon. I opened my mouth and spat out a cherry, but I hadn't even tasted it. I couldn't walk.

The cat pranced along the bar, his tuxedo front suddenly white as a near-death, and said, in an imperative tone, "Time to catch the early bird."

All of Bee's Jesus moaned.

The cat leapt up, clawing the light cord, and fluorescents hit us hard. The bartender hopped over the bar, and raised his wrist, tugging each chain, and in a moment, all the beautiful people in Bee's Jesus were gone.

Blast of light. I blinked.

I looked down. Broken glass and ice all over the floor, and a few people like me, in the middle of them, eyes sagging, stockings laddered. One of them in a bright yellow rubber dress. She looked over at me and waved, her hand shaking.

"Wanna get some eggs?" Gloria said, and I nodded, weak-kneed.

Glo and I got married and then we got divorced.

We spent too much time at Bee's Jesus. I got to know the regulars, the margaritas and the Manhattans, the Sazeracs and the Bloody Marys, but I kept ordering the Old Fashioned, and Gloria kept ordering the gin martini, as I eventually figured out she always would. She fell hard for her drink, and I fell hard for mine.

Eventually, we started taking them back to our place, the four of us, him sitting at our table in his white and silver suit, and her there in her sequins, lipstick on her cigarettes.

We moved out to the suburbs, but the gin martini didn't like it there. He'd stand outside, looking down the tree-lined, holding a shaker in his hands, and complaining about the quality of the ice. The two drinks sat in the car, in the afternoons, and sometimes Glo sat with them. Eventually, the martini took off, but the Old Fashioned stayed. After a while, Gloria went back to the city too, breaking my heart and all the tumblers at the same time.

She bought the bar, and moved into the apartment upstairs with him.

Every night, or so I heard, she could be found dancing in the middle of the floor with five or six guys in silver, the band blasting. She hired some pit bulls, and they kept the door down while she danced. Gloria had fucked a German at Bee's Jesus one time, she'd told me at some point in our marriage. At first, this wasn't worrying. It was when she added Shepherd to the mix. She said it like it was no thing. It seemed like a thing to me.

Now the dog seemed like a better option than the martini. She turned to drink, and then she turned again and wrapped herself in his silver arms. He spun down into her, his diamond shining.

I kept waiting for her to come home, but she'd never really loved me, and so she never really did.

The redhead put herself on ice, and now when I tried to dance with her, sugar cubes crushed under our feet, and everything got sticky and sour. Her skin was cold and hard, and she kept her mouth full of cherry stems, but never any cherries.

"I miss the martini, So & So," she said at last, her dress falling off her shoulder, sequins dripping from her hem. "And I miss Such & Such. I miss the way he tended."

I tried to kiss her. She turned her head. I tasted a new spirit.

"What's that?" I asked her, and she looked away.

"Dry vermouth," she said, and looked at me, with her liquid eyes. "He gave it to me." Something had changed in her. She wasn't an Old Fashioned anymore. She'd been mixing.

She swizzled out the door one morning early, and I knew she'd returned to Bee's.

I cleaned out the cupboards. I quit drinking, cold turkey. I became a cop and tried to forget.

But soon the bar was back on my radar again. Trouble there all the time. It was a blood-on-the-tiles known failure point, and the boys at the precinct knew it well.

And now, the call, the murder. I had a feeling I knew who it might be, but I didn't know for sure.

"Pull over," I said to Gene. Glitter, shining in the headlights.

"You sure you wanna do this?" he asked. "I know you got a soft spot for Gloria, but we gotta arrest that broad, we gotta do it, no matter your old flames."

"That fire's out," I said. It was.

I saw the cat then, his tuxedo shining. I saw his tail, the letters reading N-O. I saw him run out the door of Bee's Jesus and into the street, and then I saw Glo, right behind him. She shook her shoulders back, and looked at the cruiser, like she didn't care. She walked over to the window and looked at it until I gave up and rolled down.

"You got no business here, Jimmy," she said. "Somebody called in a false alarm."

She looked at me with those same acid eyes, and I felt etched. Nothing like a long-ago love to bring back the broken.

"Stay here," I said to Gene. "Do me a favor. One."

Gene sighed and set a timer, but he stayed in the car.

I walked down the alley behind Gloria, and Gloria held out her fingers to me for a second. Just one. We were the old days.

I saw him shining, his white and silver leg, dumped in the alley like the caller had told me he would be. I knew who the caller had been. I knew her voice. I knew her muddles. She couldn't let a guy stay in the street. She wasn't all bitter, and she had a soft spot for martinis.

I saw the cat, and I saw the band. All of them out in the street, like I'd never seen them. The pit bulls and the bull hounds.

The cat looked up from what he was doing, his teeth covered in blood. Red all over the white front of his tuxedo shirt.

"Sadsack," he said. "You knew this place, but it's gone."

I could hear his purr from where I stood, appalled, as he bit into the gin. The dogs and the cats. All of them on top of the martini, making it go away. There was a pool on the cobbles, and I could smell juniper berries.

"Another one back in the shaker," said the cat, then shook his head, gnashing. "Hair of the dog," he said, and spat.

Something caught the light at the end of the alley. Golden-brown sequins. I tasted ice. I could see her mouth, cherry red, shining out of the shadows, and then she stalked away.

Gloria looked up at me, and shrugged. The whites of her eyes were red. Her hands shook. The sun was rising.

"He used to be clean," she said. "You remember, Jimmy, you re-member how he was. You remember how he was. But he got dirty. I'm getting away from this town. This bar. I shut things down in there."

A cocktail walked out the door of Bee's Jesus, and I watched her come. All in crimson, her perfume spiced and salty. She knelt beside the remains of the gin martini, and stretched her long green-painted finger-nails over his face. She lay down on top of the corpse, and as I watched, the gin dissolved into the Bloody Mary.

"No chaser," said Gloria, and smiled sadly. "She'll take him away."

The Bloody Mary stood up in her stilettos, wiping her hands on her dress, and took Gloria's hand in hers.

"See you, Mister Nice Guy," said Gloria. "Bar's closed. I have a plane to catch. Somewhere sunny. Somewhere I can get a drink with an umbrella."

I watched Gloria and her new drink walk away. As she went, I saw her unfasten something from her wrist. A leather cuff decked in long chains. She dropped it in the gutter. I watched her turn the corner, away from the glitter, and then I watched the sun rise, shining on the mountain of ice outside the former door of Bee's Jesus.

"No dead body," I said to Gene. "Just ice and glass. What can you do?"

I took myself to the cleaners. Blood all over my shirt front, hair of the dog on my knees. I smelled bourbon and cherries, juniper and re-gret. Gloria and her gin.

"Ah, it's Such & Such," said the martinizer. I was no longer an Em-peror, if I'd ever really been. "I cleaned your dirty laundry," he said. "But some stains don't come out."

He handed me a white shirt not mine. He waved me out the door and back into the brittle light of the morning.

Revels in the Land of Ice

Tim Pratt

For I dance
And drink, and sing,
Till some blind hand
Shall brush my wing.
—*William Blake, "The Fly"*

"So you want to break into Iceland?" I sat on a cracked stretch of sidewalk on one of the quiet, run-down side streets a few blocks from downtown Berkeley. It was a warm March afternoon, I had a bottle of homemade rose-infused vodka in a brown paper bag at my side, and my oldest (in terms of age) friend was talking crazy again. Life was good.

Crater shook his head. (This was before he got swallowed whole.) "It's pronounced 'Ice-Land,' Aerin—like, a magical land of ice. Not like the country Björk comes from. 'Icelandic' minus the 'ick.'" He was sitting beside me, but his hand crept over toward the bottle so I picked it up and moved it to my other side. He'd just take a swig and make a face and say he couldn't understand how I drank that shit, and I wasn't about to share with someone who didn't appreciate what I had to give. Now that we weren't sleeping together I didn't feel the need to be particularly giving and likeable, and overall we'd gotten on better since then—certainly we saw each other more clearly. "Fine, it's the land of ice. You want to break in for some kind of party?"

"Not break in, per se. I mean, in a legal sense, yeah, but it's not like we'll need crowbars or anything. The place has been closed since 2007, but people go in and out all the time. Urban explorer types and every graffiti artist who's ever bothered to shake up a can of spray paint and homeless people looking for a place to sleep and cats and rats and birds."

"Sounds delightful." I unscrewed my bottle and took a sip. Like drinking perfume, except that sounds bad, and it wasn't bad.

Crater shrugged. "I don't care too much about the sorry state of the place. Maybe a little twinge—I did learn to skate there as a kid, and even played hockey when I was a teenager. It should be a historic land-mark. Founded in 1940, and owned by the Zamboni family, the same ones who invented the ice-resurfacing machine. But then again, nostal-gia's poison. I try to let the past be the past."

Sometimes I forgot how old Crater was, not that I knew exactly — probably a little over twice my age, call it forty or so. He sometimes made offhand comments about seeing punk bands in London and that must have been way back, prehistoric times. Me and him were barely even born in the same century. But he knew a lot of things, and he was funny, and sexy for an old guy, and never condescending, which is the one thing I can't stand.

"Iceland itself doesn't matter, but there's going to be a breach in there." Crater had that far-off look in his eyes, like he was seeing through time and space, or maybe like he was stoned. "There was almost a breach in the same location back in '07, that's why the powers that be *really* closed the place. They made some bullshit excuse about how the place was venting danger-ous levels of ammonia from the cooling system and it was too expensive to fix, but that's just the cover story. Somebody in city government was clued-in, there's usually one guy who knows what's *really* happening underneath the skin of the world, so he brought in some people to seal the breach— fucking posers from Europe, all crystal balls and amulets and magic words—but they did a shitty job, like wallpapering over a hole instead of filling it in. I'm pretty sure their half-assed ritual actually triggered the Al-um Rock earthquake."

Sometimes I didn't know what Crater was talking about, and this was one of those times, but I kept drinking and listening.

"Anyway, all the charts, all the stones, the bells and books and candles, everything I've got tells me there's going to be another breach, in the same spot. But nobody else realizes it, I don't think—nobody's paying attention anymore. They think the site is stable, and anyway, it looks like a short-duration breach, maybe just a few hours of accessibility from this side."

"You're saying Iceland is going to...what? Turn into a doorway to Hell?"

"It's not Hell. Or Fairyland either. Or Summerland or Abaddon or anything else you've heard of, or else it's all those places. Or those places are just neighborhoods there, good parts of town and bad parts of town. It's just...the Other Place."

"We're still talking about the land of demons and fairies and stuff though."

He shrugged. "Demons are denizens of the Other Place who breach and possess people. Fairies are...more subtle. Sometimes they seduce, sometimes they steal people away overtly, and sometimes they make trades where they always get the better end of the bargain—demons do that last one too. But demons, fairies, whatever you call them, they're all takers." Suddenly he grinned, and he looked younger, young enough to be my older brother instead of my dad. "But if you're smart you can take something from *them*. It's been a long time since I've wriggled through a breach. I'm ready to do it again."

"Why?"

"Because it's a great party, for one thing. The denizens of the Other Place get intoxicated by the connection to our world, I think. You can't even really call it a party—it's a *revel*. It's primal. There are drugs you can't imagine, things made for alien physiologies, but they have effects on humans you can't believe. And the wine, or what you might as well call wine...How old do you think I am, Aerin?"

My real name's Stephanie, but I changed it when I went goth for a while in high school and it stuck, sort of, in certain circles. (My family still calls me Steffie. They're incorrigible.) "Like, a hundred?"

He smiled again and the lines around his eyes crinkled. "You're not nearly as far off as you think, love. I turned seventy last month."

I made a noise, like a snort. No way he was that old. He didn't even exercise, he just smoked weed and drank whiskey and read books and talked all day. Plus I could handle sleeping with a forty-year-old, call it life experience for my art, but *seventy*?

"I don't feel it," he said. "My body's still aging, but slowly. I can't be sure, but I think it's because I had one glass of wine, stolen from a revel I stumbled upon in the middle of a field—in the middle of *nowhere*—hours outside London. I was on a road trip with some assholes and we had a fight and they shoved me out of the van and

I just started walking in the pissing rain, no idea where I was, or where I was going. And then I saw these...tents, like white silk pavilions, but they weren't made of cloth, they were made of beams of moonlight, or spiderwebs, but somehow they kept the rain off. And there were lanterns, but when you looked closer they were just floating balls of luminous gas. I thought it was a costume party, at first, but...no costume is *that* good." He ran a hand through his short hair, which was barely sprinkled with gray. "I got a drink, and it tasted like summer rain and honey and embalming fluid. I snorted something blue and crystalline a woman offered me, except she wasn't a woman, she was mostly something like a salamander crossed with a crystal chandelier, except I didn't notice that at first. Just being at the party was like being on hallucinogens *anyway*, the music played inside my head and the bass line followed the throb of my heartbeat, and after I took the drugs it got weirder...people kept beckoning me, and then someone else started shouting at me, and a couple of people—except they weren't people—started fighting, and I realized they were fighting over *me*, who got to keep me. Or maybe they said 'eat' me. So while they were distracted I stumbled off, and I fell asleep somewhere. I woke up beneath an overpass in Manchester with a hangover and a nosebleed, and I swear I puked up some gold coins, except after a few minutes they turned into leaves. The weirdest thing was? I'd been gone for two weeks, according to all the clocks and calendars in *this* world. Time isn't the same for them, that much of the old stories is true. Ever since that party I've been...quasi-immortal. And interested in this kind of thing. Which is why I became a student of—"

"The mystic whatever, yeah, I get it. That's a good story. Almost as good as the one where you went caving and found artifacts from a lost race and a monster spoke to you from a hole in the ground and knew the name of your childhood imaginary friend."

"That's not nearly as good a story," Crater said. "That thing barely even spoke English. So anyway. Want to come to the revel with me? Maybe become immortal, or the next best thing? My charts say...two months, exactly, from today, there'll be a crack between our world and theirs. Or not a crack exactly, more of an *overlap*. I call it a 'breach' because it's like what a whale does, when it jumps out of the water, and there's a moment when part of it is in the air and part is underwater—when it's a creature of both worlds. That's what the Other Place does: it breaches into our world. You should come. It's a once-in-a-lifetime kind of thing. Unless your life's as long as mine."

"Fine, I'll go." I figured he was having me on, but I assumed he was going to take me to some kind of secret party in the abandoned building, people taking advantage of the space before it got torn down or turned into condos or a sporting goods store or something. Sure, he'd told me more outlandish things, and shown me one or two things I couldn't explain, but a breach? "What should I wear?"

He laughed. "Nothing too sparkly. They're attracted to bright things, and never forget, we're crashing their party." Suddenly his expression went serious. "And in the next couple of months, especially in the last couple of weeks before the breach...be careful. You know how earthquakes have foreshocks and aftershocks, tremors that happen around the big quake? Breaches can be like that. Stuff can get...weird, for a little while. Things fall from the sky. Guys walk into fields and vanish in full view of their friends, nothing left but their boots."

"I'll lace my boots real tight and carry an umbrella." He laughed, and we said our farewells not long after.

As near as I can figure, I was sitting bored in a sociology lecture the next morning when Crater got swallowed by the sinkhole.

I heard about it on campus, from a couple of old professors talking on a bench while I walked by—one said "Crater" and "Couldn't recover his body" and I stopped and said, "Wait, what happened to Crater?" figuring there couldn't be too many people with that name.

The profs were both gray-haired, one male, one female, with identical ponytails, onetime hippies turned academics living the tenured dream at UC Berkeley. "Did you know him, young lady?"

I nodded. "We hang out sometimes, yeah, he was teaching me about..."

"Magic?" the other one said, and clucked his tongue. "He used to get in trouble when he taught here, showing off his sleight of hand and reading the Tarot, getting...overly friendly with the undergrads."

I'd had no idea Crater ever taught anything, much less at Berkeley. He lived in a tiny apartment in the thick of student housing, even though he wasn't a student, except, he said, "a student of the arcane." He'd never pulled a quarter from behind my ear or shown me a Tarot deck, either. I wanted to say, "It wasn't *like* that, I practically picked *him* up," but that wasn't the important thing.

"It sounded like you said something about his *body*." I crossed my arms and looked down on them as sternly as I could, pretty funny I guess coming from an eighteen-year-old in a long skirt and silver bracelets.

"I'm so sorry, dear. There was a terrible accident. A sinkhole opened up right underneath him while he was walking downtown. The sidewalk just collapsed, and he dropped straight down. There were witnesses, and they called for help right away, but the rescue personnel couldn't even find the bottom of the hole, and then there was another subsidence and the sides of the hole collapsed, filling it in again..." She shook her head. "If you give me your contact information I can let you know if there's a service, or—"

I just backed away. "No, that's okay." I didn't want to go to his funeral, or I guess it would be a memorial, with no body to bury. I'd never had anyone close to me die before—a great-uncle I barely knew, that was it. Certainly no one I'd *slept with* had died before.

As I hurried away, I heard one of the oldsters on the bench say, "Crater was a great teacher, despite everything. I remember when he taught my Intro to Anthropology class..."

The sinkhole opened on Shattuck Ave., the main street that runs through downtown (just a couple of blocks off Milvia St., where Iceland sits in all its graffitied glory). Crater hadn't vanished in the heart of downtown, around the movie theaters and the library and pubs and restaurants and shops, but several blocks south, where it was mostly just the self-storage place and old folks' homes and car lots.

I went to see the hole, which was as wide as the whole sidewalk, though by then it was more a shallow indentation partially filled with rubble. I figured in a day or two the city would fill it the rest of the way in, level it off, and pour concrete over it. An unmarked grave for Crater. Maybe if I came over when the cement was wet I could draw an upside-down pentagram there, or his birth and death dates, though for his birth date I'd have to put a row of question marks.

The hole was blocked off with chained-together sawhorses, with a sprinkling of orange cones around the perimeter, the whole thing wrapped up with yellow police tape like too much ribbon on a gift wrapped by a child. I couldn't get too close, not that I wanted to. None of it made sense. How had he disappeared? Weren't there pipes under the sidewalk to snag him when he fell? Hell, a train tunnel ran underneath Shattuck, though I wasn't sure if it went under exactly that spot. How had he just disappeared? I know the Bay Area is earthquake country and the ground isn't as solid as it seems, but, damn.

Something glittered in the weeds by the sidewalk, and I squatted down to look. At first I thought they were gold coins, but they turned out to be crinkly leaves cut out of gold-colored foil or something. There was a broken wineglass beside the leaves, the cup part still whole, the stem broken off beside it. I picked up the cup and sniffed. It smelled like antifreeze and pickle juice.

Crater had warned me. Foreshocks, and aftershocks. I thought about taking the leaves or the glass fragments home but I just left them beside his grave.

Maybe I should have gone to his memorial, but I didn't want to hear other people talk about Crater. He was fixed in my mind in a certain way and I didn't want that to change. He was this funny, smart, dirty old man, who seemed pretty wise but was probably at least half full of shit, and he always treated me with respect and listened to me (instead of just pretending to listen to me so I'd be more inclined to take my pants off, which naturally made me even *more* inclined to take my pants off for a while), and even though he mooched my food a lot he always had great weed. And he did show me some impossible things, which I assumed were tricks at the time, but maybe they were more. I could hardly believe the people at the memorial would really be his friends—not his real friends. He said all his real friends were dead. He said that's why he was making friends with me: because I was young enough maybe he wouldn't outlive me.

And while I had a lot of people I hung out with, people I knew from class and my housemates and all, in a way Crater was the only real friend *I'd* made since I moved across the country to go to college at Cal.

Look, I'm not stupid. Older guy, younger girl, okay, I've read books, I've seen movies, I've got friends. And maybe it started out that way—I was a way for him to scratch an itch or feel young or powerful or whatever. But I got something out of it, too, and after the sex parts stopped, the other parts got better, and we went from using each other to meaning something to each other.

So I couldn't just let him die without doing something to mark his passage.

One time laying together in his narrow bed, after we'd known each other for a month and been fucking for three weeks and five days (with about three more weeks to go), Crater stroked my bare shoulder and said, "What is it you *want*?"

I said something like, "I wouldn't mind a cigarette."

He chuckled, but it wasn't a real laugh, it was being nice to the college girl who'd decided to sleep with you, so you'd better humor her. "No, really. If you want to learn magic, you need a reason. A smart man once wrote that magic is the art of getting results, but if you don't have any results in mind...unfocused power is dangerous."

"What do *you* want?" I countered.

"To live forever, and feel good doing it," he said. "What about you?"

"I don't even know what I'm *majoring* in yet, Crater." His first name was Archibald, which sounded too old-fashioned to say out loud, but Archie sounded too young and dumb to fit him, so mostly people stuck with his last name. "You can't ask me what I want in some big universal sense."

"When you figure it out, let me know. We'll work out how to help you get it."

Of course I *did* know what I wanted. I wanted to be a poet. Maybe every girl—especially those with a goth phase—writes poetry, but I'd always been serious about it. I studied. I went to readings whenever I could, to listen to other poets, who were mostly terrible but sometimes sublime. I wrote a lot and tore most of it up. I knew more about scansion and lift and enjambment than I'd ever let anybody realize.

Sometimes I thought I was pretty good at writing, and I'd include some of my poems here, except fuck you, I don't have to prove anything to you. Besides, pretty good wasn't nearly good enough. I wanted to write something that would turn people inside out and make them question the shape of the lives, the way poems by Ellen Bass or Adrienne Rich or Nikky Finney did to *me*. I wanted to see the world clearly and convey that clarity to others. Or else I wanted to see a *different* world: to have visions, and see trees filled with angels, the way William Blake did. Part of sleeping with Crater was thinking I needed to fill up my life with more experiences so I could have things to write about. Part of my interest in magic—or magick or magyk or whatever—was wanting to penetrate the ordinariness of this world to find a brighter world beyond.

I tried to write a bunch of poems about Crater after he died but mostly I just threw them away, and in the weeks that followed I visited the bit of sidewalk where he'd been buried (it looked like the rest of the sidewalk again, except the concrete was newer and cleaner) and stood there like a moron and talked to him. Somebody had cleaned up the broken glass and leaves. Or else they'd turned into regular leaves, because they were bits of the Other Place that had breached into our world and couldn't last, or something. I didn't really believe that, but I didn't not believe it, either. (Like Walt Whitman pretty much wrote: Do I contradict myself? So the fuck what. I contain multitudes.)

I bought an actual wall calendar (I know, who does that? It's not like I don't have a phone) and hung it on my wall and circled the date Crater had said there was going to be a breach at Iceland. I didn't know what I was going to do that night, except I was pretty sure I wasn't going to hang out in my apartment and watch bad horror movies with my housemates. The night was just a week before the end of my freshman year, and I had important final exams to study for, but there's important and there's *important*, and maybe I'm not that old or wise but I'm old enough to know the difference.

When the night came I dressed all in black, dark pants and hiking boots and a black shirt and a black hoodie. I remembered some stuff Crater told me, so I wore the shirt inside-out under the hoodie to confuse "second sight," whatever that means, and I carried seven small stones he'd given me in my pocket. He claimed the rocks were from all seven continents, and that they acted as a "locative diffuser," meaning they'd make me harder to track by magic. (When I told him I didn't believe you could track things by magic, he got a map and a piece of string and a chunk of lodestone and did a little ritual, and after that he led me to the place on campus where I'd lost my ID a week before, stuck right there half-underneath a log in the eucalyptus grove. We'd done some serious making out in that grove. The smell of eucalyptus still makes me a little hot, even all these years later.)

I also took a silver-bladed ceremonial knife in a leather sheath he'd given me because it was sharp enough to make me feel safer.

The sign outside—reading "ICELAND" in big, rectangular retro-looking blue letters—is the best-preserved part of the old skating rink. The ruined Iceland is a big, low building, painted in fading blue and dirty white, shaped sort of like a warehouse, with windows and front doors all boarded up and scrawled with graffiti. The back of the place is built partly into a hill, which *does* give it kind of a barrow/fairy-hill vibe, though I'd never noticed that before. There are small parking lots on either side, closed off by high chain-link fences intermittently topped with barbed wire, and the fences extend for the full length of the building on both sides. The front steps are scattered with garbage, and homeless people sleep there a lot, in the covered entryway. But there's a place where the fence has been sliced open, leaving a gap big enough to squeeze through. From there you can just scramble up the hillside to the building itself or onto the roof, where some of the boarded-up windows are only sealed in theory.

I waited until there was no one around, then wriggled through the fence and made my way up the grassy hill. I found one of the loose boards and pulled it away, then peered inside.

It was dark, and after a moment's debate I decided to risk using a little flashlight. I shone it around inside, and the place was pretty depressing. The bleachers where people used to sit to watch hockey were still there, but the floor of the rink was covered up (of course, I don't know what I was expecting—a pond?). The walls inside were just as heavily tagged as the ones outside, maybe more so. The place looked pretty much like a high school gymnasium after the apocalypse, and smelled like pee, cat and human both. There were no revels here. But there were no people, either, as far as I could tell, so I wriggled in through the window to the bleachers and sat on the top bench. Coming here was pointless, but it was the last thing I'd planned to do with Crater, so screw it, this could be my memorial. I just wished I'd brought a flask of booze. And that he was here to share it. I'd have shared gladly, even if he did always insult my taste in—

That's what I was thinking when everything changed. My ears popped painfully, and my eyes watered, and I almost fell off the bleachers, because the world *tilted*, and I thought, earthquake?

But it wasn't an earthquake. It was a breach. An overlap. Two worlds inhabiting, briefly, the same space.

The old ice rink became a ballroom, but it was *also* still an ice rink— complete with a gleaming oval of white ice, and figures dressed in elaborate gowns and peculiar costumes gliding around. The bare metal support struts cluttering up the ceiling were hung now with paper (I guess?) lanterns glowing pale green, in fanciful shapes: dragons, jellyfish, spiders, castles, swords, antlered skulls. Moss and vines and streamers dangled, too. There were long tables heaped with food and bottles and pitchers of various liquids, the tables drifting around on the ice as if *they* were skating, and somehow there was never a collision. There were box seats high up on the other side of the ice, and musicians in those, playing harps and bagpipes and flutes and drums, some dressed in tuxedoes and some in zoot suits and some wearing nothing but rags, and the music that came out was inexplicably all bells and violins. There was a scented smoke in the air, not quite colorless, sort of a golden mist, and my head swam with the flavor. I came down off the bleachers carefully—they were full of people now, sitting and chatting and drinking and laughing and screaming, except they were only people at first glance. At second glance they were mostly animals, and sometimes objects. On a third glance they were a little of all of the above.

There were lights shining in various levels of brightness from various directions (not always from obvious sources) and no one except for me appeared to cast a shadow. I clutched the sheathed dagger in my pocket, and felt the stones clattering in my other pocket, and stepped down to the ice.

I was glad I'd worn my hiking boots, because the tread kept me from sliding around. The ice wasn't mirror-smooth, anyway, more beat up, like people had been skating on it for hours, which maybe they had, in the Other Place. I tried to count, or even to estimate, how many people—or "beings" maybe—were there, but I gave up. Scores, anyway. Sometimes three people would seem to merge into one, and sometimes one would break apart into many, like a flock of birds scattering. There were antlers and snouts and earrings and, I swear, a man-sized egg wearing a waistcoat, going past on skates. He did a double axel jump right in front of me.

I moved among the crowd, and no one seemed to pay me any mind, though they moved out of my way. Something like a small mountain wearing crushed red velvet and something like a bear with a fish bowl for a head stepped away from a slowly-drifting table covered in empty crystal goblets...and there was Crater, holding a bottle, filling the glasses. He was dressed in a red-lined opera cape and an old-fashioned tuxedo instead of scruffed-up denim and leather, but when he saw me, his smile was warm and human.

"You made it!" he said, not shouting, but somehow I heard him clearly despite the music and the noise of the revelers.

I almost jumped at him and wrapped him up in a hug, but he was still pouring, so I just shuffled and gaped. "You're *alive*."

"In the Other Place, even the rocks and the water are alive, so I guess it's no surprise I am, too." He kept pouring, and I wondered if he was planning to fill all the glasses on the table, and how that small bottle could possibly hold enough liquid to do so. Then I noticed that every time he poured, a different colored fluid came out—amber and red-orange and purple and pink and every color of sunsets and the rainbows you see shimmering on oil slicks.

I touched his arm, and he paused in his work. He reached out with his free hand, brushing my cheek. The back of his hand was so cold it burned. "They took me. I'm sorry. I...never really got away, I guess. They were aware of me all the time, the way you keep an eye on your toddler at the park to make sure she doesn't wander too far. And the extra time they gave me, the extra life, came with a price. I'm serving. But...at least I'm serving in heaven." His smile was weak.

"Come with me." I grabbed his hand, even though it was like clutching a bag of ice cubes.

"You should go," he said. "You haven't been here long, maybe it's only morning back in our world by now, or the next afternoon—"

He stopped talking, and I became aware of a figure standing close behind me. I turned, but the guy—or whatever—sort of half-stepped around, just out of sight, and no matter how quickly I spun, he remained almost behind me, just glimpsed from the corner of my eye. Eventually I stopped twirling, because I was getting even more dizzy, and I felt like an idiot, or a dog chasing its tail. I had the impression the creature standing behind my left shoulder was hairy, beastly, and there was a rank smell like wet dog, but its voice was smooth and cultured when it said, "This one is a poet. We have wines that loosen words and send them spiraling up, up, up. Bid her drink."

Crater gritted his teeth, but he picked up a glass, filled with something the color and consistency of grapefruit juice, but glowing with an inner light. He started to offer it to me, and I was trying to decide how dangerous it would be to refuse, when Crater grunted and flung the full glass past me, into the face—I presumed—of the monster at my back. A little of the fluid splashed my face as it went by, and though I was careful to keep my mouth shut tightly, I did get a stinging drop in my left eye.

Most of it struck the target, though. There was a terrible roar, which sounded like sheets of paper being ripped, and then Crater was flinging glasses in all directions and shouting at me to run.

I didn't run, though. I gave him my silver knife—*his* silver knife—and he looked at me in surprise, then plunged the blade into one of the glasses. When he drew it out again, the blade was shining like the last coals in a campfire.

We ran for the bleachers. Almost no one tried to stop us—mostly they ignored us, or doubled over laughing—but the few who did move to block our paths fell back when Crater slashed at them with the knife. I sprinted up the steps, mounting them two at a time, and while Crater wasn't *that* fast, he was close. The window I'd come through was still there, a little rectangle of freedom, and I scrambled through into darkness.

I was sure, *sure,* that Crater wouldn't follow me. Something would stop him first. Or he'd get his upper body through the window, and then something would grab him by the ankles and drag him back in, his face frozen in an expression of longing and terror and regret. Or he'd make it all the way out but all the years he'd put aside by magic would fall on him at once and he'd turn into a skeleton and then into dust, right before me.

Instead he collapsed on his back on the hillside, the dagger in his hand just a silver blade again, and stared up at the sky. "You saved me," he said. "While I was there, it didn't feel like I needed saving, but now...I know I was a slave. I would have stayed, and done my time, but they wanted you to *drink,* they wanted to give you something, too, so they could take you later. All that time I thought I stole from them, but they just set a hook in me so they could reel it in later—"

I leaned over and kissed him on the mouth. He was warm, as warm as ever before. When I pulled away, he blinked at me. "Aerin...I know I said you're an old soul and age is just a number and all, but, let's be honest. I'm way too old for you. Or maybe it's just that you're way too young for me."

"No shit. You're too old for my grandmother. I just wanted to shut you up for a minute. Shouldn't we get away from here?"

He shook his head. "Climbing out, I think it was like popping a soap bubble. The connection is broken. That's just empty space in there again. The revel was a trap. It's easy to get in, but you're not supposed to get out so quickly. You have those stones in your pocket, don't you?"

I nodded.

"I'm so glad I gave you the real thing and not some rocks I found in a park or something." He sat up and groaned.

"What now?" I said.

"You should be safe. I think. You didn't drink or eat anything— right?—and the stones in your pocket will make it impossible for them to fix on your location. You're carrying the earth of everywhere."

"But what about you? Will they come back for you later?"

"It was nearly fifty years before they came *this* time. With luck, the difference in our timeline and theirs will work in my favor. But all the same...I think I'd better leave town. I haven't been to Europe in a while."

I sighed. "I thought you were dead, you asshole. And now you're leaving for Europe? I guess that's better than you being in the ground or a butler for demons."

He touched my cheek again. "Aerin, are you crying? For me? I'm touched, seriously."

I rubbed my eye. I wasn't crying. The eye was just watering from being splashed by that drop of strange wine.

The little while at the revel had translated to an entire day of time in our world—not that my housemates noticed my absence—so I'd missed an exam, but I claimed terrible gut-twisting viral agony and got permission to do a make-up test. I almost didn't take it. I thought about dropping out and following Crater to Europe, but I didn't think I'd become the person I wanted to by being someone else's shadow, so I just helped him pack up a few things and pillaged the most interesting books and booze from his apartment and gave him a kiss on the cheek before he left for the airport.

After he was gone, I sat on a log in the eucalyptus grove on campus, where we'd first met, and later talked, and later did things other than talking. I closed my left eye, and looked at the trees, and they were just trees, tall white pillars, an invasive species that didn't belong in California, but were beautiful anyway.

Then I closed my right eye, and looked at the trees with just my left eye, the one splashed by wine from the Other Place.

The trees weren't full of angels, but they were filled with other things, even stranger and more luminous and breathtaking, with wings of ice and lace and twilight, and though I could see them, I was almost certain they couldn't see me.

I opened both eyes and took out a little red notebook and a black pen and began to write poems for the rest of my life.

Bess, the Landlord's Daughter, Goes for Drinks with the Green Girl
Sofia Samatar

1. Pink Ice

Bess and the Green Girl are out for drinks. They're at a club called Pink Ice, where everybody gets a lollipop at the door. Rumor has it the lollipops are poisoned, or at least drugged. Their white ink messages—JUICY, KISS ME—glow in the dark.

Bess and the Green Girl sit at the bar and twirl lollipops on their tongues. They look fabulous. They're both wearing high-heeled shoes with pointy toes. Bess's are yellow. Her image gleams in the mirror behind the bar: round red mouth and high-piled hair. She wears a white blouse with a lot of ruffles over the breast.

The Green Girl is wearing an oversized T-shirt that says LIVELIVE-LIVE. She has long, flat hair and terrible posture. A jumble of plastic bead necklaces covers her throat. She crunches lustily on the nub of her lollipop, gnawing it off the stick. The Green Girl has surprisingly large, strong teeth, and so does Bess. They've talked about whether your teeth keep growing afterward. Bess doesn't think they keep growing, but maybe you get a new set, the way children do. She dips her lollipop into her vodka and cranberry.

"This place is the best," the Green Girl yells.

"Love it," shouts Bess. The music is physical, invasive. She can feel every note in her bones.

"It's even better than that place with the smoke."

"Mm," Bess agrees around her lollipop.

"It's like, I feel like I'm getting an injection."

Pink Ice is an injection of noise and movement and beauty and youth. Boys and girls crowd in, waving lollipops in the air. They wear black boots and sparkly hair-bands, black lipstick and sparkly eye shadow, black lace stockings, everything black and everything sparkly.

The Green Girl seizes Bess's arm. "Look! I want that!"

There's a girl in a feather stole.

"You want that? *That*?"

"What?"

"It's feathers!"

"So?"

"Chicken feathers! It's horrible!"

The Green Girl rolls her eyes. "Can you open your mind, please? Even a tiny bit? There is an entire world beyond cardigans."

"Just because I have *taste*," says Bess. She does have taste, she gets it from magazines. She gives the Green Girl a playful kick with the tip of her shoe. The shoe leaves a dent in the Green Girl's spray-tanned leg.

"Ugh," says the Green Girl, bending down to rub out the dent. "Would you *stop*?"

"Sorry," says Bess.

"'Sokay," says the Green Girl. She shakes back her hair and brightens. "I love this song!" She jumps down off her stool and shimmies into the crowd. Her T-shirt's so huge her skirt doesn't show. She looks like the other girls at Pink Ice: fabulous and starving and sparkly and lost.

2. T-shirts

A thin boy in thin jeans asks Bess to dance.

Bess dances.

Bess and the Green Girl love to dance.

Bess and the Green Girl love to dance and drink and take little white pills and little colored pills and they love to go home with boys.

They love shopping and shoplifting and the movies.

Also, the Green Girl loves making her own T-shirts. She gets these big white T-shirts and rips off the sleeves, and then she puts messages on them in Sharpie or in puffy, candy-colored iron-on letters. The T-shirt mania started when Bess and the Green Girl were rummaging in boxes at Goodwill, and the Green Girl found an old shirt that said I WOULD DIE 4 U. "Hey!" said the Green Girl. "That's us! That is so us!" Her eyes were huge, silver, ecstatic. She bought the T-shirt and wore it every day for a month. Then she started creating her own T-shirts. The first T-shirt she made said I DIED 4 U. Bess refuses to go out with the Green Girl when the Green Girl is wearing this shirt, because how tacky can you get?

The Green Girl has a shirt that says DEAD BEAT. She has one that says BASTA and one that says CONQUER. She has one that says I WANT YOU GREEN. She has even made a couple of T-shirts for Bess. One of them says CLIPPITY CLOP. Every once in a while Bess wears it to bed.

3. Roman Holiday

At first, they didn't want to be themselves. They started as men, of course. They had a lot of sex. But after a while they began to feel stranded and strange. It was, the Green Girl explained, as if you'd lost something important, like your phone, and soon you'd remember what it was and know that your life was ruined. A looming, anguished feeling. So then they stopped being men, and were women instead. Sometimes they were old women, and sometimes kids. Sometimes they were even men again. They have been clowns and cowboys. But mostly they're who they were, only smarter, and with better clothes.

They have been all over the world. Last summer they went to Rome with Ophelia. Ophelia is always asking to hang out with them. They're still not sure how they feel about this. "She's okay," says the Green Girl, "but, sort of like, I don't know—weedy?" Bess thinks "tragic" might be a better word, but "weedy" works too. On the Rome trip, Ophelia went to bed early every night and cried herself to sleep, and Bess and the Green Girl sat up with their feet on the coffee table, little nubs of sponge between their toes. They waited for their toenails to dry and flipped through the shiny magazines they'd stolen from the lobby.

"The thing is," the Green Girl said, "she hasn't moved on. She's sort of like *stuck*."

"She's probably never been a man," said Bess.

"If she has," said the Green Girl, "I will literally hang myself."

They went out on the balcony and watched the cars. It was peaceful out there, like outer space. The next day they escaped Ophelia long enough to take pictures in a photo booth. The thrill of it came from circling around a truth they were discovering at the same time: that they liked each other best.

Rome was also where the cops came to their door, and they had to fade. They rematerialized in Sydney. Ophelia wasn't there. She texted them later and said she was feeling really hung over and dehydrated. Which, said the Green Girl, was sort of hilarious when you thought about it.

4. Bess's Type

The thin boy dancing with Bess is not her Type. He looks humble and sad, and he backs up politely when another boy crashes into him. When the song ends Bess thanks the thin boy, explains that she has a boyfriend, and heads back to the bar for another drink. She eyes the bartender, who is cute. He doesn't pay any attention to her; he's the cold, professional sort, always wiping things down. Boring. It's too bad, because he has the cruel profile and capable restless hands by which Bess's Type may be recognized anywhere in the world.

Bess's Type is well known to the magazines. He appears in advertisements, wearing ragged jeans, wearing beautiful suits. He is often holding a bottle of cologne. In the cologne ads he comes with a folded strip of paper that you can peel up in order to smell him. Bess's Type smells like grass and rain and leather and freshly split wood. He has notes of citrus. He has Commitment Phobia. He has eleven erogenous zones you don't know about. If you answered "Yes" to more than six of these questions, he is Verbally Abusive.

Bess's Type is trouble. He will come to a bad end. His mother loved him too much, or not enough. He is filthy rich, or just filthy. He is in prison, stabbed, shot down like a dog on the highway. He is riding, riding, riding.

Bess often stays up late checking off the boxes in magazine quizzes. *Yes. Yes.* The scratch of ballpoint pen, the shiver of recognition. The quizzes tell her that he is still here. And if he is still here, then so is she.

The Green Girl says: "My Type is the Type with a pulse."

5. Ten Hours from Now

Ten hours from now, Bess and the Green Girl will meet for breakfast at this place on the beach. The Green Girl will have more cash than Bess, but she will have only one shoe. She has ripped off the bottom third of her T-shirt and fashioned a bandage out of it. She limps, leaning on Bess, gasping with laughter, her blue toenails crusted with sand.

They sit by the big window and order coffee and trade stories. These are all stories you've heard, or overheard, or told.

"And then I was like—"

"And then he was like—"

"And then he goes, 'Why don't we try—'"

"He's like, 'Why don't we go—'"

"He's all, 'It's kind of loud in here, why don't we go somewhere else?'"

The Green Girl orders her coffee with whipped cream on top. She dips her tongue in the cream. The Green Girl needs to put some more spray tan on. She's looking green. She needs a shower. She needs more perfume. She needs, she needs. Bess needs too. She needs a new shirt. She needs a manicure and some lipstick.

After breakfast, they will go shopping and get all the things they need. Yay!

They shop with big handfuls of crumpled bills. They steal as much as they buy. They get the Green Girl a new pair of heels in creamy gray suede. The salesgirl says, "It complements your skin!" Bess and the Green Girl get lots of compliments. They get full makeovers, they get their hair done. Bess loves the smell of salons, sharp and hard as an open pair of scissors. The smell makes her eyes water. She loves the efficient little *zip* when she gets her eyebrows waxed, although she no longer feels any pain. She loves being surrounded by serious work. The girls at the salon work on themselves and each other with the concentration of embalmers. They are themselves and also not themselves, inside and outside, like ghosts. Bess feels wistful. What's it like to live like this when you're still alive?

6. Photographs

Bess keeps the photographs from Rome in her purse. A strip of black-and-white images, Bess and the Green Girl smiling, pouting, batting their eyelashes. In one photo they wear big glamorous sunglasses. Bess and the Green Girl are glamorous people who stay at the best hotels and converse in hotel language. When they run out of money, they rob people in parks. You'd be surprised how easy it is to make a person faint. In one of the photographs, the Green Girl points a finger at the camera, thumb cocked: POW! But the Green Girl doesn't need a gun.

Bess pores over the photographs. She pores over her own face. It's a pampered face, plump and smoothly powdered, the face of a queen or an heiress. The face of someone who doesn't know how to suffer. Which, Bess thinks to herself, is sort of hilarious when you think about it.

7. The End of the Green Girl's Story

So I went to check out the window and there was one of those metal fire escapes, right? So I opened the window and climbed out and started going down. I couldn't hear him anymore, but I knew he was in there somewhere screaming his head off, because I kept passing apartments where lights were going on. One window lit up right in my face, and there was this guy standing there in his shorts with his hand on the light switch, and his face was like, what the fuck? So funny, I swear to God. But when I got to the bottom the windows were all dark, so I guess they couldn't hear anything down there. Anyway, I jumped down and took off through the parking lot. Barefoot! Carrying my shoe! Like hey, don't mind me, I'm just another random ghost girl with a shoe. I ran for ages, I don't even know how long. I ran through all these back yards and a park. And then it was like, you know what? Nobody's chasing you. Why are you running?

So then I just walked. I walked down the sidewalk under these big old trees and looked at the houses. Everything was dark except one house at the end of the street. I went up close and looked in the window and there was an old lady sitting there at a table sort of laying out strips of yarn. She had all different colors of yarn. She had my favorite color, that dark teal color, and your favorite color, and everybody's favorite color, and she was just laying them out in rows and then switching them around, and then she'd lean back and put her head on one side, like this. Like hmm, does that look good? And then she'd frown and move them some more. She had on a sweatshirt and this big purple scarf with sequins. The scarf was a little bit rad, actually. She had crooked gnarled-up old lady hands and she moved the pieces of yarn like they might fall apart any minute. She seemed like, you know the Fates? She seemed like the Fates, except there was only one of her instead of three, and all her pieces of thread were cut. They were cut but she didn't throw them away. She kept moving them around. It seemed like she had something in mind for them.

8. The Creed

Bess sits at the bar at Pink Ice and orders another vodka and cranberry. The Green Girl is still dancing in the crowd, her hair and skin spangled with the glitter that falls from the ceiling, her flat little breasts bouncing under her T-shirt. Other girls dance around the Green Girl, a tangle of elbows and hair. Bess closes her eyes and breathes in slowly, smelling salons and mascara and sweat. Delicious smell of girls who dance as if it's already the end, as if they secretly know that tonight they will die for love.

She opens her eyes. The cute bartender smiles. He strolls over to her, wiping the bar. "Abandoned?" he shouts over the music.

Bess smiles. "I guess."

He says something like "shade."

"What?"

"That's a shame!"

They lean close to talk.

"I'm Evan," says the cute bartender.

"I'm Bess."

Somebody calls him; he steps away to pour drinks. He'll be back. He'll say something about the surprise, a girl like her, alone. He'll ask about the boyfriend. For him, she'll say there isn't one. There really isn't. You don't get everything back.

You could, of course, if you wanted to. You could do what the songs say. You could keep waiting, you could keep listening for those hoofbeats on the road. You could go on waiting for him and you could kill yourself over and over and maybe there would be a kind of satisfaction.

Bess said this to the Green Girl once, and the Green Girl said: "Please tell me you're high."

It was after the photographs, at a restaurant in gold light. Bess said: "But I miss him." She felt like crying.

The Green Girl smacked the table. "Damn it! Are you going Ophelia on me?"

The Green Girl took out her eyeliner and scribbled on a napkin. She wrote: THE CREED. Bess has the Creed in her purse, she keeps it with the photos. The Creed goes like this:

1. There's more than one way of haunting.
2. We didn't get enough and we are back for more.
3. No moaning I am more than a voice.
4. LIVELIVELIVE

The bartender slices lemons with his capable restless hands. Bess doubts she'll get a shot at the cash register before he takes her home: he's too professional. Still, there's the wallet. And there will be warmth. There will be kisses, arms around her. God, she longs for it. She's freezing.

She won't let him get past the ruffled blouse, to the black wound underneath. It's not that the screaming bothers her, when they find out. But some things, thinks Bess, are private. The Green Girl doesn't agree. She always says the screaming's her favorite part. Ten hours from now, wearing only one shoe, the Green Girl will gasp with laughter over the screams of the man who will take her home tonight, his retching, his flailing arms, his *Get out get out, please go away, oh God, a corpse!* It will be pretty much the funniest thing ever. And then the Green Girl will tell the story of the woman with the threads: old Fate. And that story will stay with Bess all day. At the hair salon, at the mall, she'll keep thinking about it. What do you do with yourself, where do you go, after your thread's been cut?

There's more than one way of haunting.

We didn't get enough and we are back for more.

More what?

Tomorrow night Bess will say: "Let's go find that old lady." She'll walk with the Green Girl, hand in hand beneath the evening trees. The world will seem strangely quiet, the streetlamps veiled in mist. But the old woman's window will glow through the dusk as vibrant as a heart. The ghosts will hover, then tap gently at the glass. Poor ghost girls, always on the outside, always cold. "Let us in," they'll call. "Please let us in. We're lost."

Now the bartender's back. He's still pretending to wipe the bar, preserving the distant air of Bess's Type. He raises his eyebrows. "Your friend's having a good night," he says, and Bess turns and sees the Green Girl in a cage.

The cage gleams above the dance floor, high on the wall. On some nights, Bess guesses, there's a professional dancer in it. Tonight, it's the Green Girl. How did she get in there? Was the cage unlocked? Did she fade and materialize, or did she use the stairs?

"Oh my God," groans Bess. "She is a total exhibitionist."

Evan laughs. Bess gazes up at the Green Girl, resigned, disgusted, and happy. The Green Girl grips the bars and swivels her hips. She flings her hair back, throwing off glitter. She looks utterly alive. People on the dance floor are starting to grab their friends' arms and point up at her: *Look at that girl!* Now they're cheering, jumping higher, fists in the air, all the Pink Ice kids with their feathers and fake IDs and borrowed cars, with their devious feral expressions of children raised by alcoholics or wolves.

The Green Girl is their incandescent queen. She melts the snow. They would like to pull down the cage and take out the lovely sparkly goddess inside. They would like to sacrifice her on an altar. They would like to read a poem in which she dies and dies and dies.

The Green Girl snarls. She eats all the death wishes and never gets full. Her body snaps, light and flexible as a whip. Her face is blanched by the lights, distorted with joy. "Yeah!" she screams. "Woo! YEAAAAAH!" Bess can hear her over the music.

Blood and Sequins

Diana Rowland

"Pellini, see anything?"

I lowered the binoculars, passed them to Boudreaux. "Looks clear so far." We lurked within a rented van parked on the far edge of the Bayou Skate roller rink lot. A huge banner draped the front of the sprawling building, proclaiming the 60th anniversary of the *World Famous Gator Skater's Mardi Gras Costume Contest*. A line of people waiting to get inside stretched around the corner.

My partner did a careful scan of the area. "If there's anyone in there who might recognize us, they'll probably be in costume, so we're fucked as far as that goes," he said. "But I don't see any familiar cars either." He took a long drag off his cigarette, flicked the butt out the open window. "And once we get our masks on, we should be in the clear."

I gave him a tight, satisfied smile, then opened the side doors of the van. "Let's roll."

Boudreaux donned his horned headpiece—an elaborate, iridescent white construction of papier-mâché, crystals, and sequins. It was still a little freaky to watch my wiry partner transform into what we'd dubbed the Crystal Incubus. Clawed gloves, shimmering fabric, a couple of thousand crystals, and cleverly constructed, leathery white wings that sparkled with every move completed the illusion. No way in hell would anyone recognize him.

Using the van's rearview mirror, I slipped eerie red contacts into place, then smeared shimmery black stage makeup around my eyes, the only skin that would show through the matte-black mask. Once I had it on, I pulled the hood of my robes further forward, then stepped back to assess what little reflection I had in the dark gloss paint of the van. Meaty. That's what I usually called myself, but I knew better. I squeaked by the departmental physical only because, at forty-something, I was old enough to be allowed to walk the requisite mile and a half. It'd been a long time since I'd given a crap that my belly hung over my belt and my pecs had long ago morphed into man-boobs.

But none of that showed in the costume. The cut and fall of the long robes, the wide sleeves, the jewel-studded belt, the deep hood, all suited my form nicely. Where Boudreaux was all white sparkle, my getup was shadow and darkness. Sure, I had my share of black sequins, crystals, and even glitter, but the effect was a subtle shimmer rather than gaudy overkill. Huge folded wings constructed of about a billion feathers ended almost two feet above my head, and six-inch platform shoes added to the effect of towering height. Goddamn, I was one bad ass Dark Angel.

And right now, we were about to go into the sneakiest undercover of our lives. But this was no police operation. This wasn't two Beaulac Police Department homicide detectives trying to nail a suspect.

No, me and Boudreaux were there to enter the most prestigious Mardi Gras costume contest in St. Long Parish. Attendance was limited to three hundred, and tickets were pricey and hard to come by. Costumes were required, but the entry fee for the contest was obscene, so only a small portion of the partygoers actually competed. And once I had the costumes underway for this year, I'd called in a couple of favors to land tickets.

There were hell of a lot of things I really sucked at—cooking, car repair, hell, even police work at times—but I sure kicked ass at making cool-as-shit costumes. Not that anyone else back at the station knew...or would *ever* know. Any cop caught wearing sequins or spandex would never live it down. I didn't have much of a reputation anymore, but I intended to hang on to what little I had.

Which was why we were skulking in a parking lot, making damn sure we were in the clear before heading inside.

I locked the van and stuffed the keys into the belt pack under my robes, then we headed toward the entrance. It'd taken more hours than I wanted to admit to perfect the art of walking in the funky shoes, but it resulted in the awesome illusion of me gliding along with my robes skimming the ground.

Doors were tricky with my wings, but I'd practiced that too, and made it through without mishap as old school disco music surrounded us. Boudreaux handed over our tickets and joined the line to get us registered under our usual aliases. No way would we risk getting found out by putting our real names down.

I took a half-step back to make room for the wide gold brocade skirts of a domino-masked woman dressed as an eighteenth-century French noble, tall wig and all. Her mouth was pressed into an angry frown as she joined the line a couple of people behind Boudreaux. A few seconds later she startled as one of the staff members taking registrations snapped his pencil in half. Frowning, I watched the guy stand and storm off. *Huh. Guess he was sick of costumes.*

Boudreaux returned from registration as the music changed to a techno beat. "All set. There's a lineup on the rink in about an hour, but apparently most of the judging takes place before that. The judges are in the crowd. Could be anyone."

"Got it," I said. "We're on as soon as we walk in. Everything look okay on me?"

"Yeah. Bad-ass. Let's go win this thing."

I pushed down sudden nerves. The Dark Angel and Crystal Incubus were the best things I'd ever created, but that didn't mean shit if they didn't have the same effect on other people. "Come on. And remember not to slouch."

Boudreaux snorted and straightened his shoulders. "And you remember to keep your fat ass upright and not fall off those platforms."

We headed into the rink area, both of us itching to get a solid look at the competition. The harsh bass vibrated through us, mingling with the scent of perfume and sweat, with a wisp of pot thrown in. Banks of expensive-looking lights and mirrors dominated the ceiling in the center of the room, and what appeared to be brand new, sparkle-flecked red carpeting covered the wide area that surrounded the entire skating floor. Everything looked shiny and in good repair, and I wondered how the hell a roller-skating operation could keep up with that sort of budget.

A few dozen skaters circled the rink, most wearing simple costumes that probably weren't entered in the competition. The Green

Hornet and Kato. Captain Hammer and Dr. Horrible. A grandmotherly type doing cool jumps and spins, dressed as Little Bo Peep. But there were some impressive costumes as well. A two-person dragon whose occupants somehow managed to skate in decent tandem. A chick in a barely-there steampunk get-up skating backwards with ease.

Boudreaux heaved a sigh beside me. "It's too bad neither of us can skate worth a damn."

I grimaced. "Fuck it. Second place ain't bad." First place was five grand, plus a week in Cabo for two, all expenses paid, but I knew our chances of winning that were slim to none, even with costumes as kickass as ours. Problem was, it was a goddamn skating rink, which meant that you lost major points if you couldn't actually *skate* in the costume.

I'd tried. That was three weeks ago, and my ass still felt bruised to hell and back.

"Yeah, second place would be okay," he replied. "Two grand would cover the costume costs, plus some."

My gaze skimmed the crowd. The majority of people milled, drank, and posed in the carpeted area. Only a handful of patrons in contest-worthy costumes weren't skating at all—including us, a pair of zombies who looked so real I could damn near smell them, a yeti, and a Minotaur with ingeniously constructed hooves.

"Or third place," I suggested, my wince hidden by my mask. More likely we'd manage to score one of the lesser prizes—Best Duo, or Most Original. The cash prizes for those were a lot smaller, but at this point we'd take what we could get. This was a tough hobby to pursue on a cop's salary.

The French woman passed by, face twisted in anxiety and frustration, craning her neck and looking around as if trying to find someone. An abysmal Rocky Horror followed her, then the zombie couple I'd seen earlier. *Damn.* Their makeup, facial prosthetics, and tattered Mardi Gras partygoer outfits were seriously impressive. Better than ours, maybe.

A strangled cry yanked my attention from the zombies, and I turned in time to see the Rocky Horror guy drag the cheap black wig from his head and rip at it as though determined to tear it to pieces. Not even three seconds later he stopped and stared at the shredded wig in his hands as if wondering what happened to it.

Boudreaux let out a low snort. "Someone found the good drugs."

"I'd do the same thing if I had a wig that bad," I replied with a chuckle.

We moved through the crowd while I carefully used the gliding stride that was so important for the overall effect of the costume. Now that we were in the midst of the throng I saw heads turning our way. Relief mingled with pleasure at the approving nods and appreciative smiles. Boudreaux made the perfect counterpoint to my sinister height and bulk. Small and lean, he carried off the white spandex and sparkle flawlessly. Who woulda ever thunk that scrawny Boudreaux, who looked more like a meth-head than a cop, would look so damn good in glitter?

I did, I thought with a grin. *That's who.*

We continued to work through the crowd, pausing frequently to pose for photos, and finally managed to stake out a good spot by the rink where we could size up the competition. Steampunk girl skated by again, followed closely by someone dressed like a giant raccoon. A dark-haired, well-muscled man wearing devil horns, a red jacket, and no shirt skated the perimeter of the rink as he watched the others. Maybe a judge? Recognition stirred sluggishly, but I couldn't place him for the life of me, and his red makeup didn't help either.

"How the hell does she keep her tits in that top?" Boudreaux murmured, eyes on Steampunk Girl.

"Double-sided duct tape, probably," I offered. "Maybe she didn't use enough and we'll get a show later." I allowed my imagination to explore that possibility for a few seconds. Devil Horn Guy skated past again, and I nudged my partner with an elbow. "Hey, Boudreaux. Does that devil guy look..." I trailed off, all thoughts of steampunk or devil horns vanishing at the sight of the new skater. "Jesus fuck all, check out Butterfly Girl."

Her costume was simple, but devastatingly effective. Diaphanous fabric of shimmering blues and purple flowed from the underside of her arms and connected to thin straps around her perfect thighs, giving the impression of wings when she lifted her arms. Body paint covered her toned but lusciously curved body from head to toe in beautiful swirls of color accented with glitter.

"Holy shit!" Boudreaux said, voice somewhat strangled. "Does she have on *anything* except body paint?"

"Thong," I managed, eyes following her. "And skates. Doesn't look like much more." Exhaling a shuddering breath, I nudged Boudreaux. "C'mon, we need to keep moving so all the judges can see us."

We continued through the crowd, pausing repeatedly for more photo requests, but my eyes kept going back to Butterfly Girl. She skated past, spun, skated backwards, and if I hadn't known better, I'd have been sure she was looking straight at me.

I wasn't the only one watching her, either. Devil Horn Guy leaned against the far rail talking to a couple of men wearing suits and sparkly Mardi Gras hats. The devil's gaze followed Butterfly Girl, and he gestured toward her a couple of times. I couldn't fault him for that. She made a great conversation piece.

She glided toward the gap in the rink railing and exited, but to my shock she moved directly toward us. Her eyes traveled over me, from floor to the top of my wings, her full lips parted slightly.

"Jesus," I muttered, suddenly glad the folds of the robe would hide my growing boner.

Before I could think, she stumbled and fell into me. By some miracle I kept my balance on the platform shoes as I caught her, and even got a handful of boob in the process. Yeah, there was nothing but bodypaint over those puppies.

She clung to me as she got her skates under her, not shifting away from my hand on her boob. Hell, if she wasn't gonna pull away, I sure as hell wouldn't either. I breathed silent thanks for the last-minute decision to use makeup on my hands and forego gloves.

"I'm so sorry!" she breathed. "The mat caught my skate. Can you forgive me...my Lord?" Her green eyes gazed up at me through long lashes tipped with gold as her meaning slid through me. It was the costume. The whole Dark Angel thing was a turn-on for her.

My boner was fine with that. And so was I, for that matter. I could play this game.

Even though my voice was naturally deep, I consciously lowered it even more. "All is forgiven."

She continued to keep her amazing tit pressed into my hand. "I was coming over to see you," she murmured, tipping her head back to look fully at the mask, dark hair tumbling in waves down her back. I stifled a groan as she shifted her hip to slide against my erection. Mouth dry, I ran my thumb over her nipple, then had to hold back a shudder as she pressed closer. It had been a long...*long* time since anyone had shown even the slightest sexual interest in me, and even longer since I'd had actual physical contact—with anything other than my right hand.

And yeah, I knew it wasn't middle-aged, overweight Vincent Pellini she was coming on to, but what the hell. The Dark Angel had landed me an arm full of something I wouldn't get any other way.

"You have captured my attention, little butterfly," I said, keeping my voice deep.

She undulated her hip against me. "Maybe I could capture something else later."

Oh, Christ Jesus! Was she offering to fuck me?

But before I had the chance to question or agree or anything else, the music suddenly faded.

"All contestants to the rink for line-up, please!" a cheery voice announced over the PA.

I hesitated. Swear to God, I seriously considered tossing a year of work and well over a grand in expenses in order to pursue my chance to bang this chick.

Then I sighed. There was no fucking way she would go through with it. At the most I might get to cop a few more feels and, even as amazing as her tits were, they weren't worth throwing away all the work Boudreaux and I had done.

I gave her boob a gentle parting squeeze. "Find me after this, and I will allow you to capture much more." Hey, it was worth a try, right?

Her hand found my cock, squeezed lightly. "Promise, my Lord?"

I almost forgot to answer. "You have my word," I said, willfully managing to keep my voice steady.

Butterfly Girl looked over at Boudreaux, then back up at me. "And your friend too." With a final stroke of my cock, she pulled back then turned and headed onto the rink.

I stared after her, mouth hanging open, thankful for the cover of the mask.

"What the hell just happened?" Boudreaux asked.

Swallowing hard, I found my voice. "A goddamn sexy as hell butterfly wants to fuck an angel and a demon. Jesus! I ain't never taking this thing off."

My partner stared after the painted ass until it disappeared in the throng. "Let's go win this thing so we can get to what happens after."

I made a few final adjustments to both costumes, then walk-glided out to the rink with Boudreaux and found our place in the line between the two person dragon and the Minotaur. A shimmer of purple near the other end of the line caught my eye, and I smiled as Butterfly Girl did a cute little spin before settling between Robin Hood and a Bird-thing in an elaborate feather mask. Now that my dick had calmed down I could ruefully admit to myself it was unlikely anything would happen later. Girls like that didn't come on for real to guys like me—costume or not. Didn't matter. She'd given me one hell of a fantasy to take home. Not quite as good as a week in Cabo, but still pretty damn nice.

As soon as the lineup and posing was complete I turned to go, then paused as I saw the French lady approach Butterfly Girl. For a brief moment I allowed my fantasy to expand to include her. Hell, it was a fantasy, right?

But Butterfly Girl didn't seem very pleased when Frenchy took her wrist. She wrenched her arm away and stepped back, her chopping hand motions and angry face telling me she didn't want anything to do with whatever Frenchy was saying. Behind them, Robin Hood abruptly turned and yanked the feather mask from Bird Lady, then viciously stripped the plumes from it and threw it all to the floor. A shoving and shouting match ensued, and Butterfly Girl took advantage of the distraction to push her way past the zombie couple and disappear into the crowd.

"And that completes our judging!" the announcer cried before I had a chance to track where Butterfly Girl went or why the hell Robin Hood seemed to hate feathers. I shifted my focus back to the announcer, but he simply went on to say that the prizes would be presented in an hour.

Figured, I thought as the music returned to its earlier volume. They wanted people to stick around and continue to drink. I hated waiting, but at least I could just relax and enjoy posing for pictures.

Shouts from across the rink drew my attention to a scuffle that had spilled out onto the skating floor. *Yeah,* I thought sourly. *Keep feeding everyone alcohol.* For an instant I thought Frenchy was involved in the altercation, but she stalked away with a scowl to reveal that the fight appeared to be between a ballerina and Rapunzel. The zombie couple and the dragon people quickly broke them up, but Rapunzel's wig had been trampled and the ballerina's tutu lay in shreds.

"Chicks fight dirty," Boudreaux said, snorting.

"That's why I don't get involved in that shit," I shot back. Frowning, my gaze sought Frenchy in the crowd. *The guy who broke his pencil. Rocky Horror and his wig. Robin Hood and the plumes. And now this.* "Did you see where the French chick went? Sure seems like trouble follows her. I wonder if she's instigating it."

A hand touched my arm and I turned, prepared to pose for a photo. My breath caught as Butterfly Girl smiled up at me, looking beautiful, sexy, and utterly fuckable.

"I am yours, my Lord."

Blood pounded in my ears. All of my police training, all of my life experience, all of the fantasizing I'd done since she made her proposal earlier hadn't prepared me for this moment. I stared at her, mouth hanging open behind the mask, feeling as though her hand had squeezed the power of thought and speech from my brain. Then I groaned. A hand squeezed something all right, but it wasn't my brain.

I drew a breath and remembered in the last instant to deepen my voice and play her game. "I will make use of you now, little butterfly."

"Yes, my Lord," she said in a breathless way that made me harder than her touch had. "I think I know a place. Come through the green door on the back wall in about five minutes. Your friend, too."

"Go. Prepare for your Lord." I knew it sounded cheesy, but if it made her hotter, I was all for it.

She backed off and turned away, all beautiful bare tits and ass, made even more alluring by the thin layer of body paint that masqueraded as cover. And to my delight, she'd exchanged the skates for sky high stilettos.

I turned to Boudreaux. "Dude," I said, voice slightly strangled. "We're gonna fuck a butterfly."

His throat bobbed as he swallowed. "Okay, I just gotta ask it. You sure she's not a hooker?"

It was a question I'd avoided asking myself. "No, not sure at all," I said, suppressing the sigh. Damn, it would suck shit if she was. I just wasn't at all into buying sex. "But she hasn't asked for any money or favors," I continued. "If she does, we'll deal with it then. I think the costumes turn her on, and we just happen to be the lucky sons of bitches wearing them. I'm not gonna look too hard at it."

"Gotcha." Boudreaux pressed a packet into my hand. "Good to go. Or come," he added with a snort of amusement.

Grinning, I tucked the condom under my belt and spent the next few minutes fidgeting and posing for more pictures. Who'd have thought sequins and platform shoes would get me laid?

I finally nudged Boudreaux. "Green door. Let's go."

Butterfly Girl waited in the hallway on the other side. "I know where we won't be disturbed."

I glanced around, a little wary. Light shone from side doors far down the hallway to the right, but the left looked quiet and vacant. What if she'd made us as cops and was leading us into a setup? I had my ID and phone on me, but Boudreaux and I had left our guns in the van. My eyes went back to her, and my horniness won out over wariness. "Lead on, little butterfly," I commanded.

"As you wish, my Lord." She turned left, then went down another corridor and led us to the door at the very end. We followed her into what appeared to be a seldom-used storeroom, though I was so busy watching her ass it could've been the food court of a mall and I wouldn't have batted an eye. She stopped and turned around by a desk near the far wall, dropped her tiny thong to the floor and leaned back, legs spread enough to make the invitation obvious.

"Sweet Jesus," I muttered under my breath as I moved to her, then cleared my throat. "Are you certain you wish to offer yourself to the Dark Lord?" Godalmighty, I sounded like an idiot, but I also wasn't about to bang this chick without one hundred percent consent.

She slid a hand down my cock through the robes. "Please fuck your slut, my Lord."

Sure as hell sounded like consent to me. I put a hand on her gorgeous tit, gave it a light squeeze, then pulled the condom from where I'd tucked it in my belt. She was hot as all hell, but I didn't want kids *or* diseases. To my surprise, she took it from me, opened it, then looked up with her head in an *I'm waiting* tilt.

I quickly lifted my robes, and in a matter of seconds she had her hands on my boxers, my cock out, and the condom on me. With that accomplished, she reclined on the desk in a sensuous slow move, and drew her legs up to rest those lovely stilettos on my shoulders. *Sweet Jesus!*

She shifted her head to the side, looked beyond me, and gestured for Boudreaux to move around to the other side of the desk. I almost laughed imagining his face behind the mask when he realized she intended to give him a BJ at the same time.

I stroked my hands down her thighs as Boudreaux scrambled to the other side of the desk. *This is really happening!* I thought as I rubbed my cock against her wet heat. *This gorgeous chick really wants me to fuck her!*

The *click-thwack* of the door opening startled me like a teenager caught under the bleachers. I tried to take a step back and ended up in an arm-windmilling stumble as I fought to stay upright on the god-damn shoes, and only an awkward grab at a set of shelves kept me from falling on my ass. I finally managed to look toward the door, only to see Frenchy struggling to get her wide skirts through the doorway.

Butterfly Girl sat up to stare at the intruder, anger and shock warring on her face. "Brigitte! I told you I don't want to talk to you."

"Who is this?" I demanded, drawing myself up straight again.

Butterfly Girl glared at Frenchy a.k.a. Brigitte. "Someone who I thought was my friend until she ditched me with no explanation. Caused big time trouble for me and *others*." Her mouth tightened. "I swear I'll call David in if you don't get the hell out of here," she told the other woman. "I probably should anyway."

What the hell? I glanced at Boudreaux, but he could only give me a baffled shrug in answer. I sighed. Just my luck. So much for scoring with a very willing hot chick.

Brigitte finally made it through the door and closed it behind her. "Jasmine, I swear I didn't ditch you. Please don't call David." Her face twisted with what looked like desperation. "You have to open your eyes and see that he's not so damn wonderful! He's the one who set me up with the john who...who messed me up. And he wants to *sell* you. That's what I came here to warn you about."

Shit. Not what I wanted to hear.

Butterfly Girl a.k.a. Jasmine lifted her chin. "Newsflash. He sells me every damn day. And that's okay with me. More than okay!" She narrowed her eyes. "No one fucked you up. I saw you the next morning, and you ran from me. You know he'll kill you if he finds you here."

Brigitte gave a humorless laugh. "Kill me? That's one thing he'd have a really hard time doing now."

Shit. A couple of hookers, talking about killing like it was a given. And me with my weapon in the van.

I adjusted my wilting cock then pulled my mask off and dropped it on the desk. "Both of you stop right now and tell me what the hell is going on." I glowered at them.

Brigitte ignored me. "I'm talking about *selling* you," she told Jasmine, eyes wide with distress. "The kind where you don't come back, where you don't get a say anymore." She held up a digital recorder, pressed a button. A man's voice spoke. *Jasmine's next. The deal should be done next week. We'll get her packaged up and ready to ship out as soon as we get through the Saturday night shit.*

Brigitte punched the button again, and silence hung in the room.

Double shit. I knew damn well we were right in the middle of the "Saturday night shit," not to mention prostitution, human trafficking, and who the hell knew what else. I met Boudreaux's eyes. He gave a slight nod and pulled his phone out of the pouch at his belt. Time to get some backup.

Jasmine hugged her arms around herself, face pale. "That...was David," she whispered.

Without warning, Boudreaux stripped off his headpiece, snapped off one of the horns with an angry twist, then casually set both pieces on the desk as though nothing had happened and returned to his phone call.

I stared at him. "What the hell, dude?"

He merely gave me a baffled look. "What?"

Scowling, I snapped my gaze to Brigitte. Every time someone freaked and broke something, she was there.

Unfortunately, right now I had more important things to deal with. "Who is that on the recording?" I demanded. "Is this some kind of white slavery thing?"

Brigitte gave a tight nod. "Sex slaves, and worse. David's deep into some nasty shit. He got sick of being just a pimp, even a high-class one. And dealing ecstasy wasn't enough. Jasmine and me, we've got to get out of here. "

Boudreaux ended his call and put his phone away, then jerked his head up. "Oh shit. David?" He asked, stress in his voice. "David Wohlreich?"

I cursed as I put the name to the face and the pieces clicked into place. "Yeah, David Wohlreich. We saw him out on the floor. The devil guy who looked familiar." I knew the narcs had him on their radar for prostitution and drugs, but human trafficking took it to a whole new level. I'd been too busy watching tits and ass to recognize him earlier. If I had, I wouldn't have done something stupid like go to the back with one of his prostitutes.

But before I could come up with a brilliant plan to get out of this mess, the door opened again and the two zombies entered.

"I need to see everyone's hands, please," the man said in a mild but commanding tone, leveling a gun at us and moving with an effortless grace. The woman followed him in, closed the door, and took up a position with her back to the wall.

Sweat stung my armpits. No doubt this pair belonged to Wohlreich. Did they know we were cops? "Look, we don't want any trouble," I said and held my hands out to the side to look as nonthreatening as possible. "We were just leaving."

"No, you're not leaving just yet," the gun-wielding zombie said. Now that we were in normal lighting I could see that he was dark-skinned behind the makeup, with plenty of lean muscle under the latex. "Everyone against the wall, please," he continued, "and keep your hands where I can see them."

Brigitte's eyes darted nervously, and I had the feeling she was about to bolt, even though there was nowhere to run. "Are you here to get rid of me?" Her voice quavered.

I took a slow step backwards while I searched for any opportunity to turn a suck-ass situation into a merely crappy one. It wasn't looking promising. "Just stay cool, Brigitte," I said softly. "It's gonna be okay."

"He's here for me. I know it," she said in a shaking voice. "I...I think I'm like him."

"Like him?" I asked, baffled.

The zombie ignored me and kept the gun steady. "That's right, Brigitte. We need you to come with us."

She shook her head frantically. "No. Please. I don't mean to cause any trouble."

"I know you don't," he said, still utterly calm. "We're trying to help you. It's getting worse, isn't it? People breaking things around you?"

I knew it! She *was* the cause of the weird freak outs.

Terror streaked across her face. "You can't help me! You're going to find a way to kill me!"

Boudreaux looked sharply at her. "Find a way?" he asked, in an echo of my own thought. "What the hell are you talking about? Dude has a gun."

The zombie kept his focus on Brigitte. "I'm not here to kill you, though I know exactly how to do so if I wanted to," he said calmly. "But if you don't let us help you, you'll cause trouble around the wrong person, and you *will* get killed. Time is short, we're in the middle of a hornets' nest, and we need to go. *Now*."

Brigitte trembled for a few seconds, then lifted her chin. "Okay, but I'm not leaving without Jasmine."

He gave a slight nod. "If she's willing."

"Who the hell are you?" I finally blurted. "You're not working for Wohlreich?"

The zombie shifted his attention to me, eyes keen. He hesitated a second, then lowered his weapon, to my relief. "No, I don't work for him. And we should probably continue this discussion outside."

I glanced over at Boudreaux then back to the zombie. "Sounds good to me."

"Wohlreich has a handful of men here running girls and drugs down at the other end of the building," he informed us, radiating calm authority. "We're heading for the back exit. I'll take point and my partner will take the rear. Let's move."

My gut told me this dude was military or law enforcement. "What agency are you with?" I asked, peering at him and the woman.

"That's classified."

I snorted. Likely Feds of some sort. "I'm Pellini, and this is my partner, Boudreaux. We're with the Beaulac PD." I ignored Jasmine's sharp intake of breath. Yeah, I definitely wasn't gonna be banging a butterfly tonight. I snagged my mask off the table, slipped it on, and pulled my hood up. Better to stay in costume as we escaped.

The zombie didn't offer a name in return, to my annoyance. After a quiet word with his partner, he opened the door a crack, listened for a moment, then moved out.

"We'll give him ten seconds, then we're moving," the zombie woman said quietly. She was in damn good shape beneath the latex and fake gore as well.

I turned to the others. Jasmine still looked shell-shocked from the bomb Brigitte had dropped on her. "C'mon, ladies," I said. "Let's get the fuck out of here." I took Jasmine by the elbow to prompt her to move and headed through the door, heart pounding.

As we stepped into the hall I saw zombie guy duck into an office further down. A second later, Devil Horns a.k.a. David Wohlreich and the two men in suits and sparkly hats rounded the corner, deep in conversation and heading our way.

"Okay, sweetheart," I murmured to Jasmine, "talk us out of this."

Wohlreich looked up, took in the sight of our little group as he approached. "Jasmine, sweetie, we've been looking for you."

To my relief, she pulled herself together enough to smile. "Hey, babe. I, uh, had some work to do." She tipped her head in my direction.

Wohlreich's gaze raked me before returning to her. "Good girl. You about done? These gentlemen would like to get to know you." He gestured to the men with him.

Her smile turned brittle. "I...I'm just walking these guys out."

"Do so, then come right back in." His tone was mild, but it was clearly an order. His gaze went past me and settled on Brigitte. His eyes narrowed, and I saw recognition there. *Aw crap.*

In a swift move, Wohlreich reached to the small of his back and pulled a gun. "Nobody do anything stupid," he said, voice dangerous. "Who do we have here besides Brigitte?"

Fuck this noise. No way was I gonna end up on the wrong side of a hostage situation. And no way was this dipshit hurting the girls. Snarling behind the mask, I channeled my inner Dark Angel, then turned sharply and whacked Wohlreich hard with my goddamn wings.

As Wohlreich staggered, the sparkling white of Boudreaux leapt past me and tackled the asshole while I shielded Jasmine and Brigitte. Sometimes being "meaty" was damned useful.

The suited men backpedaled as they reached for their own weapons. I caught sight of someone else coming toward us from the end of the hall, but even as I registered his presence the zombie guy stepped out of the office and took him down in swift and flowing moves that ended with the newcomer dropping like a stone. I'd never seen anyone move that fast. I almost felt sorry for the man.

Wohlreich's gun skittered down the hall as Boudreaux slugged him, but the suited men had their weapons out and on us.

I turned and seized Brigitte's wrist, locked my eyes on hers. "Get pissed!" I urged her. Somehow she made weird shit happen, and she'd looked angry or upset every time. I was even willing to risk that I'd be the one to freak out. Hell, at this point it couldn't get much worse. "C'mon, you hate these pricks!"

She stiffened, and for an instant I thought she would protest, then her eyes locked on the two men. As I watched, her lips curled back from her teeth in a feral snarl, fury etched into her features.

Then everything seemed to happen at once. One of the suited men let out a scream of rage and hurled his gun at the other man, striking him in the shoulder. Two gunshots ripped through the air, and I saw the zombie slam into the wall, blood splattering the dingy white. Beyond him, a new shooter advanced from the corner.

I shouted at the girls to get behind me, even as zombie chick leaped forward and laid into the now-unarmed suit man with a police baton. Boudreaux delivered another hard punch to Wohlreich, but I saw the second suit man raising his gun to take my partner out. Letting out a growl, I ripped Boudreaux's wings off, then whacked suit man as hard as I could with them. The leathery wings looked delicate, but all that pretty sparkle rested on a steel support, and the blow knocked the asshole back hard.

Unfortunately, not hard enough to take him completely out, and he got off a wild shot as he staggered back. I heard the *ping* of a ricochet and Brigitte's scream, then I let out an *oof!* as something punched me hard in my left side.

I looked up to see the shooter down the hall with his gun leveled at me. *That sonofabitch shot me!* And he was about to do so again, I realized as the pain in my side spread like a flow of lava. A smirk curved his mouth as he stepped forward. There was nowhere for me to go, and we both knew it. I tensed, but before he could tighten his finger on the trigger, zombie guy abruptly pushed off the wall and hit the shooter in the back of the neck with an elbow strike so hard the *crunch* echoed through the hall.

The gunman crumpled to the floor. I clamped my hand to my side and leaned heavily against the wall as I did a quick assessment of the scene. Boudreaux rolled off Wohlreich and stood, shaking out his right hand. Somewhere in all of this the zombie chick had taken out the second suit man. Impossibly, zombie guy was still up and moving, coughing blood. How the hell? I'd *seen* him take two in the back.

Zombie chick collapsed her baton and rushed to him, shoving something that looked like a packet of yogurt into his hand. The music from the rink stopped, and I heard the mumble of the announcer. Everything grew weirdly quiet other than our heavy breathing.

Looking behind me, I saw Butterfly Girl murmuring reassurances as she pressed the crumpled fabric of one of her wings over a wound in Brigitte's right forearm.

My knees buckled, and I slid down the wall, landing hard on my ass, wings twisting and gouging me. Sirens in the distance were like sweet music. "Shit. Boudreaux, we got three shot...and multiple suspects down. Don't know if there are more. Call it in."

Boudreaux nodded and pulled out his phone. Zombie guy coughed up a gout of blood, then sucked down whatever was in the packet. He took another one from the woman, then came toward us—moving really fucking well for a shot-up guy. I stared at him. I'd watched him get shot twice, center mass, with no body armor. There was enough blood on the floor, wall, and his clothing to confirm that.

"Don't call me in as a gunshot victim," he said, radiating authority, then looked past me toward Brigitte. "Her either."

"What the fuck's going on?" I asked hoarsely.

The zombie woman pulled out another packet and gave it to Brigitte.

"Classified," he said, and sucked down the contents of his second packet. "And I'd very much appreciate it if you would treat it as such."

Boudreaux gulped, then seemed to realize the dispatcher had been repeatedly querying him. "Uh...This is Detective Boudreaux. Got...uh..." He faltered, seeing the same thing I was—the wound on Brigitte's arm closing up like magic. "Officer down," he managed, voice unsteady. "Gunshot. Five suspects down, building not cleared. Need backup and EMS."

My vision seemed a little fuzzy, as did my brain. The zombie guy crouched by me, and I squinted up at him. "Can you give me some of that miracle drug?"

"Wouldn't work on you. Sorry," he said. "We're physiologically different. That's all I can say about it right now." He paused, leaned closer. "Look, it's really important to a lot of people like Brigitte, like me, that none of this gets out."

I let out a weak snort. "Yeah. Sure. Like anyone would believe us." I cocked my head toward Brigitte. "What's up with her? The anger and the breaking stuff?"

His quiet gaze went to her. "She's giving off a...scent that affects some people. We'll help her."

That made as much sense as the rest of it. In other words, none. What the hell kind of agency did he work for anyway? "Just get the girls out safe, okay?"

He looked up as the sirens wailed closer. "I have to go. Name's Kyle, by the way," he said as he stood. "We'll take care of the ladies."

I had to really focus to understand what he was saying, but I managed to lift my hand a few inches in acknowledgment. I wanted to tell him that he'd better take damn *good* care of the ladies, but I couldn't seem to get the words out. He said something else, but it was lost in the fog closing in around me. I had a vague sense of people moving away, then other people coming in. Lots of shouting, and someone laughing, then the fog grew thick and everything went quiet.

Someone's raspy breathing woke me up, and after a moment I realized it was mine.

"Vince? You back among the living?"

Boudreaux. Hospital. My throat hurt and I focused on working enough moisture into my mouth to swallow. Against my better judgment, I forced my eyes open. "Yeah," I rasped.

"It's about damn time." Boudreaux stood beside the bed, wearing a set of oversized, navy-blue PD sweats, streaks of white makeup and glitter on his face and hair.

"So it all happened?" I asked weakly. "Butterfly Girl. David Wohlreich. The weird shit with the zombies that we're not going to talk about?"

"Yep. It all happened, and you got your ass shot. Just got out of surgery about an hour ago."

I managed a smile. "We really almost fucked a butterfly?"

Boudreaux shot me a nervous grin. "Yeah. Almost. "

"And made a huge goddamn bust?"

"We're heroes. Broke up a human trafficking and ecstasy operation. Go figure."

"Hot damn!" I said, then groaned, remembering. "Shit. Does everyone in the department know about the costumes?"

"What do you think?" He snorted. "No way was *that* gonna stay quiet."

"Fuuuuck. Well, I guess if you're gonna wear sequins, best to do it while being a hero." I said, managing a feeble smile.

"We'll never live it down, but it's better," Boudreaux said, then grimaced. "The costumes are a mess. Blood all over them. Wings trashed."

"I think I need morphine," I said, only half kidding. "Damn. Probably best to cut our losses and move on." My gut clenched with a very real pang of loss.

"Can't do that. We gotta have them back in shape in two weeks."

"Huh?"

Boudreaux grinned. "We have to be ready for the photo shoots in New Orleans."

It took a few seconds for that to sink in, then I *got* it. Mardi Gras ball appearances. "You mean we won?"

"Yep. The whole shebang. Grand prize." His grin widened. "The Dark Angel and Crystal Incubus took it home even without skating. Oh, and you have flowers," he added while I was still trying to process that we'd won. He plucked the card from a simple arrangement of lavender roses and held it out for me.

I frowned over at the flowers, took the card. "The department doesn't usually send roses," I said.

"Nope, they sure don't."

He looked like the cat that ate the canary, which told me he'd already taken a peek. I rolled my eyes and slid the little card from the envelope. A glittery holographic butterfly on the front gave me my first big clue, and I felt a slow smile spread across my face. Inside, was a red lipstick kiss and *Get well soon, my Dark Angel*, signed *Your Little Butterfly*.

I dropped the card to my chest. "Oh man, this is bad."

"It is? How could that be bad?"

"I have a boner for a butterfly and I'm stuck in the goddamn hospital."

Boudreaux laughed, and hooked his thumb toward the flat blankets. "In your mind, maybe."

"That's good enough for me right now, man." I smiled, already planning a new costume. "Good enough for me."

Two-Minute Warning

Vylar Kaftan

Katya strapped on her new dancekill gear, hoping she looked intimidating. She glanced around the room. Everyone looked strong and flexible, like acrobats; some wore modded gear she couldn't even identify. She shivered. This Game was off-grid. Nearby, a hundred other rooms were packed with champions itching for the Game. Most of these were ranked league players, attending with hidden faces and jailbroken gear. Some of the more aggressive mods could wreck her gear, or even kill her—and that was why the pros played the illegal Games. For excitement. She didn't belong here.

But she had to find her brother Yuri.

The gate chimed and the anti-grav sphere blossomed open. White-tiled pillars and bridges curved through space, winding miles deep like intricate lace. Silver glitter spiraled in from the glassy surface. Like sequins tossed in the air, the players swarmed through the snowglobe. No one used their real tag in the illegals; the altered dancekill suits shimmered in thousands of authentic-looking patterns. All styles of guns, both legal and not, glinted in the lights.

Katya's tag for this Game was turquoise glow with scattered gold skulls, which no one would associate with her. No one could shoot for the first two minutes, so Katya zoomed toward the thin silver cloud at the snowglobe's center. As she bounded through space, the white tiles she touched flashed to her pattern. She could only afford the standard five-minute colorlock, but that was okay with her. She preferred to score points by tagging players, not buildings.

She wedged herself above an inverted staircase, readied her shields, and waited for the signal. Not many noobs in this Game, for sure—no wonder the pros played here in secret. Katya stared at her readings, wishing she had come only to play. The Game was seductive. She wanted to immerse herself in the maze—to become a force of pure damage. Unstoppable. For a true player, grayspace was flatland—a useless shadow of working, eating, and counting the seconds until the next Game. Like Yuri always said: only the Game was real. Her whole body hummed. Katya tapped the channels for her favorite soundtrack: *Brazen, with Purpose (#5)*.

The sphere flashed. All the shimmering suits thrummed to full power. Lasers cut the glittery air, like rainbow beams of sunlight through a dusty sky. Dancekillers dove from platforms, angling themselves toward better positions, shooting rivers of energy. Several competitors floated idly past, their darkened suits like magnets for tiny robot predators. Everyone knew the nightwolves programmed scavengers to steal the best gear so they could upmod it untraceably. Katya's gear was expensive, and she'd spotted three scavengers already stalking her.

As shots criss-crossed over her position, she ignited her tracker, hoping no one glommed on the energy. She was in luck. Yuri was nearby, just on the other side of this formation—but he was geared up like crazy. He wore a hackshield and a 400-level fadewall. Even worse, at least eight opponents could shoot his position. Reaching her brother alive would take all her skill. Katya was good, but not brilliant. She'd scored fifth in the Junior League competition at age 17, category bronze—but fifth was still losing.

A blast caught her attention and she glanced sideways. A black bomb smoked on a nearby ledge. Five darkened bodies floated nearby. Black mods were expensive—and permanent. Katya had heard of them but never seen one in action before. They were even more terrifying than she imagined. The scavengers were already stripping the pieces from the wreckage.

Holy shit, thought Katya, steeling herself, *they're actually dead. Not just back in grayspace.* She touched the two-minute-warning grenade at her hip to reassure herself, then gritted her teeth and checked her readings. She knew he'd hold position—the records proved he hadn't moved in his last hundred Games nor fired more than five shots. That was why she'd brought the grenade. Yuri needed a lesson. She closed her eyes and focused on her soundtrack until the rhythm thumped through her like a battlecry. Time to solo.

Katya vaulted through the laser fire toward Yuri's position. Her shields warped as energy blasted her. Someone's supershot crackled lightning at her feet. Katya aimed at the source and fired. She'd paid a fortune for this modded gear, from a connection it'd taken months to find, and now it was time to see if her purchase was worth it. She wielded her triple-guns like hammers, obliterating opponents where they flew, like a goddess raining justice on the battlefield. She could get ten shots off, in four directions, in half her normal time—and her new central blaster ruptured most shields. *Game on.*

Wildness rushed through her, a power surge unlike any league game, and Katya knew she would never go legal again. Not after experiencing this. For the first time, she understood why Yuri lurked in the illegals, wearing nearly-impervious shields and never drawing attention. This Game made the leagues fade into grayspace. She understood Yuri better, but she couldn't let him continue here. Not the way he was playing.

Her guns were everything she'd dreamed of, but her armor failed the test. She took heavy losses in her legs, so many hits that even her 300-ultrashield collapsed. Her legs darkened as she tried to push off an overhang; off-balance, she crashed and ricocheted upwards. She arched her back to dodge another blast and dove roughly toward Yuri. No chance of surprising him now. If he fired, she was done for. She hoped that even in the chaos, he'd recognize the hidden sig she broadcast. She tumbled toward him, her waist and torso darkening to oblivion.

She struck a wall hard and grabbed an outcropping. For a moment, Katya felt as slow and heavy as a grayspacer, interacting in real time, where moving and talking happened as if through mud. The nightmare soaked her mind with sludge, and then drained away in a wash of color. She hung onto the corner where she'd crumpled, with her two glowing arms atop a knocked-out body. Her tracker hummed against her neck as she looked up. Yuri bounded toward her like a moonwalker, authenticating her secret sig.

Katya, what are you doing here? he typed, the familiar font drifting across her screen. *This is the deadly Game.*

Just like him, never noticing his little sister had grown up. Katya air-typed, *I've come for you, Yuri. You have a problem. You're always in the Game.*

His text dripped a scornful font. *Should I stay in grayspace then? That hellish place full of unwritten rules, which gives status to the unworthy? At least in the Game I know where I stand.*

No, she accented firmly, *but you've grown timid. You lurk in corners and watch the crossfire. You no longer play the Game; you just hide here.*

What difference does it make how I play? I'm here. Don't you remember, Katya? All the nights I taught you to dancekill. The Game is all that matters and you know it. So what if I spend every waking hour here? Why shouldn't I? This is my life!

Katya closed her eyes, remembering those vivid nights dropping through zero-gee, hugging the training pillars, shooting targets like fish leaping from water. Her big brother catching her, guiding her, holding her hand. He taught her to win. In the Game, life's blandness fell away, the hodgepodge of manners and society that ultimately meant nothing. The Game was where she felt alive, so bravely explosive in a world that finally made sense. Yuri was right—the Game was what mattered. And nothing was worse than watching Yuri coast through the Game without playing, like a ghost unable to haunt the living.

Yuri, you're no longer alive. You've built your own private grayspace here in the Game.

She tugged the grenade from her hip and pulled the pin. Black smoke curled around the pair of them.

What did you just do? he asked with dagger text.

She smiled, though he couldn't see her face. *Two-minute warning. Game on, Yuri.*

Yuri cursed in a barbed-wire font. *You murdering bitch! Goddammit!*

Katya rolled away before he shot her. His blast fired over her head. She fell off the wall's side, clutching at tiles. Overhead Yuri soared, his guns sweeping toward her, as she scrambled into a deep, tiled archway. She watched on radar as Yuri zoomed away, as she expected. He knew the Game deep down. He would kill as many opponents as he could before he died himself. That was what a grenade was good for: waking people up. And now Yuri was thriving. Alive again, playing the Game.

Katya dug in her heels and defended her position. She wished she could be with Yuri about two minutes from now, when he realized he was still alive. She couldn't afford a real two-minute-warning grenade, but this replica had worked just as well.

Inside Hides the Monster

Damien Walters Grintalis

Hidden by the shadows, the dying siren crouches on a rooftop, her wings curled protectively around her body. Each time the door across the street opens, a swell of music rushes out, like a bird escaping a cage. To Lygeia, the notes taste of desperation. Of fools and folly.

A sign above the door reads *The White—A Circus of Extreme*.

Lygeia wrings her hands together. She shouldn't be here—it isn't safe this far inland—but she can't bring herself to move away. No one can see her. Still, she curls her wings even closer and peeks through the dark feathers. Even here, she can hear the water of the harbor, a gentle lullaby that reminds her of what she is and where she should be.

Her mouth twists. Should be?

Humans no longer answer her call, no matter how loud she sings, no matter how hoarse her throat becomes. She presses one hand to her side where pain lives beneath her sea-cold flesh, an ache that will only grow worse as it spreads, a hunger than cannot be assuaged by mere meat. The stories about her kind say they sing to lure, to charm, and when their captives sleep the sleep of a spell so ancient it has no name, the sirens tear them to pieces. But the stories never say why.

There is always a why.

A group approaches, the women in tight miniskirts and mesh and lace tops; the men in ruffled shirts with their hair tumbling over their foreheads. Lygeia's feathers rustle. Her mouth waters. She leans forward, catches herself, and rocks back onto her heels, her talons scratching on the roof. It's far too dangerous for her to be so close to so many, yet she cannot tear herself away.

The door opens again and the music emerges. Something about girls and film. Another group draws close, disappears inside. Following the call of the music? But how can they ignore her for this? Her song holds the dulcet tones of a hymn, the beauty of sunrise dancing across the surface of the ocean, the gentle play of wind against skin. This music is filled with screeches and thumps, like angry gulls fighting over a clam. It's nothing more than noise, grating noise filled with empty notes, a temporary sweetness pretending to be a song, yet even more people are approaching. If she learns how to make these sounds, will they come to her as they once did?

Another lean forward; another rock back. The music makes her head and heart ache. With a grimace, she unfurls her wings and takes to the sky, heading back across the water toward home.

This time, she hides in a sliver of darkness between two buildings. Across the street, a young woman pauses and turns, and, for a moment, Lygeia is certain the woman can see her. But no, she's only adjusting her dress, a shimmering gold bit of fabric that drapes and clings.

The door opens and a snippet of music creeps out, imploring her to relax. Lygeia frowns but hums the melody soft and low while the pain in her side pulses in time. The woman pauses again, glancing over her shoulder. Lygeia hums louder. The woman shakes her head, disappears through the doorway, and Lygeia bites back a snarl. She cannot take what she needs by force. She's tried. A messy affair, a waste of time and energy, and the emptiness inside remained even as she licked the last traces of blood from her fingers and talons.

Lygeia creeps close to a glass pane on the roof. Through it, she sees bodies pressed together in a glittering miasma of color and heat. Women dressed in strips of fabric carry trays to and fro; cigarette smoke rises in curls; contortionists twist on a dais; on another, a man breathes fire. On silken ropes hanging from the ceiling, men and women in gold spin upside down in slow circles with their arms outstretched.

When she places her hands against the glass, the music's steady, repetitive rhythm thrums beneath her palms. Her lips curl back from her teeth; her talons leave gouges behind.

Just one human. That's all she needs.

She isn't to blame; the curse belongs to sirens and humans both. Without a human's warmth, a siren cannot live, and the only way to draw the warmth is through the spell that weaves inside her song. But they must come of their own volition, and if her song no longer lures...

She growls, low and deep in her throat, snaps her wings open, and leaves the roof behind.

On her lonely bed of rocks, Lygeia plucks her feathers one by one, gritting her teeth against the pain, wiping the blood away with splashes of water. Molting season would make it easier, but she can't afford to wait. The ache in her side is a steady, throbbing reminder, as if a part of her has been scooped out and the wound filled with saltwater.

She scrapes the rough edge of a stone across her talons, wearing them down and down and down. Again, there is blood and pain, but the talons, like her wings, will grow back. She touches a hand to her side. Unless she dies first; then her wings or lack thereof will not matter.

It isn't fair. She's never been greedy; she's only ever taken what she needs to survive and no more. Yes, she's killed, but not from want, not from cruelty, but to break the bond of the spell. It's the only way — too much warmth and a siren will die, boiled from the inside out by an inescapable heat. This is why her kind must be careful and lure only one at a time.

Naked, she swims to shore, her back afire from the holes in her flesh. She slips unnoticed onto a boat rocking gently in the marina and searches through it, but the only clothes she finds belong to a man. The third boat she searches holds what she needs — a short dress, tall boots, red lipstick, paper money. She wrings the water from her hair and dresses quickly, listening for voices the entire time. Her exposed legs are indistinguishable from a human's, but the boots pinch her feet into a shape unlike her own and make her steps awkward. The hurt, though, is not nearly as strong as the one in her side.

Her heart races as she approaches the door, but she smiles when a man holds it open. If he senses that she's different — other — he gives no sign. She feels the pull of his warmth, but steps away quickly. Without her song and the spell, his warmth is only a bitter reminder of what she can't have. Yet.

When she steps into the main room, for a moment she forgets to breathe, to think. She's spied on humans before, peeking in windows to see bodies writhe beneath tangled sheets, to hear whispers of conversation, but she's never seen anything like this. There are so many of them. And the noise—

It's chaos.

Strings of tiny lights are draped across the ceiling, giving the illusion of a star-filled sky. The carpet is a rich turquoise; the walls are papered in a shocking shade of pink. Tables are scattered throughout, all with shiny lacquered tops and red metal legs. Women in short pink and black striped dresses and high heels carry trays of rainbow-colored drinks. The fire-breather is nowhere in sight, but the performers hanging from the silk ropes are twisting and spinning. The contortionists are bent in improbable shapes and, on another dais, a man swallows a sword fashioned in a style Lygeia hasn't seen in a hundred years. People stand shoulder to shoulder, all laughing smiles and brilliantly colored clothing, like peacocks strutting to impress a mate.

She's never been around so many before. She places one hand on her chest, moves back toward the door, then stops and exhales sharply. Without her song, she's in no danger. She could stand amid a crowd of ten thousand humans.

The music is so loud she can feel it in her feet, her lips, her fingers. How can they willingly listen? There is no nuance, no subtlety. It's as brash, as garish, as the clothes they wear. She's lived for one hundred and fifty years, only to be undone by this? No. She will not allow it. The urge to rend flesh and bone flares hot and bright, but she forces a smile to remain on her face.

This is not her fault. They've forced her to this. If they'd answered her song, she would not be here. She would be safe and whole, not mutilated. Her kind should never suffer such debasement. She clenches her fists, swallows her anger.

The music changes and a shower of gold confetti falls down like rain. Like a mermaid's tears. She holds out her hands, collects the shimmer on her palms. The new song speaks of rapture. She forms the words of the song without a sound, hating each and every one, but committing them to memory nonetheless.

A man steps toward her, his eyes appraising the swell of her breasts, the curve of her hips. He moves close and reaches out a hand, but when his skin touches hers, he hisses in a breath, audible even over the music, and draws away, his eyes puzzled. The cold always surprises them. But instead of leaving, he reaches out again. A line of unease traces its way up and down her spine. What was she thinking? Coming here was a mistake. She doesn't belong with them.

She pushes past the man and heads for the door.

Lygeia watches the waves while the pain radiates inside, like an angry flower blossoming under her skin. An empty boat bobs on the water, each swell carrying it further away. Why he landed on her island, she doesn't know, and when she sang, pouring her heart and every bit of her pain into the song—first her own music, then the noise of the humans—he didn't fall under the spell.

She pressed her body against his, desperate for the warmth that would not come, and finally, in frustration, she split his skull open with a fist-sized rock. Gulls swoop and squawk, fighting over the remaining scraps of flesh.

She watches the man's boat drift away. The pain inside grows stronger. How long must she suffer? How long will it take for Thanatos to stake his claim and carry her to the underworld?

The man at the door smiles again, whether in recognition or by rote, Lygeia neither knows nor cares. The smile she gives in return feels tight and as awkward as the boots on her feet, but he doesn't seem to notice. She isn't even sure why she came, but she still holds a small sliver of hope. Maybe she didn't stay long enough the last time. Maybe she didn't listen to the music closely enough.

The gathering place is even more crowded tonight. The fire-breather is back, spitting out long orange plumes, each one accompanied by cheers from the people gathered round his dais. The silk ropes hang empty, but the contortionists are performing their act with slow deliberation.

One of the women walks by with a tray and offers a drink to Lygeia. Their fingertips brush together, a whisper of skin on skin. The woman gasps. Leans close.

"If you're cold, you shouldn't stand here underneath the vent," she says.

Lygeia nods, although she doesn't understand. The woman's warmth is so close, but so far out of reach. Lygeia lifts her hand instinctively to touch, but the woman is already stepping away.

She sags back against the wall.

The liquor is cold and sweet on her tongue, like a secret, a wish. She takes tiny sips as the music plays. Crying doves, walking Egyptians, girls who want to have fun. Heat blooms inside her, not from the people or the liquor, but from the thought of such debasement. Is this what she must become to survive? Mindless babble instead of eloquence? Cacophony instead of symphony?

A sharp twist of agony in her side pulls the breath from her lungs. Surely her ancestors would deem death a better end. Yet the rhythms, once fixed in the mind, are hard to dislodge. Much like a thorn in the flesh.

The song changes again and again, she breathes in the notes, memorizes the words. Slowly, slowly, she can feel the music slipping into her, tracing patterns on her vocal chords, imprinting hateful harmonies on her lips and tongue.

A man with pale hair sculpted into artful waves walks by and smiles. "Want to dance?" She shakes her head. A few minutes later, another man, dark-haired this time, asks the same question. Again, after a shake of her head, he vanishes into the crowd.

Each song rolls into the next without pause. A song of tainted love becomes a look of love and then sweet dreams. Nonsense and whimsy, yet she begins to tap her foot in time.

A group of women cry out as another song starts, and they turn in circles, singing along. Lygeia winces at the lyrics. "You spin me round?" Had a child written them? The smile she's been so careful with falls. Yet her body is moving with the music, too.

When the song ends, a shower of pink confetti falls from the ceiling. Lygeia feels it land on her arms, but doesn't brush it away. The pain in her side seems faded. Distant. Her thoughts, too. She presses half-moons into her palms, but it doesn't help. It isn't the liquor; their concoction doesn't hold a candle to a sailor's homemade whiskey. It's the music. It's hypnotic in a way it should not be.

She wants to cover her ears, but her arms feel encased in lead; wants to run, but her feet seem to have forgotten how. She squeezes her eyes shut. Thinks of her home beyond the harbor, in the cold waters of the bay. She thinks of a sailor's last gasp of air, his heartbeat slowing down to nothing at all. She doesn't understand what foul sort of magic this music holds and why it should hold her so.

Then she feels a familiar tingle in the back of her throat. No, not here. Not like this. It's far too dangerous; there are too many people. She covers her mouth with a hand and staggers forward, pushing and shoving through the crowd.

"The bathroom is that way," someone says.

"Don't puke on me," another shouts inside a cruel laugh.

She nearly sobs when the door comes into view. Then it opens and a huge group of people flow in. So close. Too close. And their skin is warm and inviting. Lygeia tries to nudge someone aside, but someone else steps forward and pushes her back. She feels like a strand of seaweed caught in a whirlpool; all she can do is wait for the spiral to cease. All around her, the warmth presses in. Taunting. Teasing.

A song begins to form in her throat, and she swallows the notes. *Not safe. It's not safe.* The pain in her side pounds in time with her racing heartbeat. Sweat runs down the center of her spine, burning the wounds. Her fingers tremble. And the music rushes over her again and again and again. She shoves her elbow in someone's side, drawing a glare, but a small space opens up and Lygeia pushes forward. The door is now only a few feet away. Another elbow. Another exhalation of surprise. Another space. And forward she moves.

The song bubbles up, straining to break free, but it's wrong. The notes gouge the inside of her throat and stretch her vocal chords; the melody is a stone scraping across her tongue. It's not *her* song, but something tainted, something horrific, yet it screams with the need for release.

She holds her hand even tighter, mashing her lips painfully against her teeth. Moves forward until she stands before the door. When her fingertips brush the wood, someone opens it from the other side. She staggers forward and her hand comes away from her mouth as she reaches out to the doorframe to stop her fall. The song surges up through her throat, up and out. Not a song at all, but the dreadful cry of a seagull with a broken back, the wailing of a mermaid with a severed tail. An abomination.

She clamps both hands over her mouth, but it's too late. Footsteps rush toward her. Hands touch her skin, their warmth flowing into her. The pain in her side melts away; the pain in her clipped talons and back, too. She can hear the beating of their hearts, the expansion of their lungs, but something is wrong. Their hands tug and pull and their eyes are not vacant, their mouths are not slack. She sees desperation and a furious hunger, as if they want to tear *her* to ribbons. It isn't right. This isn't the way it's supposed to be, the way it's always been.

"Stop," she commands, but they don't obey.

She squirms and twists, trying to get free. The warmth turns to heat and she's burning up, boiling, because there are too many; they'll kill her. She shrieks a banshee's wail, but it does nothing. Of course it does nothing. The only way to break a bond is death, but there are too many and her talons are too dull. She was a fool. Such a fool.

She pulls free of the hands and breaks into a run. They follow behind, crying out in dumb need. The soles of her boots slap hard on the sidewalks, the asphalt. Buildings pass in a blur. Hands touch her skin then fall away. She runs faster and faster, smiling when she begins to smell the tang of the harbor. The water draws closer and closer and still they follow.

She dives into the water, tasting dead fish and pollution, but her arms and legs kick true and her body slides through the harbor murk like a river serpent. She hears the splashing of many bodies in the water, feels a hand wrap tight around her ankle and pull her under. She kicks hard. Something—a nose? a jaw?—crushes beneath the heel of her boot. She surfaces and swims faster.

She may not possess a mermaid's gift of breathing beneath the water, but she can swim for a long time. The humans might survive the waters of the harbor and the bay, but they'll never survive the ocean, not even in the thrall of this unnatural bond. She has to believe that exhaustion or drowning or a combination of both will eventually claim them one by one.

If she has to swim all night and all day, if she has to travel to the other side of the ocean, she will get away from their grabbing hands and the corruption of their music. Her real song is still inside—it has to be—and she'll find people who will answer her call. She won't give up. Not now. Not ever.

But behind her, the splashing continues, a hand grasps, and she goes under again.

Bad Dream Girl

Seanan McGuire

"There are three parties involved in any conflict: you, your opponent, and the terrain. Get the terrain on your side as fast as you can. If that means bribing a mountain, well. Stranger things have happened." —Alice Healy

A nondescript warehouse in Northeast Portland, Oregon
Now

Fern was doing speed trials around the track again, her head down and her arms pumping as she raced against her own personal record. I sat on the bench with my elbows resting on my knees, watching her go. There's practically nothing in the world that can keep up with a sylph going full-tilt. A sylph on roller skates is in a weight class of her own. Fern was going fast enough that it seemed like she should have been leaving a contrail, and I could see half the team mentally taking notes as they watched her go.

It was really a pity they wouldn't be able to put any of her techniques to use. Fern skated the same way the rest of us did. It's just that she had a variable density while she skated, and everyone else had to content themselves with the boring old laws of physics.

Fern finished her last official lap around the track by thrusting a fist into the air, accompanied by the approving whoop of our coach. Four other girls promptly piled onto the track with her, trying to match her pace even as she was starting to bleed off her momentum. I snorted amusement and bent forward to check the laces on my skates. If speed trials were finished, it was time for more formal practice, and they were going to want me paying attention for that.

"Yo, Thompson." I raised my head to see Carlotta—better known as "Pushy Galore" in this setting—skating toward me. She jerked a thumb at the girls now circling the rink. "You going to get out there this practice, or are you going to keep weighing down the bench?"

"I was waiting for Fern's speed trials to finish," I protested, bowing my head long enough to check my laces one more time before pushing to my feet and skating smoothly forward to meet her. "Did she beat her record?"

"The girl's a machine, I swear." Carlotta shook her head. "One day she's going to be reclaimed by the secret government lab that built her."

"Yeah, probably," I agreed, stealing a glance at the clock. We had thirty minutes left before we had to cede the warehouse to its next tenants, a bunch of local college students who were probably planning to use it for a rave. I checked that my helmet was strapped firmly in place, flipped Carlotta amiably off, and joined the girls circling the track. Fern grinned as she passed me in the pack, looking totally serene. I grinned back. We all have our happy places. For Fern, going as fast as she possibly could was the key to personal satisfaction. For me, it was...well, a little different. But a good roller derby practice was close enough.

We had half an hour. That could be all the time in the world, if we spent it right. I put my head down, stopped thinking about anything but the moment, and let myself just skate. It was a wonderful feeling. When I did that, I could understand why Fern risked herself the way she did, showing off for a bunch of humans who probably wouldn't appreciate it if they found out the real situation with her.

When I skated, I was happy. It was a pity it could never last.

Thirty minutes passed all too fast, and the bell found us returning to the benches where we'd left our street clothes, stripping off our protective gear and sniff-checking skate pads before grimacing and shoving them into our bags. Mine smelled like something had died in them. I was going to be doing some serious scrubbing when I got home, assuming nothing potentially fatal came up en route.

"Hey, Annie."

I looked up at the sound of Fern's voice, and smiled. "Hey, Fern. That was some awesome skating out there today."

Her periwinkle-blue eyes widened as she asked, anxiously, "I didn't do anything wrong?"

"No," I assured her. "You were perfect." If any of our teammates heard us, they'd assume we were talking about her speed trials.

What she was *actually* asking was whether she'd pushed her density-reduction trick too far, blatantly breaking the laws of physics, rather than just goosing them a little the way she usually did. She hadn't crossed that line yet. When she did, I'd tell her. It was part of my reason for being in the league. Cryptids like to have fun as much as anybody else, and when you're a cryptid girl with a fondness for tattoos, piercings, loud music, and the sound of roller skates endlessly circling a wooden track, that fun is likely to take the form of women's flat-track roller derby. Which is where I came in.

My teammates call me "Annie Thompson," or "Final Girl," when we're actually prepping for a bout. At home, my name is Antimony Price—no less ridiculous than my pseudonyms, I know. I'm the latest in a long line of cryptozoologists, and it's my job to keep people like Fern, who just wanted to skate without being hassled over the fact that she's not human as such, from getting into trouble.

That, and I really, really like the sound it makes when an opposing team's jammer gets her skull bounced off the track. It's this sweet sort of hollow *boing* noise, and remembering it can help me resist the urge to punch my older sister in the face.

Roller derby: it's good for more than just interesting bruises.

Fern—whose derby name was "Meggie Itwasthewind"—beamed. She sobered again just as quickly, and said, "Coach really wants me to go out for jammer."

"And I really think that's a terrible idea." Fern's speed was a function of her density. When she dialed it down, she moved faster, but had less inertia behind her. If she tried jamming at her full speed, she'd run into the opposing team's blockers and find herself with no momentum left. She looked so downcast that I added, "Besides, it's way more fun to watch them slamming into you and realizing that you're heavier than you look." The inverse of Fern's density trick made her virtually impossible to shove aside. Watching the other team try to shift a five-foot-nothing girl who seemed to weigh more than the Incredible Hulk was pure comedy gold.

"You really think so?"

"I do. And it'll get you into a lot less trouble." I tucked my skates into their bag. "See you at the bout on Friday?"

Fern nodded, her smile returning. "I can't wait."

It had been an informal practice, with skaters from all four of the teams in the league coming together to use the space. Most of the girls had been from my team, the Slasher Chicks, or from the Concussion Stand. That made sense, since we were the teams that would be skating against each other on Friday. The other two teams in the league—the Block Busters and the Stunt Troubles—would have their next bout in two weeks. It was a good schedule. I just had to hope that this season, I'd be able to show up for more than half the bouts.

Elsie was waiting for me outside the warehouse, the windows in her little Honda rolled down and Taylor Swift blasting on her car stereo. I gave her a sidelong look as I slung my skate bag into the backseat. She grinned and waggled the fingers of her left hand at me in a wave that couldn't have been more girly if it had been accompanied by rainbows and the smell of cotton candy.

"Howdy, sweet cousin of mine," she said, in an exaggerated, utterly fake Southern drawl. "You need an escort away from this den of sin and depravity?"

"You met your last three girlfriends here," I said, getting into the front seat. "What is wrong with you today?"

"I got sneered at by some girl whose hair has never been conditioned," she said, dropping the accent. "If I'm going to get looked at funny for not being counter-culture enough, I'm going to earn it."

"Elsie, you're a succubus," I said flatly, and buckled my seatbelt. "You're more counter-culture than most of these girls would know what to do with. Now please, I beg of you, change the CD."

"You're no fun at all," said Elsie, and pressed the button to switch her car stereo back to my usual default: the local college-run indie station. The soothing tones of Halestorm assaulted our ears. "How was practice?"

"Good. I think we've got a good chance of stomping the Concussion Stand in this weekend's bout."

"Uh-huh." Elsie seemed to be paying more attention to her lip gloss than to the road as she pulled away from the curb. It was a ruse, at least if her flawless driving record was to be trusted, but it still made me grateful for modern advances in automotive safety. "You realize that you start talking derby and all I hear is 'blah blah hot chicks hot chicks piercings tattoos hot chicks yay,' right?"

"I keep telling you to strap on a pair of skates and meet more of those hot chicks for yourself."

"Honey, I do fine pulling from the stands." Elsie shot me a sloe-eyed look. I snorted in amusement. Even if I liked girls—which would have made my teenage years a lot easier, since all the other kids in my high school assumed I was a lesbian no matter what I did—I wouldn't have been into Elsie. I don't date relatives, especially not first cousins.

Elsie greeted my snort with a grin, finally turning her attention to the road. Good thing, too; what looked like half the players from the Concussion Stand were skating across the street, having switched their competition gear for standard rollerblades. "Want me to flatten them?"

"No, they're nice. Besides, their primary jammer's a chupacabra, and that means she's sort of my responsibility."

"Kill a bunch of humans, whatever, kill one chupacabra..." Elsie shook her head. "Our priorities are skewed, screwed, and..."

"Tattooed?" I suggested.

"Doesn't start with an 's,' but I'll allow it this time." Elsie waited for the Concussion Stand to pass before she hit the gas again. "Okay, this time I promise I'll listen: how was practice?"

"Good. Normal. Relaxing. Carlotta knocked me on my ass twice—I'm going to have a pretty spectacular bruise tomorrow—and Fern broke her record on the speed trials. Again." I settled in my seat, cheerfully recounting all the little dramas and delights of the day. Elsie listened attentively, asked questions when the narrative called for it, and generally acted like she gave a damn, which was all I could really have asked from her.

It's funny, really. My big sister says she wants to go into professional ballroom dancing and it's like our parents can't support her fast enough. I join a regional roller derby team—in a league with no fewer than five cryptid players, mind you, which means it's worth keeping an eye on, and that doesn't even start to touch on the cryptids in the national derby community—and I'm lucky if they remember I've got a bout. That's what being the youngest of three will do for you, I guess. I'm neither the heir nor the spare. I'm the annoying child prodigy blowing things up in the backyard, and inching closer to "former child prodigy" with every passing day.

We pulled up at a stoplight. Elsie took the opportunity to check her hair in the rearview mirror. She needn't have bothered; it was perfect, as always. Elsie was a master of the art of the wash-and-wear cut, keeping her naturally blonde hair in the sort of artful bob that should have made her look outdated, but somehow only made her look more modern. The constantly changing color of the tips helped, of course. This week, the bottom inch or so of her hair was My Little Pony pink, a shade distinct enough from Barbie pink to have triggered a lecture the one time I got the two confused.

"Hot date tonight?" I asked.

"Carlotta," Elsie said, and flashed an almost sheepish smile. "She called."

I bit back the urge to yell at her. Elsie's five years older than I am. If she wanted to date Carlotta, that was her business, not mine. And yet... "Aren't you going back to school at the end of the summer?"

"Mmm-hmm. That's what makes this perfect. She and I both know that we can't possibly get serious."

"Again."

"Again," Elsie allowed reluctantly. She looked resolutely out the windshield, shoulders squared, trying to appear every inch the responsible driver. "Carly knows it's not going to be like last time. We're just having a little fun."

"Elsie..."

"It's not going to get serious."

"Okay," I said, dropping the issue. "Whatever you say. Hey, can we swing by Killer Burger on the way home? I would murder for a milkshake."

Elsie looked relieved. "Sure," she said, and kept driving.

Elsie and I have always had a slightly strange relationship. She's the girly one in our generation, even when compared to Verity, who knows how to tango in four-inch heels. Elsie understood nails, makeup, and hair care years before anyone else, and even threatened to go to cosmetology school before she realized she'd cause serious issues if she spent that much time in physical contact with straight humans. I wasn't kidding when I called her a succubus. My Aunt Jane met and married a very sweet man when she was in her twenties, and it was nobody's fault that he turned out to be an incubus, making their two children— Elsinore and Arthur—a succubus and another incubus, respectively.

Incubi and succubi are just the male and female forms of a single species, the Lilu. Both can make themselves irresistibly attractive, with a dose of empathy on the part of the males, and a dose of persuasive telepathy on the part of the females. Their specific talents are geared to work best on members of the opposite sex, which could have been a problem, if Elsie hadn't come out of the closet at age eleven, and if Artie hadn't been nursing a ten-year crush on our cousin Sarah, who also isn't human. (She's a cuckoo. Sort of a giant parasitic wasp with an improbably nice rack. Why nature decided that telepathic ambush predators needed to look like manic pixie dream girls straight from Central Casting is anybody's guess. Seriously. If anybody has a good guess, I'd love to hear it.)

Elsie got a lot of persuasive telepathy and danger sense, and very little pheromonal "I'm too sexy for this song" magnetic attraction to the opposite sex. Artie got very little danger sense, which explains his thing for Sarah, a decent amount of empathy, and a *lot* of sexy, sexy pheromones. Thus explaining why he spent most of his time avoiding girls he's not related to. Blood relations thankfully get immunity to the otherwise irresistible urge to jump my geeky cousin's bones.

Of my three cousins, I get along best with Artie, who shares my love for comic book conventions, monster movies, and doing dramatic readings of the old family diaries. Sarah comes second, although spending time with both of them at the same time has been known to make me homicidally cranky. Elsie and I had always been each other's last choice for companionship...but then Verity moved to New York, taking Sarah with her, and Artie decided to lock himself in his bedroom-slash-basement to avoid possibly coming into contact with any girls. Alex was in Ohio, and suddenly Elsie and I were the last ones standing.

(Sure, she could have spent her summer break with her parents, but there's "dealing with a cousin you don't have much in common with," and "spending your summer with Aunt Jane." Even if Aunt Jane *was* her mother, that was a fate I wouldn't have wished on my worst enemy. Besides, Elsie had a car, which made her supremely useful, and she took an interest in roller derby, at least inasmuch as it presented her with an endless stream of hot girls in tight shorts. Everybody won.)

Elsie started chattering about nail maintenance techniques. I closed my eyes, enjoying the dull throb of my newest bruises, and let myself zone out to the pleasant mix of my cousin's voice, the alt rock blasting from the radio, and the horns of all the people who were surprised to realize that Portland has traffic.

It was a good day.

So here's the 4-1-1, before you get confused and hit Wikipedia looking for the family back story: we used to belong to a global organization called the Covenant of St. George, which has "kill all monsters" as its mission statement, and "die die die" on its official letterhead. The Covenant is not made up of terribly nice people. Which isn't to say that my family is made up of terribly nice people—I've read too many of the old diaries to believe that—but we're slightly less horrible without cause. Existence isn't cause. Intentionally killing and eating people, that's another story.

Like most organizations made up of homicidal assholes, the Covenant didn't take my family's resignation well, and they followed us to North America, where they proceeded to wipe us out, at least according to the official record. It was actually a pretty clever trick on the part of my grandparents, one which left the Covenant convinced our family line had been wiped from the face of the Earth, and left us free to pursue our work in private. Said work generally takes the form of keeping the human natives from marching on the cryptid natives with torches and pitchforks, while also keeping the cryptid natives from deciding the human natives would go just swell with a nice Chianti.

(As if. Everyone knows human flesh pairs best with a microbrew from the same region, since that way the drink will echo the subtle flavors of the meat. Having now fully made my transition into Creepytown, I will continue.)

Being officially extinct has its good points—I freely admit that—but it also comes with the occasional complication. For example, we're expected to be combat-ready at all times, and to have experience working with people outside the family. How we're supposed to accomplish these things without ever putting ourselves on the Covenant's radar is left as an exercise to the individual trying to train. Verity's answer was ballroom dancing. Alex's was soccer and fencing. Mine was karate, followed by tumbling and gymnastics, until I got too good and could no longer risk performing in public. I needed a new outlet and training platform after that.

Enter roller derby, the sport of queens. Drunk, belligerent queens who probably couldn't walk without slamming into walls, and were now on roller skates. Oh, yeah. Good times. I could explain the rules, but at the end of the day, if you're not planning to strap on a pair of skates and knee protectors, you probably don't care very much. Most people don't. (People who do are heartily encouraged to put on a black and white jersey and join the wonderful world of the non-skating official. On their backs are the palaces of derby built.)

Here's what's likely to matter at any derby bout that you might choose to attend. At any point in time, there will be ten girls on roller skates on the track, coming from two different teams. Four of the girls from each team will be blockers, the position played by Fern and Carlotta. The last girl on each team is the jammer, the position I play. The jammer wants to circle the track a lot, and the more she does this, the more she scores. The blockers want to prevent her from circling the track. They do this by, well, blocking. Sometimes, girls slam into the track while moving at high speeds. That's the price of doing business, when the business is roller derby. Each team consists of between ten and fifteen players, so as to have replacements for the ones who fall down during play. My team, the Slasher Chicks, has at least two jammers during any given game—usually me and our team captain, who skates under the name "Elmira Street."

There are four teams to a league, and a whole lot of leagues to a geographical region. Individual teams skate against each other; so do individual leagues. The league I belong to, the Silver Screams, is one of three centered around Portland, Oregon. When not playing roller derby, I enjoy comic books, classic horror movies, blowing shit up, and setting traps for anyone stupid enough to come within twenty yards of my family home.

It's a living.

Getting from Portland to my house meant driving for an hour down increasingly small and unassuming side roads, until we were finally shunted onto a gravel logging path that would have been perfectly at home in a movie with a name like *Wrong Turn on the Way to the Murder Cabin, Part III: The Revenge of the Dude*. Elsie pulled up in front of the closed gates that protected my family's heavily-secured complex from casual visitors, door-to-door salesmen, and Covenant attacks.

"Can you punch me in?" she asked. "I don't know this week's code."

"That's because you keep getting me to punch you in all the time," I said, and slid out of the car, walking around to the keypad.

A few numbers later, the gates were swinging open, and Elsie and I were rolling merrily up the driveway toward home sweet suspiciously prison-like home.

Don't let me give the impression that my family doesn't have a nice house: it's perfectly pleasant, for a place that looks like it was built by the Munsters after they became extreme survivalists. We have everything from blast shutters and triple-reinforced glass to a colony of ravens living in the tree outside my window, where they provide both early warning services and a valuable early-morning alarm clock (whether I want it or not). It's just that living under lock and key in the middle of nowhere can get a bit, well, oppressive sometimes, which explains why I spend so much of my time fleeing to Portland under any excuse I can come up with.

The front door was standing open. That was pretty normal. Once someone's past the front gate without setting off security, we assume that either they're authorized, or that a door wouldn't stop them. Elsie parked next to Mom's minivan and we both got out of the car, heading up the porch steps and into the house.

"Mom? Dad?" No response. I knew they had to be on the property—their cars were there, and they'd never leave the front door open if they were going out. I just didn't know where. After a few seconds of contemplation, I decided not to give a crap. I turned to Elsie. "Oreos?"

She grinned. "Oreos."

One thing I have to give my parents: they sure know how to stock a pantry. Five minutes later we were seated at the kitchen counter with a plate of assorted Oreo cookies and tall glasses of 2% milk. (Yes, you can have assorted Oreos. Original, Double Stuf, mint, fudge-dipped...the possibilities are endless and the heart attacks are optional.)

"I am giving up women in favor of Oreos," declared Elsie, dipping a Double Stuf in her glass.

"I'll tell Carlotta you said that."

She wrinkled her nose. "Okay. I'm giving up all other women in favor of Oreos."

"It was worth a try." I glanced toward the breadbox. "You can come out now. I see you."

Head bowed and whiskers slicked back in supplication, a brown mouse crept out onto the counter. It would have looked like an ordinary household rodent if it hadn't been wearing a cape made from a paisley silk scarf. "Priestesses," it squeaked, head still bowed. "I Come to Beg a Boon."

"Mouse wants cookies," I said to Elsie.

She nodded. "I can see that."

"Should the mouse get cookies?"

"Well, you know what they say..."

The mouse raised its head, looking hopeful. "What do they say of the giving of cookies to mice, o Polychromatic Priestess?"

"If you give a mouse a cookie, he's going to want a glass of milk," said Elsie.

"And if you give a mouse a glass of milk, you're going to get a musical number." I nodded to the mouse. "Yes, you can join us for milk and cookies."

"Hail!" shouted the mouse, humility forgotten at the promise of baked goods. "Hail the Festival of Giving a Mouse a Cookie!"

It seemed like the room was suddenly full of mice. They swarmed out from behind every cabinet and kitchen fixture, covering the counters in a furry blanket that respectfully stopped a foot from our plates. Countless tiny black eyes watched intently as I prepared two more plates of cookies, careful to load them with each of the available types of Oreo. When I was done I put the plates down next to the toaster. A great cheer went up from the mice. They descended on the cookies like locusts on a field of wheat, singing our praises all the while.

Elsie and I sat back with our snack, watching them. After a while, Elsie took the last Double Stuf and commented, "Aeslin mice are better than cable."

"Amen," I agreed. Given the choice, I'll take talking religious mice who revere my family as gods over CNN any day. Anyone with any sense would do the same.

The ruckus went on for the better part of an hour. My parents eventually showed up—they'd been outside, collecting eggs from the henhouse and duck nests, and were entirely unsurprised to walk into the massive rodent musical number already in progress. They were equally unsurprised by my new bruises, the fact that Elsie had a date, and my desire to eat upstairs in my room. Eventually, Elsie went to her temporary bedroom to get changed, and I just went to my room.

Family. When they're far away you miss them, and when they're close, you wish they'd go away.

Friday found me strapping on my skates and artfully "bloodstained" knee and elbow guards as I waited with the rest of the Slasher Chicks. We looked like we'd already been attacked by a serial killer, thanks to our uniforms: blood-spattered white tank tops and pleated camo-print miniskirts short enough that they were only appropriate for certain kinds of parties. Derby was one of the appropriate kinds.

The Concussion Stand was prepping on the other side of the track. Their-red-and white usherette costumes were definitely tidier-looking than ours. Tidy isn't everything.

Elsie was sitting dead-center in the front row of bleachers, trying to show support for her cousin and her not-girlfriend-really-honest at the same time. It wasn't working the way she'd intended: instead of sitting in neutral territory, she'd managed to surround herself with fans of one of the two teams currently skating. The girls in black and blue were the Bad Idea Bears, out of Beaverton. The ones in various shades of pink were the Rose Petals, from Wilsonville. Going by the sea of pink around Elsie, she was in Rose territory.

And those Roses had *thorns*. Their jammers barely seemed to obey the laws of gravity, and I'd seen two of their blockers eat track, get back up, and keep skating without seeming to realize they'd fallen. If they hadn't been losing, I'd have started to suspect them of being Oread ringers. Oreads don't feel pain the way humans do, which is why they usually politely abstain from full-contact sports. It's not fair to put a moving mountain in a contest with people who are made of nothing sturdier than meat.

The Bad Idea Bears skated clean, fast, and coordinated. The Rose Petals were enthusiastic and they had a great tolerance for pain, but it was going to be a while before they were skating on the same level.

Then things changed.

It was a blink-and-you'll-miss-it moment. The jammer for the Bad Idea Bears was in the lead, circling the track like her faux-fur-covered ass was on fire. Then, with nothing between her and another pass, she began losing speed. It wasn't a block. It didn't look like exhaustion. She just...stopped skating, drifting slower and slower until she had lost all momentum. Her arms fell to her sides, but her hands never touched her hips to signal the end of the jam. Since only the lead jammer could stop a jam in the middle, play technically continued. She was still on her feet, after all.

Confusion spread through the stands as people stood up, demanding to know what the hell she thought she was doing. Someone booed. Someone else shouted for a referee to intervene. The jammer from the Rose Petals kept going, encountering less and less resistance as the rest of the Bad Idea Bears clustered around their teammate. I didn't know her name, but I could see her well enough to realize that her eyes were unfocused, and that she was starting to wobble.

The jammer from the Rose Petals circled the track one more time. And the jammer from the Bad Idea Bears fell forward, her eyes rolling back in her head. She hit the track so hard that the thump of her helmet bouncing off the floor echoed all the way to the back of the bleachers. The crowd went suddenly silent. For a split second, it felt like no one dared to breathe.

"Medic!" shouted a referee, running for the fallen jammer.

The auditorium snapped back into life. Referees, non-skating officials, and medical staff swarmed around the girl, obscuring her from sight. At first, there were the usual jokes and nervous chuckles about seeing someone eat track hard. Then, as the medical staff didn't call for them to resume play, the laughter died.

"What happened?" whispered Fern.

I glanced to the side to see her standing at my elbow, her helmet in her hands and her eyes as wide as it was physically possible for them to go. The three drops of blood she had painted on her cheek looked more like strawberry jam, but her worry was very real.

"I don't know," I said, looking back to the track. "She was fine, right up until she stopped skating. I don't think..." I paused, reviewing what I'd seen before I said, "I don't think she was okay when she stopped. I think it just took a little while for her body to realize that it was time for her to fall over."

"Is she going to be okay?"

"I wish I knew." I shook my head, still watching the officials as they obscured our track. We were already ten minutes into what should have been halftime, but that wasn't important. What mattered was the girl, lying on the wooden floor with her eyes closed, and the people who surrounded her.

Get up, I urged silently. *Come on, whatever your name is. Get up.*
She didn't get up.

After twenty minutes they called the bout in favor of the Rose Petals and removed the fallen Bad Idea Bear—whose derby name was "Bear-ly Legal"; I didn't catch her real name, largely because no one was throwing it out there—from the track. Most of her team went with her.

Carlotta skated across the empty track to the Slasher Chicks side. The halftime music had started, but no one seemed to be in a partying mood. "What the *fuck* just happened?" she demanded.

"I don't know," I said. "Are they taking her to the hospital?"

Carlotta nodded, expression grim. "They're talking about whether they're going to let us skate tonight."

I paused before I said anything, choosing my words very carefully. "If they've taken her to the hospital, is that really something that we should be worrying about right now?"

"Yes. No. I don't know." Carlotta shook her head, shoulders slumping. "I don't understand what happened. I saw her stop, but I thought she was trying to give the other team a fair chance or something stupid like that. I didn't realize there was anything *wrong* with her."

"I don't think it would have made a difference if you had," I said. "You couldn't go onto the track during active play, and her teammates didn't catch it either. As soon as she went down, the medics moved."

"What if she had a stroke or something?"

"God, Carlotta, I don't know." I grimaced. "I really don't. I wish I did. But hey, we have like ten minutes before halftime is *supposed* to end, and they can extend it as long as they want to while they figure out whether or not we're going to skate. Why don't you go make out with Elsie behind the bleachers? You'll both feel better, and I promise to send Fern to fetch you if they say we're going to skate."

Carlotta blinked before smiling gratefully at me. "You know, I wonder every time we talk why I didn't recruit you to the Concussion Stand when I had the chance."

"Because I look better in bloodstains than I do in bruises, and because if you were my team captain, it would be inappropriate for you to put your hand down my cousin's pants," I said promptly.

Carlotta laughed, flipped me off, and skated away.

I turned to Fern. "I don't think it was a stroke."

"Me, neither," she said.

"So what was it?"

Fern frowned. "I don't know, but something about it wasn't right. She stopped too slow."

"What do you mean?"

"Physics says that momentum and inertia are real things that really do stuff, okay?"

I was pretty sure the actual physical laws of reality were more complicated than "real things that really do stuff," but I was willing to go along with it for the moment. "Okay," I agreed.

"If she'd been having a stroke, either she should have fallen over immediately because she lost the ability to keep her balance, or she should have tried to stop herself while she figured out what was going on. She didn't do either one. She drifted until she ran out of momentum." Fern shook her head. "That's not a stroke. That's something else."

I blinked. Sylphs have a reputation amongst the cryptid community for being a little, well, empty-headed. Given how much time they spend insubstantial, I can't say the reputation isn't at least somewhat justified. But I'd never considered that Fern might need a sophisticated understanding of physical forces if she was going to keep moving while changing her personal density.

"So...what do you think it is?" I asked.

Fern frowned. "I think—" she began.

Elmira Street's arrival cut her off. Elmira was wearing a red-and-green-striped tank top instead of the standard team white. It went with her theme, so we never objected. "The referees have decided to continue play," she said, without preamble. "They're giving halftime another ten minutes, since some girls still need to finish suiting up, and then we're on. Meggie, Final, you're on the starting line."

"Okay, Captain," said Fern.

I just nodded.

Elmira turned and skated away, presumably to rustle up the rest of her wayward lambs. I checked the straps on my kneepads before straightening up and looking to Fern. "Can you go get Carlotta?" I asked. "I want to do a few laps and warm up before I'm expected to jam."

Fern smiled beatifically. "I'll see you in a minute," she said, and started skating off toward the bleachers. I smiled after her retreating back and joined the throng of roller girls from all four of the day's skating teams as they circled the track.

During actual gameplay, there's no such thing as "the fast lane" or "the slow lane." There's the "moving at the speed of play" lane, and then there's the "getting knocked on your ass and praying no one skates over you" lane. During warm ups, people tend to be a little more charitable, if only because it's no fun to bruise the opposing players before the game begins. I started on the outside, where the traffic was at its slowest, and began working my way into a groove.

Skating works different muscles than any of the other things I do; that's part of why I like it so much. Verity is faster and Alex is stronger, but I'm the only one in my family who can smash a watermelon between my thighs. (Not a skill that makes me popular at parties, but it has its uses, and it's definitely helped with my trapeze classes.) I skated slowly, listening to the cues I was receiving from my body, until I was sure everything was in proper working order. Then I merged into the main group of girls, sliding smoothly in between a Rose Petal and one of the Concussion Stand blockers—Shomi d'Money, who had the remarkable ability to stop dead while moving at top speed, and who had knocked me out of the track with that little trick more than once. Shomi smiled when she saw me. I smiled back. Until the whistle blows, we're all friends here.

Fern blew past me on the inside lane, already moving at a speed that had half the girls shifting over to get out of her way. Some of them looked after her with envy, others with disbelief. Fern just giggled, still accelerating.

If Fern was here, that meant Carlotta had been roused from behind the bleachers. I glanced to the stands and saw Elsie reclaiming her spot, surreptitiously smoothing her pink-tipped hair. I smiled—and then I blinked, smile fading into confusion.

One of the Rose Petals was sitting behind Elsie, a sated expression on her face. She was still wearing her pink-and-green uniform, although she'd added a zipped-up hoodie over the top of it. Without her helmet, her hair was frost-white, cupping her cheeks in a perfect bob. She looked like a cinema idea of a roller girl, too perfect and unbruised to be real.

She caught my eye and smiled lazily. I wrenched my gaze back to the track. There was another Rose Petal skating three girls ahead of me. I sped up, pushing my way through the pack until we were skating side-by-side.

"Hey," I said, a little overly-loud, to be heard above the clatter of skates against the track. "I'm Final Girl."

She frowned a little, giving me a sidelong look, before asking, "From the Slasher Chicks?"

I nodded.

"Cool. I'm Triskaidekaphilia—you can call me Trisk."

That made her the team captain, if the roster I'd seen earlier was correct. "Nice to meet you. We have a match next month, right?"

"Only if you beat the Concussion Stand," she said, laughing.

I laughed back. It didn't even sound fake. "Right. Oh, hey—one of your players is in the bleachers behind my cousin, and she looks super familiar. Do you know her?"

Trisk glanced to the bleachers. "White hair?"

"That's the one."

"That's Adrienne. She's one of our jammers. She's the one who got that last power jam in and won us the game." Trisk grimaced. "That sounded really heartless, didn't it? She was our jammer during the last skate."

"It's cool, I understand." I kept my pace matched to Trisk's. "Has she been skating with you long?"

"She just transferred from a team in Colorado." Trisk's smile shifted as she apparently reached some conclusion about my reasons for asking. "Look, you're super-hot and all, and you've got a great rack, but she doesn't swing that way."

"What? Oh! No, not why I was asking." My cheeks burned red. "*I* don't swing that way either. My cousin does, and she wanted me to ask." Elsie wouldn't get too angry at me for using her as a cover. I hoped.

"Ah. Well, tell your 'cousin' that she's not going to have any luck there. Now, if she wanted to pick a different kind of rose, she might find what she's looking for." Trisk blew me a kiss and sped up, easily vanishing into the pack.

Cheeks still burning, I bent forward and focused on getting ready for the match. When I looked at the bleachers again, Adrienne was gone.

The Slasher Chicks defeated the Concussion Stand by a twenty-four -point margin, skating to victory thanks to some impressive block- ing (aided by Fern's ability to slide in front of the opposing jammers and suddenly become practically immovable), one too many technical fouls by Carlotta, whose seat in the penalty box might as well have been permanently reserved, and one hell of a power jam by yours truly. (Power jam: when the lead jammer is in the penalty box and the remaining jammer can go and go and go with no one to call off the round.) We were going on to the next match, where we would be skating against the Rose Petals.

"What kind of name is 'Rose Petals' for a derby team, anyway?" asked Elsie after the match, as we were en route to the diner where we were having the first stage of the after party. Fern was in the backseat, trying to get the last of the fake blood out from under her fingernails. Carlotta had her own car, thankfully. The conversation I wanted to be having wasn't exactly human-friendly.

"A lousy one," I said, propping my open laptop against my knees. "Did you see the jammer with the white hair?"

"Uh—which ones are the jammers again?"

"The ones with the stars on their helmets. Me."

Elsie nodded. "Right. Um, no, I didn't notice any jammers with white hair. Is she on your team?"

"She's on the Rose Petals. She's new, and she was the jammer in the round where the jammer for the Bad News Bears collapsed." I pulled up a browser window, typing in a search for "roller derby" and "Colorado." "She was sitting behind you in the bleachers for a little while during halftime."

"Oh. No, I can't say I noticed her."

"Me neither," said Fern, from the back.

"Something's off about her." I switched my search to images, scrolling through page after page of Colorado derby girls until I spotted a familiar white-haired figure photographed mid-jam. The caption said that the picture was taken during a bout between the Rocky Mountain Rocketeers and the NCOs. A little more digging produced her bio. "'Ivana Cutya is a recent transfer to the Rocky Mountain Rocketeers. She hails from chilly Wisconsin, where she skated with Cheesetopia for the past year. Her interests include roller derby, roller derby, roller derby, and none of your goddamn business.'"

"Friendly," said Elsie. "Why are you so interested in this chick? I thought you didn't like girls."

"You're the second person today to assume that I can't be curious unless I'm also horny, you realize." I returned to the search engine, typing in "roller derby injuries Colorado." The results were extensive, and unnerving. "Okay, this isn't good."

"What?" asked Fern.

"There were fifty-seven on-track accidents last year in Colorado. Thirty-five of them involved the Rocky Mountain Rocketeers, and twenty involved girls stopping or collapsing on the track for no apparent reason. I don't have all the game rosters yet, but the ones I do have all show that Ivana was jamming."

"So you think she was cheating somehow to help her team win? Uncool," said Elsie.

"More than half the injuries were to her team," I said. "Fern, can we drop you off? I think I need to go home and study."

"Sure," said Fern. "No party?"

"Yeah, Annie, no party?" said Elsie, turning big, sad eyes on me.

"You're semi-dating a derby girl," I pointed out. "You don't need me to get into the party. You'll have more fun if I'm not there, since you won't have me bitching every time you and Carlotta decide to start making out."

"Homophobe," said Elsie without heat.

"I don't like PDAs, no matter who's doing them," I countered. "You can drop me off at home, turn around, and come straight back to join the drunken debauchery already in progress."

"I'll text you if we move to Marnie's house," added Fern, almost shyly. "She has a pool."

"A pool, Elsie," I said. "Imagine how much more fun you can have at a party with a *pool* if you take me home first so that I can do my research and you can stay as late as you want."

"I hate you."

"That means you'll take me home, right?"

"I do, I really hate you. Are we sure that we're related? Because I think you're actually my punishment from God."

"That's how you *know* we're related," I said, and kept typing.

An hour later, I was back in my room, sitting at my desk, and staring at way too much data for one person to handle. Ivana had only skated with the Rocky Mountain Rocketeers for a year before she transferred to the Rose

Petals, half-recruited by the team captain, Cylia "Triskaidekaphilia" Mackie. Before that, Ivana had been with Cheesetopia, and before that, she'd been with the Toronto Maple Griefs. And the trail kept going. It's surprisingly difficult to follow a derby girl from team to team, especially if she doesn't want to be followed. There were gaps in Adrienne-slash-Ivana's timeline that could most easily be explained by the assumption that I was missing some of her team postings.

I needed help. I needed someone who had even less of a life than I did, because he had spent all his time hiding from the prospect of social interaction. I booted up Skype on my laptop, and sure enough, he was online. I sent a chat request. When that was ignored, I sent another one. And another.

After five minutes of a chat request every thirty seconds, my headset beeped, and Artie's voice demanded, "What did I ever do to you?"

"Oh, the usual, but that was when we were much younger, and I've virtually forgiven you by now," I said, copying all the links I'd been able to find thus far into an email and hitting "send." "Check your inbox. I just sent you some links."

"Uh-huh, and...?"

"And I need your help." I quickly outlined the situation with Adrienne.

When I was done, Artie asked, slowly, "So is there anything to actually indicate that she's doing this?"

"Not as such."

"She just creeps you out, and that is somehow enough to launch a full-scale investigation."

"No, she creeped me out, and that was somehow enough to trigger a simple web search. The results of said simple web search have motivated me to launch a full-scale investigation. But Artie, I think I'm missing some of the teams she's skated with, and it's possible that this is all a really shitty coincidence."

To my surprise, Artie laughed. "I should mark today on my calendar. 'The day Antimony admitted coincidences happen.'"

"Look, will you help me or not?"

"I'm already helping. The witty repartee has been covering the sound of my frantic typing. You missed five teams—no, whoops, six. That's minimum, not absolute, but it fills the holes. Anything else came simultaneous with something on the list, or before the list begins."

That was an unnerving thought, since the list we had already went back five years. "And? Does the pattern hold?"

"Hang on." This time, he stopped talking, and I could hear him typing. After what felt like fifteen minutes but was probably more like ninety seconds, he said, "Yes, it does. I'm sending you the links. From what I can find, the weird injuries and fugue states seem to accompany her from team to team."

"So it's not a coincidence."

"Not unless she has an invisible friend who really likes making derby girls pass out."

"Unlikely but not impossible." My computer beeped as Artie's email arrived. I opened it, beginning to click the links. "What confuses me is that she goes for her own team, too. It's not just something that helps whoever she's skating for win."

"That's assuming she has any control over what she's doing." A note of barely-concealed disgust crept into Artie's voice. "She could be like me, you know. Maybe she doesn't even know what makes the people around her keel over."

I thought about the way she'd been watching the girls circle the rink. She'd looked assessing, even predatory. "I don't think that's it," I said. "Whoever and whatever this girl is, I'm pretty sure she knows exactly what she's doing."

"Well, I'm happy to help with research. Just don't ask me to come to a bout."

I wrinkled my nose, even though he couldn't see me. "How did you know I was going to invite you to come and see her for yourself?"

"One, I've met you. Two, you've been trying to get me out of the basement all summer. It didn't work when Warren Ellis came to town for a signing, and it's sure as hell not going to work for roller derby."

"You're no fun, Arthur Harrington."

"So I've been told." The sound of typing came through my headset again. "I'll keep digging around to see if there's any other trace of her, but there's not too much for me to go on. I can't even tell you for sure if Adrienne is her real name."

"It's real enough for me. Look—thanks for your help on this. My team's skating against hers next month, and I'd really rather not get whammied by something I can't identify."

I could practically hear Artie smile. "That's what family is for, right? Now log onto *World of Warcraft*. I want to go kick some monster ass."

"Yes, sir," I said. It was going to be long night. We might as well spend it killing things we didn't have to feel guilty about later.

The weeks before our bout against the Rose Petals passed in a haze of research, training, and setting pit traps in the woods around our property. The pit traps were for practice—it's never a good idea to sit back and rest on your laurels—but the rest was to get me ready for my first formal encounter with the mysterious Adrienne. After a month of chasing down every trace she'd ever left on the Internet, Artie and I still didn't know her last name, where she was from, or what she did outside of derby. The white hair didn't seem to be a wig, but that didn't make it a viable distinguishing feature: her failure to wear a wig when she skated didn't mean she didn't wear one in her off hours.

Was she a student? A truck driver? A waitress with wanderlust who sought out the nearest derby league every time she moved? Or was she some kind of psychic vampire, moving on when her food supply started to get suspicious? And most troubling of all, could I skate a good jam with this many questions cluttering my head?

"Thompson!" My team captain came up fast on my left, scowling at me. We were in the middle of warm ups. I was supposed to be weaving around my teammates, preparing for some hard skating. Instead, I was gliding around the track at a smooth, unvarying pace, too distracted by my thoughts to do anything but keep myself from falling over. "Is there a problem?"

"I banged my knee yesterday on the counter at home," I said, choosing a believable lie. "I'm fine to skate, I just need to loosen it up before I start doing anything fancy."

She looked at me suspiciously. Elmira Street was one of the best jammers in the league—top four, definitely. But I was better. "Are you absolutely sure about this?" she asked. "Because this is the last match before Regionals, and if you want to make the All-Star team, you need to have a solid record to carry you there. It's good right now. You fuck up tonight..."

"I know. I'm not going to fuck up tonight." I flashed a toothy smile in her direction. "I'm going to skate circles around those Roses."

"I hope so, Thompson. You've had a really good season. I don't want you to blow it."

"I won't," I said, and sped up, finally putting my back into it as I bent my knees and began to weave my way around the track. The faster I went, the easier it became to focus on skating, rather than allowing myself to worry about what the Rose Petals' jammer was likely to try. By the time the whistle blew to clear the track for the evening's first match—the Stunt Troubles vs. the Grim Grinning Girls—I felt like my head was finally clear. I joined the rest of the Slasher Chicks on the left-hand bleachers, where we'd be able to watch the skaters without getting in the way.

Our position came with the unexpected bonus of giving me a perfect view of the Rose Petals—and most importantly, of the white-haired jammer with the bad track record where her teammates were concerned. The fabled Adrienne seated herself squarely in the middle of her team, watching the derby girls who now circled the track with that same predatory interest that I had observed on our first meeting. She was scoping out the skaters the way a cat scopes out songbirds, watching first the individuals and then the flock, determining their weaknesses.

I was making some pretty big assumptions—maybe she just liked to stare at people—but a large part of my training had focused on trusting my gut, and my gut told me that I was right about the way she was looking at those skaters. I lightly elbowed Fern, who was sitting next to me, and motioned with my chin toward Adrienne.

"What do you think?" I asked softly, my voice almost drowned out by the roaring of the crowd.

Fern followed my gaze to Adrienne and blanched. For just a second, her weight seemed to decrease on the bleachers until I might as well have had nothing beside me. "She looks hungry," Fern whispered.

A commotion on the floor wrenched our attention back to the track, where a group of girls had formed, unmoving and shouting for the referees. One of the medical staffers was running toward them. I stood, trying to get a better look, and caught a glimpse of a girl in Stunt Trouble green lying at the middle of the crowd. She wasn't moving.

Fern tugged on my wrist. "Annie, look," she said, her thin voice barely audible above the shouting.

I didn't need to see which way she was pointing. I looked up, and there was Adrienne, still sitting in the same spot on the bleachers...but her eyes were closed, a look of serene pleasure suffusing her face. She looked like a woman who'd just had a really good orgasm, or a really good slice of pizza: satiated and fulfilled on a deep, primal level. Everyone around her was shouting. Half of them, like me, were standing up. And Adrienne just sat there, smiling like everything was perfect.

Maybe for her, everything *was* perfect.

Play was halted until medical could take care of the blocker from the Stunt Troubles. By the time they had her bundled off to the hospital, accompanied by her anxious boyfriend and two of her teammates, it was too late to get through a second match. The Rose Petals and the Slasher Chicks would not be playing against each other this season.

Elsie came to find me in the bathroom as I was stripping off my gear. She looked worried. "Annie? Are you okay?"

"I'm frustrated, I'm irritated, and I'm not going to skate tonight, so no, I'm not going to the after party," I snapped, shoving my kneepads into my bag. "What about you?"

"Um, I'm going to drive you home, and then I'm meeting up with Carly for a little private time. The blocker who fell down, Hailey Mary? She used to skate for the Concussion Stand, and Carly's really shaken up about it."

I blinked, cheeks going red. Elsie wasn't even a skater, and she knew more about what was going on in my league than I did. "Oh, hell, I didn't even think of that. I can find my own way home if that would work better for you..."

"I can drive her home," said an unfamiliar voice from behind us. We turned to see Adrienne standing in the bathroom doorway, her helmet held against her hip and a small smirk on her face. She looked faintly amused, like everything was a play being put on just for her. "I've got to get up early tomorrow, and giving someone else a ride is a great excuse for missing the party."

"I don't think—" began Elsie.

"That's so great of you, thank you so much," I said, cutting my cousin off before she could refuse Adrienne's offer on my behalf. "We haven't even been introduced yet, have we?"

"Not really, but I've seen you around. I'm Ivana Cutya. You're Final Girl, right? You're on the Slasher Chicks. Pretty cocky name if you ask me. Are you that sure you'd be the one to survive if we all wound up in a horror movie?"

"I'm sure," I said. "Good catch, though. Most people think my name just means I'm the last one to stop skating."

Adrienne snorted amusement. "On a team with a horror movie theme? Yeah, right. Most people are morons. Anyway, one of your teammates told me you lived somewhere out east. That's the way I'm going, so I'm happy to take you."

"Cool. Let me get my stuff."

Elsie's hand clamped down over my wrist as I reached for my bag. She pulled me close, smiling sweetly as she said, "It's really no trouble. I think it's best if I drive my cousin home."

"No, *really*, Elsie." I pulled myself free, smiling back as I willed her to understand what I was going for. "Carly needs you, and it'll be good for me and Ivana to get to know each other a little better."

"Know thy enemy," said Adrienne.

I glanced back at her. "Yeah," I said, after a momentary pause. "Exactly what I was thinking."

Adrienne was a good driver: calm, confident, and unhurried. She broke the speed limit on every street we drove down—she was a derby girl, after all—but she stopped for red lights and never did anything I could interpret as dangerous. The GPS on her dash spat out periodic directions that would lead us to the house of an old classmate of mine who lived three miles from my parents' house, as the crow flies. It was a small ruse, but enough that I didn't feel bad about potentially leading a predator home.

We were most of the way there when Adrienne said, "I saw you watching me during the match today. You want to tell me what that was all about, or should I guess?"

"Sorry. Your hair it's just so...white. How do you manage that without bleach-frying it into straw?"

To my surprise, she laughed. "Oh, please. 'Your hair is so white'? This is derby. I think you're the only girl with undyed hair that I've seen in the last week."

Stung, I reached up and touched one reddish-brown braid. "I henna," I said.

"Henna is not the same as dye, little girl, just like temporary tattoos are not the same as real ink, and bravado is not the same as bravery. Why were you really staring at me?"

"I remembered you from the match last month. The one where a Bad News Bear got hurt."

"Ah, so we start telling the truth." Adrienne turned down a side street. "I'm the new girl, so I'm a good place to point the finger. They talk about you, you know. Unfriendly, stand-offish, but always so ready to tell tales out of school. I'm on to you, Final Girl. You think you can survive the horror movie by refusing to drink, smoke, or fool around with boys. Well, you can't. Not if you decide to fuck around with monsters instead."

"What are you—"

She slammed her foot down on the brakes. I jerked forward against my seatbelt, gasping at the impact. "Get out of my car."

"*What?*"

"You stared at me. It was rude and it made me uncomfortable." Adrienne's expression was unreadable in the dim cabin light. "Now I'm throwing you out of my car in the woods at night, which is rude, and should make you uncomfortable. You're not a threat, Final Girl, and we're even. Get out."

"...Right." I got out. Quickly, since I was more than a little afraid she'd start the car while I only had one foot on the pavement. Hugging my bag to my chest, I slammed the door. She hit the gas, and roared off down the road, vanishing into the trees. "What a bitch," I said wonderingly.

Somewhere in the dark, an owl hooted loudly. I sighed and slung my bag over my shoulder before turning to start the four-mile trek home. At least I wasn't much further than I'd planned to be. If Adrienne had been trying to scare me, she'd failed. But she'd told me one thing for sure:

Whatever she was, she was afraid of me.

I dialed Elmira's number at the crack of noon the next day, which was the earliest I figured she'd be out of bed and ready to deal with derby questions. "Hello?" she said, sounding faintly muzzy, like she'd just woken from a deep sleep.

Oh, well. Too late to avoid waking her now. "It's Annie Thompson—Final Girl. Do you have a second?"

"Oh my God, Annie, what *time* is it?"

"Noon."

She groaned. "You're a morning person, aren't you? I thought morning people were banned from roller derby."

"Technically, the morning ended when the clock struck twelve."

"Yeah, but you were awake to make the call." There was a rustling sound from the other end of the phone. "God, my mouth tastes like the wrong end of a cat."

"There's a right end?"

"Don't quip at me, it's fucking noon. Talk fast, Thompson, or I'm finding an excuse to kick you off the team."

"It's about Regionals."

There was a pause before she said, sounding much more awake now, "You want to know if last night's cancellation means you're not going to make the All-Star team. That's why you're calling me first thing in the morning."

"Um. Yeah."

"Fuck. Couldn't you have waited until I was awake?"

"I'm sorry, but no. It's really important that I make the team." The league Adrienne skated for had already posted their roster. She was jamming for them at Regionals, and that meant it was vital that I not only be there, but I be on my skates.

"*Every* derby girl thinks it's important that she make the team. *Every* skater wants an excuse to put on her skates one more time. *None* of them think it's important enough to call me while I'm still in bed."

Shit. "In my defense, most people are awake at noon."

"Well, I'm not." Elmira sighed. "Last night's cancellation will have no impact on your overall stats, okay? You have exactly as much of a shot as you did before Hailey Mary ate track."

"Is it a good shot?"

"Why do you care?" Now Elmira sounded suspicious. "You didn't care this much last year. I'm pretty sure you fucked up a few times on purpose so you *wouldn't* make the All-Stars. What aren't you telling me?"

I hesitated. Finally, I said, "There are some things I can't discuss. But it's important I be able to keep an eye on things, and that means I need to be on the All-Star team. That's what's going to keep me in the best position to help out."

"Is this about the girls who've been blacking out during play?"

I didn't say anything.

"I'm going to take that as a yes. Look, Annie, I don't know what your deal is—nobody knows what your deal is. You're a good skater, and you're about as friendly as a wolverine in a box."

"Has the box been shaken?" I ventured, trying to make a joke.

"Yes," said Elmira, without amusement. I wilted. She continued, "But that's not the important part. I've seen you with Meggie, and with Princess Leya, and with the other skaters who are...special. I'm pretty sure that whatever your deal is, it's about helping those girls cope with their...difabilities."

"Like different abilities," I said. "Nice portmanteau."

"We're just going to ignore the part where normal people don't use the word 'portmanteau' in conversation, and you're going to answer a question for me. You're going to answer it honestly, or I'm hanging up, and I won't take any more calls from this number. Do we have a deal?"

"Yes," I said reluctantly.

"Are you trying to make the All-Star team this year because you want to protect us from whatever's causing the accidents?"

"Yes," I repeated, more firmly this time. Protection was familiar ground, even if discussing it with the captain of my roller derby team wasn't.

"All right. I'll keep that in mind when I put in my recommendations. Don't fuck it up, Thompson, or I'm going to figure out who got left off the roster to make room for you, and then I'm going to help her kick your ass."

"Aye-aye, Captain."

"Fuck you," she said, and hung up on me.

A roller derby All-Star team is sort of like one of those Capcom fighting games, the ones where characters from all different franchises would come together to kick each other's asses. Each league fields an All-Star team made up of the best skaters from that league's teams. In the case of the Silver Screams, that meant that our All-Stars would be drawing from the Slasher Chicks, the Concussion Stand, the Block Busters, and the Stunt Troubles. A normal derby team will have between ten and twenty players, with five of them taking the floor during each jam. The All-Star team for our league was hard-capped at twenty. No matter how you cut it, for some of us, the skating season was over.

Practice was called as normal. Elsie dropped me off out front, and I walked inside the warehouse only to be promptly grabbed in a headlock by Carlotta. I managed, barely, to restrain the urge to grab and break her wrists.

"There's the bitch of the hour!" she crowed. "How's it feel to be hated and envied by your peers?"

"Like I can't breathe," I said, making a show of ineffectually shoving her off. Carlotta didn't budge. I wasn't really trying. "Let go. This isn't funny."

"Wow, your life is tragedy. Your cousin got the looks *and* the sense of humor." Carlotta released me. "The All-Stars roster is up."

I straightened, blinking at her. "It is? And?"

"And you're one of the four jammers to make the team. Congratulations." Then she grinned and punched me in the arm. "I may even stop most of the opposing players from turning you into a thin stain on the floor."

"You're on the team?"

"Co-captain and blocker bitch extraordinaire for the third year in a row." Carlotta put two fingers in her mouth and whistled shrilly. Heads turned our way. She beckoned them over. "Come on, girls! Say hello to your new teammate!"

Girls from all four teams in our league—including, I was relieved to see, Fern and Marnie—swarmed around me, laughing, while Carlotta raced off to intercept another All-Star who had just come unwittingly through the front door. Fern flung her arms around my neck in a hug that was substantially friendlier than Carlotta's chokehold. I laughed and hugged her back.

It's nice to be a part of something. That's what derby's really all about: finding a place where you can be a part of something. And I tried to hold fast to that thought as our captains—Elmira and Carlotta, because what every hard-ass needs is someone even harder—put us through the most grueling practice I had ever experienced in my life. After an hour on the floor, I was ready to die. After two hours, I was ready to kill. After three hours, I was ready to die again, but I was too tired to be sure I'd do it correctly.

The whistle blew to mark the end of our session. I collapsed onto the mats, panting and staring up at the ceiling. Elmira skated into view, smiling sweetly.

"A little tired, Thompson?" she asked.

"I hate you," I replied.

"Same to you, perky girl," she said, and skated away. "Remember, you asked for this."

I groaned as I rolled into an upright position. Inwardly, I was rejoicing. I had what I wanted: I was on the All-Stars. I was going to skate against Adrienne, and she was going to learn what it *really* meant to be afraid of me.

Assuming I was capable of moving under my own power by then. Closing my eyes, I lay flat on my back and waited for the feeling to come back into my feet.

The weeks between the roster going up and the final matches of the season dissolved like sugar in hot water, wisping away into nothing but cloudy memories and the smell of topical muscle relaxants. Elsie and Carlotta broke up, got back together, broke up again, and got back together again. My father sat me down for a talk about priorities after I skipped my third hunting trip in a row due to practice-related exhaustion.

"It's okay, Daddy," I said. "The season's almost over. I just need to make it through the last game without eating track, figure out what the hell this Adrienne girl is and what she's doing to the other players, neutralize her, and hang up my skates until the next season starts."

"Even so, it's taking up a lot of time," he said.

"Think of it as a hunt—I wouldn't have gone out for the All-Stars if I wasn't chasing a potential danger. So now I'm hunting."

My father raised an eyebrow. "You know, hunting normally doesn't involve quite this much blunt force trauma."

"That's because you're doing it wrong."

That seemed to close the discussion: he agreed that I would be allowed to resolve the Adrienne situation as I saw fit, made me promise to help him randomize the traps in the woods around the house, and let me get back to work.

Artie and I spoke daily during the run-up to Regionals, referencing and cross-referencing as we tried to figure out what Adrienne could possibly be. Finally, the night before the match was set to begin, he said, "We're down to four possibilities. She's a previously unknown form of gorgon who can stun with her gaze but doesn't need to wear glasses to avoid doing it—"

"A step below the lesser gorgon? That seems pretty unlikely."

"I know, but it fits the symptoms, if we assume that it would be a power reduction comparable to what's seen between the lesser gorgon and the Pliny's gorgon."

"Possible, not probable," I allowed. "Next?"

"Succubus."

"Wouldn't Elsie have noticed her?"

"Succubi notice incubi, incubi notice succubi. We don't notice each other." He sounded deeply uncomfortable taking the conversation onto such potentially personal ground. "Elsie always knows when Dad gets home, but I never do."

"This is one more reason you should come down to Portland for tomorrow's match. You'd be able to spot immediately if she's a succubus."

"And if she wasn't, I'd be packed into a warehouse full of excited, sweaty girls, many of whom have been drinking." I could actually hear Artie's full-body shudder through the Skype connection. "No, thank you. There are much more pleasant ways for me to die."

"You're going to have to deal with girls again someday, Artie. If nothing else, Emerald City Comicon. You know it contains females."

"Yes, but those are familiar girls. They're girls I know how to avoid."

I sighed. "Right. So succubus is still on the table—what's our third option?"

"She could be a mara."

The word was vaguely familiar. I paused, dredging through the recesses of my memory as I tried to find a set of characteristics to go with the name. Finally, I ventured, "Aren't mara another form of succubus?"

"Closely related, but not quite the same. I'm sending you over the file on them now. They come in both male and female varieties, and their victims are generally assumed to have dropped from 'exhaustion.' The symptoms sound a lot like what you've been seeing in the affected players."

"That's not good." My computer beeped as Artie's email arrived. I opened the attachment and started skimming. A line in the first paragraph caught my eye. "Wait—they feed on the life energy of their victims? That's not very neighborly."

"No, and they *are* succubi in the sense that they need intelligent food or it isn't very nourishing or filling. They tend to go after sapient species, but that's about it. Mara aren't picky eaters."

"Can this get any more charming?"

"A mara who's fed recently can project bad dreams onto her enemies, and can even use that as a way to increase the 'volume' of available food, since fear makes people produce more immediately accessible life energy."

I eyed the computer. "I hate you. You make this shit up just to hurt me."

"Blame evolution. I'm just the messenger."

"I do blame evolution. Every morning I get out of bed and say 'how can evolution fuck me over today,' and every day, evolution finds a way. What's our fourth option?"

"Something we've never heard of before."

"...wow. Way to look on the bright side." I glanced at the clock next to my bed. "Hell, it's almost midnight. You *sure* I can't convince you to come to the match, Artie? You'll enjoy it. It's Regionals."

"Every time you say that, I picture the kids from *Glee*," said Artie. "I'm sure you'll have a wonderful time slamming into your enemies and fighting the good fight, but I'm going to have to decline. Dropping an incubus into a roller derby arena strikes me as one of those things that gets included in your obituary."

"Live fast, die young, leave a good-looking corpse?"

"No, thanks."

I laughed. "Good night, Artie."

"Good night, Annie."

I was still laughing as I climbed into bed, turned off the light, and tried to convince my over-taxed brain that the best thing it could do was let me sleep. My brain wasn't listening. That was nothing new. Eventually, soothed by the steady creep-creep-creep of the frickens outside my window, I slipped into unconsciousness.

"Welcome to the Pacific Northwest Women's Flat Track Roller Derby Association Regional Semi-Finals!" shrieked the announcer, a skinny little man who looked like a cross between Walt Disney and Grandpa Munster. He was mugging for the microphone like he was on stage at Madison Square Garden, not standing on a raised platform near the edge of a makeshift roller rink. I had to respect his dedication to his art, even as I questioned its value. "Are you ready to *roller derby*?!"

The crowd shrieked approval, indicating that it was, in fact, ready to roller derby.

Carlotta and Elmira had pulled us all off to the side as we arrived, and were reviewing the day's assigned matches with us. "We're skating third," said Elmira. "Who we're skating against is yet to be determined, but we're going to kick their asses and skate all the way to the final round. Who's with me?"

General cheering and a few middle fingers greeted this inspiring speech. I yawned, covering my mouth with the back of my hand.

"Tired, Thompson?" asked Elmira.

"Tired of standing around not getting any skating done," I said.

"Then go sit your butt down," she said. "It's going to be a while."

The whole team took that as an invitation to scatter. Some moved toward the concessions and vendors that took up the front half of the warehouse where we were holding Regionals. Others went to sit amidst the sea of roller girls that ringed the track, avidly watching the skaters who were starting to circle. I scanned the bleachers until I spotted Elsie, holding down a prime piece of real estate in the very front row. Motioning for Fern to follow me, I skated over and plopped down beside her.

"Did you remember to grab breakfast before we left the house?" I asked. "I'm starving."

Gravely, she produced a foil-wrapped packet of bacon from inside her purse and handed it to me.

"You are my absolute favorite cousin with bright red hair," I said, pulling out a piece of bacon and munching it as I considered her new dye job. Finally I ventured, "Showing team colors?"

"That, and I figure I may as well come pre-dressed for a blood bath." Elsie grinned. She was wearing a Silver Screams league T-shirt, a denim miniskirt, and fishnet stockings that were practically predestined to wind up discarded on the floor of Carlotta's apartment. "What's the plan?"

"Sit, watch, wait," I said. "The Poisonous Garden—that's the league the Rose Petals belong to—will be skating in the second round, and if they win, they advance. Assuming they keep winning their brackets, and we keep winning ours, we should get to skate against them in round six, around seven o'clock tonight."

Elsie blinked. "That's seven hours from now."

"You can do math." I withdrew another piece of bacon. "For now, we watch."

The first round match involved teams from two leagues I wasn't particularly familiar with. Their fans were enthusiastic, whooping and hollering until one of the teams skated their way to victory. No one collapsed on the track. I looked around the stands, but I didn't see Adrienne. That made sense: her team was one of the next up. She was probably off with her coach and teammates, getting a few last-minute instructions before the game.

You're lucky, I thought, as the winning team took their ceremonial lap around the track, slapping palms with the waiting spectators. The thought was directed to the losing team as well. None of them had been drained and discarded by a potential mara. That was a win in my book.

We finished the bacon. Carlotta joined us, bringing gluten-free vegan cupcakes from one of the vendors. I didn't complain. Never look a gift cupcake in the mouth. Elsie snuggled up to Carlotta. I leaned forward, waiting for the next bout to begin.

It wasn't a long wait. The Poisonous Garden took the track, amidst cheers and boos from the stands. Their opponents, the Beaverton Honeys, got the same reception. I tensed a little as the Honeys skated out. The Bad Idea Bears belonged to the Beaverton Honeys, and the jammer who'd collapsed during the Bears' solo bout against the Rose Petals was part of the pack. If mara liked targeting the same snacks more than once, that girl could be in serious danger.

Adrienne skated with the rest, a vision in her green-on-green uniform. She was smiling. And she looked hungry.

The whistle blew. The bout began.

I won't bore you with a blow-by-blow—describing every play of a roller derby match is like describing every random monster encounter in a game of D&D. It's fascinating if you're into that sort of thing, and deadly dull if you're not. The first interesting thing happened during the second jam, when I saw Adrienne intentionally bleed off momentum during her jam in order to "accidentally" brush her fingers against the wrist of a blocker from the opposing team. She recovered speed quickly, but the damage had been done; the lead jammer called off the jam, and the Poisoned Garden came away without any additional points.

"Did you see that?" I murmured to Elsie.

"Could've been an accident," she said.

"And I could've been a kindergarten teacher, but I'm not, and neither was that."

Carlotta gave us a curious look. I smiled wanly and turned my attention back to the floor.

A new jam was beginning. It started normally, with the jammers trying to fight their way through the pack and claim the lead. The jammer for the Beaverton Honeys was the first to break free. Adrienne followed at an almost leisurely pace, seeming to put no effort into taking the lead. The pack pursued them, maneuvering to cut off avenues and force the jammers into undesirable positions.

All except for that one blocker from the Beaverton Honeys, who was falling behind the rest of the pack. She was still skating, but she looked confused, like she no longer knew where she was. One of the referees blew the whistle, and the blocker was escorted off the track for medical reasons. She was barely standing up on her own when they got her to the chairs, and once seated, she collapsed forward, head between her knees.

I glanced at the track. Adrienne was standing amidst the crowd of confused, concerned girls with her eyes closed, a serene expression on her face.

"That *bitch*," I hissed.

Carlotta followed my gaze. "What?"

"I—" I stopped, shaking my head. "Nothing. Ignore me."

"I've been ignoring her for years," said Elsie.

That seemed to be enough for Carlotta, who shook it off and went back to watching the game. I leaned forward, elbows on my knees, and waited. *Soon*, I thought. *I'm taking you down.*

The bout continued.

The Poisoned Garden beat the Beaverton Honeys with no further mysterious accidents. The Silver Screams beat the Coastal Cruisers, meaning that both leagues moved on. We'd be skating against each other that night.

I borrowed Elsie's keys before I snuck out behind the warehouse, pulling my phone out of my bag, and dialed the house. My mother picked up on the second ring, with a cheerful, "We don't want any."

"Mom, how do I stop a mara?"

"Aconite and unicorn water, same as a succubus," said Mom, without hesitation. "Why? Is it a mara that's been hurting your little roller derby friends?"

"I'm not in third grade anymore, Mom," I said, scowling at the phone. "But yes, I'm pretty sure that it's a mara. She hasn't killed anyone, and I don't feel like killing her, but she has a pattern of hunting derby girls, and I need her to stop." Mara might have to feed on humans to survive. That didn't mean she needed to be going after people who were on roller skates and had the potential to be seriously injured if they collapsed.

Sometimes being a cryptozoologist means admitting that monsters have a right to exist, no matter how much you might disapprove of them. From there, it's just a matter of minimizing the damage that they can do.

"Well, you just be careful. Mara aren't very fond of being stopped when they're feeding."

"Is anyone? I've seen what happens when you come between Dad and a cheesecake."

She laughed. "Do you need any supplies, or are you set?"

"I brought my kit," I said, and started walking toward Elsie's car. I had at least an hour before I'd need to be on the track again—longer if Adrienne decided to munch on someone else and slow down the course of play. "I'll call if I need backup."

"Okay, honey. Don't stay out too late."

"I'll be home by dawn." I hung up, dropping the phone into my bag before unlocking and opening Elsie's trunk. Aconite and unicorn water wasn't a difficult blend to put together, especially since—if mara worked like succubi—I didn't need to worry overmuch about the ratios. I just needed to dump a bunch of aconite essential oil into a spray-top perfume bottle full of unicorn water and I was good to go.

No one noticed me as I slammed the trunk, tucked the bottle into my bag, and walked back to the warehouse. I kept my head down, watching for signs that I was being followed, until I had rejoined Elsie and the others in the stands. Fern was gone, replaced by Leya; Carlotta was still there, her head resting comfortably against Elsie's shoulder.

Elsie caught my eye. "Well?" she mouthed.

"Aconite," I mouthed back, exaggeratedly.

She wrinkled her nose and inched away from me, causing Carlotta to grumble. Aconite has a weirdly sedative effect on succubi and their relations. It blocks their powers, which can be good, but it also makes it hard for them to resist suggestions, which can be bad, especially if you're the succubus in question.

I shrugged in sympathy and turned back to the track, where two more leagues were duking it out for the right to progress one more slot in the rankings. I leaned forward, making myself comfortable, and for a little while, I forgot about anything but the sport that had brought me to this old warehouse filled with laughter and the sound of wheels endlessly circling the track.

During the halftime between round five and round six, Carlotta and Elmira gathered the members of the Silver Screams into a huddle, assigning our positions for the first jam. I was going to be the opening jammer; Elmira would take second jam, and so on, until one of us needed a break. That's when Leya would take her turn. Our blockers were set, and we had a decent idea of our overall strategy — all of which would go to hell the second we hit the track, because that's the nature of the game.

"Everybody know what they're doing?" demanded Carlotta.

"*No!*" chorused the rest of us, in gleeful unison.

"Good. So what are we going to do?"

"*Let's drink some beer!*" we all shouted.

"What else?"

"*Let's smoke some pot!*" Everyone in the nearby stands was shouting with us now, even the people who weren't necessarily fans. It's hard to resist that kind of battle cry.

"I can't hear you!"

"*Let's have premarital sex! I love premarital sex!*"

"Then let's win this!"

Whooping and cheering, the members of the Silver Screams swarmed the floor, joining the throng of Poisoned Garden skaters who were already circling. I scanned the pack as I skated through, finally spotting Adrienne on the other side of the track. I smiled sweetly at her. She sneered and sped up, moving out of my line of vision.

"This is going to be a fun, fun game," I muttered to myself, and focused on warming up.

I was just settling into my groove when the whistle blew to mark the end of halftime. We all skated to our side of the "bench," plastic chairs set up for the players to use when they weren't on the track. All around me, girls double-checked their safety equipment, put in their mouthguards, and adjusted their helmets, looking for all the world like they were going to war.

"How's my arterial spray? I was trying for a sort of 'sexy slasher victim' look."

Exactly like they were going to war. "It looks good," I said to the skater who'd asked, and pulled the perfume bottle out of my bag, spraying the contents liberally all over myself. A few players glanced my way, but shrugged and dismissed whatever I was doing without asking about it. The aconite didn't have a strong smell, and there's nothing in the rules against being damp at the start of play. Portland wouldn't have any roller derby at all if we required players to be dry.

The whistle blew. We took the track, and I was unsurprised to see Adrienne—Ivana Cutya now that we were in play—lined up next to me, crouched in the starting position. The whistle blew again, and the jam began.

Ivana took an early lead, forcing her way into our assembled blockers with a surprising ease—at least until she ran up against the unexpectedly solid obstacle that was Meggie Itwasthewind. Nobody moves a sylph who doesn't want to be moved, and by the time Ivana broke free, I was through the pack and accelerating, well on the way to establishing my position as the lead jammer.

"Final Girl leads the jam!" crowed the announcer. I put my head down, shutting him out along with all other distractions, and focused on my dual goals for this jam: scoring points for my team, and catching Ivana before she could start draining anyone.

Being the lead jammer meant that only I could stop the jam, but it also meant that I was starting out ahead of Ivana, and it would be suspicious if I dropped back to catch up with her. I put my head down and skated like I'd never skated before, until my thighs and ankles were burning and the people in the stands were just blurs. The Poisoned Garden blockers tried to grab me, but I was fast, determined, and willing to do whatever it took to catch up to Ivana without drawing attention to myself.

An illegal hip-check sent me flying out of the bounds of the track. I silently thanked the gods of derby as the offending player was escorted to the penalty box and I skated back into position. Ivana had taken advantage of my temporary loss of momentum, and was almost level with my position. I sped up, but not as fast as I could have, and let her draw up even with me. It was easy to "stumble" as I brought my hands to my hips, ending the jam just as my bare skin collided with hers.

The look on her face was worth all the crap I was going to be taking from my teammates over my clumsiness. I smiled sweetly, spitting out my mouthguard.

"What's the matter, Ivana?" I asked. "Don't you like my perfume?"

"You little—"

The whistle cut her off as the referees called us into position for the next jam. I took a seat on the sidelines while Elmira Street took my place on the track. Ivana had also been rotated out, for a jammer I didn't know. She glared at me from her seat. I kept on smiling.

That smile stayed on my face all the way through the first half of the match, even when a badly-timed block sent me sprawling into the guard rails. I'd have a bruise down my side for the next week. That didn't matter. I just kept skating, taking every opportunity to brush my aconite-coated body against Ivana. It was almost like a game, but the cost of losing would be high. There was no telling what a pissed-off mara would do to me if I gave her the opportunity.

The whistle blew for halftime. Laughing and groaning, the players scattered, heading for their seats, for the restrooms—and, in the case of one white-haired mara, for the back door of the warehouse.

"Oh no you don't," I muttered, grabbing my bag off the chair where I'd left it. I waved to Elsie, making sure she saw me, and skated after Adrienne.

The warehouse backed up on a vacant lot. It was the sort of weedy, unkempt place that always seemed to show up in low-budget horror movies. The sun had set while we were skating, and the moonlight glittered off the broken glass scattered through the weeds.

Adrienne was waiting for me. I would have been disappointed if she hadn't been.

"What the fuck do you think you're doing?" she demanded.

"Playing roller derby," I replied. "Fairly, without using preternatural powers to disable my opponents, I might add. That's dirty pool."

"What?" She blinked, and then she laughed. "The aconite wasn't an accident, was it? You're targeting me."

"Only because you're targeting roller girls," I shot back.

Adrienne shrugged. "A girl's got to eat. What do you care, anyway? I haven't gone after you. You're too sour to be worth eating."

"You said I wasn't a threat. Maybe I just wanted to prove you wrong."

"You haven't proven a damn thing."

"Haven't I?" I skated closer. She backed away. No matter how much bravado she was projecting, she didn't want to risk more aconite touching her skin. "I know what you are, mara, and I want you to stop preying on derby girls. I know you have to eat. I know you serve a purpose. But draining people who are skating at stupid speeds around a closed track is just plain malicious. Someone's going to get hurt."

"I like roller derby," she said. "I like winning. So what if I make it a little easier on myself every once in a while? There's no law against draining the energy of your opponents. I've read the whole derby handbook, and that is nowhere in there."

"Then maybe it's time for an amendment," said a familiar voice. I glanced back. Elmira was behind me next to Elsie and half a dozen cryptid skaters were lined up behind them. Some of them I knew personally; others I knew in passing, from my casual "okay, yeah, that girl there's a..." record-keeping. None of them looked amused.

Elmira's presence was a surprise that I could deal with later. I looked back to Adrienne. "Looks like you're in the minority here."

"You did this?" The speaker skated forward to stand beside me. It was Trisk, the captain of the Rose Petals. She looked profoundly disappointed, like a little girl who'd just learned that there was no Santa Claus. "Ivana, how could you?"

"Like you're one to talk," Adrienne snapped back. "You eat luck."

"I eat *bad* luck," said Trisk. "And I never eat anything while we're skating. That's dangerous. What you've been doing is dangerous."

"It has to stop," I said. "You can either stop it on your own, or—"

"Or what?" sneered Adrienne. "You'll kill me?"

"I can't kill you. You haven't killed anyone, and you haven't received a warning." My family's code for killing sapient cryptids is strict, and it makes no exceptions. If your life isn't in danger, you don't kill unless the individual in question has already knowingly killed members of a sapient race, and even then, you have to give a warning first. Anything to show that we're not trying to play judge, jury, and executioner to the entire cryptid community.

"So basically, you can't do anything," said Adrienne.

"Yes, we can," said Trisk. "You're off the team, Ivana, and when I turn in my reasons for booting you, I'm going to make it clear that you have exhibited behaviors unbefitting a derby girl."

"I'll back her up," said Elmira. A murmur went around the other girls as each of them agreed to turn in their own complaints.

I shrugged. "Looks like you're going to wind up banned from flat track derby. You'll need to find another hunting ground. And I'll be watching you."

"*You'll* be watching *me*?" snarled Adrienne. "Oh, you stupid little bitch, you have no idea what you've just done." She lunged for me, hands hooked into claws—

—only to hit the ground hard as Fern barreled into her. From the impact, I guessed that the fast-moving sylph had increased her own density as far as it would go just before she slammed into the mara. I winced.

"That had to hurt."

Adrienne made a choking noise, clutching her stomach. "Who do you think you are?" she wheezed.

"Oh, that's easy." I pulled the perfume bottle out of my bag, dumping the last of the aconite and unicorn water mixture directly onto Adrienne's chest. She sneezed and glared. I smiled. "I'm the Final Girl."

With that I turned and skated back inside. Everyone else followed, except for Adrienne. That was fine with me. She wasn't my concern anymore.

We won, by the way. But that was never really the point, now was it?

A Hollow Play

Amal El-Mohtar

Dear Paige,

I'm heading out of the flat tonight, for once, since Anna invited me out to a cabaret thing. Funny how it happened—for weeks she's been casually asking what I'm doing after work, but never following up after I say some variation on "derby practice" or "watching cartoons." I guess it's taken her until now to decide I'm someone she'd actually choose to hang out with in her free time. That should make me feel good, right? But I'm actually terrified. Because it's been so long since—I don't know, since I've had a friend? That sounds horrible. And it's probably not true, if I sit and think about it properly. What I mean is, since I've had a friend the way I had friends in Canada. When it was easy, you know? When I could click with someone and just feel this trust, this knowledge that we both liked each other equally and in the same way, when I could take for granted that I could say things and have them be understood. Like with you. It feels like forever since I've had that. A year, at least.

So anyway, I feel like I might have that with Anna—but we're always at work, and all the conversations we have are sandwiched between people ordering flat whites and the occasional biscuit. When it gets quiet, though, sometimes we really talk, about serious things, heart things. I've told her a bit about you. She told me she's trans—which isn't a secret, it's okay that I'm telling you—and we talked about how basically we're both always coming out, we can never be wholly done coming out.

I guess I'm terrified of messing this up somehow. Being boring. Not being into the show that she's really excited about. Being—yeah, okay, being an obnoxious North American in the company of British people, even though Glasgow's about a million times better than London for not making me feel that way.

Right, it's time to go. I'll write more later.

Love,
Emily

Emily stood in the doorway to the Rio Cafe and looked around, half-convinced she had the wrong place. The word "cabaret" had conjured up visions of illicit underground doings populated by white-faced pianists in dark, shabby suits, coaxing notes of tragic joy from their instruments. But this was just a really nice pub, full of comfortable, brightly coloured wooden booths perpendicular to a long bar. There were some smaller tables and chairs to the right and back of it, blackboards with specials written on them, and nothing that looked like it could be turned into a stage.

Make sure you get there early, Anna had said, *it fills up fast.* Emily shrugged, manoeuvred her way to one of the small tables toward the back, pulled a pen and a leather-bound journal from her bag, and resumed writing.

Dear Paige,

So, I'm here, but Anna's not , and I awesomely left Memoirs of a Spacewoman *at home in spite of knowing I'd have two hours to kill, so I figure I'll just keep writing to you.*

Cabaret! I have no idea what to expect. Have you ever been to a cabaret show? I wasn't sure how to dress for it either—when I asked Anna she just laughed and told me to use my imagination—so I'm wearing the red top you gave me, the button-down one with the sleeves that flare out and curl from the elbows. I can't believe I still have it—it's been, what, ten years, three moves? It's not fitting so great now—since I started taking derby more seriously (I'm EMILY THE SLAYER now! Strong like Buffy!), my arms have gotten huge, and you should see the butt on me—but it's still pretty and I love it, and it still matches my favourite earrings best.

I should probably tell you more about Anna, since obviously there's more to her than being trans and my co-worker. She's really great, and really cute—she just cut her hair short last week and dyed it bright orange-red, so she looks kind of like Leeloo from The Fifth Element. *She's vegan (sometimes I swear she likes the fact that I'm not, because it gives her an excuse to play "Meat is Murder" on loop in the cafe for the duration of my lunch break, which no one notices, because it sounds like every other Smiths song except the good ones, which she refuses to accept no matter how many times I explain it), an amazing cosplayer, and getting into burlesque. She hasn't performed in public yet, just for friends in her living room, but she's been developing this number that involves a chef's hat, mixed greens, and oversized serving implements.*

We're not dating or anything. I've only known her for about a month, though it feels like way longer — and I refuse to entertain a crush, because she's been in a closed poly triad for a while and they're kind of going through a rough patch that she hasn't told me much about. So I'll tell you more about this cabaret thing instead.

It's called SPANGLED CABARET ("spangled" is apparently one of about a million words that also means "wildly drunk" in the west of Scotland) and it happens once a month in this cafe, and Anna's been coming to it forever, basically. She really wants to perform here sometime once she feels confident enough.

It's also where she met her partners, Lynette and Kel. Kel's genderqueer and prefers "they" as a pronoun, so I'll try to keep this from getting confusing: they work nights at the airport, but Lynette's a performer, whose stage name is Lynette Byrd; her thing is apparently to dress up like a bird and sing?

Oh, she's just coming in. I'll write more later.

Love,
Emily

"Ooh, well done," said Anna, grinning, hooking her jacket over a chair. "These are the best seats in the house. Can I get you a drink?"

"The finest wines available to humanity," Emily declared, capping her pen and shutting the journal. She smiled up at her. "Something red?"

"Will do."

Emily watched her head to the bar. Anna, as usual, looked amazing, in a turquoise chiffon dress with ruffles at the neckline waving their way asymmetrically down the front, cinched at the waist with an orange belt that matched her hair.

She was also alone. When Anna returned with their drinks, Emily asked, "So, where's Lynette?"

"Oh, she can only hang out after her act. Something about 'diluting the effect'—" Anna made air quotes and rolled her eyes, "—if she mingles with people beforehand. I hope that's okay—I thought we could have a little more time to talk before launching you into poly drama."

Emily chuckled. "That's fine. It's really cool to see you outside of work. You look awesome."

Anna grinned and tossed her short hair back dramatically. "Why thank you. So do you. That's a great blouse."

Emily blushed, looking down at her shirt. "Thanks, it was a gift—"

"It's very Romantic! Poet sleeves, fountain pen, leather-bound journal—excellent ensemble, though of course leather's murder too." Anna's smile was teasing. "It's beautiful, though. Where'd you find it?"

"Oh," she said, blushing hotter. "It was also a gift. From the same person. My best friend. The one I mentioned, Paige." She paused, uncertain how much more to say. "I write to her in it."

Anna blinked. "What?"

"You know, instead of letters. We each have one, and we write to each other in them whenever the mood takes us, and when they get full, or half full, we post them to each other. We've been doing it for years—ever since she moved out west." She dropped it into her bag again, zipped it shut.

"That's so cool." Anna grinned. "You've actually found a way to make snail mail slower."

"Shut up! Not all of us want to have our phones embedded in our palms."

"Lies and trickery. You, too, lust for the Singularity in your heart of hearts."

"Those aren't even the same thing!"

The wine was good, the conversation easy. Emily felt herself relaxing, becoming aware of how little effort she was making, how unnecessary it felt to play at being wry and unaffected and vaguely disdainful of anything she passionately loved. By the time the lights dimmed and a tall man in red spats and cerulean trousers announced the beginning of the show, she was feeling excited.

The first act was a startling realisation of Emily's earlier expectations, as a short bearded man unfolded a keyboard, flicked his

coat-tails behind him, and sat down to play something melancholi-
cally sinister while a young woman in layers of fringed and shimmering fabric, loops of large white beads, and a flapper's red head
scarf expertly drew a violin bow along the edge of a saw. The result
was equal parts mournful and uncanny.

"That," shouted Emily over the subsequent applause, "was
amazing. Is it all like this?"

Anna smiled. "Not quite."

The next act saw Emily covering her face while an attractive young
man hammered nails up his nose.

"Come on," chuckled Anna, "it's not that bad! It's mostly tricks,
anyway."

"Anna, he's *bleeding*! He stuck a needle up his arm and *drew blood*."

"He's a professional!"

"His hands are shaking! This can't be right!"

"It's just part of the whole blockhead routine, honest. I've watched
him do it loads of times."

"Really?" She dared a peek between her fingers, winced, and
covered her eyes again.

"Really. Well. Not the needle, I think that's new, but the nails are
standard. Oh, come on, you can't miss this, he's going to swallow those
razors and knot them together in his throat—"

"*Hey*, I need the loo and we should have more drinks. Same
again?"

"Sure, sure. Coward."

Emily stuck her tongue out and beat a hasty retreat.

It was equal parts the half-light, the show, and the wine, but the
Rio had clearly slipped somewhere just slant of real. Navigating the
distance between table and toilets felt like lucid dreaming. She
passed men with moon-white faces in bowler hats; she washed her
hands next to a woman in scarlet lingerie with mouse ears and a
cheese-grater crotch. It felt like a secret carnival, like a place a runa-
way could call home.

She sat down again just as the blockhead was taking a bow, thankfully none the worse for wear. Anna looked positively fond as Emily
pushed a new glass of wine toward her.

"You've got the look," Anna said, smiling.

"The look?"

"Of the hooked. The enchanted. You're one of us now."

"Just like that?" Emily looked dubious. "By running away from the blockhead?"

"It takes all sorts. I can't *wait* for you to see Lynette. She's usually on toward the end." Anna fiddled with a napkin. "She's...something else. I could go on and on about her and not be able to say how."

"Are things..." Emily hesitated. "I mean, is it okay if I ask..."

Anna shrugged. "Things are things. The weirdness is mainly between Kel and me, but obviously Lynette's involved too, she can't not be. But—I can't really talk about it, sorry."

"That's totally fine. I don't want to pry! I just don't know what to expect, at all."

Anna chuckled. "That's probably for the best."

Once the applause died down, the emcee stepped forward to announce the final act, and encouraged everyone to stay precisely where they were.

Then the lights went out.

The cafe buzzed for a minute until a spotlight clicked on, shining up from the floor, illuminating a woman seated on a tall stool. But not completely—shadows striped her face and body, and as Emily took the scene in, she saw that the spotlight was shining through an ornate bird cage, projecting its bars against the wall and woman together.

When Anna said Lynette would be dressed as a bird, Emily had imagined something a bit camp, a bit silly, maybe a bit sexy into the bargain. She hadn't expected this tall, solemn, slender creature of angles and air, delicate golden-brown feathers sprouting from the shoulders, hips, and hem of a long white dress worn over slightly incongruous brown boots. Thick dark curls were piled on top of her head, against which leaned a high, feathered fascinator. There was an air of honey and copper about her, a shimmering sweetness. Emily's breath caught at the sight.

Lynette Byrd lifted her chin and regarded her audience coolly, head sharply tilted. When she parted her glittering lips and spoke, her voice was a sweep of warm light in the dim.

"Green finch and linnet bird! Nightingale! Blackbird!"

"How is it you sing!" shouted the audience members as one, making Emily jump a little in her seat. Lynette smiled.

"An oft-repeated question. Why does the caged bird sing? Why does it not embrace silence in protest, refusing to give up the thing for which it was imprisoned? Why, day after day, does it warble and sway from perch to perch, trilling its essence out in unrepeatable sequence for the benefit of its captors? *I am trusted,*" she laughed, suddenly, a sound like glass bursting, *"with a muzzle and enfranchised with a clog; therefore I have decreed not to sing in my cage."*

With that she closed her eyes and leaned her cheek against the feathers on her shoulder, looking for all the world like a bird asleep.

Silence, then. Emily looked at Anna uncertainly, wondering if she should clap, but Anna was gazing at Lynette in rapt adoration. No one else seemed to think it was over, either. An uncomfortable minute passed, then two. A few people closed their eyes; a couple were staring intensely at their phones; one man nearby was moving his mouth without making a sound, and Emily realised he was counting. She looked back at the stage. Lynette remained completely immobile. The sound of the bartender wiping crumbs from the counter became noticeable. She heard people shifting a little in their seats, though none spoke.

Emily frowned and looked down at her own phone. Had it been four minutes? Four minutes of—

Her eyes widened in sudden understanding. Before she knew what she was doing, she had gasped "OH!" out loud, to the shock of just about everyone else in the room.

She clapped her hands over her mouth in a panic and looked at the stage, but Lynette hadn't moved—it was only every other head in the cafe that had swung toward her, some frowning, some biting down a laugh, some laughing outright. Anna stared at her in an astonishment that bordered on reproach. Cheeks flushing, she fixed her eyes on the floor and tried to will it into melting away and taking her with it.

But only for another thirty seconds, as Lynette's performance of John Cage's "4'33" came to an end. As people began to clap, Emily raised her head again.

Lynette had opened her eyes and was looking directly at her. She seemed amused.

"The reason, ultimately," she said, stretching her neck from one side to the other, and rolling back her feathered shoulders, "is that silence is terribly boring, no? Let us jubilate."

With that, Lynette launched into the most unearthly rendition of Sondheim's "Green Finch and Linnet Bird" Emily had ever heard. It was like sugar melting into caramel, hearing that bright, glittering song dimmed into a smoky minor key and twisted, stretched into so unlikely a shape. To listen was to feel her heart dragged over burrs, each turn of lyric snagging and pulling at her. By the time Lynette was asking the birds to teach her to be more adaptive, Emily had a pain in her throat and wet cheeks. Anna was quietly sobbing next to her.

Emily stretched out her hand without a word. Anna took it and squeezed.

It was like nothing else. She broke us open and read our entrails, I swear. It was like her art was a kind of sewing, a stitching together of things you'd never have thought could go together seamlessly. Hah. I just noticed how Seamstress is like a portmanteau of Seam and Mistress. Seam. Seem. Mistress of Seams and Seemings.

I'm pretty drunk right now by the way.

So she's a Seemstress. She ended the show with a flick of her wrist, throwing a black cloth over the birdcage, and the spotlight clicked off. She didn't take a bow. She's drinking with Anna, now, they're talking, and I'm hiding in the bathroom because I can't bring myself to look at her even though I really want to talk to her and tell her how amazing it was. She came toward us after, and she looked at me in this way and said "I truly enjoyed your contribution," and I just clammed up. I was so mortified. I don't think she even meant it to be mocking but I couldn't bear it. So I just sat there and got redder and redder and Anna took her attention off me, which is fine but I just felt like I'd failed, made the worst impression, and I just really needed to tell you about this right away, while it's all still hurting, the good and the bad of it, all together. I needed to tell you. I always need to tell you and you're not — you're never —

I wish — I wish you could have been here. Everything would be better if you were. I wish we could be talking about it right now. I wish — God, Paige, I miss you so fucking much. I miss you.

The ceiling came into focus first, and it was wrong: much too high, and the familiar pale-orange stain that usually greeted her when she woke wasn't there. Then the smells: unfamiliar laundry detergent mixing with coffee like her father had it, with cardamom. The sound of water running, one wall over. Suddenly she bolted upright and took stock of the strange room, the strange bed, and the dull orange light coming through unfamiliar window slats from a street lamp outside. Still nighttime, then.

She felt sick. Still drunk, obviously; the room kept threatening to spin, and her vision was anchored to a slow, awful churning in her belly. Was this Anna's place? Blearily, she swung her legs out of bed, and saw that she was still dressed. Quietly, she padded her way out of the room and into a dark hallway, toward the sound of water. She was thirsty. Her mouth felt full of sour cotton.

Light slanted into the hall from the half-open door to what she thought must be the bathroom; maybe Anna was brushing her teeth? She pushed it the rest of the way.

Lynette Byrd stood on one foot, lifting the hem of a white night-gown, one knee delicately raised above a bathtub filling with water. But her feet—Emily stared, blinked, shook her head, couldn't stop staring.

From the ankle down, Lynette's feet were the leathery, taloned, four-toed feet of a bird.

Lynette's eyes met hers, and she tilted her head as she had in her performance, but it had the look of a raptor now. Emily staggered back, watching Lynette's upraised knee lift higher, those talons flexing, swivelling away from the tub and on to the floor, clicking.

"Seemstress," she gasped, and the room spun faster and faster until she tumbled backwards into the dark.

When Emily woke again, it was to morning light filtering through the blankets over her head and whispering voices in the hall. She ventured a peek over the sheets, and saw Anna and Lynette in animated conversation, while someone who shared Lynette's height and colouring stood silently by with arms folded. Kel? They had short-cropped black hair, sharp cheekbones, and human feet.

Lynette's remained disconcertingly taloned. She hadn't imagined it.

Emily rolled over and burrowed deeper into the blankets in search of oblivion.

"Hey," came Anna's voice, gently, from beyond the duvet. "Morning. How are you feeling?"

Emily tried to part her lips to say something intelligent and managed a tiny croak of misery. Anna patted her shoulder.

"Have some water. Come on, we won't bite. What do you remember?"

Slowly, Emily sat up, taking in the company. Anna, in pink flannel pajamas, looked concerned. Lynette without her make-up and feathers was still devastatingly beautiful: her black hair was a long sideways braid over her shoulder, and her light-brown cheeks still had a hint of glitter to them. Her eyes were as black as her hair. She looked less like a magical bird-woman and more like someone from Emily's own family now—as did Kel, who was looking at Emily with distrust.

She accepted a glass of water and took small, careful sips. "Lynette has bird feet."

Anna winced. Kel muttered something under their breath that sounded like it was probably rude. Lynette waved her hand.

"We will speak of that later. I think Anna meant from earlier in the evening."

"Oh." She hadn't given it much thought. "I remember—sitting with you both, and then going to the bathroom, and, um." The shame of it, locking herself in a stall and crying, washed over her in a nauseous wave. "I guess Anna came in to check on me after a while. I don't remember much else."

"You seemed very upset." Lynette looked at her curiously. "I was concerned that I had said something to hurt you. Then you fell asleep, and Anna didn't know where you lived, so we brought you here instead."

Emily bit her lip, stared into her glass. "I'm so, so sorry—"

"It's no trouble, truly," said Lynette. Kel snorted at that, and Anna smacked them on the arm and glared. Lynette ignored them, focused on Emily. "*Did* I hurt you in some way?"

"No, I'm—I was just so embarrassed. About the John Cage thing. Everything had been going so well until that point, and now I've fucked everything up, and you—you're being so *nice*—"

"Emily." Anna looked pained. "You haven't done anything wrong."

Emily looked at her, and felt something tightly wound in her release. She felt suddenly ragged with relief.

"Really? You're not angry?"

"Angry?" Anna stared at her. "Emily, you just found out my girlfriend's part bird and you're worried about what *I* think?"

"I think," said Lynette, "that we should have some coffee. Would you like that, Emily?"

"Yes, please." She looked at Kel uncertainly. "Are you—are you going to curse me or erase my memory or something?"

Lynette blinked. So did Anna and Kel. All three of them looked at each other. To Emily's discomfort, they all burst out laughing.

"That," said Lynette, "would be terrible manners."

"That's—not a 'no,' though." Emily had the feeling of being in a dream, of watching herself having this conversation. Lynette only smiled, looking as if she was enjoying herself.

"Emily, if you'll forgive me the presumption, what is your surname?"

"Haddad."

"Then we both hail from places where hospitality is sacrosanct, and one would not offer coffee to a guest to whom one intended any harm. Come. Let us have a *sobhiya*."

The coffee tasted of home, of dawns spent with her father in comfort and certainty and safety. Kel remained quiet, and Anna's focus was on them more than Emily, but Lynette was shockingly easy to talk to. Emily found herself pouring out the history of her last year: the Master's degree in library sciences in London, how unbearable she'd found life in the city, how brutal the sarcasm that passed for affection, how she only hated herself more for not being able to banter with her colleagues and their friends, how she never felt entirely welcome among them.

"It's like everything I took for granted about friendship, and language, about what's polite and what isn't—it's not a default. We're taught—I was taught—that it's somehow universal, to be kind and open and welcoming and sincere, and it's not. And worse, it's not that it's *bad* not to be that way, there. There, it makes sense, how closed off and distant and biting everyone is. It's just a different way of being, that's all. But it's hard not to feel like everything about me is *wrong*— the way I laugh, the things I laugh at or don't. My words, my accent, the things I think are cruel. It's like, to live there, I needed to...tailor myself. Cut off bits that don't fit, or stuff them away, and sometimes I'd look in a mirror and just not recognize myself for the silence."

Kel stood up, abruptly.

"I'm going to bed," they said, gruffly, in a low voice. "Sorry. Long night."

Emily faltered. "Okay."

"I'll join you," said Anna, getting up. "Just for a bit."

Kel muttered something by way of assent. Anna looked apologetically at Emily before following Kel and shutting the door behind them.

"So," said Lynette, sipping her coffee from a tiny porcelain cup, turning her attention back to Emily. "Where were we. You finished your degree, yes? Why not go home to Canada? Why come to Glasgow instead?"

"Oh—" she sighed, swirled her coffee around her cup, watched the patterns the grains made against it. "I love my family, and I miss them. A lot. But—I'm queer, and they're not okay with that. I mean," she rushed to say, "they're not horrible or anything. We've had the 'we'll still love you no matter what' talk and whatever. But I just—I never really dated anyone when I was home. At all. And suddenly here, awful as everything else got, I went on dates, I flirted with men and women, and—part of me is more *me* here, I guess. I'm not done with that yet."

"Even though everything else feels wrong?"

Emily chuckled, not without bitterness. "Yeah. I'm crying you a river, I know." She finished the rest of her coffee in a gulp. Lynette leaned forward and poured more.

"It's the plight of the displaced, Emily. The stuff of song and story. People here are fond of saying that all the most loving songs about Scotland are written by those who left." Lynette replenished her own cup, and lifted it contemplatively. "One leaves home, one misses it; one makes a home as best one can, with the materials at hand, knowing it will never be what one had; but there are reasons, always good reasons, why one left in the first place." Before Emily could ask anything, Lynette smiled. "But, Glasgow? Why not stay in London?"

"Honestly?" She smiled a little. "I'd never been to Scotland yet, and I loved the names of Glasgow's derby teams. *Irn Bruisers*? *Maiden Grrders*? Seemed like reason enough."

Lynette laughed, and Emily found herself thinking of flowers. She took another sip of her coffee, and waited.

"Well," said Lynette, a touch of amusement still there, "I suppose it's my turn. Do you know what a Peri is?"

Emily blinked, brain flashing through Patricia McKillip, *Doctor Who*, and hot sauce. "Er—"

Lynette smiled. "That's quite all right. Whatever you do, don't read the Wikipedia entry. Nineteenth-century Englishmen with their books and operas did more to secure ignorance about us than the Severing of Seventy Bridges. Suffice to say we are a kind of— what you would call spirit. We are not human, though we sometimes enjoy human form. We have a world, our own world, that overlaps and intersects with yours," here Lynette clasped her hands together, fingers interweaving, "and in which we are ourselves. But without access to it—" Lynette fixed her gaze on somewhere just over Emily's shoulder, as if the world she spoke of was just there, "—we are less. We lose our ability to shift our shapes, to fly, to be flame or water. We become solid, locked. We," she drew her gaze back to Emily, "cut off bits that don't fit, or stuff them away, and sometimes we look in a mirror and can't recognize ourselves. We are wrong. We are *less*." Lynette paused to sip her coffee, and licked her lips thoughtfully. "Though we are also sometimes more."

Emily felt a lump rising in her throat. "How?"

Lynette lost, for a moment, the air of knowing amusement she'd worn for most of their acquaintance, and looked only wistful. "I was no performer, back home. I had no art. It was here, in this place, that I found my voice." When she smiled again, it was soft, and pained. "I did not learn to sing until I was shut in a cage."

Emily frowned. "Shut? But—didn't you leave on purpose?"

She shrugged. "To the extent that being forced to flee is 'on purpose.' Kel and I—"

"Wait, Kel's a Peri too?" Emily stared. "But—Kel's feet—"

Lynette chuckled. "We all have different tells. Were Kel to show you their back, you would see two lines of black feathers angled along their spine. May I continue?"

She flushed. "Please."

"We were...'Exiled' is perhaps not the right word. Our country is at war, Emily. We are, in a sense, refugees. We fled, and the door shut behind us. Kel wants nothing so much as to go back, to fight, to die, if necessary. I do not. As much as I long for wings again—" Lynette's voice caught, and she looked down, and shook her head slowly. "—No. For better or for worse, I am making a life here." She chuckled. "Though it is difficult not to laugh, or weep, when someone asks me where I am 'from.'"

"I sort of know what *that*'s like," Emily murmured. "'Where are you from?' 'Canada.' 'Yeah, yeah, where are your *parents* from.'" Emily mimed throttling an invisible neck, and Lynette chuckled. "It's not as bad here, actually. Mostly people assume I'm American." She paused, thoughtful. "So—why doesn't Kel go back?"

"Ah." Lynette put down her cup, folded her hands in her lap. "They cannot afford the cost."

263

"The cost?"

"Indeed. Our world is the source of our power; when the way is open, we can shift our shapes, fly, find things that are hidden or missing, carry our lovers across the world in our arms if we so choose. When the way is shut—" Lynette shrugged. "—there is a cost to open it. At present it is as if Kel and I have been stripped of citizenship, and must apply for visas instead of coming and going as we please. And, as with visas, there is always the chance that after having paid the price and sent in our paperwork, our application will be rejected all the same. ...Are you all right?"

Emily nodded, tight-lipped. "Sorry, I just—what do you mean, find things that are hidden or missing?"

"It's just an ability we possess." Lynette looked at her curiously. "A function of our nature."

"Oh." She nodded again. "Please go on. What *is* the cost?"

Lynette considered her for a moment longer before answering. "It is...an elaboration of the usual shedding of a form. For us, to open the way, we must give up a whole person. A sacrifice, if you will."

Emily stared at her. "What, you mean—you have to *kill* someone?"

Lynette shook her head. "Not kill. Give up. Relinquish. But it only works if the person is precious, beloved. For me—if I were to cut out my tongue, I might be able to open the way back. I would be giving up who I have become here, my art. Once on the other side I might easily choose a different form, one with a tongue, perhaps one with a more beautiful voice—but I would lose Lynette Byrd, whom I have come to love, and I would never have her again. That is *if* the sacrifice is deemed sufficient."

"So, Kel—"

"Kel loves nothing about who they are here. Every moment spent in their body is torment. Kel never kept one body for long, understand—if you comprehend gender on a spectrum of male and female, think of us as possessing gender along a spectrum of fluid and fixed. It is agony for Kel to be in one body, to be static, to be observable always in the same way." Lynette sighed. "It is an exquisitely devised exile. We must love something so much that we could never wish to give it up—and then give it up. So long as Kel despises their body, they cannot shed it, and so long as they cannot shed it, they will always despise their body and the world it is forced to inhabit. The only things they have come to love, while here, are the River Kelvin, from which they take their name—and Anna. But not enough. Kel is too willing to give them up. I had hoped that perhaps with Anna—with someone who understood the pain of a body that feels wrong—" Lynette shook her head. "As soon as Kel began to feel deeper affection for her, they sought to barter it for passage."

Emily blinked. "Kel tried to give Anna up?"

"Yes." Lynette looked pained. "There is a ritual we do, by the river, to open the way home. Anna participated, willingly—but it wasn't enough. The trap works too well. Kel might have once loved me enough for the leaving to hurt sufficiently, but—" she closed her eyes, briefly. "—It is hard for them, that I will not give up myself to pay for the chance of our passage. And so it goes. The magic must be cruel, to work. It must feel like the tearing of a page."

Emily felt a sudden pang—a tug in her belly, like cresting the topmost hill of a rollercoaster, teetering on the edge of the plunge.

"So, without your powers, you can't open the way back, and until that way is open, you don't have your powers?"

Lynette opened her eyes again, and nodded. Emily bit her lip.

"And could—anyone open up the way? By giving something up?"

"In theory." Emily felt her cheeks flushing beneath the sudden intensity of Lynette's gaze. "What are you saying?"

"I'm saying—suppose someone wanted you to have your powers. For something specific. Would you—could you help them, if the door was open?"

Lynette said nothing for a long moment, while Emily met her eyes. When Lynette finally spoke, it was gentle.

"What have you lost, Emily?"

She pulled her backpack onto her lap, unzipped it, pulled out her journal, and put it on the table between them.

"My best friend."

Dear Paige,

I told Lynette about you. It was hard, at first. For so long you've felt like a secret I've been keeping on your behalf. My best friend, to whom I write—who never writes back. My best friend, whom I've known for half my life—but who hasn't spoken to me in over a year. My best friend, who was going to travel with me, share a home with me, be up against the world with me—who vanished into air and darkness and didn't tell me where she was going.

It was hard, but it got easier.

I told her how afraid I've become for you. I told her about your depression, how you'd been withdrawing for a while, that it got worse once we had extra time zones between us. I told her about the unanswered phone messages, e-mails, postcards. I told her about how I called your work one time just to see if they could tell me you were alive, and how they said they'd laid you off a week earlier, and didn't know how to answer my question about whether or not you were okay.

She asked me if I was prepared to find out that you're dead. I told her that I knew you couldn't be dead, couldn't possibly be, because I'd know. I'd feel something snap. I'm sure I would.

She told me to prepare for the possibility all the same.

So this is the last I'm writing to you in here. I'm giving you up—sort of—to find you. It may not work. It may not be enough. But I told Lynette that I'm giving up years of myself in here, too—the me who is best friends with Paige, who is happy and secure and confident, who can see friendships come and go because at her core is this one, this unshakeable soul-twin sister-friend who'll never leave her.

So long as I've been writing in here I've felt like I could still be that person, because by writing to you I am conjuring you, I am keeping you in existence, and if you exist, so do I. And maybe if I find you—if Lynette can find you—she said Peri magics include carrying people through the air, so—if you're in trouble, if you're hurt—I can't even think about that but I have to trust in something, that this will be okay, somehow. That I can still be some kind of me even without you.

I love you. I'm giving you up.

Emily

Lynette and Kel had gone ahead, saying they had preparations to make. Anna watched as Emily laced her boots in the entrance to their flat. "I can't believe you're doing this. *Why* would you do this. You hardly even know them."

Emily shrugged. "It's not for them. It's for Paige. And—for me."

"Bullshit."

Emily flinched and looked up, hurt. "What possible other reason could I have?"

Anna folded her arms, looked away. "Whatever, I don't care."

"Do you not want me to do this?"

Anna rolled her eyes. "Think about it for two seconds, Emily."

"But Lynette said you wanted—"

"*Fuck* Lynette." Anna brushed a lock of hair behind her ear. "Look, I just—I love Kel. I fucking love them. And it's—hard, to make peace with losing someone for their own good, to know that you're the price of their happiness, and to agree to pay that price and then have it not be enough, because actually they didn't love you enough, you know?" She exhaled, pushed the heel of her palm into her eye. "And here you are, having only just met them, making some kind of huge weird sacrifice, and if it works—" Anna choked. "—If it works, then I lose Kel, and nothing about it was noble, nothing about it was *my* sacrifice. I'm just another failed attempt to get home."

"That's not true," said Emily, shocked, standing up so quickly she stumbled. "Anna—"

"Shut up. Go to the river, do whatever needs doing. I get it. Been there, done that." They looked at each other through tears. "I hope you find your friend."

Then Anna walked into her bedroom and slammed the door behind her. Emily tried not to cry as she let herself out.

They stood together beneath the Gibson Street bridge over the River Kelvin, having climbed over the fence and down to the water's edge. Emily clutched her journal to her chest and shivered as Kel waded into the water barefoot. Once the river reached their hips, they stopped.

Emily could hear Kel murmuring something to the water. Lynette stood next to her, wearing her cabaret costume and clutching a fistful of flower petals. She spoke quietly.

"You know what you need to do?"

Emily nodded.

"Very well. Kel is almost finished asking the river's permission to pass through." She looked away. "I hope this works. I don't know how Kel will bear it otherwise."

Emily swallowed, thinking of Anna. "I hope it works too."

Kel stopped speaking, and began undressing in the water. As they removed their shirt, Emily saw the two long black lines of feathers running to either side of Kel's spine like sutures, glinting in the dim light.

Kel turned to look at them, and nodded once. Lynette closed her eyes. "It's time."

She drew a deep breath, cast the petals into the water, and began singing the Arcade Fire's "My Body is a Cage." While she did, Emily took a few steps into the water and opened the journal. She looked down and couldn't help but read a line—from an early entry, a happy day, speaking of how exciting it was to be in England, how she'd been to the Sir John Soane Museum and tried to count all the busts for science.

As she grasped the page and pulled, she couldn't tell if it was she or the paper who was tearing.

Then she staggered. The world tilted, and she felt herself struggling to hold her breath. Something was happening to the water—a churning where it had been still, a circling of light flooding upwards around Kel. Emily tore another page, and another, throwing each one into the river, sobs welling up as she did, cutting into her throat every time she read, in spite of herself, a snippet of something Paige would never read, never know—her conviction that a different sun shone over London, made of syrup and smoke; the dream she had on Halloween after her first gin and tonic; her first kiss with a woman. She'd meant to share it all with Paige, had written it all out for her, and if Paige didn't have them, how could she?

Lynette was still singing—*set my spirit free, set my body free*—but she sounded farther and farther away. Emily could see the light around Kel brightening, and Kel—Kel was changing. The twin lines of feathers on their back were growing out, covering more and more skin, and Kel's body was blurring in and out of the water. Could it be working? Was it enough, after all? Would she find—

Lynette's song ended, and half a beat after the final note Emily heard her say, as if she were shouting from a vast distance away, *look into the water.*

She looked. In the same brightness she had seen shimmering around Kel, there was Paige.

The sight sank into her like a knife. There was Paige, in a laundromat—she was seeing her from behind, her long pale hair twisted up into a bun. She was taking washing out of one machine and putting it in a dryer. She was humming something, happily.

Overwhelmingly, Emily knew she was happy.

I can bring her to you, thundered Lynette's voice, *if you wish. In half a moment or less.*

She did wish. She wanted, so badly, to have her in front of her, to rage and scream *how, how could you be happy and all right and not speak to me, why wouldn't you, what did I do wrong, what.*

Paige was happy, washing laundry, and had her back to her. Emily stretched her hand into the water, choking on everything she wanted to say. But she'd said it already, into the river, as Anna had said it to Kel.

She drew her hand back.

"No," she whispered. "She's fine where she is."

Then the light dimmed, the river smoothed, and Emily found herself weeping into the down on Lynette's shoulder.

Dear Emily,

This is probably cheating, but you never specified the size of journal required, and a palm-sized Moleskine is still a Moleskine, and that means journal, so. Here I am, writing to you in a journal. My penmanship peaked in Primary 6. I hope you're happy.

I'm sorry for—well, everything. I hope I didn't hurt you too badly by keeping away for a while—that's why I'm writing in here, for now. I figured maybe we both needed a little space after what happened. But—well, I miss you. I miss talking to you. This is a piss-poor substitute, actually. But I guess it's better than nothing, and I think you might like, maybe, to know that I pay attention to the things you say even if I also tease you about them a little.

So I don't know how long I'll keep this up—it's a small book, and it's not meant to replace anything, obviously. It couldn't. I don't know how you'll feel about it when I give it to you. I just want you to know, basically, that I still really like you, that I think you're grand, that I'm grateful you're not a jerk, and maybe if you're up for it we could go to Nice N'Sleazy's sometime for a gig? I think you'd like it, the ceiling lights are covered in paper shades with clubs, spades, hearts, and diamonds on them.

Oh, you're just coming in for your shift. I'll write more later.

Love,
Anna

Just Another Future Song

Daryl Gregory

As they pulled him out of the oxygen tent, he asked for the latest party.

"Oh, Mr. Jones," one of the nurses said, amused. "We wouldn't forget *that*." The nurses, women in gray smocks with pale faces, moved in and out of view, murmuring in conspiratorial voices.

Something important had happened. Something that he should remember.

A great moon face leaned down into his line of sight. The man smiled with teeth of brass. "Welcome back, Jonesy." He had a thick Brixton accent. Another man leaned in, a twin of the first. The same brow as blunt as an anvil, the same thick neck. But this second man was stone, not all smiling.

Mr. Jones opened his mouth to cry out, but all that escaped his lips was a rasp. He tried to lift his arms to protect himself, but his limbs would not respond. He knew these men, these brothers, though he could not remember their names. They were there in their strange black smocks when he died. The one who never smiled had held him down while tiny knives ripped him apart, cell by cell.

"The orderlies will take care of you from here," the nurse said. And suddenly they were alone.

They lifted his willow-boned body, moving his limbs like a puppet's. They dressed him in silk pajamas and a lush smoking jacket of deep purple, then set his feet into slippers of black cashmere. Finally, they placed him in a red velvet chair with silver wheels.

The smiling one crouched to look him in the eye. "No fun and games this time, eh, Mr. Jones?" he said. "No wandering about, doing mischief?"

Mr. Jones didn't know what he was talking about. What mischief could he possibly do? His entire body felt weak as paper.

They pushed him across marble floors, through a corridor of high, arched windows. Outside it was dark, but spotlights raked the windows, casting disturbing shadows. Eventually they reached a large room walled in glass. *A solarium*, Mr. Jones thought, though there was no sun here, only the dark and those roving lights, diffused by fog or grime, pawing the windows. The brightest light in the room was cast by the face of the huge television screen. It was ten or twelve feet wide and half as tall, a miniature cinema. In front of it, dozens of ancient men and women sat slumped in wheelchairs as ornate as his own. The occupants were mottle-skinned and half-bald, jaws agape. The light of the screen flickered in their wet eyes.

"I..." The word came out in a whisper. "I want..." He wanted to see the doctor, but fear closed his throat.

The smiling brother ignored him. "Attention everyone," he called. "Don't want to miss the *celebration*." His voice was waxy with sarcasm. The brothers parked Mr. Jones in the center of the room, then set about positioning the other patients around him. Some of the old ones cried out, twisting to keep the screen in sight. Others were asleep, or simply inert.

The stone-faced brother pushed a large, wheeled cart into the circle. Atop the cart was a white cake bristling with dozens and dozens of black-topped candles, so many that Mr. Jones could not quite read the words on the cake's surface. Was that his name? It seemed to be the wrong one entirely.

The silent brother produced a match, flicked it alight with a long fingernail. He began to touch the tops of the candles, moving unhurriedly, lighting row upon row. The match somehow never gave out or dwindled. The cake disappeared beneath a rippling expanse of flame.

"How many?" Mr. Jones asked. His voice seemed strange to him, like a rake dragged across a cave floor.

"Oh, yer but a lad of five-and-twenty," the smiling brother said. He clapped a hand on Mr. Jones' shoulder. "Times twelve. Give or take." He laughed hard.

Mr. Jones pictured twenty-five twelve-tone octaves, climbing higher and higher. He could not be that old. No human being could.

"Won't you honor us, Jonesy?" the orderly asked. "You used to *love* to sing."

Mr. Jones shook his head.

"Aw, don't be shy. Bang a gong."

Mr. Jones was surprised to see a young face in the audience. The teenager stood at the back of the room, watching the proceedings: hands in black jeans, a swoop of black hair streaked with orange hanging over one eye, a scarlet mouth. The teenager caught Mr. Jones's eye and nodded.

The smiling orderly turned Mr. Jones in his chair and shook his head in exaggerated disappointment. "All right, then." He bellowed to the crowd, "The rest of you, then! One and *two!*" He beat his arms in the air, and a few of the elderly patients began to wheeze and squeak like a carousel winding up. The song stuttered to a halt before they got to his name. Mr. Jones scanned the room, but the teenager had disappeared.

The brothers wheeled the patients back to their spots before the gigantic screen. Mr. Jones watched the cake burn.

Finally they came for him. The smiling brother inserted Mr. Jones into the front row of the audience, only a few feet from the screen. "Best seat in the house for our birthday boy," he said. A huge plastic dial was set to C-15. There were thousands of other channels.

The orderlies left him there. He was relieved to be away from them, but he did not want to look at the screen. He'd watched enough TV in his life.

Yet. Images danced to get his attention. Thin young men in white suits, old-fashioned sailors, fought each other in a dance hall. As he watched, the figures became three dimensional, and the TV became not a cinema but a stage.

Someone behind him touched him on the shoulder, and a low, soft voice spoke into his ear. "You're not that old. Remember that." He looked up, then leaned out to the side, trying to catch a glimpse of the speaker, but he—or she—was already gone.

The old man next to him laughed. "Look at those cavemen go," he said.

Mr. Jones waited for the voice to return. The images, however, kept drawing his eyes to the screen. Soon he was nodding, smiling. He forgot about his fear of the orderlies, and the uneaten cake, and the teenager with the orange-black hair.

The images never ceased. There was no plot that he could sense, no order to the scenes, yet still he could not look away. He did not know how long he watched. He only came to himself when the orderlies pulled him away from the screen to wheel him to a small bedroom in another wing of the building.

The walls were gray. Above the bed, a picture of a spaceship hung at an odd angle.

"See?" the smiling orderly asked. "Home sweet home." He tugged the blanket almost to Mr. Jones's chin. Thick fingers caressed the wrinkled skin of his neck. "Warm as gravy."

"When can I see the doctor?" Mr. Jones asked.

"That's not the question you should be asking," the smiling one said. "No, you should be asking yourself, how did I get in this position? Third time's the charm, Jonesy. Twice't you took the hard left turn out of here and twice't we brought you back. The third one, now..." His grin was yellow. "...the third time they're going to take yer word for it. Them's the rules."

The silent brother flicked out the lights. The brothers stood in the white rectangle of the doorway for a long moment. Finally they closed the door.

Mr. Jones lay in the dark. The pillow, the sheets, smelled strongly of bleach. What did the orderly mean, hard left turn? Memories tumbled past his eyes, but he was unsure if these were images from his life or things he had seen on the screen. A tuxedo shirt draped over metal chair. A long-haired man, pale and naked to the waist, turning over white cards, one by one, each card inscribed with a sentence. And this: a dark-skinned woman with beautiful cheekbones lying in a bed, naked, one knee cocked, smiling at him. He longed for all the stories behind these images.

There were no windows in the room, but Mr. Jones felt that many hours had passed since they put him to bed. The wheelchair was against the wall, four feet way. He slid the bedclothes off him, and then put one foot to the floor, then the next. He leaned forward, one hand braced against the headboard. His thighs trembled as they took his weight.

The orderlies caught him as he was moving toward the chair. Standing was against the rules. But walking? That was right out.

"Watch yourself, Jonesy," the smiling orderly said as they set him into the chair. "We won't have your shenanigans."

They wheeled him out to the solarium, where the other patients were already waiting. Again Mr. Jones asked for the doctor.

"No special treatment," the smiling orderly said. "You know better than that."

Mr. Jones regarded the screen. He didn't know what time it was. The lights were low.

He leaned back.

A soft voice awoke him. No, that was the wrong word. He was awake, but dreaming. Or perhaps the TV was dreaming for him.

"The Moon boys are away," the voice said. It was low and sweet. "Care to spend some time together?"

"Who are you?" he said.

The figure leaned around the wing of the chair, bending low to look him with kohl-rimmed eyes through a curtain of orange and black hair. The thin, powdered face belonged to a child not much older than sixteen. "Call me Jeanie."

Jeanie steered the chair out of the pack and around the other side of the huge screen. There was another hallway there he didn't remember seeing before. But then again, he remembered so little. This teenager pushing him had been watching him from across the room yesterday, he was almost sure of it.

This corridor's wooden floor was weather-streaked and smelled of mildew. It seemed to stretch on forever.

"Where are we going?" Mr. Jones asked. "Out?" He could not hide the eagerness in his voice. Perhaps it was panic.

"I don't have the permission sets for *that*," Jeanie said. "I'm just a visitor, here to see an ancestor—*ostensibly.*" The accent was American. He was afraid of Americans.

"You're a spy," he said.

Jeanie cackled with delight.

The teenager pushed his chair through French doors, and then they were outside, in a winter's garden, the chair rattling across uneven bricks. The sky was gray, heavy with mist, and the air was cool against his face. Stone planters like great funeral urns stood in rows, most empty but a few topped with brown, dying plants. Jeanie gave him a final push, nearly jolting him from his chair, and then jumped in front of him and stopped him with hands on his bony knees.

"I've been *sent*," Jeanie said. "To rescue you."

A low stone wall curved in front of them. Beyond the wall the ground rose steeply, so that they seemed to be at the bottom of a bowl. Leafless black trees rose up into fog. The top of the hill was invisible.

"This is the limit," Jeanie said. "Outside, but not out. The rest is up to you."

The rest? He wanted to go inside. He wanted the TV.

"There are people waiting for you out there," Jeanie said. "People who remember you."

"Who?" he asked.

"People who *love* you. Who know who you *are*."

"I...No. I don't want..."

"If you stay here, you'll die," Jeanie said, standing with hands on hips like Peter Pan. "You've tried to end it a couple times already. If you do it again they won't revive you, no matter what your mental state is. Do you understand? Those are the rules."

The talking went on for a long time. Rules. Explanations. Technical considerations. Why was he outside? It was cold out here. The teenager filled the air with words.

A hint of movement caught his eye. He look up the hill, into the fog. Something dark and low to the ground slipped behind a tree.

"What is it?" Jeanie said. Then: "Oh shit." But the teenager was looking over his shoulder, at the doors they'd come through. Jeanie grabbed his hand, scrawled something there with a black pen.

"I'll be waiting," the teenager said, and then kissed him on the lips, quick as a kitten's bite.

Jeanie scampered atop the wall, then vanished. Mr. Jones wanted to yell a warning. There were wild animals out there! But the door opened behind me, and he did not want to give the spy away.

"Ah, there you are," a man said. A BBC presenter voice.

Mr. Jones put a hand against the top of one wheel, pushed down. The chair barely turned.

"Come out of the garden, Mr. Jones," the man said. He patted Mr. Jones' arm as if they were old friends. Perhaps they were. "You'll catch your death in the fog."

"You're the doctor."

"Why yes. Very good. Do you remember my name?"

He could not.

"Benway," he said. "Doctor Benway. At your service. I understand that you want to talk with me now, rather than waiting for our usual?"

Mr. Jones nodded.

"Absolutely not a problem. I have an hour free. Would you like to go inside?"

The doctor's office was everything Mr. Jones expected, and more so. A set decorator for a 1962 film about a psychiatrist would have made no alterations.

"I hope you understand my concern," Dr. Benway said. "If you feel at all...out of sorts, I hope you know that my door is always open." He made a show of sucking on his cigarette. Mr. Jones stared at the tip of it. He did not remember being a smoker, but he felt as if he must have been one; in fact, he might have smoked quite a lot.

The doctor said, "And are you?"

Mr. Jones looked up.

"Out of sorts?" the doctor asked.

"No, I'm...Yes. I want to go home."

"Home." Dr. Benway said. "*Home*. That's a tricky one." He tapped his cigarette into a glass ashtray that was large enough to serve hors d'oeuvres. "Unfortunately, Mr. Jones, that window has closed."

"Window?" Mr. Jones asked.

"We transferred you here just in time. A few days longer and you'd have been in no position to accept the offer. That position, of course, being six feet under."

Mr. Jones opened his mouth in shock, then shut it.

"Apologies, apologies," Dr. Benway said. "In a previous revival you laughed at that joke. *Loved* it. Still. The point is..." He showed Mr. Jones the gap between index finger and thumb. "You nearly missed it. He who hesitates is lost. Upload-wise."

"Upload?" Mr. Jones asked.

"A terrible term," the doctor said. "Inadequate and inaccurate. There is no software, only hardware. Look inside the body, and where would we find this *self* that we are all so fond of, if not in the hard stuff? All those care-fully grown patterns of neurons and synapses in your head, the web of glial cells, the millions of calcium ions loaded up and ready to spring...Oh! And not just in the frontal cortex, not even the whole brain, but down to the emo-tional centers in the brain stem, down into the spine, down and down and down into the hundred million neurons of the enteric nervous system—"

The doctor finally noticed Mr. Jones' confusion.

"The *gut*, Mr. Jones. The so-called second brain. But why stop there? What about all those nerve pathways running hither and yon through your old body? Where do we draw the line of what must be copied, and what may be left behind? Do you see the problem?"

"He don't, Doc."

Mr. Jones startled in his chair like an infant. He hadn't even heard the orderly enter the office. No, both orderlies. The Moon boys, Jeanie had called them. They slid into position on each side of the doctor like a pair of rooks.

"Never does," the smiling one said. "Wasting yer breath."

"No," the doctor said. "He's getting it. You are getting it, aren't you, Mr. Jones? We're making a breakthrough."

The silent orderly stared hungrily into Mr. Jones' eyes.

Mr. Jones looked down, and saw that there was writing on his palm. Instinctively he closed his fingers to hide it. "I want to go back to my room," he said.

"To do what, exactly?" the smiling brother asked.

"I think what my associate means," Dr. Benway said, "is that there's nothing more important right now than solving the problem before us. Namely—"

"Namely that you're fucked," the orderly said. "Neurologically speaking." His silent brother nodded.

The doctor raised his hands. "Not your fault, of course. Dementia is quite common in the aged, especially someone like you who is extreme-ly...well. Systems break down. And in your case—in the case of everyone here in the Temperance Building—we had to take you as-is. Because it's all or nothing. There is no you that is not that which is, do you follow?"

"Please..." Mr. Jones said.

"He ain't following shite," the orderly said. "This lad's insane."

The doctor took a breath, then seemed to mentally back up to take an-other run at the problem. "Even if we could tell the difference between what was 'damage' and what was the result of the 'natural' action of your mind—which we can't, not with anything approaching certainty—we could not return you to some idealized 'true self'—because who can say what that would be? Only *you*, Mr. Jones. You have to give your permission for us to operate on you. And not just vaguely—you must understand the risks. The laws are quite strict on this matter."

Operate? Mr. Jones thought.

"Get to the conundrum, Doc," the orderly said. "Then we can get him off your hands."

The doctor frowned, but even he seemed unwilling to make eye contact with the orderly. "The *conundrum*, as my associate puts it, is this: what if the state of your brain is the very thing that prevents you from giving your permission?"

He opened his hands as if displaying the final card in a magic trick.

The three of them watched Mr. Jones.

They want inside my head, he thought.

Dr. Benway recognized his distress. "You don't have to decide now," he said. "We've got all the time in the world."

Mr. Jones pretended to watch the screen. But then, as soon as he felt the orderlies had left the room, he squeezed shut his eyes. He kept his eyes closed for the rest of the day, until the orderlies came to move him back to his room.

"We know what you're up to, Jonesy." The smiling orderly leaned in so that his lips grazed Mr. Jones' ear. He whispered: *"You want out."*

The orderly straightened and waggled his eyebrows. "Show him, brother."

The silent one stood on the other side of the bed. In his hand was a huge kitchen knife, the blade tall as a head of cabbage, hefty enough to cleave bone.

"I'd ask if you recognize it," the smiler said. "But of course you don't. And you'll never get your hands on it again. Fool us once, Jonesy. You ain't getting out of here that easy."

Mr. Jones lay in bed, watching the strip of light beneath the door, waiting for the Moon boys to return. They were right, he was filled with an urge to flee—but to where? There was something he needed to do, but he could not recall what it was.

He was afraid of falling asleep. Finally he eased out of the bed and stood, one hand braced against the headboard. His legs held him.

He made his way in the dark to the doorway, flipped on the lights. He blinked against the glare.

He opened his palm. In shaky letters was written: MIDNIGHT GARDEN.

At first he could not remember who had done this to him. Then he remembered the garden, and the girl—or was it a boy?—with the black and orange hair, the red lips. Little Jeanie. But when was midnight? There were no clocks here.

Then he thought, *If there are no clocks, then now is as likely to be the right time as any.* He pushed his cold feet into his slippers and pulled on the purple jacket.

He opened the door an inch, listening for footsteps. Then he pushed the door a fraction wider, and saw that the corridor was empty. Which way was the solarium? Left? Right? Doors stretched away in both directions.

He chose a direction, instantly forgetting which one he'd picked. He dragged a hand along the wall to steady himself, lifting it as he passed each doorway, hopscotching past number after golden number. At some point he must have forgotten to put his hand back to the wall because he was walking steadily now. As soon as he realized this, he tried to forget that, too. The trick was to pretend that he was not so old, not such a cripple. He was not *dying*. No, these were his golden years.

The light globes on the walls around him began to sputter. He stopped, looked back. The hallway behind him had become banded with dark, half the lights out now. Far down the hallway, something animal-like slipped into one of the deeper shadows. He glimpsed gleaming fur and red eyes.

He wished he had the orderly's knife. He had wielded it once, evidently. Why hadn't he hidden it for himself where he could find it?

The lights in his section of the hall suddenly went out. He forced himself to move faster. Then all the lights went out, up and down the hall. He froze, his heart drumming in his chest. He turned in the dark, trying to adjust to the gloom.

Then something touched his arm. He cried out and jerked away.

A face leaned close to him. Jeanie said, "Look at you, walking." The teenager tugged his jacket a little tighter.

"There's something coming," he said.

"We're close," the child said.

Somehow Jeanie knew the way through the dark. A pair of doors opened and then they were outside, in the garden. The teenager helped him up onto the low wall, then said, "You have to step down yourself. That's the rules."

Permissions. Rules. He remembered her trying to explain, but did not remember the explanations.

He stepped down, stumbled, but managed to stay upright. He expected some sign that he'd crossed a barrier, some inner chime or outer alarm, but there was nothing.

Jeanie held him as he struggled to get his legs to move up the hill. He breathed hard in the wet air. At any moment he expected pursuers—the animal he'd glimpsed, or the brothers—to appear behind them. But then the fog enveloped them and he lost sight of the Temperance Building. He walked with Jeanie's hand in his, pulling him onward, until suddenly they broke through the fog.

Suddenly they were walking on a wide city street. The many lanes were empty of cars, and all the streetlights were dead. The only light came from a hazy moon drooping between black skyscrapers, and from a scattering of small fires burning in high windows. The tops of the buildings were jagged as if they'd been chewed off.

Mr. Jones looked at Jeanie in confusion. "What happened?"

"It's Hunger City," Jeanie said, as if he would recognize the name. As if it would explain everything. "Do you like it?" Jeanie was not being sarcastic, but proud.

Mr. Jones thought, How could anyone like this? It was some hell version of Manhattan. A ghost town. He got a sudden flash of the real New York: the densely packed streets, young people in bright clothes, and the cars, so many shining cars. He knew by the feel of it that this was an old memory, imprinted on the brain of a very young man.

"This is awful," he said.

Jeanie seemed disappointed. "We thought it would trigger something for you."

The teenager led him down the block. Mr. Jones heard things moving behind them, paws tapping across the rubble. But Jeanie, whose ears must have been better than his own, said nothing, and so he said nothing.

Jeanie led him across expanse of cracked concrete, toward a glass and steel monolith rising up behind it. As they entered its deeper shadow, Mr. Jones glimpsed red eyes in his peripheral vision. He turned, but there was nothing there.

"Watch out." Jeanie put a hand on his chest, pushing him back, and something heavy slapped the ground a few feet in front of them. A coil of rope, dropped from above.

He looked up. The rope trailed down the side of the building, twitching like something alive. Another shape dropped toward the street.

"Here he comes," Jeanie said. "A regular Tarzie."

It was a man, his body twisting around the rope as he slid down it. He hit the ground in a crouch. His face was painted with a white grinning skull.

"This is Jack," Jeanie said.

Jack rose, extended a hand.

"Your hands are smoking," Mr. Jones said.

"So they are," the man said, grinning. He clapped his palms and ashes puffed the air. "I just want to say, I'm dead honored. Your work means so much to me. Obviously." Despite the Halloween paint, he managed to look sheepish.

"Were you followed?" Jack asked Jeanie.

"Yes," Mr. Jones said.

"The Moon boys are back in the Temperance Building," Jeanie said.

"They'll figure out he's missing soon enough," Jack said. "Better hurry." He whistled, and figures began to move out of the shadows of the building. A skeletally thin man in a 19th century bathing suit; a limbless woman, wriggling across the ground; a dwarf, less than three feet tall, in an immaculate tuxedo. A larger figure loomed out of the dark—a man, almost eight feet tall, naked except for the brass tubes that wrapped his body. The bell of a sousaphone sat on his left shoulder like a second head.

Mr. Jones backed away from them. "What do you want? I don't have anything."

He felt a tug on his jacket and turned. A pair of bald-headed school girls, joined at hip and shoulder, grinned shyly at him. They had two outside arms, and in each they held a single drum stick.

Jack smiled. "Isn't it obvious? We want to be your band."

"No," Mr. Jones said. "Never again."

"Oh, we think you'll change your mind," Jack said, and the freaks—Mr. Jones could only think of them as such—burst into laughter.

Jeanie gripped his hand. "Let me show you the body."

Jeanie led him into the building, a vast space hollowed out by destruction. The teenager guided him over tumbled heaps of cement, under drooping ceiling tiles and loops of electrical cables, around the black mouths of unguarded elevator shafts. Most of the band stayed outside, but Jack and a few others followed them inside, keeping to a discreet distance. The school girls giggled in anticipation.

The body lay on a metal slab, surrounded by candles. It was a man, naked and pale, with red-orange hair streaked with black. The body sparkled in the light as if it were dusted with diamonds.

"It's for you," Jeanie said. "A birthday gift."

Mr. Jones stepped forward. The face of the naked man was beautiful and alien. Red, glittering paint divided the face in a lightning jag. Mr. Jones touched an index finger to the face, ran a finger along that red stripe. He rubbed finger to thumb, feeling the grit.

Jack appeared on the other side of the table. "Let me show you how to get in." He touched the head of the body, where the bright hair met the pale skin, and pressed down. The skull parted, then opened like a flower. There was nothing inside.

"Now you," Jack said.

"Get away from me," Mr. Jones said.

"Don't be afraid," Jeanie said to him in a soft, reassuring voice, and then touched his forehead, directly above his nose. He felt himself tipping back.

Someone had placed a chair beneath him; he thumped into it. The dwarf in the tuxedo stepped back, nodding as if to say, *You're welcome*.

"Open your hands," Jeanie said, and he did as he was told. The child reached up, above his line of sight, and then brought down a glowing, pulsing object. It was shaped like a brain, but it seemed made of neon. A ribbon of light was connected to the base of the brain and ran past his cheek to, he supposed, his own skull.

"This is your noetic module," Jeanie said.

It was so beautiful. He touched the top of it, between two glowing folds, and it seemed to expand in his vision, like a microscope zooming in. (But it did not feel like a microscope, it felt like a telescope, bringing distant stars into focus.) Lights flashed, but there were vast sections that lay in shadow.

"It's only a representation," Jeanie said. "But also an interface. Do you understand? You can go all the way down to the bottom —"

"Atomic even," Jack said.

"—of the acquired substrate."

Jack squatted beside him. "Just slip it into the new body. The metaphor will actualize the transfer, as well as perform other up-dates to the module. We built it to fix some of your current, uh, difficulties."

Mr. Jones frowned, trying to remember what Dr. Benway had said. "But the new body won't be me," he said.

"That's not a bad thing," Jack said. "You're a mess."

"It will be *mostly* you," Jeanie said. "The rest we've modeled with everything we know about you, your true nature."

"Sure, there were disagreements," Jack said. "Some of us insisted on looking to your later work."

"The dance albums," Jeanie said. "Regrettable."

"But in the end we all agreed—*this* is the you you're meant to be."

Jack held out his hand, and the small man in the tuxedo handed him a gleaming pair of scissors. "Once you've inserted the module, you've got to cut the connection. We can't do you it for you."

"Permissions," Mr. Jones said.

"That's right!" Jack said. "Exactly right."

"And what happens to...me?" He touched his sternum.

"*You* are in the module. But this old body will just...*poof.*"

But Mr. Jones was no longer listening to them.

He was gazing deeply now, so that he seemed to be inside the module, the light surrounding him. His thoughts flashed by, de-lighting him. Then he became aware of the thought about his own thoughts, and laughed. He was himself watching himself...and this thought, too, came under his scrutiny...and *this* thought...

He felt himself lurch, spinning into free-fall. The beams of lights coursing past him slowed, became dollops of mercury. *So beautiful...*, he thought (and saw this thought, too, slipping past him like a spangled parade float) *...but so constrained*. The more he looked, the more he noticed the frayed connections, like bridges that had been sundered, and sections as dead as the ruins of Hunger City. He reached out toward a seam of black, pricked at its edge...

He lay on his side, the cement floor rough against his ribs. What had happened? He'd been inside the noetic module, learning it. But now it lay glowing beside him, still tethered by a thread of light to the unseen socket in his head.

Someone was screaming. Bodies all around the room were in motion. He couldn't understand what was happening. Then he realized: the Moon boys had found them.

The smiling brother held a length of pipe that he might have picked up in the debris. He swung it in the direction of the giant, forcing him to step back. The big man moved awkwardly in his suit of brass tubes.

"Ceci n'est pas une pipe," the orderly said, and laughed. He jumped forward and swung again, striking one of the tubes with a *clonk.* "I revoke your privileges," the orderly said calmly, and the giant disappeared in a flash of light. The tubes clanged to the floor.

A dozen feet away, the silent orderly held Jack by his throat. The great kitchen knife, the weapon he'd shown him back in the Temperance Building, was in the brother's hand. He thrust it into Jack's gut, and Jack made a sound like a door creaking open. The orderly grimaced—it was the first change of expression Mr. Jones had seen cross the man's face—and twisted the knife a quarter turn.

Jack...shattered. A thousand pieces clattered into the dark.

Mr. Jones sat up in horror. The members of the band were charging toward them. And in the dark, skulking outside the perimeter, were the wolf-shapes that had been following him. They were not engaged in the fight, but circled around it, waiting.

"Damn it," a voice said. It was the tiny man in the tuxedo. He was staring at the spot where Jack had disappeared. "This is all going to hell."

The silent orderly turned and nodded toward the dwarf, as if inviting him to dance.

The man in the tuxedo smoothed down his oil-black hair, straightened his cuffs. "Well then," he said.

He took two quick steps and threw himself at the orderly, yelling with surprising savagery. He tackled the man at his thighs, sending him stumbling backward.

Mr. Jones heard a moan. On the other side of the metal slab, out of sight of the orderlies, Jeanie lay on his—or her—back. Still alive, but there was something wrong with the child's skin. It fizzed with light, like lasers turned back on themselves. Jeanie had been wounded.

A voice behind him said, "Making love to your ego, Jonesy?"

The smiling orderly, done with the giant, strode toward him, twirling the pipe in one hand like a batsman warming up. "These peoploids must have taught you that trick. But you can't just be waving yer old N.M. around where it might get hurt."

There was a double shriek. The bald girls lurched on too many legs to throw themselves in the orderly's path. They raised their drum sticks like knives and stabbed at his face.

They are heroes, Mr. Jones thought. *Risking everything for me.*

He tucked the module under one arm, then pulled himself up. The pale, lovely body waited for him on the slab, the skull open like a cradle.

Just slip it in, Jack had said. *Actualize the metaphor.*

He could become someone else. This was a world in which all forms were malleable. These freaks had fashioned themselves into shapes that would please him. They'd built an entire city for him. And this shell they'd designed for him, this beautiful diamond-flecked man, was exactly what they dreamed him to be. It would make him into their dream. He wouldn't be who he was now, but he could escape. He could beat them.

The girls screamed in harmony, the tones a third apart. Mr. Jones looked back just as the orderly drove his pipe between the twins, tearing them in half. "Revoked!" he shouted. The bodies fell in opposite directions like a split tree. They hit the floor and each vanished in a spray of sparks.

Mr. Jones stifled a shout of fear. The orderly winked at him. "Come here, Jonesy. Time to get back home. Yer missing all the good shows."

Mr. Jones lunged for the new body. But the silent orderly was already there, squatting obscenely over it. The kitchen knife was in his hands. He swiveled his head to regard Mr. Jones.

The old man realized he wanted nothing to do with the body. It was just another type of trap. Designed by those who loved him, but a trap none the less.

"Go ahead," Mr. Jones said. "I don't want it."

The orderly shrugged, then plunged the knife into the body's chest. It did not twitch or react. There was no blood.

"No unauthorized transfers," the smiling orderly said. "Them's the rules."

Mr. Jones had already backed away. He held the module in one hand, and the fingers of his other hand were pressed into one of the creases.

"Careful now," the orderly said. "You don't want to be fiddling with that."

Mr. Jones plunged his hand wrist-deep into the module. Yet in another way, he was deeper than that. All the way in, submerged and surrounded, where thoughts became languorous as dripping mercury. He'd already learned a great deal about the flaws and dead zones in his mind. Now he was eager to make repairs.

The silent orderly jumped onto Mr. Jones's back. They went down together, and Mr. Jones's hand came free of the module with a cartoon *pop!*

Mr. Jones laughed. The sound was low and came from far back in his throat. "Wham *bam*," he said.

The smiling orderly hesitated. "Okay now, Jonesie" he said. "Time to put that brain back where you found it."

Mr. Jones nodded. He reached above his head, then set the noetic module into the cavity, as if crowning himself. His skull accepted the module and enfolded around it. The orderlies bent to lift the old man, but he raised a hand to stop them. He got to his feet by himself. His smile was one they had not seen before.

"What have you done, Mr. Jones?" the orderly asked.

"That's not my name," the old man said. He slipped off the smoking jacket, let it fall to the ground. Mist rose from the neck of his pajamas.

The skin of his face began to crackle and fall away like buckling ice, exposing a new surface the color of indigo. His eyes shifted color: one to green, the other to blue. His body assumed a new shape, and the pajamas slipped from him.

He'd lost memories, he was almost sure of it, but other, older memories that had been irretrievable for the old man were now accessible to him. He remembered some of the things that belonged to him. He remembered the dogs.

"Mr. Jones—" the orderly said, but his smile was faltering. Wolf shapes padded out of the dark, more than a dozen animals, their red eyes fixed on the Moon boys. As they stepped into the circle of candles, the light glittered on their diamond collars.

"Revoked," the indigo man said. The dogs leaped.

Jeanie gazed up at him through light-splintered eyes, still trying to maintain cohesion.

"You changed," Jeanie said in wonder. "All on your own."

"Is there anything you want me to do for you?" he asked.

Jeanie smiled shyly. The indigo man kneeled beside the teenager and placed his lips against Jeanie's. He allowed a bit of deep purple to smear against the child's own lipstick.

Jeanie sighed. "This body you're wearing—I don't recognize it. Is it from '72? '74? Something in the 80s I missed?"

"Oh little Jeanie," he said, and rested the teenager's head gently against the rocks. "When have I ever repeated myself?"

The Electric Spanking of the War Babies

Maurice Broaddus &
Kyle S. Johnson

Everything was inextricably tethered to the box in George's closet. He stood on his tiptoes and let his fingers find the familiar edge of the old shoe box on the top shelf in his closet. He pulled it down carefully and carried it over to the bed, where he laid it with quiet reverence. Though it had become a weekly routine, George never lost sight of how important the ceremony of dressing was to him. Clothes made the man.

After a moment of silence, he popped open the lid and withdrew his most prized possessions: his well-worn-yet-still-fresh pair of robin's egg blue quad skates adorned with rhinestones in geomantic formations. They were his talisman. His key.

A Dr J poster hung next to one of his namesake, George "The Iceman" Gervin, behind him. They were his childhood heroes. He had grown up wanting to ball just like them. The ritual, however, felt every bit as if he was turning his back on childish things. He was ready. His two-toned blue bell-bottoms hugged him tight in all the right places. His sideburns trailed down to his chin. He tucked a pick into his sculpted Afro, leaving only the raised fist that was its handle visible. All that remained were his shoes. He slid the first one on, and the familiar wave swept down over him. Before he lost himself, he paused and shouted toward the crack in his bedroom door.

"Going out for a while, Momma."

From behind a curtain of beads which separated the rooms down the hall came a muffled cough and then her voice, weak and half-asleep. "Oh, is it Thursday already? Where has this week gone?"

"Yeah, it's that time again."

"Be careful, baby. The war is almost here," she whispered.

"What you say, Momma?"

"You have fun now, okay? Don't be out too late."

"Sure thing, Momma." George tried to ignore how tired she sounded. She'd been hustling all day to feed his brother and sisters. He couldn't help but think they'd be better off with one less mouth around. George returned his attention to the second skate, sliding it on easily. Pulling the laces tight, he rose to his feet. The energy coursed through him. He felt blue electricity. He felt alive. He felt free. Looking himself over in the mirror, George tugged the wide collar of his polyester shirt and watched himself disappear into the person he became every Thursday night. He was no longer George Collins. The transformation was complete. He was Shakes Humphries, the baddest mofo on eight wheels.

The Sugar Shack was an oasis in the riot-torn city. No matter how angry folks got, burning buildings and tearing up their own stuff, they left the Sugar Shack alone. It was sacred ground, but it wasn't a place for heroes. Everything was so dark and gritty in those days, one long shadow drifting into an endless night.

This wasn't how it was supposed to be, a broken world filled with broken people who reveled in their brokenness. A world populated by anti-heroes, misunderstood villains, and heroes with feet, legs, and torsos of clay, where those who stood tallest fell first. Part of him remembered an echo of how things used to be, of a time where men and women were proud and bold, which confused him because this was all he ever knew. He put it down to a childhood dream, to something he'd read in a comic or seen on the television in his youth. Something he'd lost himself in, laying on his belly in the living room, while Momma was at a revival meeting.

The streetlights burned to life on either side of the street, guiding Shakes in like the open arms of a neon goddess. A few kids ran past him trying to make it home or risk getting the switch for being caught out too late. Though rough, the neighborhood was home. Whether he was George or Shakes, he stood as tall as the world would allow, had always done everything he could to help out his little brothers and sisters. He felt like the hood thanked him in its own way by keeping him and his momma safe. But from the moment his skates touched the asphalt, he knew he was being watched. He scanned the shadows, anxious but not wanting to betray his cool. Whatever stalked him waited.

"They're spying on us." A man knocked over a trashcan in the alley. "With their satellites and drones and eyes in the sky. We can't hide from them." *Don't look up.* "That's how they capture your face and run off with it to another world." The man stumbled toward him. "Can I get a dollar, young blood?"

"What for?" Shakes knew his answer from the booze on the man's breath.

"Information about the revolution isn't free. No one believes me though. No one ever believes me. Belief is the key."

"Don't look up. Got it." Shakes handed the man a dollar.

The old drunk stuffed it into his pocket and offered daps, an appreciative smile, and a slurred, "Good looking out."

Shakes accepted his offerings. "Stay strong, brother."

Shakes hustled into the skating rink. His name rang out as soon as he entered. The neon pink words "Sugar Shack" bathed the back corner of the rink. A mural of the solar system covered a full wall of the building, lit up by the cascading lights. George rapped with some of his boys, slapping palms and clutching hands in the secret handshakes of the initiated. The DJ raised his fist in salute, the rhythmic bobbing of his head persistent.

"Our very own star child, Shakes Humphries, is in the house. Show him some love, boys and girls, cause this is an aaaaall skate!"

The strains of the Bar-Kays bumped from the speakers. With a series of crossover moves to remind them of who he was, Shakes eased into a groove and his boys fell in step with him. They soon formed a train, imitating the intricate dance routine of The Temptations in precise lockstep. They made that rink grunt.

A series of figures stepped from the shadows. It took Shakes a few seconds to process what he was seeing. The brother at the front was protected by a hard plastic shell adorned with panels of little neon lights and buttons. Everything was fiery pink. Despite the seeming bulk of the suit, his movements were smooth and natural. Where a face should have been, Shakes saw only his reflection in the obsidian sheen of the orb fastened to the raised neck of the armor.

Who is this dude? Some kind of spaceman?

The others emerged from the darkness, their suits identical but for the yellow color. In their hands, each held what appeared to be a child's toy, like Nerf guns except with hard purple polymer for their carapaces. Despite the resemblance, Shakes knew then that playtime was over.

"Sweet Christmas," Shakes muttered.

Two of them covered the front door, another stood by the rear exit. No one reacted to them, as if only Shakes could see them. Three more emerged from the shadows by the wall of lockers muttering a low chant. "Psychoalphadiscobetabioaquadoloop. Psychoalphadiscobetabioaquadoloop. Psychoalphadiscobetabioaquadoloop."

The rink was covered by a thin layer of mist that rose like a flood, reeking of lemon-scented Lysol.

The leader spoke behind his mask, the voice modulated to sound high by an otherworldly Theremin. "Your time's up, sucker. High time you come with us. Make it easy on yourself. You don't want it getting tough out here."

The head spaceman fired into the air. The rink erupted in chaos. Tables overturned as people scurried for cover. People tripped over one another, rushing about blindly. Screams drowned out the music except for the throbbing bass line.

A hand clapped down on Shake's shoulder. He turned to find a fine sister wearing a fox-fur coat and pink hot pants, revealing her bare midriff. Her matching pink sunglasses, trimmed with glitter, were tucked into her Afro puffs. For all of the surrounding panic, she was ice.

"My name is Mallia Grace." She held her hand out to him. "Come with me if you want to funk."

Mallia melted, her skin sloughing like wax giving way under its own weight. Shakes raised his hand, but it pooled, rain streaking a windshield in a hundred rivulets. He tried to take Mallia's hand, but they merged together, their bodies falling into a co-mingling mess. He tried to hold onto her, find some grip on her reality, knowing they'd mix into a single bowl of cosmic slop to be poured down the drain, discarded and forgotten. He resigned himself to their ultimate dissolution, hoping maybe this time the light hanging at the end of the darkness would be kinder...

Shakes opened his eyes. His head pounded, his stomach queasy, but he tried to not throw up on the chair. His throat tight and dry as the pants clinging to Mallia's behind. And with that image jolting him to full consciousness, he forgot his thirst and tried to find his cool. His chair faced out over a throng of people in the club beneath him. He wasn't in the Sugar Shack anymore. The place was too packed, too clean. The building seemed like a hollowed-out warehouse. Metal gleamed along each of the three tiers of space like the polished rib cage of a huge beast. Gaudy lighting — fuchsia, olive, purple — flashed, pouring over the sea of bodies beneath him. Every last person was dancing, moving, loving, and grooving. Far removed from judging eyes, they were people who knew they were out of sight. Everything was sweating, even the room, beaded with condensation from the rising heat. Shakes realized the room he was in was a huge clear bubble, suspended somewhere above the third level.

The stage was at the far end; the six-piece band on it wove through an uptempo rendition of "Pop That Thang." A double stack of what appeared to be Marshalls, triple stacks of Ampeg SVTs, a chorus of speakers pulsing as one great wall of music. On a separate stage above the fray was an oversized set of drums, but like no kit he'd ever seen before. Nearly translucent, each pounded kick produced rhythm as color. It had been the bass line that brought him back around, a defibrillator shockwave through his chest. Like the *thump-thump-thump* of a brand-new heart.

He knew Mallia watched him, so he strapped on his cool again and turned his head back slightly. "You didn't have to drug me. I'd have come quietly."

All business, she passed on the lingering innuendo. "Oh, baby, I didn't do a thing."

"My man, you flat out fainted. You missed all the action." A brother in a pink coat and chartreuse bell-bottoms said. Stars and crescent moons had been shaved into his head, as if his skull streaked through the cosmos while he bobbed his head. But the rings on his bare feet seemed too affected, as if he were trying too hard to create a look he wasn't entirely comfortable with. He was slick with perspiration and trying not to show that he struggled to get his breath back.

"Don't make it sound so glamorous. It got thick in a hurry. We lost one of our own back there and we don't have many of us to spare," Mallia said. "Shakes, Weary Nation."

Weary gave him a head nod. "You look a little rough. You may have caught some of their steam. That shit'll fuck you up like a blast of LSD."

Shakes caught his next words in his throat and turned back in full toward the people below, whooping their appreciation as the tune ended. "Who were they?"

"Afronauts," Mallia said with matter-of-factness to her voice. "But don't you worry, sugar, the man's gonna be up to see you in a minute. Just sit tight and it'll all be explained."

The lights changed and stayed there, bathing the masses in an otherworldly green. The band wasted little time, the horns bleating out, jumping right into some "Tower of Power."

"Aw, I love this song, man. Love it."

Shakes turned toward the heart of the bubble-room, toward the figure striding toward the long zebra-print sofa in the middle of it. He was lithe and graceful, majestic in a shimmering golden vinyl jumpsuit that seemed painted on him. The platform shoes he glided in on made him tower like a golden titan.

"How'd it go?" Mallia asked.

"They tightened that ass," the golden man said.

"Yeah, I bet they were stroking on that," said a man in a buccaneer hat from which long braids snaked. He wore matching buccaneer boots, but the only other items he sported in between were a diaper and a smile.

In a long chain of motion, smooth enough to have been rehearsed, the golden man snatched a drink from the hand of the buccaneer, knocked it back, and flung the glass away before reaching the couch. When he got there, he stopped and looked it over like it was offending him, shook his head in disapproval, and turned to face Shakes. The table between them sat low and was covered in LPs. *Hot Buttered Soul. Mother Popcorn. Stand! Innervisions.* The essentials.

"It's a fitting tune, ya know? For this situation we have ourselves here. So I just gotta figure it out. You drunk as a skunk? Maybe you're loose as a goose? Or maybe, maybe, maybe, you're high as a fly?"

"I don't have a damned clue what you're talking about." Shakes swallowed the saliva pooling in his mouth from his still-sour stomach.

Hands on his hips, the golden man leaned over the table and inspected Shakes. Something in his face softened. To Shakes, it almost looked like surprise or maybe relief. "Or maybe you're the real deal."

He turned to the buccaneer who had taken to inspecting his own muscles in the doorway mirror and shooed him out. When the door closed, the golden man reached behind his back and yanked a string from the vinyl jumpsuit, releasing the hidden girdle built in. His midsection bloomed, a full belly pressing hard against the gold and stretching it to its limits. He sighed and plopped himself down on the couch, throwing his feet over the stack of records and sending some spilling to the floor.

"So you probably want it straight. You have no idea. Yeah, I can dig that." The golden man stroked his belly as if in his final trimester, still getting used to his bulge.

"What the hell is going on here?" Shakes asked. At the steel of his voice, Mallia took an aggressive posture, but the strange man waved her off.

"Shoot. You really have no idea who you are, brother?"

"I know exactly who I am. Never been in doubt."

"No you don't. Not even close. You just one of them cats. You practically glow. You ain't Shakes. Yeah, I know about that name. Know your momma called you George, too. But that's not how I know you, oh no. No, you are the inheritor of the Funkenstein spirit. Intergalactic Master of The Funk, Emperor of The Grove, Ambassador of The Rhythm, The Heart and Soul of Rock and Roll, Martian Prince Come Down From His High Obsidian Tower on Mount Bump, Dr. Funkenstein. And I've been looking for you for a long, long time."

"You higher than a mug," Shakes said.

"We don't have much time." The golden man planted his feet firmly in the shag carpet, stiffened his spine and leaned forward.

He was going for serious, Shakes knew, but the whole act played just an inch shy of cornball. It was when the strange man took off his star-framed glasses and Shakes saw it there in his eyes that he shut his mouth and opened his mind.

"I'm tired. Every night I go out there to that crowd, tripping off the music. We're out there, doing our thing, every night making promises.

All about that sanctified testimony. They never ask questions, you know, because they want to *believe* it. So they believe us, believe the things we say, and we let it grow. When we hit the break, we let the whispers start. 'I think I hear the mothership coming.' But I'm just out there faking the funk, man. All hype, no love. Was a time when I could hear that mothership coming, too. But that's been a long time now, and now I'm an imposter. All because we need them to believe."

"Believe in what?"

"In all of it. In the mothership connection. The funkentelechy. In the Star Child. In you. Their groove powers us. We want to go home and we need you to lead us there." He pointed a multi-ringed finger out to the bouncing masses. "They're the fuel. You're the engine."

Prophetic pronouncements never went down well on an empty stomach. Shakes never thought there'd come a time where he actually craved Sugar Shack's chili fries. He didn't know how he was supposed to feel. Hearing the story reminded Shakes of this one time at the barbershop when he was a kid. He'd listen to all the older men, huddled in a corner as if they all belonged to a club he wasn't a part of, discussing mysteries of life he'd never understand. Mostly women. They'd said things with such certainty, like how ladies loved full beards. All George wanted to do was grow a full beard, to prove that he could hang. But his hair came in patches. He'd study his face in the mirror, lift his chin, examine the sole patch on the side of his face. "Next time you have to go to the bathroom," the men at the shop said, "dab some pee on your face. Hair'll come in thick then." Of course he believed it. He came out, stinking of piss, to peals of laughter from the men. Wasn't often that he was taken for a sucker after that.

"Look here, Agent Double-O-Soul..."

"We can't explain it to you." The golden man looked tired all of a sudden. "You have to experience it. I'm into something I can't shake loose. Mallia?"

"Don't be scared. You ain't no punk." She motioned for Shakes to follow, and he'd follow her shake anywhere.

Mallia led him toward the crowd below them. The buccaneer moved to the golden man's side, cinching him back up into his suit in preparation for taking the stage. When they reached the smaller bubble that would transport them to the first floor, Mallia leaned into Shakes's ear.

"I can see why he believes in you. The Star Child's been talking you up, and I didn't really believe it. But now? Yeah, okay, I'm on board."

"Yeah?"

"For sho."

"How do you know?"

"It's just one of those things. Can't explain it. You just know when you know."

The crowd hushed, a track on pause, waiting, breath bated as the Star Child slithered to the microphone like a whispered word, his fingers wrapped slowly around the mic stand, taking it as surely as he would his manhood, confidently, sex everywhere, everyone turned on, and his lips moved, forming the hiss, "Shhhh...y'all hear that," and they roared their approval that they could, oh yes they could, "I...I think I can...yeah, I think I hear something way, way up there," oh yes, they heard it too, "it's out there," finger erect pointing up toward space, "can't you hear it moving out there behind the stars, it's looking, and oh, it's powerful, but it needs a little help," they swayed in anticipation, wanting to know how they could aid the cause, "oh, you see, the mothership relies on a sense of smell, that's right, and it needs to pick up your funk," kinetic, the band hummed behind the Star Child, kept them on their feet, the pulse of the bass not giving them a chance to sit down, their words brought to life, their feet stepping with them, sacrifices to the altar of the Funk, "we need this funk uncut if you want the mothership to find us, children," their eyes rolling back, their mouths moving, like the Holy Spirit falling down on them causing them to speak in tongues, chanting the words, *Psychoalphadiscobetabioaquadoloop-Psychoalphadiscobetabioaquadoloop-Psychoalphadiscobetabioaquadoloop*, his voice rising, "no, no, I don't think you understand how far out there it is," moving faster, "so far out there, so you gotta Funk it up better than that," the crowd writhing, building toward it, "I wants to get funked up, we've been down here for so long, too long we've been trapped in the Zone of Zero Funkativity, so long now, from way back, kings and queens and presidents and cabinets and dictators and real fakers and," the crowd fed it back, thrumming like an organic bass drum, setting the tempo, "OH MY LORD," he exploded, the crowd swooned, the chant burst forth, *Psychoalphadiscobetabioaquadoloop- Psychoalphadiscobetabioaquadoloop*, the words hit Shakes's ears and found familiarity there, something distant, some far-off place, somewhere proud, the crowd hit its mark, achieving climax and riding it down on the hook of the backing band's bass line, and the Star Child turned his back to head off stage, with a little more dip to his hip, with a little more bounce to the ounce, picking up a little bit more of what he was putting down, smiling to no one in particular.

They crowded around Shakes off-stage, maybe without meaning to, maybe on purpose, his gravitational pull absolute. Their eyes tracked his every twitch and breath, their gazes filled with something expectant, as if even to watch him was to be enlightened. Shakes flinched but didn't buckle; their scrutiny unsettled him, leaving him with feelings of both vulnerability and being creeped out, like having garden gnomes watch him undress. Like they'd scoop him up and slam him down onto an altar at any moment, plug the knife in and cut a bit deeper, draw some more blood for the good cause. But he had plenty of practice putting on cool that he didn't have anymore.

"You ain't from around here," Shakes said.

"No, we're not. We're reality explorers. Funking cosmonauts," the Star Child interrupted as he stepped back into view.

"Afronauts. Like the ones that jumped us?"

"No. *Funkateers*. We're about peace and the groove. Afronauts, they're a different school of cats entirely. We all access the groove the same way. *Psychoalphadiscobetabioaquadoloop...*" The Star Child closed his eyes, lost in a moment.

"...to different effect. They take our message for weakness. They see love and dance as a plague...and they're the cure."

"The war crept nearer..." Shakes whispered.

"At this point, no one remembers what incursion into whose space started things. There's always been a rivalry between the Star Child and Professor Bereft of Groove," Mallia said. "They're both Leos."

"Man, we were like brothers back in the day. We came up together in the same band. We had all these hopes and dreams, wanted to make music no one had heard before. And we were good, too. No one could get with us. Then everything got funked up, and not in a good way. We got caught up. We each had a song to sing, had to go solo, do our own thing. It tore up the group. All anybody seems to remember after that is the hurt." The Star Child's attention drifted far away, seeing it all again, feeling it once more. For as accomplished as he was at faking the funk, he couldn't hide his pain. "Our reality was obliterated. We pushed through what we could, and whatever made it into this world resonates as things of music, of fiction."

"There were stories. Rumors of a child, sent down..." Mallia started.

"Just hype." The Star Child didn't want to go into it any further, but Shakes could sense something. "All that's left is in dance and rhythm and making love and partying past your momma's curfew. That's all we've got left, and we're hoping it's enough. There are some out there who are attuned to it. Agents of the Funk. Music, love, the groove, it awakens something way down deep and lets them see glimpses of what we were. It lets them dream of what we could be again."

"We make the music to fill in the gaps, like holes in our DNA. To make ourselves whole again."

"To believe us into reality," the Star Child said. "I have a relic from our world that I need to show you. It will..."

Psychoalphadiscobetabioaquadoloop. Psychoalphadiscobetabioaquadoloop. Psychoalphadiscobetabioaquadoloop. Psychoalphadiscobetabioaquadoloop.

The chant seemed to come from all around them. The lights fluttered. Darkness took shape, spaced folded on itself. Silhouettes shuffled in the night. A thick wave like dry-ice fog swallowed the dance floor, riding up George's legs and into his nostrils. A familiar smell, like citrus-scented disinfectant. Then a voice, like a wiggle in the ear, spoke.

"Citizens of the universe, we are here to reclaim the mothership."

They lie to you, George. You don't exist. You're nothing but a pack of baseball cards without gum. You are little more than the liner note drivel, ripped from the ravings of a fringe cult transcribed while riding shotgun on a bad LSD trip. This isn't the real world. But you know that, don't you? You aren't some savior figure struggling to come to terms with your messianic consciousness. Look at you, George, you are a boy, not a man, having a drug-induced dream. If your mother could see you now, you'd be the death of her, George. You know what's best for you, right? Get a nine-to-five. Get married. Consume. Obsess. Covet. Never question. Never wake up. Never wake up. Never wake...

"...up, Shakes! Hump your ass!" Mallia had him by the wrist, dragging him behind an overturned table across the floor. Through the fog, all around him, he could see the trampled bodies, could hear the screams. His fingers scrabbled over the floor to gain some kind of hold for leverage, but his fingers only found discarded clothing, still warm, and the grains of sand that he knew had once been people. He felt sick, coming down off a bad trip.

"What's going on?"

"Damn it." Mallia leaned over, her breasts heavy on his chest, as she checked his eyes. "Their gas is still affecting you. I hoped you would be more immune to it."

"You're beautiful."

"Apparently not." Mallia palmed a rod in each hand. With a flick of her wrist, they extended into batons. She caught him staring at them. "For defense purposes only."

"Defending who?" Shakes asked.

"Get up! We need to get you somewhere safe. The Star Child's using the artifact to hold them off. I don't know how they found us. They didn't..."

...think of your brothers, George. Of your sisters. Think of what will become of them without you. Think of your home. Think of your hood. Think...

"...they're sending everything they got at us." A bad mama jamma, Mallia leapt into the fray, delivering a roundhouse kick that shook the roof off that mutha. Then she battered him with the batons, twirling them with the ease of drumsticks. "That's Professor Bereft of Groove's lieutenant leading them. He must know that we've found you. He must know that..."

...you can still have a future. There's something more out there for you, but you must stop this nonsense. Get back on board with the real thing, George. Get your head out the stars and come back to Earth. You need to...

"...snap out of, Shakes. We're doing this all for you. You're the real thing."

"The words are gone." Shakes stared at his hands, making sure he had the appropriate number of digits.

"They're coming out of your mouth."

"Funk you. They're not there. They're not there, I'm telling you." Shakes trembled. "No, wait, somebody's in my head."

"Then fight him."

Unsteady at first, Shakes rose to his feet, letting Mallia's voice pull him through the noise. Through the smoke, the screams of the people rushing past, as thick and clunky suits of brightly-colored armor chased them. The high squeal of a dozen Theremins laughed at them, cutting them down with glee. One of the Afronauts stood there, his fiery pink and purple Bop gun aimed toward Shakes's heart. He could sense the smile behind the obsidian orb, hear the cackling of laughter, and the mocking tone of his words.

I am transmitting ideas directly into your reality, crooked and unoriginal. You fell into my grandest trap: prepare to become the greatest story ever untold.

The muzzle of the Bop gun flared, but then the Star Child was there. He leapt, waving an object that looked like a flashlight. He screamed. He fell.

But all Shakes knew after that was the light.

Who am I?

Another pointless dream lost in a crowd of pointless dreams. Hunched over in the dark, gyrating, bumping, grinding in dance to relieve that pressure. The ship. Hurtling through space. The ship was mother. My true mother. That knowing noise, the constant thrum, giving myself over to the music. The dance itself is the most intense rush, taking me out of this world to that place of possibilities. Holy funk, the engine of life and creation, like collard greens, KYs, and cornbread for the soul. Where everything that could happen, has happened, a cosmic conflagration, subatomic rhythms in collision. Where reality is the imaginary story.

I am...

"...waking up. I'm making it up. I'm...cosmically aware," Shakes said. "Sweet Christmas, this is deep."

Vibrations poured through his body, a deep soul spasm, and leapt from him into the surrounding walls, then reverberated back to him. Panels along the walls lit up. The walls hummed to life. Neon everywhere, blinking to life like the eyes of long-dormant beasts. Somewhere deep within the building, something pulsed to life.

"This building...*it's* the mothership," the dark Afronaut said. Shakes felt his fear through the modulation.

"Look here, Mr. Wiggles." Shakes turned to the black-clad Afronaut, its onyx-domed body seemed frozen in time, space-locked. "Y'all think you so slick, so cool, but you nothing but a daggone fool. Everybody's got a little light under the sun."

Shakes felt his mind becoming a weapon of love, flexed it like fingers and reached into the Afronaut's mind. He was struck by the image of maggot-laced meat. Shakes heard the music in his heart, the pounding drum. The bass line kicked though his soul. His feet took off with the groove, skating in a circle about the man. His skates never seemed to leave the ground, round and round he went. Shakes opened his mind, allowing more funk to wash into his soul. He watched it crash down in a great pink wave. A torrent of groove washed out the silt of Unfunkiness, whipping beneath the surface, brushing out the dead and breathless at the bottom.

"No. No more. I hate water. I never learned to swim!" The Afronaut clutched at the sides of his orbed head, trying desperately to claw it open, and collapsed to his knees, then fell forward.

Seeing Mallia cradling the Star Child's head, Shakes rushed to their side.

"If I'm going to be down with you, I'm down to the bitter end." The Star Child's eyes grew distant. "I can hear my mother call. I can hear my mother call. I can hear—"

Shakes stood within the bubble, bridge of the mothership. Earth filled the viewscreen, growing smaller and smaller.

"We're prepared to leave orbit," Mallia said.

"I know. I was just taking one more look." He thought about his momma, about his brothers and sisters. Had they known all along? Would they be safe without him? He couldn't say, couldn't worry about it. He shifted and turned to Mallia. "What's the plan?"

"We find more of the Funkateers, gather our forces. We will spread funk's glorious message across the cosmos if we have to. Then we'll bring it straight to Professor Bereft of Groove."

"In other words, we take it to that sucker." He nodded, turned back to the blue marble on the screen. "Where'd you learn to fight, anyway?"

"Shortest kid in the band and four older brothers." Mallia slipped her hand into his and joined him in staring at Earth. "It all seems so big. I don't know where or how to begin."

Living and jiving and digging the skin he was in, Shakes stretched his mind out, touching so many, awakening them to the possibility of everything. He turned to her.

"Free your mind...and your ass will follow."

All That Fairy Tale Crap

R a c h e l   S w i r s k y

I was supposed to go to the ball, but I spent the night licking out my
stepsister instead.

Bethesda moaned and rustled mulberry silk high up her thighs.
"There, there, no, faster, come on, faster, please..."

The friendly mice put out their eyes and ran out in trios to join a
different fairy tale.

Never marry a prince when you can eat a pussy.
  Never ride a pumpkin when you can steal cab fare.
  Never wear a ball gown when you can slink in snakeskin pants.
  Never listen to a fairy godmother.

Bethesda and I went clubbing. Everyone gave her the oddball eye
for wearing ruffled silk with fucking puffy sleeves. I laughed back
at all of them.

I seduced some refugee from the eighties who had a rainbow mohawk. Bethesda glared at us and bought herself two shots of tequila,
one of which she threw in my face.

Well, what do you expect from an ugly girl?

I danced until the eighties mohawk guy got tired and went home, and
then I danced until the bartender tried to close everyone out, and then I

danced more until it was sunrise and the bartender still hadn't managed to get away because I was dancing with him, our eyes locked across the room, him swaying like a hypnotized snake to the flute of my body.

Outside, it was pink and gray over endless city. I chose a street at random.

"Eat my body," said a house that belonged to a witch.

"Look at me," said a mirror with a voice.

"Do you want some boots?" asked a man exchanging new shoes for old.

I pulled off my heels and traded them in for knee-high go-gos.

"You look very intelligent," said the man. "I bet you could scam an ogre."

I grinned and gave him a dollar I'd stolen off the bartender.

The heroes of fairy tales are straight. And skinny, too, so they're straight and narrow.

People think this is because of heterosexism and beauty standards. It isn't. Snow White takes a cock in her scrawny cunt because she can't imagine how to be twisty.

You start out with three tools. You're pretty. You have small feet. And you can do housework.

Now become a princess.

Go on. Laugh. Shatter glass class ceilings? Yeah, right. There's a reason they call it the American *dream*. It ain't gonna happen while you're awake.

I find a hotel all lit up neon even though it's half past five a.m. Slip inside because why not? A place still partying through dawn's likely to have someone in it who'll try to pick you up by buying breakfast and staring at your tits.

Inside, it's all tattered chiffon streamers and tumbled confetti glitzing up the rug. Martini glasses are scattered on ottomans, couches, in the pots of fake rubber tree plants, half of them smashed to shiny bits.

And there: the prince. What the hell? Thought he was throwing a ball not a prom. But you can tell he's the prince on account of the epaulettes.

He's tongue-spelunking down some girl's throat. Grope, slip, grope, they change angle, and shit—that girl's face! Sharp and blunt in all the wrong angles. Hell if it's not my other stepsister, Griselda.

Suddenly, the prince's hangover pall goes from jaundice to chartreuse. His abdomen clenches. Then comes the retching. Griselda can't jump back fast enough. He spews puce chunks of half-digested pâté all down her mint green frills.

She shoves him off—"Fuck! You got some in my mouth!"

But he can't hear because he's slammed on the floor, passed out like a pine board.

Griselda gives me the stink-eye when I go over to help, which I can't blame since I'm the one who just last night threw her over for her sister. But when I turn over His Blotto Majesty so I can rifle through his pockets, one of his epaulettes falls off, and underneath there's a label for a costume shop on 44th.

"Fuck!" Griselda shouts. "A fucking fake!"

Her rant zooms off and I'd kiss her to shut her up except for the vomit.

"You're uglier when you're angry," I say.

"Bitch. Where's my sister?"

"Jealous snit. Stormed off."

"You're an entitled little slut, Cinderella."

"You want this guy's wallet or not?"

Griselda sets her mouth in an ugly snarl. Hard to describe the kind of ugly she and Bethesda've got. Everything in the right place, technically, but goes together nine kinds of wrong.

She stays all frozen grimace—can't say no, won't admit yes—till I take mercy and throw his billfold at her. He brought enough to play prince for another couple hours. Won't set her up for life, but it's not nothing. She glares at me as she rifles bills with her thumb.

"You're still a bitch, Cinderella," she says, but her bark is out of bite.

There's this thing happens when you're growing up, narrative an anvil on your shoulders, when you know you're supposed to pull yourself up by the bootstraps of your Lucite stripper heels. And that thing is: you cease to give a fuck.

Worse when everyone and her hairy-legged sister's busy telling you what it is you *mean*. Smashing you with a hammer and turning the bits into symbols, grabbing a ballpoint and writing you into a hundred ink-stained girls in diamond ball gowns, screaming bra-burning opposition to becoming passive, powerless, pampered princesses.

And what's wrong with pampering? Sounds good to me. Better than wearing the daily jewels of five-fingered bruises bestowed by the cunt who calls herself mother. Better than inhaling bleach and ammonia every morning while you're on your hands and knees scrubbing other people's muck.

Better than the taste of coal, the *real* taste of it, when the char's gone deep in your tongue, scorched every bud, turned all that supposed-to-be-pink into scalding black. After that, there's nothing doesn't taste of burning.

I tell you: when the whole world is charcoal, you take whatever bullshit they're serving because even shit sandwiches are better than fire.

Deeper in the lobby, there's a she-bear sitting on a loveseat. You can tell it's a she-bear because she's wearing a ruffled apron.

Beside her, there's a passed-out girl. Like last night's champagne, she's gone flat. Tongue lolls; limbs sprawl; hope she had a ball 'cuz today's gonna be a long-ass haul.

She-bear opens her paw. Inside, there's a tiny tea cup—on second thought, not tiny; her paw's just enormous. Silver tray on the ottoman in front of her, bone-delicate porcelain tea service painted with pastel roses. She raises the cup to her snout and, I swear, her fucking pinky claw is raised.

"What are you at the ball for?" I ask. "You someone's dancing bear?"

I shove the flat-champagne girl onto the floor and take her place. Girl grunt-snores as she tumbles onto the rug, golden ringlets flipping over her face.

She-bear rumbles disapprovingly at my incivility but won't be rude in return. Gestures with her free paw to the other cups on the tray.

There are three. Obviously.

I grab the hot one and pour it down my throat. Hiss of steam as it hits my lips. Saliva boils. Flame sears down my gullet.

Like anything's so hot I can't take it.

I open my mouth so she can see the skin bubbling on my tongue. "Juuuuuust right."

Her nose twitches with amusement. She sets down her just-so cup and grabs the oh-so-cold one. One long swallow and when she opens her mouth again, icicles glisten on her fangs. Her frozen exhalation blasts my face like frostbite.

"All right," I say. "I grant you. That was mucho macho."

She runs her tongue across her fangs to lick off the ice, regards me with an impatient *what-do-you-want* stare.

"It's paper-thin. That's what gets me. It's *always* paper-thin. Was to start with. Well, I guess it was voice-thin then. Oral-tradition-thin. There you are, you're an archetype, and you get to marry a prince who doesn't even have a name, and does either of you exist at all? Or are you just epaulettes and glass slippers? Not even *good* costumes. Oh, what the hell do you know anyway? You're a bear who doesn't even have to shit in the woods."

Her teacup slams against the tray. Reverberation sends the dishes crashing into each other. I startle-leap back, but much as I want to, I can't run; I'm transfixed by the smoldering black glare. Her maw gapes open. This time, I'm not fooled by the flowers and ruffles. Those fangs can bite down on cucumber sandwiches, sure, but they can also tear out a moose's throat, seize a salmon straight out of the river.

Glass rings as her growl crescendos.

She says, "You shouldn't make assumptions."

I shiver. "I didn't know you could speak."

"Let me give you some advice." She leans closer, snout foreshortened in my vision, breath a humid mix of rotten meat and blueberry scones. "Female to female. From someone who's been in the world longer than you have. Who's borne a cub and met a thief and slept howling winters into spring."

I rub the goosebumps on my forearms. Her ursine stare is all crags and glaciers and white-water rapids.

Along the back of my neck, where the hairs are raised, I feel a sting—not just of fear, but of hope. Maybe she has the answers to questions I don't even know how to ask.

Levelly, she stares at me. "You look stupid in go-go boots."

Here's the thing:

You can't win.

You can't win if you're a princess. You can't win if you rescue the prince. You can't win if you cross-dress and become the royal huntsman. And heaven forbid you try to slip into another fairy tale by pricking yourself with a spindle—in the real world, the only thing a spindly prick gets you is up the duff.

No one else is doing better. The mice always wondering if they're supposed to walk on two legs. The prince so vapid he can only recognize the chick he's fallen in love with by her shoe size. Your poor, ugly stepsisters who half the time are hobbling on chopped-up feet.

Animators can come in with fake smiles and truckloads of bleach and Zip-a-Zee-Do-Dah away the blood and eye-pecking birds. Postmodern lit grads in ironic T-shirts can tear you up and stitch you into Frankenstein's femme fatale.

Still there are a thousand girls resting their heads on fireplace stones. Still a thousand streaked with ash and spit.

Still a million going to sleep each night with the knowledge that no one gives a fuck whether or not they wake up.

Little cinder girls, we're raised in fire.

Either you melt and become the simpering thing you're supposed to.

Or else you temper into something calloused and unbreakable.

Ditched the hotel to search for Griselda. Was hoping I could wheedle a cut of the cash, but before I can chase her down, someone's grabbing my arm and dragging me down the sidewalk, and she-bear is right, I *am* stupid to be wearing go-go boots because if I'd chosen something else—something with steel toes maybe—I could kick this fucker in the shins and get away.

Instead, I'm shoved into a swarm of people. My assailant shouts, "What about this one?"

More people grab my arms. There are women in black sheath dresses and pink pearls, and men in ponchos and eyeliner, all talking rapidly over each other. "Could be the one! Could be her! She could work!" Hands push me down onto one of those folding chairs people take camping, and there's some guy at my feet—

Oh, look. Epaulettes again.

Gently, he tugs on my left go-go boot. Leather slips down my calf. His tongue brushes the side of his mouth as he pulls, slow-as-slow. He pants, quick and shallow. Saliva pools in the corner of his mouth. His lids lower with creepy-ass pleasure as my heel pops free. He reveals my arch and then my toes. His index finger traces my sole. "Mmmmmm."

Whole crowd's eyes on my bare foot. The prince's eyes. The eyeliner-and-pearls attendants' eyes. The eyes of the encircling ranks of morning commuters in business casual who cinch in closer so they can get a better ogle.

The prince passes off the go-go boot, and holds out his hand, impatiently. Sheath-dresses and ponchos confer. "Blue doeskin?" suggests one.

"Blue doeskin!" shout the others. "Blue doeskin!"

A ponchoed ponce presents a shoebox. Sweeps off the lid with a flourish. "Blue doeskin!"

Prince lifts out a four-inch, sling-back heel. "Doeskin. Mmm."

He leans forward to slide the shoe onto my foot. I surprise him with a kick to the stomach.

He doubles over. The pearls-and-eyeliner people flutter their hands in alarm. "Five-bow wedges?" "Studded cowboy boots?" "Gladiator sandals?"

I lurch to standing, awkward with one foot bare and the other go-go heeled, and grab Prince Droolface by the collar. "I always figured a fucker that obsessed with shoe size had to be a fetishist. Look, fine by me, okay? You want me to wear stilettos and walk your spine like a runway? Skippy. But first you tell me what you're offering in exchange."

He sputters. I grab one of his epaulettes.

Patty's Party World. 'Nother fucking fake.

It's all so clear the day before you're supposed to go to the ball.

Walk away and they can't make a real Cinderella out of you.

But once you've washed the taste of your stepsister's pussy out of your mouth with a tequila shot...What then?

Now you're hungover, and your eyes are bloodshot, and you haven't slept in thirty-six hours—and still, everything you do is heading toward some kind of *meaning*.

All you wanted to do was run off so you could say, "Her? That's not me. I'm someone different."

But Cinderella's still the center. Everything you do is bound to what she did. You're her marginalia. You're the commentary on her body of work.

Everything you do is going to be read in relation to her. You can't ever really be your own.

I'm still running—well, hobbling, given the one-shoe thing—away from Creepy-Ass McFootFetishist when suddenly I spot Griselda. She's sitting on the curb, taking coins out of the wallet once possessed by Faux Prince #1 and flipping them one by one into the gutter. They make a lonely ringing sound as they clang into the sewers.

I pause, wondering if I should set myself up with a catcher's mitt—because wasting cash? what?—when shifting clouds change the light, and my shadow tumbles over Griselda.

She looks up. Tears streak her ugly face.

"Oh," she says, looking sadly back toward the gutter. "You."

"Uh. Hi."

A big coin that looks like it might be a Susie B. clamors its way down.

"Could you stop that?" I say.

Her face snarls up. She pulls out a fistful of change, and it looks like she's going to throw it all in the gutter at once, but then she turns and hurls it in my face.

"Take it then!" she shouts.

"Um," I say.

I can't help glancing at the passersby who are now giving the crazy chicks wide berth. For dignity's sake, I probably shouldn't bend ass to collect a few dollars in change, but I pull off my second go-go anyway and start scooping quarters into it.

Griselda grunts disgustedly. "He wasn't even a real prince. I let him feel me up and everything. And he wasn't even a real prince."

She bares her teeth.

"Should have known," she says. "Thought maybe I could get some royal nookie even if you got the veil. But no. With you around, everything's fake."

She throws the wallet smack at my chest. It hits me then bounces to the ground. I bend down to get it. When I stand back up, she's gone.

You're an astute reader. So let's cut the bullshit. You've read enough metafiction to think you know where I'm going. And you probably do know because basically what I've been saying this whole time is that everything that happens from here is going to fall into one category of commentary or another.

You've probably become aware that I'm not exactly Cinderella. I'm not bricked up behind the fourth wall, but I'm not driving the bulldozer either...I'm going to go with the charitable angle and call my identity complex. But I won't argue if you want to call it confused, ill-defined, or pretentious bullshit.

For the purposes of this story, you may consider me to be any one of the following, or any combination thereof. Feel free to switch up at any time:

- Cinderella
- The metafictional compilation of Cinderellas
- A prop for anachronistic jokes
- A stand-in for the author
- The pissed-off ghost of the chick who told her story to some asshats named Grimm
- A caterpillar with sixteen feet wearing sixteen glass slippers, dreaming of smashing its cocoon and metamor-phosing into the black hole that will devour the universe

Not sure if wandering the streets is such a good idea given my luck so far, but I keep pounding the pavement anyway, walking barefoot, with the wallet in one hand and the coin-filled go-go boot in the other.

Come upon a dried-up patch of grass trying to pass as a park. Asleep on a bench, there's Bethesda. Mulberry skirt torn into a mini that makes her legs look uglier than usual.

"Hey," I say, looming.

She wakes up. Her breath smells like the bear's, but without the trace of sweet. "Shit." She rubs her eyes to get a bleary look at me. "I should slap you."

"Yeah. But you won't."

"Nah," she agrees.

That's the central difference between Bethesda and Griselda. Piss off Griz and she'll punch a motherfucker. Beth runs hot for an hour or two but can't keep grudging.

She presses her hand against her head and moans. "The fuck did you let me drink so much?"

"I'm not your mother."

"Fuck my mother. Where's Griz?"

"Sulking because she made out with some dude who wasn't a prince."

"Fuck her too, then. But not like I fucked you."

"Speaking of," I say, "That's over. No offense. Was just a one-time kind of thing."

"Figured. After mohawk guy." She shrugs. It turns into a full-out stretch. "So what the hell're you going to do now?"

"Been thinking about that."

"And?"

"Not coming up with much."

"What happened to your shoes?"

"Sold 'em for some boots." I lift my change purse cum go-go. "Then lost one."

"So you're a streetwalker who can't even keep her heels on."

"And you're a recently dumped, hungover ugly chick wearing a ball-gown miniskirt."

"So you done yet?" she asks. "This all weird enough for you finally?"

"Hell no..."

Cuz it's not, is it? Not twisty. Not really.

Even if I could somehow break us out of this place where we started...chew us free from the bear trap of our story...go someplace no one had ever heard of glass slippers and running away at the stroke of midnight...how would we even recognize ourselves then?

I shift foot to foot. Sun's making the asphalt hot. I'm regretting not having made off with the blue doeskin slingbacks.

"One idea," I say. "We should go home."

"So you can grab some shoes?"

"Yeah, but also, I bet if we toss the place, we can figure out where your mom keeps all her valuables before she even wakes up. Live hog-high for a week or three."

Bethesda smirks. "Kick the 'figuring out what to do next' thing down the road a while."

"Correct-a-mundo."

You know what? Never mind all that shit I said before. I'm none of those things.

Unless that was working for you. Then go for it. Far be it for me to tell you what to think.

But here—this is my theory. I'm not just Cinderella. Not *just*. Not *metaphorically*.

Take my situation—you could apply it all around.

Listen. We're all trying to escape archetypes. I'm trying to be *me*, not just a girl who grew up with a mouthful of ashes. I don't want to be someone that everyone thinks they already understand. Someone everyone wants a piece of.

Bet you're trying to escape, too. Trying to be more than just mother, wife, daddy's little girl, big sister, little sister, baby sis, granny, daft old biddy, crone, trophy wife, castrating bitch, conniving cunt, skank, vixen, hobag, virgin, Madonna, sweetiepie. Trying to navigate the hairpin turns between bangled bikinis, apple-pie aprons, and power-bitch pantsuits.

I bet you manage it, too. Bet you're an ice queen exec who bakes cookies on the weekends, or a demure little preacher's daughter who takes it up the ass, or the marathon runner who's going to smoke the world record that dudes think belong to them by right of chromosome Y.

Feel free to fill in the blanks with whatever it is you actually are.

But all that aside, at the end of the day, where do we stand? The archetypal feminine, the ur-woman with a capital W, she's this fire we can't run from. She's burning constantly, devouring bits of us, turning them into herself.

Here and there, we don't burn up completely. But even our ashes are her creations.

We always exist in relation to her, no matter what we do.

So anyway, Bethesda and I head home.

We pass the dude trading new shoes for old, and I shout at him that his products are crappy. Bethesda makes faces in the magic mirror until it begs her to go away. We break off pieces of peppermint windowsill to eat for breakfast, and when the witch shouts at us, we flip her the bird and grab extra fistfuls of pop rocks from the driveway.

Last night's bartender is still in the back alley, smoking a clove. In a flash of remorse for stealing his tips, I toss him the go-go full of change.

Outside a salon, we run into she-bear with ringlet-girl in tow. She-bear's smirking. Blondie's definitely too zonked out to choose her own haircut. Wonder if she's due for a knee-length weave or a pixie cut.

At the coffee shop next door, the sheath-dressed women and men in ponchos are lined up for lattes. His Royal Foot Fetishist stands outside the door, licking the blue slingbacks.

"What the—" Bethesda begins.

"Don't ask," I say, guiding her quickly past.

Couple blocks later, we see a couple on the other side of the street, gropeslurp groping. Sure enough, they change angle, and there's Griselda. This time, she's making out with a drag queen in six-inch stilettos, a sequined slink of a dress, and epaulettes made from the shards of disco balls. Least she knows this one's fake.

We tiptoe on past so we won't disturb them.

Not too long later we reach home. Bethesda grabs her key out of her bra.

She toasts. "To home sweet home."

"Cheers," I agree. "Let's rob a bitch."

And we slap each other high five.

And some of you are saying, oh look, I know what this means, it ends with female-on-female violence which pigeonholes women as jealous backstabbers, and what the hell is with the unquestioning perpetuation of the evil stepmother stereotype?

And some of you are saying, oh look, I know what this means, it's a tale of female friendship because Cinderella and her sister are forging a bond through petty theft and how often do you see stories focusing on positive female-female relationships?

And some of you are saying, oh look, a wimpy ending that refuses to say anything decisive, I could tell from the beginning this was going to be pretentious bullshit.

And some of you are wondering whether there was any point to the bear scene or whether the author just thinks bears drinking tea is funny.

And look, whatever, okay? You just go ahead and take whatever you're thinking and go think about it on your own time. Because Bethesda's searching the house, and I'm the lookout, and I really don't need your noisy-ass ruminations waking up my stepmother before we're finished.

Okay, fine, I'll tell you this one thing for sure. Right now, a thousand Cinderellas are going to steal back our childhood dignity in the form of an old lady's life savings. And then we're going to spend it on booze and clubbing and high-priced high heels.

And when we pass out drunk, we're going to keep on dreaming of becoming that black hole that will swallow the universe.

Glittery Authors & Artist

Christopher Barzak

Christopher Barzak is the author of the Crawford Fantasy Award-winning novel *One for Sorrow,* which is currently being made into the feature film *Jamie Marks is Dead* (to be released in 2014). His second book, *The Love We Share Without Knowing,* was a finalist for the Nebula and Tiptree Awards. His short fiction has appeared in a variety of venues, including *Asimov's Science Fiction, Realms of Fantasy, Strange Horizons, Lady Churchill's Rosebud Wristlet, Apex Magazine, The Year's Best Fantasy and Horror, The Mammoth Book of Best New Horror,* and *The Year's Best Science Fiction and Fantasy.* His most recent books are *Birds and Birthdays,* a collection of surrealist fantasy stories, and *Before and After-lives,* a collection of supernatural fantasies. He grew up in rural Ohio, has lived in a southern California beach town and the capital of Michigan, and has taught English in suburban and rural communities outside of Tokyo, Japan, where he lived for two years. Currently he teaches fiction writing in the Northeast Ohio MFA program at Youngstown State University.

Amber Benson

Amber Benson is a writer, director, and actor. She currently writes the Calliope Reaper-Jones series for Ace/Roc, and her middle grade book, *Among the Ghosts,* came out in paperback this past fall from Simon and Schuster. She co-directed the Slamdance Film Festival feature *Drones* and co-wrote and directed the BBC animated series *The Ghosts of Albion* with Christopher Golden. She spent three years as Tara Maclay on the television series *Buffy the Vampire Slayer.*

Maurice Broaddus & Kyle S. Johnson

Maurice Broaddus has written hundreds of short stories, essays, novellas, and articles. His dark fiction has been published in numerous magazines, anthologies, and web sites, including *Cemetery Dance*, *Apex Magazine*, *Black Static*, and *Weird Tales Magazine*. He is the co-editor of the *Dark Faith* anthology series (Apex Publications) and the author of the urban fantasy trilogy Knights of Breton Court (Angry Robot Books). He has been a teaching artist for over five years, teaching creative writing to elementary, middle, high school, and adult students. Visit his site at *www.MauriceBroaddus.com*.

Kyle S. Johnson hails from Dayton, Ohio, and currently lives...somewhere. His fiction has appeared on *Psuedopod* and in *The World Is Dead*, *Vampires Don't Sparkle*, and the *Dark Faith* anthologies. He is not terribly adept at roller skating or dancing, but he will try anything once.

Galen Dara

Galen Dara has done illustrations for *Fireside Magazine*, *Lightspeed Magazine*, *The Lovecraft eZine*, *Scape* zine, *Apex Magazine*, Dagan Books, and Edge Publishing. Most recently she illustrated the cover of *Oz Reimagined: New Tales from the Emerald City and Beyond*, edited by John Joseph Adams and Douglas Cohen, and the cover of *Geek Love: An Anthology of Full Frontal Nerdity*, edited by Shanna Germain and Janine Ashbless. When Galen is not working on a project, you can find her on the edge of the Sonoran Desert, climbing mountains and hanging out with a loving assortment of human and animal companions. Her website is *www.galendara.com* and you can follow her on Twitter as @galendara.

Alan DeNiro

Alan DeNiro is the author of the story collection *Skinny Dipping in the Lake of the Dead* (Small Beer Press) and the novel *Total Oblivion, More or Less* (Spectra). His second story collection, *Tyrannia and Other Renditions*, is forthcoming from Small Beer Press in the fall. His short stories have appeared in *Asimov's Science Fiction*, *Interfictions 2: An Anthology of Interstitial Writing*, *One Story*, and elsewhere. He lives outside St. Paul, Minnesota, with his wife Kristin and twin toddlers, Alessandra and Tobias, who every day bring new meaning to the word "mayhem."

Amal El-Mohtar

Amal El-Mohtar is the Nebula-nominated author of *The Honey Month*, a collection of spontaneous short stories and poems written to the taste of twenty-eight different kinds of honey. She is a two-time winner of the Rhysling Award for Best Short Poem and edits *Goblin Fruit*, an online quarterly dedicated to fantastical poetry. She has also contributed essays to *Queers Dig Time Lords*, edited by Sigrid Ellis and Michael Damian Thomas, and the Hugo-nominated *Chicks Unravel Time: Women Journey Through Every Season of Doctor Who*, edited by L. M. Myles and Deborah Stanish. Find her online at *amalelmohtar.com*.

Amal would like to point out that Spangled Cabaret is a real thing (though sadly no longer in the Rio Café), and that this story is deeply indebted to its participants, among them Markee de Saw & Bert Finkle, Vendetta Vain, and the Creative Martyrs. Look them up!

Daryl Gregory

Daryl Gregory is an award-winning writer of genre-mixing novels, stories, and comics. His first novel, *Pandemonium*, won the Crawford Award and was nominated for a World Fantasy Award. His other novels include *The Devil's Alphabet* (a Philip K. Dick award finalist), *Raising Stony Mayhall* (a *Library Journal* Best SF Book of the Year), and the upcoming *Afterparty*. Many of his short stories are collected in *Unpossible and Other Stories*, which was named one of the best books of 2011 by *Publisher's Weekly*. He lives in State College, Pennsylvania, where he owns far too many flannel shirts to ever be considered glam.

Damien Walters Grintalis

Writing as Damien Walters Grintalis, Damien's short stories have appeared in magazines such as *Beneath Ceaseless Skies*, *Strange Horizons*, *Interzone*, *Fireside*, *Lightspeed*, and *Daily Science Fiction*, and her debut novel, *Ink*, was released in December 2012 by Samhain Horror. Her work is forthcoming in *Shimmer*, *Shock Totem*, the anthology *What*

Fates Impose, and a collection of her short fiction will be released in spring 2014 from Apex Publications. She is also an Associate Editor of the Hugo Award-winning magazine, *Electric Velocipede*, and a staff writer with *BooklifeNow*, the online companion to Jeff Vander-Meer's *Booklife: Strategies and Survival Tips for the 21*st *Century Writer*. You can find her online at http://damienangelicawalters.com or follow her on Twitter @dwgrintalis.

Maria Dahvana Headley

Maria Dahvana Headley is the author of the dark fantasy/alt-history novel *Queen of Kings,* as well as the internationally bestselling memoir *The Year of Yes*. Her Nebula-nominated short fiction has appeared in *Lightspeed Magazine*, *Subterranean*, and more, and will be anthologized in the 2013 editions of Rich Horton's *The Year's Best Fantasy & Science Fiction*, Paula Guran's *The Year's Best Dark Fantasy & Horror,* and Jurassic London's *The Lowest Heaven*. Most recently, she co-edited the anthology *Unnatural Creatures* with Neil Gaiman. Find her on Twitter at @MARIADAHVANA or on the web at *www.mariadahvanaheadley.com*.

Kat Howard

Kat Howard is a full-time writer living in the Twin Cities. Her short fiction has been performed on NPR as part of *Selected Shorts* and selected for a year's best anthology. Her work has been included in *Stories: All-New Tales*, edited by Neil Gaiman and Al Sarrantonio, and *Oz Reimagined: New Tales from the Emerald City and Beyond*, edited by John Joseph Adams and Douglas Cohen, and in magazines such as *Apex Magazine*, *Lightspeed Magazine*, and *Subterranean*. You can find her on Twitter as @KatWithSword, and she blogs at *strangeink.blogspot.com*.

Vylar Kaftan

Vylar Kaftan is a Nebula-nominated author who has published about three dozen stories in places such as *Clarkesworld Magazine*, *Lightspeed Magazine*, and *Realms of Fantasy Magazine*. Her novella "The Weight of the Sunrise," an alternate history about the Incan empire surviving into the 19th century, came out in *Asimov's Science*

Fiction this year. She's the founder of FOGcon, a new literary SF/F convention in the San Francisco area, and she blogs at *www.vylarkaftan.net*.

Seanan McGuire

Seanan McGuire was born and raised in Northern California, land of many flat-track roller derby leagues, and even a few surviving roller rinks (although not nearly enough). She writes urban fantasy as herself and medical science fiction thrillers under the name "Mira Grant," which is sort of like having a derby name, if your team had a "destroying the world for fun and profit" theme.

Seanan currently lives in a crumbling old farmhouse with her three giant cats, her extensive collection of horror movies, and enough books to be classified as a library under local zoning laws. You can follow her online at *www.seananmcguire.com*, where she posts a lot of really random stuff. If you enjoyed "Bad Dream Girl," check out *Discount Armageddon*, the first book in the InCryptid series.

That noise wasn't the wind.

Jennifer Pelland

By day, Jennifer Pelland is a surly project manager. By night, she transforms into a glittery belly dancer and a not-so-glittery science fiction author. Okay, sometimes she's a little glittery when she writes. It takes a long time to wash that shit off completely. Jennifer is a two-time Nebula short-fiction nominee and a 2013 *Boston Phoenix* Readers Poll finalist for best author. Her work can be found in places such as *Brave New Worlds*, *Unidentified Funny Objects*, both volumes of *Dark Faith*, and her short story collection *Unwelcome Bodies*, published by Apex Publications. Apex Publications also published her novel *Machine* in 2012. She has been nominated for absolutely nothing as a belly dancer, although she's currently in a three-way tie for "Tallest Belly Dancer in the Boston Area," which isn't really a competition. The mayhem in her life is supplied by the Andy and the three cats currently infesting her home. You can find her online at: *www.jenniferpelland.com*

Tim Pratt

Tim Pratt's stories have appeared in *The Best American Short Stories*, *The Year's Best Fantasy*, *The Mammoth Book of Best New Horror*, and other nice places. He has won the Hugo Award for his short fiction, and has been a finalist for the World Fantasy, Sturgeon, Stoker, Mythopoeic, and Nebula Awards. His latest collection is *Antiquities and Tangibles and Other Stories*. He lives in Berkeley, California, with his wife, writer Heather Shaw, and their son. For more, visit *www.timpratt.org*.

Cat Rambo

Cat Rambo lives, writes, and teaches by the shores of an eagle-haunted lake in the Pacific Northwest. Her 100+ fiction publications include stories in *Asimov's Science Fiction*, *Clarkesworld Magazine*, *Apex Magazine*, and *Tor.com*. Her short story, "Five Ways to Fall in Love on Planet Porcelain," from her story collection *Near + Far* (Hydra House Books), was a 2012 Nebula nominee. Her editorship of *Fantasy Magazine* earned her a World Fantasy Award nomination in 2012. For more about her, as well as links to her fiction and information about her online classes, see *www.kittywumpus.net*.

Tansy Rayner Roberts

Tansy Rayner Roberts is a fantasy novelist with a PhD in Classics. Her books include *Splashdance Silver*, *Love and Romanpunk*, and the *Creature Court* trilogy (*Power & Majesty*, *The Shattered City*, and *Reign of Beasts*). She has won the Washington SF Association Small Press Award twice, and is a presenter on two popular podcasts: *Galactic Suburbia* and *Verity!*

You can find Tansy at her blog *tansyrr.com* and on Twitter as @tansyrr.

Diana Rowland

Diana Rowland has worked as a bartender, a blackjack dealer, a pit boss, a street cop, a detective, a computer forensics specialist, a crime scene investigator, and a morgue assistant, which means that she's seen a helluva lot of weird crap. She won the marksmanship award in her Police Academy class, has a black belt in Hapkido, has handled numerous dead bodies in various states of decomposition, and can't rollerblade to save her life.

Diana is the author of the police procedural/urban fantasy *Demon Summoner* series (*Mark of the Demon, Blood of the Demon, Secrets of the Demon, Sins of the Demon, Touch of the Demon*...are you sensing a trend yet?) and the *White Trash Zombie* series (*My Life as a White Trash Zombie, Even White Trash Zombie Get the Blues,* and *White Trash Zombie Apocalypse.*) And, seriously, her rollerblading is the stuff of comedy.

Sofia Samatar

Sofia Samatar is the author of the novel *A Stranger in Olondria* (Small Beer Press, 2013). She holds a PhD in African Languages and Literature from the University of Wisconsin-Madison, where she specialized in Egyptian and Sudanese fiction. Her poetry, short fiction, and reviews have appeared in a number of places, including *Stone Telling, Strange Horizons, Clarkesworld Magazine,* and *Apex Magazine.* She is Nonfiction and Poetry Editor for *Interfictions: A Journal of Interstitial Arts,* and blogs, mostly about books, at *sofiasamatar.blogspot.com.* She loves thrift stores, staying up late, and cheesy urban dance movies, and glitters constantly, especially on the inside.

David J. Schwartz

David J. Schwartz writes short stories, novels, rent checks, ransom notes, constitutions in code, and epics in ice unread by humans. If he had three wishes, one would be to be a rollergirl. His stories have appeared in numerous anthologies and periodicals, including *Strange Horizons, Unstuck, Asimov's Science Fiction, Apex Magazine,* and *The Best of Lady Churchill's Rosebud Wristlet.* His serial novel *Gooseberry Bluff Community College of Magic: The Thirteenth Rib* is available from Amazon; his previous novel, *Superpowers,* was nominated for a Nebula Award. His favorite Bowie album is *Hunky Dory,* his favorite Prince album is *Sign "O" the Times,* and he has no knowledge of any romantic connection between Barry White and Dusty Springfield. His website is at *www.snurri.com.*

William Shunn & Laura Chavoen

William Shunn is the author of over thirty works of short fiction, including the Hugo, Nebula, and Sturgeon Award-nominated novella "Inclination." He served three years as a national judge for the Scholastic Art & Writing

Awards, and he co-hosts Chicago's monthly Tuesday Funk reading series. In the early days of the web, he helped produce live online concert broadcasts for artists like The Cure, The Allman Brothers Band, and Mötley Crüe.

Laura Chavoen is a wanna-be geek, a data and meme junkie, and a scarf and bangle lover. In her role as a digital brand strategist, she creates social and digital programs for clients and drives innovation. In the past she executive-produced Scholastic's websites for kids, including websites for Harry Potter and Clifford the Big Red Dog, and also helped manage Scholastic's non-profit scholarship program, The Alliance for Young Artists & Writers. A former denizen of the Chicago club scene, Laura is an experienced world traveler who has run the Chicago and Boston Marathons and inline-skated across Holland.

Bill and Laura have been married since 2001, and have lived in New York City and Chicago. Their dog Ella is the world's most photogenic soft-coated wheaten terrier. "Subterraneans" is their first fictional collaboration. A soundtrack to the story can be heard on Spotify at *bit.ly/glittersub*

Cory Skerry

Cory Skerry lives in a spooky old house that he doesn't like to admit is haunted. When he's not peddling (or meddling with) art supplies, he's writing, reading submissions, or off exploring with his sweet, goofy pit bulls. If his career as a writer fails, he plans to build a time machine and travel back to the 1700s to be a highwayman, because Jonny Lee Miller made it look hot. So far, Cory's work has appeared or is forthcoming in several magazines and anthologies, though none of them are quite as sparkly as the one you're reading right now. To read those other stories, visit *coryskerry.net*.

Rachel Swirsky

Rachel Swirsky holds an MFA from the Iowa Writers Workshop. Her short fiction has appeared in numerous magazines and anthologies, including *Tor.com*, *Subterranean*, *Apex Magazine*, and *Clarkesworld Magazine*. She's been nominated for the Hugo Award, the Locus Award, the World Fantasy Award, the Sturgeon Award, and the Seiun Award, among others. In 2011, her novella "The Lady Who Plucked Red Flowers Beneath the Queen's Window" won the Nebula Award. *Through the Drowsy Dark*, a slim volume of Swirsky's feminist poetry and short stories, came out from Aqueduct Press in 2010. A second collection, *How the World Became Quiet: Myths of the Past, Present, and Future*, is forthcoming in 2013 from Subterranean Press. Visit her online at *www.rachelswirsky.com*. If Rachel ever loses track of her spouse, he can be identified via size 10 steel-toed work boots.

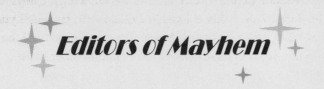

Editors of Mayhem

John Klima

John Klima previously worked at *Asimov's Science Fiction*, *Analog*, and Tor Books before returning to school to earn his Master's in Library and Information Science. He now works full time as the assistant director of a large public library. When he is not conquering the world of indexing, John edits and publishes the Hugo Award-winning genre zine *Electric Velocipede*. The magazine is also a four-time nominee for the World Fantasy Award. In 2007 Klima edited an anthology of science fiction and fantasy stories based on spelling-bee winning words called *Logorrhea: Good Words Make Good Stories*. In 2011 Klima edited *Happily Ever After*, a reprint anthology of fairytale retellings. He and his family live in the Midwest.

Lynne M. Thomas

Lynne M. Thomas is the Curator of Rare Books and Special Collections at Northern Illinois University. She's probably best known as the co-editor of the Hugo Award-winning *Chicks Dig Time Lords* (2010) with Tara O'Shea, *Whedonistas* (2011) with Deborah Stanish, and the Hugo Award-nominated *Chicks Dig Comics* (2012) with Sigrid Ellis, all published by Mad Norwegian Press. Along with the *Geek Girl Chronicles* book series, Lynne is the Editor-in-Chief of the Hugo Award-nominated (2012 & 2013) *Apex Magazine*, an online professional prose and poetry magazine of science fiction, fantasy, horror, and mash-ups of all three. She moderates the Hugo Award-winning *SF Squeecast* and contributes to the *Verity!* podcast. Lynne lives in DeKalb with her husband Michael, their daughter Caitlin, and a cat named Marie. Lynne is also a part-time Dancing Queen and grew up at a roller rink in the wilds of Massachusetts.

Michael Damian Thomas

Michael Damian Thomas is the Hugo Award-nominated Managing Editor of *Apex Magazine* and a former Associate Editor at Mad Norwegian Press.

He's the co-editor of the *Doctor Who* essay anthology *Queers Dig Time Lords* with Sigrid Ellis. Michael lives in DeKalb with his wife Lynne, their daughter Caitlin, and a cat named Marie. He can solve most of the world's problems with a cocktail, some music, and a pair of roller skates.

Acknowledgements

We want to thank all of the people who made *Glitter & Mayhem* possible. A Kickstarter needs a lot of help. Numerous people spread the word and promoted this project. We thank all of you. A special thanks goes to all of our backers. This is *your* party.

Our Kickstarter Backers:

@lintilla42
A.P. Matlock
Adam Israel & Andrea Redman
Adam Windsor
Adeline Teoh
Alexandra Pierce
Alisa Krasnostein
Alison Pentecost
Alistair Hyde Page
Allison Armstrong
Alyn Day
Amal El-Mohtar
Amber Watson
Amy E Goldman
Amy Estes
An Owomoyela
Ana Steuart
Andrew DiMatteo
Andrew Hatchell
Andrew J Clark IV
Andrew Lin
Andrew Stingel
Ann Walker
Anna McDuff
Anne Burner
Anonymous
Anonymous
Anonymous
Anthony R. Cardno

April M. Steenburgh
Arachne Jericho
Ari Marmell
Arzvi
Ashley Chatneuff
aurellia
Barb Moermond
Barry Deutsch
baywoof
Bear Weiter
Bekki Callaway
Ben Stanley
Beth
Betsy Phillips
Betty Widerski
Beverly Bambury
Bill McGeachin
Brad Roberts
Brenda Stokes Barron
Brent Millis
Brenton Clifford
Brian Sebby
Brian White
Brian, Sarah, and Josh Williams
Brit Mandelo
Bruce Cohen
Bryan Thomas Schmidt
C G Julian
C.C. Finlay

Cameron Horn
Carey Watson
Carl Rigney
Carla M. Lee
Carol Darnell
Carol J. Guess
Caroline Pruett
Catherine & Christian Berntsen
Cathy Green
Celeste Wetzel
Charlie Byrd
chelsea g. summers
Cheryl Morgan
Chia Lynn Evers
Chloe Hardy
Chloe Long
Chris Matthew G
Chris Newell
Christian Decomain
Christina Vasilevski
Christopher Mangum
Cindie Hurley
Cindy Sperry
Colleen Reed
Cory Cone
Courtney Bocci
Craig E
Craig H
Craig Hackl
Creatrix Tiara
Cylia Amendolara
Cynthia Dawn Griffin
Cynthia Ward
D Bubulj
D Taylor-Rodriguez
Dana
Dana Organ
Dani Daly
Danielle Beauchesne
Dave Freireich
Dave Thompson
Dave Versace
David Wardrop

David Wohlreich
Dawn Vogel
DeAnna Knippling
Deanne Fountaine
Deborah Stanish
Denise Gorse
Denise Moline
dixie lee ross
DJ Reilly
DJ Skw33k
Don Alsafi
Dr. Mary Crowell
Drew Glazier
Duffi McDermott
E. Kristin Anderson
Edward Greaves
Elanor Matton-Johnson
Elishabet Lato
Elizabeth Bordeau
Elizabeth Creegan
Elizabeth Fallon
Elizabeth Massie
Emily B. Langton
Emily Hartman
Emily Wagner
Emily Weed Baisch
enui
Eric Horbinski
Erika Ensign
Erin Kowalski
Erin McNamara
Eugene Johnson
Evgeni Kantor
Fade Manley
Ferrett Steinmetz
Fletcher
Fran Wilde
Frances Rowat
Fred Kiesche
Galen Dara
Gary B. Phillips
Gary J. Baker
Gary Kloster

Gessika Rovario-Cole
Ginger O
Glennis LeBlanc
Greg Jayson
Greg Roy
Gregory Lincoln
Gretchen Treu
Gwydion Vennema
Gwynne Garfinkle
Haddayr Copley-Woods
Hans Ranke
Heathyr Fields
Heidi Cykana
Heidi Waterhouse
Helen Apocalypse
Helen Truax
Herbert Eder
Holly Aitchison
Holly McDowell
Hugh Blair
Ian Mond
J Nilsson
Jack Vivace
Jackie Monkiewicz
James Bushell
james_
Jasmine Stairs
Jason Root
Jaym Gates
Jed Hartman
Jeff James
Jeff Linder
Jeff Xilon
Jen Grantham
Jen Woods
Jennie Goloboy
Jennifer Brozek
Jennifer Melchert
Jennifer Wilson
Jenny Barber
Jeremy Zimmerman
Jerrie the filkferengi
Jess Lethbridge

Jessica Cohen
Joanna King
Joanna Lowenstein
Joanne B.
John Devenny
John M Gamble
John Richards
John Seghers
Jon Christian Allison
Jonathan Disher
Jonathan Hamlet
Jordy Jensky
Joseph Hoopman
Josh Rountree
Joyce Clapp
Joyce Saenz Harris
jrho
Juha Autero
Julia Rios
Julia Svaganovic
Juliana Rew
Juliette Wade
K Kisner
K. Dikeman
Kaia Gavere
Karen Mahoney
Karen Meisner
Karen Williams
Kari Blackmoore
Kat McNerney
Kate G.
Kate Heartfield
Kate Keen
Katharine
Kathleen Luce
Kathryn L
Katie Hynes
Kellan Sparver
Kelly Lagor
Kelly McCullough
Kelly Myers
Kelly Stiles
Ken Liu

Kerry "circeramone" Jacobson

Kerry aka Trouble

Kevin Bailey

Khinasidog

Kim Riek

Kip Manley

Kitty Stark

KN Kasdorf

Kristi Chadwick

Kristin Stonham

Kristina VanHeeswijk

Kristine Kearney

Kristjan Wager

kristopher o'higgins

Kyna Foster

Larry Stein

Laura Blanchard

Laura D

Laura Pinson

Laurel Copeland

Lauren M. Roy

Lauren Vega

Layne

Leah Marcus

Lee Morey

Liari

Lindsay Walter

Lisa Martincik

Lisa Padol and Joshua Kronengold

Liz Gorinsky

Liz Peterson

Lola McCrary

Lorena Dinger

Lori Priebe

Lydia Ondrusek

M J

Marc Jacobs

Margaret Colville

Marina Handwerk

Marina Radcliff

Mark Amidon

Mark Gerrits

Mark Webb

Mary Spila

Mary Sue

Matt & Morgan Wagner

Matt White

Matthew A.

Matthew Kressel

Matthew Sheahan

Megan Lynae Sohar

Megan Scroggins

MeiLin Miranda

Melissa House

Melissa Tabon

Meredith Jeanne Gillies

Meri Aust

Michael (Mike SumNoyz) Kwan

Michael Bernardi

Michael Lee

Michael M. Jones

Michael Mendoza

Michael R. Underwood

Michael S Lienau

Michelle Dupler

Michelle LaRock

Michelle Muenzler

Micole Sudberg

Mike Douton

Mike Gucciard

Mindy Schmid

Miriam Krause

Misha Dainiak

Morva Bowman & Alan Pollard

Muriel Jackson

Natasha Yar-Routh

Nathan Hall

Nayad Monroe

Neil Williamson

Nicole Cipri

Nina Niskanen

Nivair H. Gabriel

Olna Jenn Smith

P. Gelatt

paksiegurlie

Pamela Adams

Patricia Bullington-McGuire	Sara Harvey
Patricia E. Crebase	Sara Puls
Paul Cornell	Sarah A.
Paul Hattrem	Sarah Goslee
Paul Weimer	Sarah Kuhn
Persis L. Thorndike	Sarah M. Heile
Peter Aronson	Sarah Pinsker
Peter Hansen	Sarah Smith-George
Peter M Ball	Sass
Philip Barkow	Sealey Andrews
Pornokitsch	Sean Collins
Qui-Gon Jinn	Sean Hagle
Rachel Holkner	Seth Fogarty
Rachel Sasseen	Sharyn November
Rafia Mirza	Sheila Perry
Rebecca D. Howard	Sheryl Ehrlich
Rebecca Harbison	Shira Lipkin
Rebecca Sparks & Orion Newcomb	Shiyiya LeCompte
Remy Nakamura	Silvia Moreno-Garcia
Ren Warom	Simo Muinonen
renshai	Sondra de Jong
Richard Leaver	Sonya Dent
Rivka	Stacey Jones Erdman
Robert H. Wilson	Stephanie Franklin
Robert L. Fleck	Stephanie Leary
Robert Levy	Stephen Blackmoore
robyn S	Stephen Tihor
Roger Silverstein	summervillain
Roselyne Bourgault	Suzette "Twinki Darfur" Padley
Rosemarie Brizak	Sven of the Dead
Rrain Prior	Sydney Ashcraft
Rudi Dornemann	Tahmi DeSchepper
Ruth Stuart	Tamara L. DeGray
Ruthanna and Sarah Emrys	Tamisha Martin
S M Kennedy	Tansy Rayner Roberts
Sabrina Sloyan	Tara Smith
Sally Qwill Janin	Tasha Turner
Samantha Henderson	Tehani Wessely
Samantha Rohaus	The Sables
Sandra Wickham	Thomas Werner
Sandy Coffta	Tim Sonnreich
Sandy Swirsky & Lyle Merithew	Tod McCoy
Sara Carrero	Tom Hunter

Tom Underberg
Toni Wiltshire
Tony Romandetti
Tracy Cain
Trevor Quachri
Tyler Hayes
Vajra Chandrasekera
Victoria Traube
Wesley Chu
William & Laura Pearson
William B. Emerson
Wolf SilverOak
Yoshio Kobayashi
Ysabet MacFarlane
Zoe E. Whitten

Made in the USA
San Bernardino, CA
11 September 2013